DIG YOUR GRAVE

ALSO BY STEVEN COOPER

Desert Remains

A GUS PARKER AND ALEX MILLS NOVEL

DIG YOUR GRAVE

STEVEN COOPER

SEVENTH STREET BOOKS®

AN IMPRINT OF PROMETHEUS BOOKS

59 JOHN GLENN DRIVE • AMHERST, NY 14228
www.seventhstreetbooks.com

Cover design by Nicole Sommer-Lecht
Cover image © Creative Market
Cover design © Prometheus Books

Inquiries should be addressed to
Seventh Street Books
59 John Glenn Drive
Amherst, New York 14228
VOICE: 716–691–0133 • FAX: 716–691–0137
WWW.SEVENTHSTREETBOOKS.COM

22 21 20 19 18   5 4 3 2 1

Library of Congress Cataloging-in-Publication Data

Names: Cooper, Steven, 1961- author.
Title: Dig your grave : a Gus Parker and Alex Mills novel / Steven Cooper.
Description: Amherst, NY : Seventh Street Books, an imprint of Prometheus Books,
    2018.
Identifiers: LCCN 2018024937 (print) | LCCN 2018026537 (ebook) |
    ISBN 9781633884816 (ebook) | ISBN 9781633884809 (paperback)
Subjects: LCSH: Murder—Investigation—Fiction. | BISAC: FICTION / Mystery
    & Detective / Police Procedural. | GSAFD: Mystery fiction.
Classification: LCC PS3603.O583 (ebook) | LCC PS3603.O583 D54 2018 (print) |
    DDC 813/.6—dc23
LC record available at https://lccn.loc.gov/2018024937

Printed in the United States of America

For Paul Aaron Milliken.
Here's the dedication you've been asking for.
Finally. Deserved.

1

He'd rather be at Starbucks. Or Hava Java. Or Luci's.

He'd rather be spending Saturday morning in a grubby sweatshirt and a pair of jeans, staring into the sleepy eyes of his beautiful wife, Kelly, while sipping steamy cups of espresso among whiskery hipsters who wear wool hats year-round. In the desert.

Yes, on a lazy Saturday morning, he'd rather be judging millennials.

He'd rather be reading. Or rereading. For his birthday, Kelly bought him a handsomely bound special edition of *To Kill a Mockingbird* that he's been wanting to devour, as if for the first time.

He'd rather be tossing a ball with his son, Trevor.

Or hiking at Squaw Peak.

Detective Alex Mills of the Phoenix Police Department would rather be undergoing electrolysis of the gonads on this otherwise lazy Saturday morning than being here, doing this.

Instead of staring into Kelly's sleepy eyes, Mills is staring into a hole in the ground. Not a very deep hole, maybe a foot and a half, a gash really, a pit. In this hole, staring back at him, is a dead John Doe, his arms and legs akimbo like an acrobat who fell to earth and missed the net. It's eight thirty, about sixty-five cool degrees, typical for an early-March morning in the valley. The smell of death is starting to rise. Mills guesses the body has been here overnight, that John Doe was murdered shortly before midnight—but time of death is not his job; that task belongs to the Office of the Medical Examiner. Judging by the dried blood around the eyes, the black-and-purple bruises that seep from the forehead down, the corpse's dented head, and the crater in the crown,

7

Mills concludes that John Doe is the victim of a rather unfriendly head bashing. But cause of death is not his job either. Again, the OME. Sorry to bother the medical examiner, but the fact is Alex Mills has not been denied the piety of a lazy Saturday with his wife to perform an autopsy. He's here for two reasons: to figure out who killed John Doe and to figure out why. Of course, that won't happen right now, right here, at the crime scene. Mills doesn't even know at this point if the crime scene is the place of death. Though this crime scene, it could be strongly argued, is the ultimate place of death.

Mills lifts his head from the hole in the ground. He scans the horizon. There is death everywhere. Lovely, landscaped, manicured death. Marked by statuaries of imported marble, exquisitely sculpted. Like something you'd see outside an Italian palazzo, not here at Valley Vista Memorial Gardens in Phoenix, Arizona.

A gathering of marbleized angels, birds, saints, human hands clasped in prayer, you name it—they're all frozen in time here at Valley Vista. Samuel Shine was a golfer, apparently. Mary Harrison Delahunt was a fan of roses. Gordon D. Hancock loved dogs. With such a swanky neighborhood, the property values at Valley Vista Memorial Gardens are said to be double the value of your average Phoenix home. This is where the privileged go to rest. The same luxury had not been afforded John Doe, however. His grave is marked not by marble statuary but by a cardboard sign roughly excised from a carton that was once the home of a Whirlpool refrigerator. Add a thick tree branch and some hearty duct tape, and you have a grave marker staked into the ground that reads the following:

I'm Sorry
That I fucked over everybody
I got what I deserved
And I picked the place myself

Alex Mills is shaking his head, bewildered by the fucking crazy world that produces crazy people who do crazy things when, really, people should just go to Starbucks, or their favorite coffeehouse, and fucking relax.

"We recovered the Sharpie, Alex," a crime scene tech tells him from above.

He looks up. "What?" he barks. "You think the murder weapon was a Sharpie?"

"No, Alex. I don't," the tech replies, then points to the cardboard sign. "We believe the Sharpie was the writing instrument."

Mills nods. "Right. That. Of course. Where'd you find the marker?"

"About thirty feet down that slope," the tech says. "It was resting in the grass."

"Interesting," Mills says. "Prints?"

"Hopefully."

Mills rises to his feet, gives his legs a shake to loosen his aging knees, and says, "Nice work."

He takes in the view. It is, indeed, a vista of the valley. From this acreage of death you can look across Phoenix to the raging peaks of the Sierra Estrella mountain range and, to the left, the slightly less excited South Mountain. You can think yourself a poet, for a moment, sent here by God to interpret the erosion of time and find yourself completely inadequate, if not a fool, for presuming you can interpret anything this ancient.

What you can interpret, what Alex Mills is *paid* to interpret, is the erosion of life.

He looks at this crude grave below him once more. It was dug with irregular scoops; at least that's what the skid marks from the shovel suggest. No one tried to be tidy. The dirt was tossed everywhere, the work of an amateur. Pebbles litter the grass. One of them snuck inside Mills's tennis shoe and is rolling around in there like a pinball.

Befitting the clientele of Valley Vista, John Doe is wearing a suit jacket, dress shirt, no tie, as if he came from work. Or a cocktail party.

When she first inspected the victim, homicide detective Jan Powell, a former patrol officer who recently joined the Violent Crimes Bureau, had pointed to the dead man's shoes and whispered, "Ferragamo."

If only the body had been as easy to identify as the shoes.

No wallet. No ID. No business card. Nothing. The prints came back with no match to anything in the database.

But Alex Mills has a hunch. A good hunch. You don't get to die in style and stay anonymous for long. John Doe is a VIP corpse. A member of the dead elite.

He has to laugh. And he does. Audibly. He drifts away, hoping his foolishness goes unnoticed. He has suddenly amused himself with the inevitable headline of the valley's latest murder:

DEAD BODY FOUND AT CEMETERY

For once, the media will get it right.

2

Gus Parker wakes up eye level with a nipple. That's all he sees: a big nipple in his face. He ponders the view. The entire aureole looks like some kind of solar system orbiting the sun, the individual planets obviously inspired by the hues of Mars. He'd pat himself on the back for his vivid imagination, but he doesn't want to wake her. The nipple is the property of Billie Welch. *That* Billie Welch, the doe-eyed rock-and-roll legend who's still rocking and rolling all these years after she first broke the hearts of young men and even younger boys, Gus among them. Her mysterious songs of heartbreak and solitude had been a rite of passage, had scored much of his high school encounters with love and lust, late-night drinking and drugging (nothing heavy, just the typical bong hits and shots of tequila). Eventually Gus Parker had lost track of the music of Billie Welch much the way you lose touch with an old lover. But, almost thirty years later, her career has endured and now he finds himself more often than not half-naked with her on weekend mornings.

They've been together for just about a year. Together—being altogether tentative. She plays New York, LA, London. He works part-time at Valley Imaging. He still lives in his little house in Arcadia. She still lives in a desert manse below Camelback Mountain, a few doors down from Beatrice Vossenheimer, through whom they met, the psychic matriarch of the Southwest and Gus Parker's adopted "Aunt Bea."

When she's in town, not playing gigs, Billie likes to sleep in late. Very late. Until noon, at least. She's a creature of the night, for sure, and Gus is learning that to be with Billie is to live within a time-zone-hopping jet lag; her world is upside down compared to his. This is why they can't sleep together every night. He takes his mammograms and his ultrasounds very seriously. Likewise, the CT scans and the MRIs. Billie Welch may be worth many, many millions, but Gus Parker earns his living as a multi-certified imaging technician, not as a gigolo.

"You're too old to be a gigolo," Beatrice has told him.

In his early forties, he supposes she's right.

But his feelings for Billie Welch have nothing to do with her fame or her fortune. His feelings for her have to do with the serenity in her eyes when she speaks, the intensity in her eyes when she sings, her laughter, her touch, and the way she acts toward others. He watches how kind and generous she is with friends and family, how patient and accommodating she is with fans. She sometimes talks in hippie poetry, much like she writes, but who is he to judge? After all, some people regard him as an aging hippie himself, what with his long, raffish hair, the beaded bracelets, the occasional yoga class, and, of course, the psychic visions. Contrary to his parents' fears, Gus was not going mad back in his teenage years; he was going psychic. He considers it, the psychic thing, just great intuition. Others call it a "power." Power shmower. It just is. He hears things and sees things that others don't. He can't control it or necessarily call upon it on cue like you might see in the movies or on TV, which is why he is reluctant to take on clients (though he does, mostly to relieve Beatrice of hers). When Gus says he has "visions," he's mostly referring to a visual manifestation of his intuition. Or sometimes it really is a sudden, vivid scene that plays out before his extra set of eyes, and most of the time it spooks him. When pressed, he will admit that his psychic gift has helped solve crimes. Which reminds him that he and Billie have a dinner date tonight with homicide detective Alex Mills of the Phoenix Police Department. He and Alex have worked together over the years, and they got closer, almost brotherly, on the last case.

Gus turns away from the nipple and looks at the time. Past noon. He senses that he's losing the day, but then he listens to Billie breathing and realizes that he's losing nothing. Still he thinks he ought to pick up the phone and ring the detective to confirm the where and when.

He'd like Vaguely, the best veggie restaurant in Phoenix, but he knows Alex will recoil at the suggestion (that's not psychic; that's just knowing Alex). Gus is not a vegetarian, so maybe he'll suggest Tapatio Steakhouse. It's one of the valley's hottest restaurants (at the moment) and easily one of the best, making it nearly impossible to get a table. But if there's one thing for which he doesn't mind exploiting his relationship with Billie Welch, it's getting dinner reservations.

But he better dial Alex first.

"This is Alex. You've reached my private line. If you're a murderer and you'd like to confess, please dial 911. Otherwise, leave me a message, and if I'm not up to my neck in cases, I'll call you back." *Beep.*

"Yo, Alex, I'd like to report the murder of several cattle in the Northwest section of Phoenix. They will be taken to Tapatio Steakhouse tonight at seven thirty for identification and consumption by Parker, party of four. Please call to confirm."

"Who was that, Gus?" It's the sleepy, throaty voice of Billie Welch. She has rolled away from him now, her smooth, milky white back as beautiful as her breasts; he wants to kiss her shoulder, so he does.

"I was talking to Alex's voice mail," he tells her.

He likes the taste of her skin, the scent of her musky fragrance. So many men, so many men all over the world, would kill to be lying next to this woman, even now that her golden hair has silvered in places.

"Dinner plans?"

"In the works."

Her beauty is timeless. You look into her eyes and you see years and years of everything. And yet she smiles like a little girl. Her kisses are soft and sensual. And yet she laughs like a giddy child. Her age has always been the subject of much intrigue. She liked creating mystery. Still does. Back when she first burst onto the national scene, everyone wanted to know about this doe-eyed creature with the silky voice; was she a child, or was she a woman? Gus remembers being aware of her in junior high school, fully infatuated by high school. The age thing is a moot point, after all. She's almost eleven years older than Gus, and yet her timelessness negates the difference. She, the fantasy of so many men, and he, the surfer dude schmuck who had no idea what he was getting into, still doesn't, only knows that she is not some kind of celebrity conquest for others to envy—she is as much a mystery to him, at times, as he is to her. She's very much drawn to his psychic gifts, so curious, so enchanted, and yet there's little he can explain. When people want to know about Billie Welch's new "love interest," Gus keeps a very low profile. And people do want to know. Fans and tabloids, alike.

She rolls over and smiles, and he can't fathom her beauty, the alabaster skin, the moony eyes, those lips. He embraces those lips with his and holds them there until she laughs. "You're holding my lips hostage."

"I call it a frozen kiss. Maybe you can write a song about it."

"I don't think so," she whispers. "How about 'Strange Affection'? That sounds more Billie Welch."

She refers to herself often in the third person, because Billie Welch is as much a brand as it is her name; he has come to learn that Billie Welch means many things to many people, to many people she will never know, and that's probably as hard for him to understand as his very persuasive intuition is for her to grasp. She likes to talk about it, as if his psychic gifts are more likely to inspire a song than his kiss.

She throws her arm across his chest now, and he pulls her close.

"Tapatio is right around the corner from Valley Vista," she says.

"Valley Vista?"

"Memorial Gardens. It's a cemetery. I own a plot there."

"Well, that's pleasant."

"Please don't ever bury me there."

He lifts his head and looks down into her eyes. "First of all, I'm not planning on burying you anytime soon. Second of all, if you don't want to be buried there, why do you own a plot?"

She sighs. "Just in case."

"In case of what?"

"In case I have no heirs to carry out my true wishes, my body has a place to rest, but I hate that place. It's way too gaudy for my liking."

"What are your true wishes, Billie?"

"I want to be cremated with some of my music, some of the original songwriting in my journals, and I want the ashes buried here in Phoenix, maybe here at the house."

"Not the house in Malibu? You love the ocean."

"I love the ocean," she purrs. "But I was born in the desert. And this is where I shall rest."

"Okay. But I think we're a ways off from that, Billie."

"You never know," she says to the ceiling. "Or do you?"

"What?"

"Do you ever know when death is imminent, Gus?" she asks, her eyes still fixed on the vaulted ceiling. "Can you see someone's death? Can you see mine?"

"Yes, sometimes I do sense when death is imminent. I knew my mother was dying before I knew my mother was dying."

She strokes his shoulder. "You've told me that. And of course, you wouldn't do all that work with the police if you didn't have a sense of death."

"But, no, Billie, I can't see yours," he says. "Why would I want to?"

"Just curious. I'm not asking because I'm scared. I'm asking because I'm fascinated."

And he fully believes her. He knows her to be one of the most fascinated people he's ever met. All that fascination with the universe finds its way into her music and into the way she loves, if the two are not the same.

As he rolls on top of her, the entire house erupts. A whirl of sirens surrounds them. Her body tenses. Normally when he slides himself between her legs, he hears a whimper and a soft, throaty growl of permission—not a house alarm. Bells are ringing; horns are blasting. His first reaction is to laugh. "What's so funny?" she asks.

"Nothing. Just the timing. That's all. It's like the house is having an orgasm instead of you." He rolls off her.

"Not funny." She sits up.

They're screaming to be heard above the roar of the alarm.

"A little funny?"

"Gus! There might be an intruder in my house!"

Her phone rings.

"That's the security company. Will you get it?" she asks.

He does. "No, we didn't trip it by mistake," he tells the operator. "We haven't moved all morning."

"What's your password?" the operator asks.

"Password?"

"It's 'masquerade,'" Billie says.

"Masquerade."

"Do you hear an intruder?" the operator asks him.

"Are you kidding me? The alarm is so loud I can barely hear my own voice."

"Okay, Mr. Welch, we can turn the alarm off remotely."

Mr. Welch? That's a first. "Please do." There's irritation in his voice that doesn't surprise him, what with the piercing shrill of the alarm, the coitus interruptus, and the shrinkage of his dick.

The house goes silent.

"And, now, Mr. Welch, do you hear an intruder?"

A moment of fight-or-flight tingles his spine. "This place is a mansion. Hard to tell."

"Would you like us to send the police?"

He covers the phone. "Do we want the police?" he asks Billie.

She's wide-eyed, begging him.

He shakes his head, doesn't understand.

She nods, finally, and pulls the blankets around her; Gus watches her do this, and it turns his flesh to ice. She's frightened. He's never seen her this way. "Yes," he tells the operator. "Please send the police."

He ends the call and hops off the bed.

"Where are you going?" she begs.

He looks at her, as if it should be obvious. "I'm going to check out the house."

"Like hell you are. Sit down."

"Billie, I'll be fine. Lock the door behind me. I'll be back in a minute."

"No, you don't," she insists. "I can't let you do that. You stay here until the police come."

He looks back at her, this woman clinging to her velvet security blanket; she might be a frightened doe, but she's ordering him around. Classic Billie. Vulnerable but headstrong. Lost in her music, in control of the world.

"If that's what you prefer," he replies, "but right now some robbers could be making off with your priceless guitars over in the music wing."

She grabs his hand and pulls him back to the bed.

"This is a guard-gated community, Gus! First they'd have to get past the security booth, and then they'd have to get past my driveway gate."

Her voice is gravelly. When she speaks and when she sings, her voice often sounds like the dry, hardscrabble desert that surrounds her. As if it were born of this earth. It's a good effect, the huskiness, a sexual come-on that men and women, particularly men, find irresistible, and yet her obliviousness of it makes that voice all the more fetching.

"Chez Welch is not exactly Fort Knox," Gus tells her.

"You're adorable," she says. "Trying to protect me."

He pulls her close. "Are you saying you don't need protection?"

They hold each other for a few minutes, listening to the stillness, listening for a trespass on the stillness.

"We all need protection sometimes," she says finally.

It's a line from one of her songs.

The intercom squawks, and they both stiffen, their nerves rattled. Billie rises and reaches for the keypad on the wall. "Hello?"

"Miss Welch, it's Paradise Valley Police. Are you free and able to open the gate?"

She buzzes them in. Gus throws on a robe and tells Billie he'll greet the cops at the front door while she gets dressed.

"Are you kidding me, Gus? I can't get dressed that quickly," she gripes.

"Billie, please. There are a dozen robes in the closet. Throw one on. And lock the door behind me."

Before she can protest, he's gone.

Even a year into his romance with Billie, Gus has not grown accustomed to her sleep-until-noon schedule (that's noon on weekends, 2:00 p.m. often on weekdays), which would explain his hard squint at the uncompromising Arizona sky when he opens the door to greet the two cops out front.

"Hi."

"Who are you?" one of them barks.

"Gus Parker," he replies, offering a hand for a shake. Neither accepts, letting it dangle there in its rejection.

"Where's Miss Welch?" the red-faced one asks. His head sprouts a ginger buzz cut, right above his bright red neck. The name engraved on his badge is Thelan. The other officer, more mundanely named Johnson, is leaning in the doorframe. Johnson is a tall one, towering over both Gus and Officer Thelan. What Thelan lacks in height, however, he makes up for in width, strong width, like-a-truck width, all muscle. The two of them could crush Gus into cactus pulp.

"She's in her bedroom," Gus answers. "Why don't you gentlemen come in? I'll get her."

"Do you have any reason to believe there's an intruder on the property?" Officer Thelan asks before Gus can step aside.

"Other than the alarm, I didn't hear a thing," Gus tells them. It's so quiet he can hear birds singing in the distance. The air smells crisp. A cool breeze sneaks up his robe, and he backs away from the door. "Please come in," he repeats.

"Damn, what a place," Johnson says in a whisper as the cops enter.

"My partner, here, is a rookie, still impressed by all the money in PV," Thelan hisses. "But I've been out here. Miss Welch threw one heck of a New Year's party a few years ago. Loud and late. Noise complaints."

When Gus returns to the bedroom, Billie opens the door, wearing a sweater-like robe that falls from her neck to her bare feet, with buttons the whole way down, her silvery blond tresses cascading around her shoulders to the small of her back.

"Are we headed for the log cabin?" he asks, hoping to get a laugh.

"No," she says without one. "Where are the police?"

"They're downstairs. I think they're waiting for your permission to search the house."

"Jesus," she groans.

"You want to put on some socks or slippers?" Gus asks.

"No."

The cops seem to notice her bare feet first. Johnson, puzzled, and

Thelan, amused. "Hello, boys," she says. "Go on, search the house. I'm making coffee. Want any?"

"Sure, ma'am," says Officer Johnson.

Thelan elbows him. "Uh, no thank you, Miss Welch. My partner and I will get down to business and then be out of your way."

While the officers inspect, Gus and Billie sip coffee in silence. She's writing something in her journal, probably something about fear. He won't ask; it's none of his business, but here comes his intuition, shaken to life by the house alarm, now restlessly searching for a sign of something, anything, anywhere. Here in Billie's residence, in her physical sanctuary, is a bald man around Gus's age, his features too nascent to be descript in this sudden vision. He is the shadowy intruder in a dream. He's a blur of malevolence lingering at the end of a hallway. He has stepped out of the wilderness, a man in a burly plaid jacket and a sneer on his face. He has come alive, and he's a threat, a pickax in his hand.

"What's wrong?"

Her voice brings him back.

"Nothing," he answers.

"You sure?"

"Yeah. Why?"

"You were standing there shaking your head like you do in your sleep sometimes."

"Was I?"

She puts her pen down. "Don't be evasive, Gus. It was like you just disappeared."

He smiles. "I'm right here, babe."

She scoffs. "Oh come on, Gus, don't patronize me. I know when you're having a vision."

Yes, she does. He doesn't hide it from her. He doesn't slip out of the room anymore. "I wish I could explain what I just saw, but I can't."

She sidles up to him, grabs his hand. "Did you see an intruder?"

"No."

He hates lying to her. It feels like a sting to his throat, a barbed wire kind of guilt. But it's better than scaring her.

They both turn when footsteps approach.

"Are we interrupting anything?" Thelan asks, his passive-aggressive intent loud and clear.

Billie waves them into her massive kitchen. "No," she says. "The coffee's still hot."

"Okay," says Thelan, taking a seat across from them at the big tiled island. "All we have is a good guess. Looks like someone might have hopped the wall behind the pool."

Gus and Billie look at each other. She's spooked; it's all over her face. His heart is racing. "So there was someone here?" he asks.

"We think so," Johnson replies, still standing, his head partially obscured by the light fixture above.

"But that's a huge wall," Billie says. "It's a security wall."

"But it backs up to the mountain," Thelan reminds her. "The other side is public. Not popular among hikers. But not inaccessible."

"We found some dirt at the base of the wall tracking through your pool area to one of your French doors back there," Johnson explains.

Billie is a deer in headlights. Gus pulls her close. Her expression doesn't change.

"Could be an animal," Johnson continues, "but we doubt it."

"Looks like there was some intent to enter," Thelan says. "Probably scared off by the alarm."

Gus looks from one officer to the other and says, "Look, guys, I'm not a cop, but if there's evidence that someone approached the house, wouldn't there be evidence of someone leaving?"

Something about "look, guys, I'm not a cop" amuses Thelan.

"It's likely all the dust on his shoes was loosened by the time he turned around," Johnson tells Gus. "Again, that's assuming we're right."

"Or that he entered the house and is hiding somewhere," Gus says.

"Stop it, Gus," Billie pleads. "He's a psychic, so he has his own hunches, you know."

Thelan crosses his arms and smiles. "Maybe he should go search the house, himself. We did and found nothing. No one came inside this palace of yours, Miss Welch."

"Please call me Billie. And, if you don't mind, it's my *home*."

Thelan rises, his neck redder, his chest puffier. "You got a safe room? In your *home*?"

"A what?" Billie asks.

"A place where you can safely retreat if you hear an intruder," Johnson tells her. "A secret room. With locks. Secure. Out of the way. A lot of the newer mansions out here are putting them in."

Billie shakes her head. "No."

"You might consider," Thelan begins.

"No. Not now. Not ever," she tells him.

Thelan puts his hands up as if he's directing traffic. "Hey, no problem, Miss Welch, just a suggestion."

"It's Billie," she reminds him. "I don't suppose you want to check the other side of the wall for footprints. You know, to prove your theory."

"Yeah, what about that?" Gus asks, moving closer to Thelan to equalize the machismo. It reminds him of his surfer days, of the territory wars and the testosterone-fueled competitions.

"Look, *Billie*, that's easier said than done," Thelan scolds her. "It would take us hours to go on foot and reach the other side of your wall. I said the mountain behind there is not inaccessible, but it's far, far removed from the road, with no marked trails and very rugged terrain. That's why people like you choose to live in places like this."

Gus and Billie let their silence speak volumes.

The mutual disdain at this point is palpable. The refrigerator whirs to life, and the ice-maker roars as several new cubes are hatched.

"If there will be nothing else . . ." Thelan says.

"There will be nothing else," Gus tells him. "We have a ladder. I'll take a look for myself."

"Gus . . ." Billie whispers.

"No, it's fine," he says. "Thanks, guys, for coming out. Let me show you to the door."

Johnson hesitates. "Now, it can't hurt to climb a ladder. I'm happy to do it."

"Johnson," Thelan hisses. "The gentleman just offered to show us the door."

"I know that," Johnson tells his brutish partner. "But I'd like to see for myself. Just to satisfy my own curiosity."

"Or to finish the damn job," Billie interjects, glaring at Thelan.

Thelan throws his hands up in the air and shrugs. "Whatever."

Gus insists on going up the ladder first.

"Gus, you can't climb a ladder in your robe!" Billie cries.

"I got my gym shorts on," he tells her. "No one's going to see my junk."

"That's not what I meant. You'll fall off."

He laughs and grabs the ladder with both hands. As he climbs, the sun hits his face, reminding him just how fierce the desert is and how scorching the light can be, illuminating and uncompromising. He scans the rocky gullet of the camel, unforgiving territory at best, and he looks below at the other side of the wall: there is a puzzle of footprints down there. Indeed, there was an intruder.

"Footprints," he shouts to those below.

"Okay, Gus," Billie calls to him, "why don't you let one of the officers up there now to investigate?"

"I'll be down in a minute," he assures her.

"Really, Mr. Parker, come on down and let us finish up," Thelan insists.

But he ignores the man and steps off the ladder to a spot atop the wall where he sits down and closes his eyes.

"Gus, what the hell are you doing?" Billie shrieks. "Get the fuck down here."

Again, he sees the pickax. He doesn't understand it, can't intuit it, but the image is a clue. Then he opens his eyes, leans over, and studies the side of the wall that faces the desert.

"Oh, my God, Gus!" It's Billie again. "I am so mad at you right now!"

He swallows a laugh and inventories the assault on the wall below him. Whoever was here was a skilled rock climber because the evidence shows a pathway of divots and dents from the bottom to the top of the wall. Somebody scaled the thing. Somebody was damned determined.

Gus descends the ladder and is met with a look from Billie as fierce as the sun.

"So?" Johnson asks.

"Go on up," Gus tells him. "We definitely had a climber."

Later in the kitchen the officers toss out a few theories. Billie is visibly more angered than scared.

"Why would someone do this?" she asks no one in particular. "It seems like an awful lot of work to break into a house. And then what? Grab some things and toss them back over the wall?"

"They probably weren't here to steal big things," Johnson says. "Most likely they were looking for cash and jewelry."

"They?" Billie begs. "You think there were more than one?"

"Just a form of speech," Thelan says.

"You think they targeted me, specifically?" Billie asks them.

"There's no way of knowing that," Thelan replies. "But I doubt it. The intruder probably just landed on your property randomly. But, heck, I can think of plenty of easier places to break into."

"Me, too," says Johnson with a burst of zeal. "I don't even know how you'd get back there unless you were either in top shape or super determined."

Thelan prods his partner by the elbow and leads him to the front door. "We'll write up a report and call you when it's ready," he tells Billie. But she's not listening. She's in a zone. She's far away. And Gus knows the look. It's him when he disappears.

She's pacing, and she doesn't snap out of it until the men are long gone. "I don't think I'm safe here," she says.

He doesn't think so either. He doesn't know why. But he fully understands, perhaps more than Billie, that there's more to the intrusion than money and jewels.

3

The manager of Valley Vista Memorial Gardens is a man dressed for his clientele—not the dead ones but rather the living ones who are here shopping for plots. He's wearing one of those impeccably tailored Italian-looking suits, diamond cuff links, and a diamond wedding ring. His shoes have ties to the Mafia. He has adult acne, asymmetrical, Mills notes, the way he'd note the complexion of a corpse, but otherwise a dapper man in his late thirties. His name is Ronald, and his voice is nasally.

"The media is gathering out front," he tells Mills. "They're asking if I can get a spokesperson from the police department."

Of course the media is here. Always on cue for murder. "Tell them it'll be a while."

The two of them are standing about fifteen feet downhill from John Doe's grave. The cemetery manager gestures to Powell and the small army of technicians. "How long do you think you'll be out here?"

"Probably into the evening," Mills replies. "I'll be gone before that, but the crew will stay until the scene is completely processed."

The man scowls. Do-it-yourself graves, apparently, are not good for business. "It's a good thing we don't have any services scheduled for today."

"Burials?"

"Interments," the man says. "We don't like to say 'burials.'"

"Because the mounds of dirt and the holes in the ground don't give it away?"

Ronald recoils. "Because we do more than burials here, Detective. We have mausoleums. We have a crematory. We have vaults."

Mills is aware of the offerings. He's just fucking with the guy. He's not proud of himself for doing it, but there's something about the Tony Soprano loafers with the diamond studs instead of tassels that Mills finds offensive around dead people.

"You got video cameras on the property?" he asks the man.

"No. I'm afraid we don't."

"I find that surprising, given the value of some of these gravestones," Mills says, his arm sweeping the surrounding plots.

"We call them ornaments."

Mills just looks at the guy, the sarcasm that dares not escape his mouth lodged in his eyes instead. He lets the non-ornamental look sink in and then says, "Is the place locked and gated at night?"

"Yes."

"Any idea how someone could have gotten in here?"

"Maybe on foot. But that's your job, Detective," the man says with a snarky grin. *This is my fucking Saturday*, Mills is thinking. *This man is not my wife. This fucking graveyard is not Starbucks. You asshole.*

Mills smiles back. "Who locks up? Who's the last to leave?"

"Usually maintenance. They leave an hour after closing."

"Security?"

"We don't have patrols, if that's what you mean."

"That's what I mean."

The man twirls nervously at the diamond ring, looks past Mills to the crime scene. "Do I need a lawyer?"

Mills was not expecting that question. "Not unless you've done anything criminal."

Ronald laughs out loud. "Well, of course I haven't. But I wonder if the business here could be liable for something."

Mills shakes his head. "Your price per square foot may be obscene, but it's not a crime."

"If you'll excuse me," the man says.

"I will."

Back at John Doe's grave, Mills finds the techs meticulously measuring the hole in the ground. They're entering data into an iPad.

Though he's supposed to be using a tablet, as well, he's still not parted ways with the pen and paper. He's old school that way. So is the squad, for the most part; Powell, his scene investigator, is younger but not the digital type, it would seem. She's a no-nonsense former lacrosse player who owns three dogs. She never wears sun block, which explains the perpetual ruddiness, the freckles, and the peeling skin of her nose. Detective Ken Preston is older, a lot older, early sixties, and probably has stored more knowledge about murder in his brain than all of the RAM in the world could house. While the iPad is a strain on his eyes, Preston will use it if for no other reason than to be a good sport. Detective Morton Myers, however, is still figuring out how it works. He's the doughy one, a rare guy who wears the extra poundage well because it's the kind of doughiness that obscures his age. He's thirty-seven or so, with a big, happy, Gerber Baby face. Myers is not a stupid guy. He's surgically thorough and can be alarmingly imaginative with theories when others are stumped. He's geeky for computers, but old habits, like keyboards, like pen and paper, die hard. Mills asks Myers to inspect the gate with one of the techs. Then he drifts toward the grave, where he squats.

So, John Doe, you're missing, but no one misses you.

If you have a wife and kids, you never made it home to them last night.

Come on, J. D., who the fuck are you?

Mills tries to assemble the story. It's an odd way of doing things, the story before the clues, but so often you have to think big before you know the details. Sometimes you have to make the story fit the crime, rather than the other way around, because sometimes you have no choice. Like now. Obviously it's a revenge crime. John Doe fucked somebody over. He cheated someone. Owed a drug debt. Had an affair. The killer was angry, full of fury; Mills sees it in the tattered earth. He sees it in the dented skull. And nowhere is it more pronounced, better articulated, than on the grave marker. That's a humiliation. He's guessing the killer had forced the victim to etch a final statement of contrition, and if that's not revenge, Detective Alex Mills does not know what is. He tells the tech to get hair and blood samples and to check the teeth to see if dental records will help. The usual. The tech looks at him as if she just received a bucket of obvious.

Two hours later, Mills and his squad flank Detective Sergeant Jacob Woods as Woods and a public information officer field questions from the media.

"Were there any witnesses?"

"We're guessing most witnesses in this neighborhood were asleep, eternally, at the time of the murder," Woods replies.

Woods is the kind of boss you work for, not the kind of boss you befriend. A clean-cut guy who looks as if he moonlights on a box of Wheaties, Jacob Woods is far more a bureaucratic administrator than a crime fighter. But, if it's possible, he suffers even fewer fools than Mills is inclined to suffer, and that's something to be admired, especially now, when a press conference is heading into overtime.

"When will the body be removed?" a reporter asks.

"In other words, when will you be getting the money shot you're waiting for," Woods replies. The gaggle of reporters rewards the sergeant with a brief round of self-deprecating laughter. "Actually, I can't answer that question. That's up to the Office of the Medical Examiner. Thanks for coming. We'll send out a press release when we have more information."

With that, Detective Alex Mills is done for the day. On the drive home he listens to a message from Gus Parker about dinner plans, but now, searching the dusky horizon through his windshield, at the premature stars trying to beat the darkness, he considers his lazy Saturday stolen by the ghosts of Valley Vista, and he realizes he's not up to socializing tonight.

"Maybe I should cancel Mills tonight," Gus says to Billie. "You probably don't feel much like going out after the day we've had."

"Is that a psychic vibe, or just a vibe?"

"Just a vibe. I'm human, too," he says.

She smiles. Billie calls this room her "inner sanctum." It's an entirely round room of white stucco walls at the very center of the house. A full-size fireplace, also round, like an indoor chiminea, dominates the middle of the room. A fire is lit. It was a warm day, but it's still winter in early March, and this is what Phoenicians do. After all, Gus checked the forecast, and lows could dip into the sixties tonight. Having moved to Phoenix from Seattle via Los Angeles, Gus has always found the paucity of Phoenician blood amusing. Pillows of all origins cover the floor. Billie and her band have traveled the world, and she has, over the years, developed an admiration for handcrafted pillows that reflect the cultures she's visited. She collects them, obsessively if you ask Gus. There are the beaded ones from India, the Alpaca ones from Peru, silks from China, wools from New Zealand, Aboriginal designs from Australia, and the list goes on. It's a United Nations of pillows. Also here are the two custom-made chaises she brought home from Thailand, their bases carved from native wood, the cushioning intricately embroidered to illustrate a march of sacred elephants. The "inner sanctum" is her hippie hangout, the idea stolen, she confesses, from a spa in Sedona. Sometimes she meditates here. More often she sips wine, which is what she's doing now upon one of the chaises.

"Actually, I think we should stick to the plan, Gus," she tells him. "Maybe Alex can figure this out. You know, another set of eyes besides the cops from PV."

He's sitting below her on the floor, his butt on Japan, his feet on Brazil. "That's fine," he says.

It's only a few minutes later, just as Gus rises to inspect the fire, when Alex calls. There are no phones allowed in the "inner sanctum," so when his phone jovially rings, Billie eyes him with consternation.

"It's Alex," Gus whispers. And then, he answers his phone. "Hey, buddy, what's happening?"

"Gus, I have bad news. I don't think we can make it to dinner tonight."

Gus lowers himself again to Japan (Kyoto, to be specific). "Aw, really. That sucks."

"Long day, man. Don't know if you watched the news."

"Nope. Can't say we have."

"I had a murder. Lost my entire day," Mills explains. "I'm just really beat. How about a rain check?"

Gus turns to Billie, shakes his head, and shrugs. "Sure. That'll work. But, if you have a sec . . . well, never mind. A rain check is fine."

"Never mind what?"

"Oh, nothing. It can wait."

"C'mon, Gus, you know I have no patience when people withhold information," Alex says in his *Law & Order* voice. "Don't make me interrogate you."

"We think we had an intruder today."

"You *think*?"

"Pretty sure."

"Where?"

"Here at Billie's."

"Shit. Anyone come out?"

"Paradise Valley PD."

"Lemme call over there."

"Don't know if it'll do any good."

"That bad?"

"I wasn't overly impressed."

"Say no more, bud. See you at seven."

"Really?"

"Really."

At 7:03 p.m. Gus rolls into the parking lot of Tapatio Steakhouse with Billie sitting shotgun in his SUV. Alex and his wife, Kelly, are waiting inside. "I love your dress," Billie says to Kelly, who beams at the compliment. Gus has never seen someone have such a beneficent effect on people; Billie innately shifts the attention away from herself, out of her spotlight, and onto others around her, making them feel like the only stars in the room. She once told Gus that while fame has heavenly perks, fame is often embarrassing and gauche. That may be true, but it follows her wherever she goes. Wherever they go. It's obvious, in fact, that when the hostess sees Billie Welch she sees nothing and no one else. The woman tosses her reservation book aside, excuses herself, and returns with the manager.

"We had you all seated in the main dining room tonight," the manager says. "But if you'd like a private room, we can make that happen if you don't mind waiting a few minutes."

Gus loves every inch of Billie when she's the one to speak up and say, "The main dining room is fine. But very nice, very sweet of you to offer an option."

Alex nudges Gus. "Aw, come on, can't we poach a little of your luxury?"

Over dinner in the main dining room, a moody place of dark mahogany with candles everywhere and a live jazz quartet playing in the corner, Gus tells Alex about the intruder.

"They say it was probably random."

"I wouldn't say probably random," Alex tells them. "I'd say fifty-fifty."

"I don't know that I like those odds," Billie says.

Alex smiles. "I understand. But there's little evidence either way. It's not like someone broke in and specifically targeted your guitars or your recording equipment."

"Or her demo reels," Gus suggests.

Billie laughs. "Gus wants to turn this into some kind of music caper."

"No, I don't. I'm just saying anything is possible."

"And you, the resident psychic, have no hunches about this?" Alex asks him.

"Not yet. It all happened so fast. And then we drank some wine, which tends to limit my visions."

"Kind of like driving," Kelly says. "Channeling under the influence?"

"Not recommended," Gus says.

Alex offers to come out to Paradise Valley and check the place for vulnerabilities.

"I thought that's what the guys from PV were supposed to do today," Billie says.

"Hence our dinner with Alex tonight," Gus reminds her.

"Are you worried, Billie?" Kelly asks her.

Billie shrugs, adjusts her shawl, and says, "I really don't know. When I'm on the road I have security staff, but when I'm at home, you know, I'm at home and I'm never thinking about that. Maybe I should, but I don't. I don't think fear should intrude, if you know what I mean."

"I think I do," Kelly says. "I'm married to a cop. You have to make peace with your fear. It's probably not the same thing, but it's about protecting your normal life."

"It is the same thing," Billie says with a gentle smile.

A waiter wheels over a dessert cart.

They say no to the crème brûlée, likewise the white chocolate mousse and the raspberry-kiwi torte, and they say hell no to the seven-story deep fudge and dark chocolate cascade cake.

"I don't think we'll be having dessert," Gus tells the waiter. "But coffee would be great."

Billie nods emphatically. Gus recognizes the nod. It's the nod that says, "Bring me the caffeine so I can stay up until four in the morning to write music." Then Billie turns to Kelly, leans in, and confesses something about getting older, and the women giggle like little girls. Gus is smitten all over again. As the coffee arrives, somebody's phone dings.

"Aw shit," Alex says. "Fuck."

Kelly winces. "Watch your language," she tells her husband, pointing to their dinner companions.

"Oh, please, I've been around rock 'n' roll boys my whole life," Billie tells her. "And I've out-cursed them all."

Alex rises from the table. "I'm sorry, everybody," he says, "it's a text from the PD. Something's come up from this morning's case. I have to run."

"Need help?" Gus asks.

"Help?"

"Yeah, Alex, you know, an extra set of eyes."

"Your eyes or your psychic eyes?"

"My psychic eyes."

"You volunteering? So quickly?"

"I don't know anything about your case, but maybe you can bring me up to speed."

"What are we going to do with them?" Alex asks him, pointing to the women.

"The women can take care of themselves," Kelly says with a roll of her eyes. "Take Gus's car and leave me yours, honey," she tells her husband. "I'll drop Billie off later."

But Gus hesitates. "Maybe this isn't such a great idea," he says. "I don't want Billie going home to an empty house."

"I'm not going home to an empty house," she informs the group. "I'm checking into the Desert Charm."

Eyebrows lift all around. The Desert Charm is an exclusive resort, famous for its famous clientele, in Paradise Valley. It offers secluded and quiet luxury, a private collection of bungalows where no one knows quite what happens behind its convent-like walls. And no one talks. The Desert Charm doesn't have a website.

"When did you decide that?" Gus asks.

"Just now," Billie says.

"What about clothes and stuff?"

"I'll have my sister bring them over."

"Why don't you just stay with her?"

Alex pushes his chair in. "Uh, guys. I really have to get moving."

"Go on, take Gus," Billie says. "I'll be fine in my little hideaway."

Gus is behind the wheel, listening to Alex's navigator recite directions.

"I never told you this, but I had a crush on Billie Welch when I was seventeen," Alex says.

"Everybody did."

"And yet she settled for you. . . ."

"Thanks, man."

Alex describes the John Doe murder, fills Gus in with the details.

"Wow. I think you're right about revenge," Gus tells him. "It sounds personal and angry."

"We're not going to find another body tonight," Alex says.

"We're not?"

"No. The call came in as an empty grave. No mention of a body. But apparently someone left us a message—"

Alex is interrupted by the dulcet tones of the woman inside his navigator.

"In three hundred feet," she says, "your destination will be on the right."

4

Mills can still hear the high-velocity static of the highway, but he assumes the traffic noise doesn't disturb the neighbors here at All Faiths Destiny Park. Here they are under the palms, monuments lined up in rows and columns, like a spreadsheet of death imposed on an unnaturally green template of grass. Their names, their birthdates, their expiration dates, and whom they loved are engraved into slabs of stone. Under the light of a full moon and aided by a team of lampposts, he can see everything. So orderly. So perfect. Until row 33, column 9. That's where Mills finds a crudely dug hole in the ground. The hole is not truly deep enough for a body, which might explain the absence of a body and the cardboard sign that says, "Who's Next?"

Mills shakes his head. "Aw, shit," he says to no one.

A woman, standing opposite him on the other side of the hole, is talking on her cell phone when she hears him. She ends her conversation abruptly, adjusts her navy blue business suit, and makes the short walk over to his side. "Are you the detective?"

"Alex Mills." He extends a hand, and she shakes it firmly.

"They told me you'd be coming," she says. "Is that your partner?"

Mills remembers Gus is behind him, pivots, and says, "No, just a friend. We were out to dinner when the call came in."

Gus waves. "Hi, nice to meet you. I'm Gus Parker."

"Oh, I didn't formally introduce myself," she says. "Please understand. I'm a bit shaken up. I'm Crystal Levenworth. I manage All Faiths."

Mills lifts his head, looking at her. Everything about her is tight. The bun on top of her head, the business suit, the smile. She's blond, smart-looking in tortoise shell glasses, probably in her early forties. "Did you call this in?" he inquires.

"Oh, no. I wasn't here."

"Who discovered this?" Mills asks her.

"One of our clients," she replies. "He called our after-hours number."

Gus belts out a laugh. Mills turns sharply with a warning in his eyes.

"I'm sorry," Gus says, gesturing to the surrounding plots. "But surely, no one *here* picked up the phone."

"Gus, really?" Mills groans.

Gus retreats a few steps, then shrugs.

"It's someone who owns a family plot here," Crystal explains. "His wife died many years ago. He comes out every year on their wedding anniversary, around seven p.m., to coincide with their vows. It's really sweet."

"I don't suppose he's still around," Mills says.

"He is. I asked him to wait in our office. I can take you to him."

Halfway there, around row 14, column 6, Mills collides with a bouncing brigade of white orbs, and he knows that Gus is on the verge of making some smartass joke about ghosts, so he's relieved to find that the brigade is actually a small team of crime scene techs and a photographer armed with flashlights to document evidence. Powell is with them.

"Good evening," he says. "I'll be back there in a few. Going to track down a witness."

"Cool," Powell says, and the brigade passes them in the night.

Carl Deacon doesn't have much to share. He's sipping on a can of club soda, sitting on an upholstered chair, his legs crossed awkwardly at his ankles. "I just saw it. You know, it looked weird."

Mills does a head-to-toe assessment of the guy, checking instinctively for signs of dirt or any other evidence of digging. None. Still, Mr. Deacon made the call. And Mills knows that could be the perfect obfuscation. So he does a split-second rundown: Maybe the man is punishing someone for his wife's death. Maybe he set the stage tonight and lingered here to see what kind of evidence the cops would be looking for. Maybe there's a connection between Mrs. Deacon and John Doe. Maybe, maybe, maybe.

Carl Deacon is here tonight for the annual ritual to honor the vows he made to his wife. That's sweet but strange, believable but also a tear-jerking page out of a Hollywood script. Mills is, at this point, over-thinking. "What time was it when you discovered the empty grave?" he asks Deacon.

"I got here about seven," the man replies. "I didn't notice anything unusual until I spotted that sign sticking out of the ground. Struck me as odd."

Alex nods. "Yes, that's odd, sir." The man is balding, his face weary. This is what protracted grief looks like, Mills observes. He guesses Carl Deacon is in his early to middle sixties, drives an American car, goes to church. "Did you see anyone out here? Anyone at all while you were visiting?"

"No, Detective Mills, I did not," Deacon says. "I never see anyone out here when I come to visit Katherine."

"Do you think anyone saw you?"

The man looks puzzled but says, "No. I don't think so."

"And you always come after hours?"

"I do. I like to be alone with her." His eyes begin to water.

"May I ask how she died? Your wife?"

The man looks away, tightens his jaw. "Cancer," he says.

"Do you have any enemies, Mr. Deacon?"

Deacon's face visibly downshifts, his eyes boring through Mills. "What on earth does that have to do with anything, Detective?"

"Just need as many details as possible."

"But this has nothing to do with me," the man says indignantly. "I simply made the call. That's all."

"It's my job to ask anything and everything," Mills explains. "It's your prerogative to answer or not."

The man nods, takes a sip from the can. "I understand."

"Let's just rehash what you observed this evening."

"Like I told you, I didn't observe much."

"Did you notice any cars in the parking lot when you arrived?"

"I don't think so. But I wasn't really paying attention."

The questioning lasts just another five minutes. "I'm going to give you my card, and I want you to call me if you remember anything more specific about your visit here. Anything," Mills stresses. "You know how it goes, no detail too small."

The man takes the card, hoists himself up from the chair. He offers Mills a handshake, nods, and says, "Sorry I couldn't be more helpful."

"Sir, you made the phone call. That was a major help. Good night."

Mills waits for the man to be out of sight and then instructs Crystal Levenworth to leave the can of club soda exactly where it is. "I'm going to need my techs to bag it."

"Bag it?"

"Yeah. We just need to process it."

When Crystal Levenworth follows Mills and Gus back to the gravesite, Mills can tell the woman's nerves are jangled. It's partly in her jittery walk, partly in her soft staccato breaths. "Is everything okay, ma'am?"

"Other than the vandalism of my property? Yes, all is good."

"I can understand why this would upset you," he says.

"What upsets me are all these people traipsing across my lawns to investigate a stupid prank. It's not like a major crime has been committed."

"All is not what it seems," Gus interjects.

"What is that supposed to mean?" she asks.

"It means it's too early to draw any conclusions," Mills says swiftly enough to preempt his companion.

She says nothing else until they reach the gravesite. And then, "I'm not sure if I need to remain on-site until you all are done. But my gut tells me to stay."

"It's getting chilly," Mills says. "Why not wait in the office where you'll be comfortable?"

"Are you asking me to leave?"

"We have police business."

That answer sufficiently coaxes Crystal Levenworth to retreat.

"Nicely done," Powell says.

"Thank you, Jan. You remember Gus Parker?"

"Yup," she says, her eyes averting Gus. "We almost got him killed on the cave murder case."

Almost. Mills would prefer not to flashback. It was one of their own, a homicide detective who had stalked women on hiking trails, murdering them in a bloody ritual inspired by the petroglyphs of the desert's ancient tribes. One of their own, an imposter. Gus Parker had almost given his life to bring the killer to justice. But Mills won't look back at his own miscalculations. That's of no use now. He's in debt to Gus, he knows that, and is infinitely thankful that the man, this crazy surfer dude in the desert, regards him like family and, as such, is unlikely to ever come collecting.

"Jan Powell is my scene investigator," Mills tells Gus. "Find anything interesting here?"

"We got a scramble of footprints that we're processing now," she says. "But what I find interesting is that this is obviously not a copycat. First of all, it's too soon. Second, we never released details of the Valley Vista crime scene so there would be nothing on public record to copy."

"Right," Mills says. "All of that is obvious."

"What she means," Gus says, "is that the killer, one singular killer, preplanned the order of events. This is not a whim. Not a spontaneous decision. This is all part of a preplanned mission."

"You reading her mind? Or getting a vibe?" Mills asks.

"A vibe," Gus says sheepishly.

"Do you know if the victims are preplanned as well, or just random?"

"I don't know, Alex. I need more time."

"Go for it, man. Just don't disturb the grave."

While Gus is intuiting the crude hole in the ground, Mills and his colleague debate motive. He elaborates on the revenge theory and keeps going until he sees a palpable shift on Powell's face; she's squinting at him.

"What?" he asks.

"Well, I'm not sure where all of that leads. If this cardboard sign is a message that our killer intends to kill again, we can't assume revenge. If his victims are random, then revenge makes no sense."

"Unless he's avenging some universal wrong."

"True," Powell says.

"And if his victims aren't random . . ."

"Then does he really want to kill them?"

"I don't follow," Mills says.

"If his victims aren't random, staging a murder like the one at Valley Vista and then following it with this stunt is clearly a warning," she explains. "And why would he want to warn someone who he's determined to kill?"

"To scare the shit out of them. To control by fear," Mills replies. "Unless these crime scenes aren't meant as much as a message for his victims as they're just meant to taunt us."

"You think this is fun for him?"

Mills stuffs his hands in his pockets. "It's imaginative. It's creative. So, yeah, I think he might be having fun."

"We need to go back and—"

Mills's phone rings. "Hold that thought. It's headquarters."

The dispatcher is speaking so fast Mills asks the man to take a breath and slow down.

"But I'm telling you," the dispatcher begs, "the woman sounds hysterical."

"And I'm telling you, so do you."

"Sorry, Detective, but she's in tears. She saw the news tonight, and she thinks that could be her boss at Valley Vista."

"The victim?"

"Yeah. She says she can't find her boss, something about him being a no-show for a flight at Sky Harbor," the dispatcher explains. "You want to talk to her?"

Mills is twisting his right foot into the earth, impatient with his own impatience. "Put her through."

Her name is Shelly Newton, and her voice is trembling. "I just have a sick feeling."

"Let's start at the beginning," Mills tells her. "You saw the news. You think the victim is your boss."

"I have no reason to believe it's him, but I also have no idea where he is," she says.

Beginnings often start with ambiguities, and Mills knows not to judge, but he doesn't have the patience in his blood for dead ends. He needs to work on that. His other foot is excavating the earth. "I need you to tell me why you even think he's missing."

"I already explained to the operator that my boss was supposed to be on a flight to New York City but never showed up at Sky Harbor."

"That's right," Mills says. "But how do you know he never showed?"

"Because the pilot called me."

Mills shuts his eyes for a moment, massages his forehead with his free hand. Shelly Newton breathes loudly to fill the silence. Mills has to bite his tongue. "The *pilot* called you?"

"Yes."

"I don't think pilots do that, ma'am," he tells her calmly. "How would he even know to call you?"

"Our pilot is a she, not a he," Shelly informs him. "And she'd certainly know to call me."

"What do you mean by 'our pilot'?" he asks.

"I mean our pilot," she says, exasperated. "What's so difficult to understand? My boss doesn't fly commercial, Detective."

A revelation worthy of an eye roll. "Of course he doesn't," Mills says, his sarcasm poorly veiled. "What is your boss's name?"

"Davis Klink. He's the CEO of Illumilife Industries. I already told your operator."

"I'm sorry, but he didn't pass that on. Tell me about your boss's itinerary."

Davis Klink was supposed to be on an evening flight to New York City last night aboard the company's private jet. He was scheduled to show up at the airport at 9:00 p.m. At nine forty-five, Shelly Newton received the first call from pilot Jessica Perry inquiring about Klink's whereabouts. Shelly advised the pilot to give it another fifteen minutes because Klink might have stopped quickly at home to pick up his daily shipment of mangoes from Peru. He also might have ducked into the Phoenician for a preflight facial. Though that could have been accomplished inflight had she known to arrange for the traveling cosmetician. The pilot called back at ten fifteen. Still no sign of Klink. Shelly tried reaching him on his cell phone to no avail. She told Jessica Perry to cool her jets, so to speak, thinking at the time that was a hilarious pun. She didn't start to get nervous until eleven fifteen when Klink still had not shown at General Aviation. She called the Phoenician and discovered that her boss had not checked in for a preflight treatment, not a facial, not a massage. She tried several more times to reach him on his cell. She never thought to call the police because she was sure there was an explanation for all of this. There always is. At midnight she stopped worrying and started to pray. She fell asleep praying. But now, with what she saw on the news, she is downright panicked.

"May I ask why you're the one looking for him? Does he have a wife or children?"

"Well, yes," Shelly replies. "He does. But his wife's off in Italy, and I can't reach her. She's not returning my calls. And I don't want to panic the kids."

"Can you tell me why he was headed for New York?"

"A board meeting."

"Over the weekend?"

"The board meeting was scheduled for Monday. He was booked into the Mandarin Oriental, but of course he never checked in. I called to confirm."

"Do you have any idea what his itinerary was for the weekend? Free time in the city?"

A brief silence, and then she says, "Down time. Drinks with friends. And an appointment at Armani for a fitting."

"Is there someone special he visits in New York?"

"I'm not sure I know what you're insinuating."

"If you think I'm insinuating, then you do know," Mills tells her.

Another pause. "I don't arrange affairs."

"So, you're saying he has affairs. Romantic affairs."

"That's not what I'm saying."

"Do you have a photo of your boss?"

"Of course I do."

"Would you mind sending me one?"

"I'd be happy to. Casual or formal? Mr. Klink is a stickler for details."

"Mr. Klink could be dead. In which case details won't matter to him."

She gasps. "Oh, God, dear God, I'm responsible for his every move."

"I'm sorry, Shelly. I shouldn't have said that," Mills concedes. "It's late, and I need to get off the phone. I'm going to give you a number, and I want you to send me a photo. Okay?"

"Okay."

"Does your boss have any distinguishing marks that we won't see in the photo?"

"No. I don't think so."

"No tattoos?"

"Not that I know of."

"A more recent beard, mustache?"

"No."

"Moles?"

"One. But it's under his neck. You probably won't see it in the picture."

"Does he have a dentist?" Mills asks.

"A dentist?" A curveball for most civilians.

"Yes. A dentist. We'd like his dental records for a positive match."

"Oh, oh, yes," she says. "I'm sorry. Of course he goes to the dentist."

"I don't suppose you schedule those appointments for him."

"Like I said, I schedule his life."

"Then please send me contact information for his dentist. To the same number."

There's an emptiness now, as if the line has gone dead.

"Ms. Newton?"

"Yes," she murmurs, presumably behind quiet tears. "I'm sorry. I just . . . I just can't believe. But, yes, I'll look through my files for the dentist's name and get that to you. No problem."

Mills thanks the woman for her time. "Ma'am, I can't say this enough, but you might be the first person to come forward with a truly solid lead for us."

"I hope not," she says. "If you know what I mean."

"I do." He gives her his phone number, thanks her again, and says good night.

Back at the hole in the ground, Mills feels emboldened but cautious. Even if John Doe is Davis Klink, what the fuck is the killer really up to? Gus is kneeling at the gravesite. The shadows make him look like a monk at prayer, enough so that at first Mills hesitates to approach. Powell intercepts.

"Interesting call?"

"Potentially." He fills her in, detailing his call with Shelly Newton.

"What's Illumilife Industries?" she asks.

"I have no fucking clue," he says. "Should've asked."

"No worries. That's why God created Google. I'll look into it."

The shadows have shifted, and Gus is no longer a monk. He's a beagle. Mills lowers himself to his knees.

"You're a little too close for comfort," he tells his psychic friend.

"I haven't disturbed anything, Alex."

"More importantly, are you seeing anything?"

"Not really," Gus says. "But you're not going to solve this overnight. In fact, this is just the beginning."

"So you do get a vibe?"

"Yeah," Gus says. "I get a vibe, but unfortunately I don't *see* a thing."

Alex has filled Gus in on the call from Davis Klink's secretary, and they're about halfway to Alex's house when the photograph of the CEO comes in. The detective squints at his phone and, making digital tweezers of his fingers, enlarges the photo so every splotch on the man's face is like a NASA image of Mars.

"I'm looking for the identifying mole under the man's neck," Alex explains. "But the secretary warned that the photograph might not reveal it, and it doesn't."

He zooms back out. Studies hard.

"Mole or not, there's a similarity to John Doe," he says. He shows Gus the preceding JPEG on his phone: a JPEG of John Doe staring up from the grave, as provided to him by the crime scene photographer. He swipes between the two. "Davis Klink alive, John Doe dead. I see it in the lips, the chin, the ridge below the nose. Even using a bashed-in head to compare, they're the same guy."

"You've got the trained eye, but lemme see."

Alex hands him the phone. With one eye on the road and one eye on Davis Klink, Gus tries to intuit. Davis Klink is smiling a million-dollar smile. He's got the eyes of a man who knows everything, owns everything, and will someday control everything. Sparkling teeth, sparkling eyes, sparkling champagne. In a sudden vision, the man's making a toast. Every diamond on his cuff link represents a thousand people he's cut from the workforce. Gus doesn't know this for sure, but, with a vibe that pulses through his fingertips, he senses that Davis Klink is the master of layoffs. He almost runs a red light. Slams on the brakes. Alex is not amused. Gus is about to hand the phone back to the detective when it issues a strong vibration. But the phone, itself, isn't vibrating. There's percussion from deeper inside, from somewhere in the life of Davis Klink. And it stops, starts again, a loop of memory and music.

"Gus?"

"Yeah?"

"The light's green."

"Oh. Sorry." He hits the gas. The vehicle rumbles forward.

"What's up, man?" Alex asks. "I know when you're having one of your vision things."

Gus nods. "Right. But not exactly a vision thing. I'm hearing a song. I know the words are in Spanish, but I don't speak Spanish."

"*No bueno*," Alex says. "*No bueno*."

5

Not exactly the ideal Sunday either, Alex Mills has arranged to meet Shelly Newton at her home in Chandler. Jan Powell is with him. On the way Mills calls into the Office of the Medical Examiner to inquire about a mole on the Valley Vista corpse. While waiting on hold for the technician to check, he slips into a Starbucks drive-through and decides after a few sips that Starbucks might not have the same jolt for him as it used to. "Yup," the tech says. "A mole under the chin. You want a picture?" Mills answers affirmatively and pulls into traffic.

Shelly Newton's house is a stucco-and-tile replica of every other one in her neighborhood, and, like every other one in her neighborhood, it sits on a postage-stamp lot with desert shrubbery and one anemic palm tree. Inside it's a smallish box of Southwest décor (earth tones, potted cacti, pottery, and cheap, patronizing prints of Native Americans), which happens often when people move from Michigan or Illinois to their new homes in Arizona. Shelly says she's from Minnesota, and she sounds like it. She moved here ten years ago when her husband took a job with Southwest Airlines. He's working today, but she got his permission, she assures Mills, to talk to them.

Mills can't recall Kelly ever asking his permission for anything.

The small talk ended in the foyer.

He and Powell are sitting on an overstuffed sofa opposite Shelly, who sits in a recliner. The room is bright and smells like cinnamon. She's a petite woman with a heart-shaped face. Her hair is shoulder-length and curly, not exactly what he'd call stylish, but Mills is the first to admit he doesn't understand style. There's just something dowdy about her, though she couldn't be more than thirty-five. She's wearing a pink-and-gray Illumilife T-shirt, as if she dressed for the occasion.

"I believe our victim is your boss," Mills tells her. "I've confirmed the mole under his neck. I have a picture, but it's a close-up of the mole, not the injured face."

"I'll know it."

"Really?"

"Oh, yes," she says. "I've been after him to get it checked. I set up two appointments with a dermatologist, and he was a no-show for both."

"You sound like his wife," Mills says as she glances at the JPEG on his phone.

"That's it," she says without hesitation.

"Seriously? You can tell in a split second?" Powell asks her.

The woman smiles grimly. "It kind of looks like the profile of a penis. There can't be many moles like that."

Mills takes the phone back, finger tweezes for a zoom, and nods. "Yeah, I guess you could say that."

Shelly leans in intimately. "Don't call me crazy. I'm not some kind of pervert. But it's a memorable mole. It just kind of juts out like an erection, you know, with a blob at the end and a blob and a half underneath, like testicles. You see it?"

"I said I did."

"Totally irregular as moles go," she persists. "Asymmetrical, odd edges." Then she looks away, her chin trembling. She's a portrait of grief. Tears begin to fall, and she wipes them away with her wrist.

"We're so sorry," Powell tells her. "Do you need a minute?"

The woman turns back to them. "No," she replies softly. "I tried to prepare for this. I think I knew deep down inside. It's not like him to go completely off the grid for more than a few hours."

"Then you must know what he was doing Friday afternoon," Mills says. "I'd like to account for his time before that flight was scheduled to leave."

"Well, he was scheduled for meetings all afternoon," Shelly begins.

"But he got a call from his daughter Jordan around three o'clock. It was unexpected and unscheduled."

"Would he normally require his calls with family to be scheduled?" Powell asks.

Her eyes narrow as if she doesn't understand the question. "Pretty much every second of his day is scheduled. He's a CEO of a global company. You wouldn't understand."

Mills leans forward. "We're going to have to understand if we hope to find his killer."

Shelly puts her hand to her heart and says, "Of course. I didn't mean it that way. What I'm trying to say is that Davis is always overscheduled."

"What happened when the daughter called?" Powell asks her.

"Jordan sounded really sick, like I almost didn't recognize her voice," the woman says. "But I put the call through, and the next thing I know he comes rushing out of his office, says he doesn't need the driver, and he's out the door."

"And that's the last time you saw him alive?" Mills asks.

"Yes."

"You assume he took his own car?"

"Yes."

"To see his daughter?"

"Yes."

"Devoted father," Mills says with measured snark.

"Your words, not mine, Detective Mills."

"Other children?" Powell asks.

"Two others."

"Strained relationships with them?"

"I'd rather not get into his personal life any further," the woman says. "That's a bit out of my lane."

"Your lane?" Mills asks.

"Hmm, I guess that's a corporate expression."

"Guess so," Mills says. "But you seem to run every other aspect of his life. Did you not provide personal assistance?"

"I did," she concedes, "but I just don't want to talk about it."

"Is there anyone in his personal or professional life who, in your opinion, would want him dead?" Powell asks her.

The woman fidgets in her chair, dabs her eyes. "I don't know."

"But that's not a no?" Powell prods.

"I would hope not. But I don't know. He made many unpopular moves."

"Like?" Mills asks.

She leans forward. "Look, every CEO makes unpopular decisions. He's no different. You close factories, sell brands, unfortunately cut jobs to stay profitable. If he got killed for that, alone, there'd be a lot of dead CEOs today."

That thought has occurred to Mills. For all he knows, there are more CEOs out there in shallow graves. That could be the killer's MO *and* motive.

"You probably worked closer to him than anyone at your company," Powell says, and Shelly beams proudly at the recognition. "He might have even trusted you more than anyone else."

"I often suspected that. No one had better access to him than me."

Like he was Springsteen, for Christ's sake.

"Do you recall him arguing with anyone? Or having a heated phone call recently?" Mills asks.

"Well, he had a big blowout with our human resources officer on Friday morning."

"About?" Powell asks.

"I wasn't in the room."

"Then why would you characterize it as a big blowout?" Mills asks.

"Because I could hear it through the walls. I couldn't tell what they were saying, but they were going at it."

"Did he have blowouts often with people?"

"Sometimes. He's demanding. Was demanding," she says. "About two hours after his blowout with Claire from HR, he had another one with Peter in Legal."

"Wow," Mills says. "Friday was certainly a stressful day for a man who ends up dead later that night."

Shelly shakes her head. "No. I don't think so. I don't think either of those arguments have anything to do with his murder."

"But you can't say for sure?" Powell asks.

"I wasn't there when he was killed," she says and begins to sob.

They let her weep. They let her stare up at the ceiling. They let her dry her eyes and take a deep breath.

"For the record," Mills says when Shelly recovers, "where were you Friday night?"

"Here at home with my husband."

He knows he doesn't really need her alibi, but it's an important reflex. "Do you have children?" he asks.

"Three."

"Ages?"

"Twelve, ten and seven," she replies. "Those are their pictures on the shelf."

Mills turns to look. All-American towheads, with blue eyes and bright faces, stare back at him. "Handsome family," he says.

"Thank you."

"Any way you can arrange for us to meet Claire from Human Resources and Peter from Legal?" he asks her.

"When?"

"Tomorrow."

She scrunches her face. "Jeez, Mondays are hard. They might be traveling. I can check with their assistants."

Mills says he'll call in the morning to confirm. "And one more thing, Ms. Newton? Klink's wife. Has she ever returned your calls?"

She looks down, shakes her head. "No. But I checked her itinerary. She's due back from Italy tonight."

"Did you indicate that her husband was missing in the messages that you left?"

"Not in so many words."

"What did you say?" Powell asks.

"I said I was having trouble reaching him."

"And does Mrs. Klink normally return your calls?" Powell asks.

"Greta lives in her own world," Shelly says, her tone bitter.

"When she hears that her husband is dead, she might come back to this world," Mills says. "I'll need for you to give us her telephone number, and I'll need for you to cease calling her immediately. If she does call you back, give her my contact information."

"Would she want her husband dead for any reason?" Powell asks.

"I don't know. I mean, no. I mean, how would I know?" she says, exasperated. "I told you I don't get into their personal lives unless I have to. I'm happy to help, but keep me out of their personal business."

Then yes, Mills infers, there were marital issues. Were the issues lethal? Greta Klink should have the answer to that question. Maybe she wasn't in Italy, after all.

Gus has already been home twice to walk Ivy since spending the night in Billie's bungalow at the Desert Charm. When he returns to the resort for the second time, Billie is just starting to stir. It's two o'clock in the afternoon.

"Have you been out?" she asks as she hoists herself up in bed, a sleepy smile on her face.

"Ivy."

"Oh."

"Do you want me to call room service for coffee?"

"Sure," she says, and then she adds, "Is there something wrong?"

He shakes his head. Nothing's wrong. But something, Gus senses, isn't right. He can't put a finger on it, but there's an unprompted distance between them. Nothing happened. No words were said. He came in last night to find her writing in her journal. She had asked what he discovered at the graveyard, and he told her, and, as he did, he could sense a momentary shiver within her. Then she went back to writing. And he went to sleep. Today the light around them seems more tentative than usual. In the silence of this exile, there are no expectations.

The bungalow opens to a private courtyard with a splash pool. High walls, adorned with flowers and vine, surround them. The place makes him want to go to Tuscany or maybe to a villa in Capri. The coffee arrives, its fierce aroma wafting, and they're sipping out here when Billie turns to Gus and announces that she's leaving for LA.

"When?"

"Tonight."

He nods. She's impulsive, if nothing else. And there's little middle ground with her. She can be distant like the lowest of tides, and she can be, like a high tide at full moon, all the energy you'll ever need. He's okay with that. He's still a surfer at heart, and he's had a long, dreamy relationship with the ocean. He understands it. Even now, after many years in the desert.

"I'd rather you didn't leave," he tells her. "We can stay at my place if you don't want to go back to your house."

She turns to him, confusion in her eyes. "But why would I need a place to crash, when I have the house in Malibu?"

"A place to crash? Maybe I'm misunderstanding something about us," he says.

"This has nothing to do with us," she insists. "I just need to be someplace that's mine, that's safe, where no one has broken into. I need to be in my own comfortable surroundings. Can't you understand that?"

She's not accusatory but clearly desperate for affirmation.

"I can," he replies.

"And of course you could come with."

He loves returning to the ocean, loves the house in Malibu, but the difference between them is that her week begins when she wants it to begin, and his week begins tomorrow. "I have to work," he says.

"Well I'm not going back to PV unless Alex can assure me the house is impenetrable."

"I don't think anyone can guarantee that," he says. "Besides, Alex is now up to his neck in this graveyard case."

She gets up, closing her robe around her. "Then I gotta go, Gus."

"And I can't stop you, Billie."

6

Mills is up before the sunrise. But, contrary to the plan, Kelly is up before him and she's beaten him to the shower. "Hon! I need to get out of here," he groans.

"What's your hurry?"

"Hmm, let's see . . . a killer on the loose?"

"And let's see . . . I have jury selection," she reminds him from behind the steam. "Because somebody actually caught *my* perp."

"Nice," he says. "What shit-for-brains are you defending today?"

"I told you. That pinhead who robbed the pet store in Tempe."

He laughs. "The one the cops tracked down with the fecal DNA from the goldfish?"

"Turtle," she says.

"Same difference." He feels the throb of morning wood in his briefs, and he presses himself against the shower door. "Let me in, and I'll make it worth your while."

"Are you kidding me, Alex?"

"What?"

"I can't be late for jury selection because of your erection."

"You're a poet," he says. "Not even a quickie?"

"I'll make it up to you."

"Do you know how many IOUs you've given me in the past month?"

"I'm not keeping track."

"Well, that's great," he groans. "If you're not keeping track, then how're you supposed to honor them?"

She opens the door a crack, flashes a saucy grin, and shuts him out again just as quickly. Duly dismissed, he steps out to the kitchen and pulls out the yogurt and granola for breakfast. He slices some fruit for Kelly. In the process, his dick withers and he worries that by the time Kelly's trial is over, the morning wood will be permanent pulp and he'll be beholden to Viagra. They've always been explosively compatible—not *Fifty Shades*, but still—and he misses the frequency of sex.

He just about jumps out of his skin when he hears his son's booming voice. He turns and finds Trevor hulking at the edge of the kitchen, in sweats and a T-shirt.

"What do you want? Shouldn't you be getting ready for school?"

The kid snickers. "Yeah. But I need sixty dollars."

"Sixty? What for?"

"Yearbook."

Mills shakes his head but doesn't argue. The kid's a senior, expected to get into both Arizona State University and the University of Arizona on a football scholarship. Trevor's really turned himself around after a few adolescent setbacks. His grades are stellar again, confirming that the brain he inherited is likely his mother's.

"Hang on 'til I get out of the shower," he tells his son. "In the meantime make some coffee for your mom and me."

Later, on the way into work, while listening to a pair of morning radio clowns trying to be clever, funny, and shocking, and failing at all three, Mills's phone rings. He doesn't recognize the caller but answers on the off chance that someone is calling with a lead or, less likely, that Davis Klink's killer is reaching out to confess.

"This is Greta Klink," the caller says. And that's it. She drops her name, as if that's enough. As if the dead silence is Mills's cue to jump. Instead of jumping, Mills lets the silence sink in for a moment. He listens for grief and hears nothing but the cacophony of rush hour.

"Thanks for calling, Mrs. Klink. I'm sorry I have bad news about—"

"So I've heard."

"You've spoken with Ms. Newton?"

"Yes. Shelly told me to contact you."

"Are you home this morning, Mrs. Klink?"

"I am."

"We'd like to come by and talk."

"I'll text you the address. Goodbye."

After the widow's abrupt departure, Mills swings into the Starbucks close to headquarters for another fill-up.

He's in his office, jacked up on caffeine, when about ten minutes into the workday the sergeant calls and kills the buzz. Woods wants to meet with the squad.

"I was planning on meeting with them at nine," Mills tells him. "Join us then?"

"No."

"No?"

"Let's do it now," the sergeant demands. "Gather 'em in the conference room. I'll be up in a sec."

There's nothing specific about Jacob Woods's urgency, Mills knows. It has more to do with control than anything else. Woods is not a micromanager, but he's an impatient son of a bitch and as political as anyone has ever been in the Phoenix Police Department. More political than the chief, even, and that's probably because Sergeant Jacob Woods sees himself becoming Chief Jacob Woods in the not too distant future. He'll have to wait his turn, step over a few heads on the way, but Mills has no doubt Woods will make it. Nor does he have any doubt that Woods's success will likely be on the backs of people like Mills, whose job it is to solve crime in order to make people like Woods look good. Getting killers off the street, it turns out, is collateral success.

A few minutes later in the conference room, Mills welcomes Preston, who shows up first. Myers follows next. Powell arrives last, coffee in hand, and takes a seat at the head of the table. Mills remains on his feet, waiting for the sergeant.

"Where is he?" Powell asks.

"I thought he'd be here," Mills says. "It's been ten minutes."

"You made it sound so urgent."

"I don't know, Jan," he says. Then his phone rings. It's a department number. He answers and finds himself talking to Jerry Jordan in the Black Mountain precinct.

"You sent out a BOLO for a dark blue BMW SUV?" the officer asks, referring to Mills's "be on the lookout" request that went out department-wide.

"I did."

"Got a call from a Safeway over here. They got one abandoned behind the store. Plate comes back to a company called Illumilife. Insured driver is your victim."

"Davis Klink?"

"Yep."

A wave of affirmation rises from his feet to his face. He can't hide the goofball smile from his squad when he speaks into the phone and says, "That's our SUV. Is the scene secured?"

"As we speak," Jerry Jordan tells him.

"Great. I'll send a flatbed to bring it to the lab."

"I'll take care of the transport if you want."

"That would be huge. Thanks. And hey, Jerry, if you can text me the Safeway address, I'd like to send someone over and see about surveillance video. . . ."

"I'm happy to do that, too, Detective."

Mills looks at his squad. "I got some eager folks in front of me. One of them will handle it. Just send the address."

"Done."

When Mills ends the call, he looks at the others and simply says, "Any questions?"

"No," Preston tells him. "Sounds like we got the victim's car. Great news."

"I have a question," Powell says. "Where the fuck is Woods?"

"I have no idea," Mills replies. "But in the meantime, let's get some things out of the way. . . ."

"Did I hear someone call my name?"

Powell's face goes red.

Woods enters the room, gives a nod, and takes a seat facing Mills who is standing at the whiteboard.

"We were just getting started," Mills tells the sergeant. "So, our victim is Davis Klink, CEO of Illumilife Industries, a Fortune 500 conglomerate based here in Phoenix. We have met with his executive assistant and plan to meet with colleagues at company headquarters hopefully later this morning or this afternoon. His car was just found and is on the way to the lab to get processed. Powell and I will head out after this meeting to interview Klink's surviving wife."

Everyone is nodding back at him.

The list on the whiteboard is growing.

"Preston and Myers, get before a judge and get search warrants for Klink's bank records, credit card transactions, cell phone accounts, you know, his whole life," Mills says. "We also need to know what happened when he left his office. Where did he go? Who saw him? When and where did he cross paths with his killer?"

"Got it," Preston says.

"And in your free time," Mills says with a laugh, "please run out to the Safeway and inquire about surveillance video. I'll forward you the location."

Woods clears his throat and says, "I have to make a statement to the press."

Mills looks at him blankly. Woods rewards him with a passive-aggressive smile and, in his eyes, the implicit message that Mills should get ready to jump through a hoop. Mills doesn't jump through hoops. Instead, he lets the stare down hang there. A tug-of-war. It's stupid and unnecessarily macho, but fuck it, his job is to catch a killer, not to change the sergeant's diaper.

"It's forty-eight hours today since the body was found," Woods says, relenting but persistent. "We're getting calls, like every ten minutes, from reporters. We'll release our victim's name and say we have no motive but we're pursuing multiple leads."

Woods is two o'clock, sitting, to Mills's six o'clock, standing. "Multiple leads might be a stretch," Mills tells his boss. "And please don't release his name until I'm able to talk to the wife and confirm that all next of kin know."

"Your call," the sergeant says. "What about the secondary grave at All Faiths?"

"I obviously think they're related," Mills replies. "But it's way too early to tell how or why. I think the more we discover about Klink's murder, the better we'll be able to connect the two."

"Before we have another body?"

"That's the goal," Mills quips.

"I think we need to keep our resources aimed at the killer," Powell says. "I don't think we have the luxury of chasing empty graves."

"Agreed," Mills says.

With that, Sergeant Jacob Woods is on his feet. "All right. Thanks, everyone. Good job. Let's catch our guy and have a great day."

When he's out the door, the room is quiet in his wake. They look at each other. Myers reaches in his front pocket and removes a Twinkie. He unwraps it gingerly, and there isn't a sound but the crinkly undoing of the plastic sheath. Fully liberated, the snack cake goes directly into Myers's mouth and down his gullet with minimal chews.

Powell leans back in her chair, arms folded across her chest. "What's with the cockfight, Mills?"

"Cockfight?"

"Yeah," she says, "you and Woods waving your dicks around."

"Is that how you perceived it?"

"That's how everyone perceived it," Preston says.

"I'm sorry, folks," Mills tells them. "But you know what I see? I see a dead CEO. And a dead CEO becomes a very high-profile case. And I see the governor and the mayor, maybe the entire city council—who the fuck knows?—and you know where this all leads."

"Then let's get to work," Preston says.

Mills gives them all a hearty smile. "Thanks for being the adult in the room," he says to Preston. "Plan on reconvening end of day, everyone, tomorrow morning latest."

Davis Klink lived with his family on their estate in North Scottsdale, in an exclusive subdivision called Miracle Canyon. It's guard-gated. Mills just flashes a badge, and the guard on duty waves them in.

The Klink compound sits at the back of Miracle Canyon in the shadows of the McDowell Mountains. They have horses. And riding rings. A main house of stone and glass, mostly glass (Mills counts seventeen windows on the façade alone), sits at the center of the property, flanked by outbuildings on each side, maybe guesthouses or offices. Apparently there is an indoor pool in the building to the left because Mills can see the sun's reflection shimmering on the water. Whatever it is, it's befitting a man who lords over a global conglomerate.

The driveway gates open gracefully with a quiet whisper, granting access.

They get out of their car, Powell with an appreciative whistle to the wealth, Mills with an eye roll to her whistle.

Mrs. Klink, with a uniformed woman to her side, is waiting at the front door. "Hello," she says. She's dressed as a minimalist multimillionaire, wearing a simple tight gray skirt and a sleeveless turtleneck exposing arms crafted by Pilates or tennis, or both. Her diamond bracelets are simple strands of gleaming stones. Her face, bronzed by the sun of good fortune, features a nose with the perfect pitch for a woman of her stature—that is, to say, most probably sculpted by the best plastic surgeon money can buy. The rest of her, however, looks fairly spared by the scalpel. Short, blunt, blond hair caps her head.

"I'm Detective Alex Mills from the Phoenix Police Department. This is my partner Detective Jan Powell."

"Yes," the woman says, granting them each a once-over. "I figured as much. I'll have Lola show you to my office and take your drink requests."

Mills looks at his partner and shrugs at the oddity. They follow Lola, a diminutive woman with a pensive face and quiet smile, through the marble foyer and into a vast room two stories high. A wall of glass overlooks an outdoor pool area reminiscent of the Hearst Castle; another wall is filled entirely with tropical fish, colors so dazzling and vibrant they confound the eyes. They exit the main house there, meander around the mosaics of the pool deck, and follow Lola into the outbuilding on the left. Mills shakes his head, trying to comprehend the necessities of the über wealthy, as they pass through a spa-like setting, like something you'd see on a cruise ship, with the indoor pool, a kidney-shaped Jacuzzi with room for twenty, he guesses, two massage tables, a sauna and steam room, and all of it is just staged there and waiting for barely a soul to use. But surely it's a conversation piece, the whole place. Lola leads them into an office at the end of a long hallway, more marble, more glass. A Spartan desk and chair, an exquisitely sculpted Italian sofa, the same color gray as Greta Klink's outfit.

"Mrs. Klink will be with you shortly," Lola tells them as they sit. "What will be your beverage of choice?"

"I think we can do without," Mills tells her.

"But Mrs. Klink insists," Lola says. "A glass of wine, perhaps? I can have Leo mix you a cocktail if you'd prefer. He's in the kitchen preparing lunch for the house. But he wouldn't mind at all."

"We're on duty," Mills says. "But thank you anyway."

"Then I'll bring in a selection of juices, unless you'd like coffee."

Mills gives her a friendly, amused laugh and says, "It won't be necessary, really."

When Lola ducks out of the office, Mills and Powell are quiet, staring at each other, then around the room. The walls are charcoal and completely unadorned. A few ornaments reside on the desk. The detectives' prying eyes shift to the door at the sound of approaching heels. The click-clack on marble grows louder. Greta Klink enters, a glass of wine in one hand. She sits behind the desk. "I'm sorry you won't join me for a drink," she says.

Mills understands the importance of staying hydrated in the desert, but the emphasis on beverages in this household mystifies him, especially now, given the circumstances. "Mrs. Klink, we'd like to ask you some questions about your husband," he says.

"First of all, please call me Greta, and second of all, I'm not sure I'll have the answers you're looking for. We never discussed the minutia of Illumilife."

Mills shifts his body, gives her an angle to consider. "We're not here specifically to ask you about his business unless you believe his business is somehow connected to his death."

She smiles thinly. "I have no reason to believe that, but I thought that would be your assumption."

"We assume nothing," Powell tells her. "When was the last time you spoke to your husband?"

"I can't recall, honestly. Probably on Thursday of last week," she replies. "If he went missing on Friday night, then, yes, probably Thursday."

"And you were in Italy?"

She nods. "Milan. I bought him a new briefcase to celebrate the acquisition."

"Acquisition?" Mills asks.

"Yes," she says, beaming. "Illumilife bought out Portman Brands last month. Everyone's talking about it."

"I don't follow business news," Mills tells her. "But contrary to what you said a minute ago, it does seem like you followed his business."

"Well, of course," she said, clutching the wine glass. "Of course I follow the business. What I mean is that we don't discuss the details or the inner workings."

"Do you have a career yourself?"

"I'm just returning to work as a management consultant," she says. "I left my career to raise a family."

"How many children?"

"Two of ours, together. One from his previous marriage."

"Do they all live here?"

"Douglas, my stepson does," she replies. "The girls are at boarding school in Flagstaff."

"So you last spoke to your husband on Thursday from Milan," Mills says. "Was there anything remarkable about the conversation? I want you to think really hard about what he said. In fact, I want you to recall any recent conversations with him when he might have expressed any anxieties or concerns. What was bothering him?"

She sighs. Her face, like a fifth sterile wall in the room, has not yielded an expression. This ice queen won't melt. Not even now, talking about her dead husband. "I can't think of anything," she says. "Really, I've been trying. I've been racking my brain trying to remember something important."

"Had he argued with anyone to your knowledge?" Powell asks.

"Look," the woman says, leaning forward, "someone who does what my husband does for a living argues with people because arguments lead to better decisions. Of course there were conflicts. You don't lead a major, global company without running into conflicts. They happen several times a day. Let's not be naïve, Detectives, my husband was entrusted with the livelihoods of thousands of employees, thousands of stockholders. He made unpopular decisions. He rubbed some people the wrong way. But look at the stock price. It's up thirty percent from two years ago. That's why they pay him what they pay him."

Mills lets a few seconds linger, allows her dissertation to hang in the air. Then he shifts again, squares himself to her, and says, "Let's cut to the chase, Greta. Can you think of anyone who would want your husband dead?"

She takes a sip of wine, puts the glass down with a clink. "Like I said, he made some unpopular decisions. Some people were not in favor of the acquisition. But I can't imagine anyone killing Davis over business matters."

"Names?" Mills inquires.

"Names?"

"Do you have names of people who opposed your husband's unpopular decisions?"

She laughs. "How could I possibly? There could be thousands of people out there."

"Thousands," Powell says. "Wow."

"Anyone prominent?" Mills asks. "A thorn in his side?"

"You can always ask the board," Greta Klink suggests. "Or any one of the chief executives."

Lola enters the room, stops just inside the doorway. "Mrs. Klink, can I get you another glass of wine?"

"Please," the lady of the house replies.

Mills pulls up a JPEG on his phone. It's Davis Klink posing in the morgue. Maybe this will break her. He puts it on the woman's desk. She notices it as soon as Lola leaves the room. "What's this?" she asks.

"I'm sorry to have to share this with you now," Mills tells her.

"Why would you show me this?"

"To make sure we're talking about the same man."

She pushes the phone back to him, and it almost falls to the floor. Then her folded hands hit the desk, her jewels banging the surface. "I know my husband is dead, Detective Mills. You don't have to prove it."

"Again, I'm sorry," he says. "But I'm puzzled by your demeanor."

"My demeanor?"

"He means you don't appear all that upset by the news," Powell suggests. "Were you and your husband on good terms at the time of his death?"

"What on earth do you mean? I loved my husband."

"Were there infidelities?" Powell asks. It's always better when the woman asks that question.

Greta Klink looks away. She does this odd, pursing thing with her lips. Then she looks down at her hands and says, "That question is too personal."

"You should answer it," Powell says. "If you want to help us catch your husband's killer."

The woman looks at Powell fiercely, then at Mills. "I don't see how this"—she waves her hands at both of them—"is helping."

"How long had you been in Italy?" Mills asks.

"Three weeks," she says.

"Is that a typical vacation?"

"It wasn't all vacation. I did have some R and R, but I was visiting with several clients."

"As far as we know, the last family member to speak to your husband was your daughter Jordan. Is that correct?" Mills asks.

"That's what I've been told," Greta says. "But I can't confirm that."

"Why not?"

"Because—"

Lola enters the room, quietly places a glass of wine on the desk, and retreats.

"Because," Greta continues, reaching for the glass, raising it to her lips, "we're a bit estranged, my daughter and I."

"Estranged?"

"We don't get along. But she's daddy's little girl. Wouldn't surprise me if she called him because she had a runny nose. All the way from Flagstaff!"

"And do you know when your other children last spoke with their father?"

"Douglas said he spoke with Davis over breakfast Friday morning," she replies. "They usually get up at five to run together if Davis isn't traveling. Joanna, my other daughter, said she hadn't talked to him all week."

"We need to speak with all of them," Powell says. "I'd imagine they're home, now, given the circumstances."

Greta shakes her head. "I didn't want to pull the girls out of school until I make funeral arrangements. Douglas flew to Atlanta to get his grandmother."

"Your husband's mother?" Mills asks.

She nods. "They'll be here tomorrow. She's devastated."

"Of course," Mills says, lifting himself from the sofa. "We'll be in touch to arrange a visit with your children. Thank you for your time." He hands her his business card. "If you think of anything, anything at all that might help, please call. Even the seemingly most minor details, Greta, could prove to be an important lead for us. Something doesn't seem right? You let us know."

"I will," she says, rising to her feet. She offers a firm handshake to both of them. "I'll have Lola show you out."

Jesus, some people. Jesus, some families. They've been riding in silence for several minutes now, thawing out from their visit with the ice queen at the Klink compound. Mills has been shaking his head the whole way.

"Alex, please stop shaking your head, and say something," Powell begs.

"I'm dumbfounded."

"You and me both. The grandmother is devastated. Did you hear that?"

"I did," he replies. "But the wife, not so much. Not a tear in her eye. Not a frown on her face. That was a fucking weird interview."

"We've got to dig deeper with her," Powell says. "There are stories there. Big, complex stories, I think. Like he was having affairs, or she was having affairs, or both of them were screwing around. This puts a mistress in play, or a boyfriend. Or anyone who could benefit from Davis Klink's death."

"Like a child," Mills says. "Who stands to inherit a fortune."

"I'm going with adultery."

"We're forgetting the empty grave," Mills points out. "If another body turns up, our theories, however shitty they might be at this point, are probably out the window."

"Unless it's the body of Greta Klink."

7

Mills is eating lunch at his desk when he gets a call from Shelly Newton at Illumilife. She says two of the chief executives have been freed up to meet with him at three o'clock. She says the whole company is in shock, that people are openly grieving. It's as if the whole building is mourning, she says. But her voice sounds chipper. So at least he has that to look forward to.

"Hey, Shelly, I have a question, if you don't mind," he says.

"I hope I have an answer."

"Why would Mr. Klink's daughter call him all the way from Flagstaff if she were sick? What could he do for her here? I doubt he bolted from the office to drive up to Flagstaff. That doesn't make sense."

"I'm not sure she was calling from Flagstaff," Shelly says. Then she laughs for a second and says, "You don't know Jordan. She's had a habit lately of sneaking off campus and coming back to Phoenix to party with her friends. Especially on the weekends."

"How does she get here? Does she have a car at boarding school?"

"No cars allowed," the assistant says. "But she has this boyfriend—"

Mills takes a swig of water. "Name?"

"Of the boyfriend? Hmm. I can't recall."

"Try."

"I'm so sorry," she says. "They come and go, you know."

"Go down the alphabet, or something," Mills suggests.

"Pardon me for saying this, but I think you're overestimating the importance of the boy," she replies. "He likely has nothing to do with this whatsoever."

"I'd rather overestimate than underestimate. It's my job."

"Right," she says. "Let's see, Glen was a few months ago. Mohammed was before that, and that's a name that's easy to remember, right? She dated a Jack, but that was last year. And so was—what was his name?—Antonio? Oh, now I know! A is for Antonio. B is for Bradley. She's dating a guy named Bradley."

"Last name?"

"No idea, sorry."

He jots down a note to follow up about the boyfriend. "That's okay, Ms. Newton. We'll see you this afternoon."

Despite what his doctor said about watching his cholesterol, Mills hates these fucking lunches of salad and fruit. He looks at it with disgust and imagines, for a minute, a pastrami sandwich as thick as a suitcase. Unlike most men in midlife crisis, Mills is craving pastrami, not a Porsche. His joints ache, his hair is saltier, but he has no interest in proving his virility by jumping out of planes or fucking other women. How could he? He's married to a collector's item—a funny, sexy, smart, strong woman who gets more beautiful with age. Besides, he still gets morning wood, and that counts for something, even if Kelly shows more interest in her law reviews than in his dick.

Illumilife Industries occupies a gleaming skyscraper on Central. Mills counts fifteen floors of glass and beams, but he's squinting against the glare of the sun, so he might be off by a floor or two. A typical glass monolith, like so many others in the valley, the tower lacks its own fingerprint. Not so, on the inside. The lobby, a pyramid-shaped atrium, is a spectacle of refracted light. Two security guards stand behind a massive block of marble, upon it a sheet of raised glass, apparently their desk. Life-sized replicas of Illumilife's products, however, form the true welcoming party. Apparently Illumilife Industries makes everything. Car and truck tires bounce up and down like yo-yos from an automated track high up in the atrium. Several bicycles, all somehow mechanized, climb the walls at different heights. A mobile of life-sized baby cribs dangles from the roof. The security guards, Mills can now see, are standing on treadmills, slowly walking to nowhere as they greet Illumilife guests. Shelly Newton appears from behind the bank of glass elevators.

"Welcome," she says. "Our foyer is quite the experience for newcomers."

"Your company makes all this stuff in here?" Powell asks.

The woman smiles. "And more," she says as she escorts them to an elevator.

The elevator glides them to the executive floor, which lords over everyone. Up here, the floor-to-ceiling windows offer a 360 degree view of the valley's mountains. Shelly leads them to a small sitting area that takes its minimalist cues from the Klink's marble-and-glass Miracle Canyon home. From here they can see the arthritic fingers of Squaw Peak. The view is so detailed Mills can count the veins.

"You'll be meeting with our chief legal officer first," Shelly says. "He'll be with you in a minute."

Mills thanks her.

Fifteen minutes later they're still staring at the Peak. Mills can understand fifteen minutes. But he can't understand thirty. As thirty minutes come and go, Mills figures there's a certain narcissism embedded in the internal clock of a corporate titan that renders the schedule of anyone else meaningless; either that or there's been an explosion at a tire plant in China. At forty-five minutes, a young millennial toothpick with hair down to her waist approaches them. "I'm so sorry," she says. "Our executives are so crazy busy. It's really hard to keep them on time. Peter will see you now."

She leads them into an office, a space larger than most studio apartments. The office features a living room setting; the official working desk of Peter Tribble, Chief Legal Officer (so says the name plate); a collection of museum-quality leather chairs at his desk; a wet bar; and one of those miniature putting greens. A man enters and closes the door behind him.

"Peter Tribble," he says with a British accent. "Chief legal officer. Pleased to meet you. Sorry for the delay. A meeting went over."

Handshakes all around.

"Please join me at my desk," he says.

Mills eyes him before the man can sit down. He's a short guy, probably no more than five-six, maybe five-seven. He's youngish, late thirties maybe, younger than Mills would expect for a chief executive of a major company. Peter Tribble has small eyes, a happy, almost babyish smile. His skin lacks color, but his shirt (no tie) is turquoise, so that helps. He's wearing white skinny jeans with a studded belt. No jacket.

The man leans forward, ready to emphasize, as soon as he sits. "First, let me assure you, we're all stunned to learn about what has happened to Davis," he says. "We have not communicated this externally until we know that his next of kin have been notified."

"They have," Mills tells him. "And it's all over the news, so I'm sure it's out there externally, if not by you."

"Fine, but that's quite different than the arduous and painful task of messaging this to our stakeholders," laments the chief legal officer.

Mills goes poker face and stays there. This is how he deals with people who presume to talk from a marble pedestal. The accent doesn't help.

"You should know that as much as I want to help in your investigation, Detective Mills, my job is to also represent the best interests of the company."

Poker face.

"So you may have questions for me today that I cannot, out of the best interests of the company, answer."

Poker face.

"I will not be able to hand over any corporate records, or any documents whatsoever, without a subpoena."

Poker face.

"That's not to say we'd argue every subpoena in court, but we may have information that is either highly confidential, sensitive, or proprietary that we will insist on protecting."

Poker face.

"That said, let me assure you that we want to do everything we can to help you apprehend a suspect."

It's one thing when an American sounds supercilious, but when a Brit sounds supercilious, you want to punch him in the face.

"Are you following me?" Tribble asks them.

"What were you and Davis Klink fighting about on Friday?"

"Excuse me?"

"You were overheard having a heated argument with the CEO on Friday afternoon before he left the building," Mills says.

The man lowers his head. "A good argument is good for business," he concedes. "But, I'll admit this was worse than most."

"You're only admitting that to us because we have several witnesses who heard the shouting. Right?"

He smiles. "Yes. Imagine so. We did have a serious argument. One of our executives might have done something that could have compromised the integrity of the business," he explains. "This person came to me with the disclosure wanting to know if any law was broken or if the company would have legal grounds to terminate based on the questionable actions taken. Davis was furious that this person didn't go to him first and that I didn't tell him as soon as I learned of the problem."

"Does this person have a name?" Mills asks.

"I'm not prepared to release that at this time," the man replies.

"In the best interests of your company?" Powell asks.

"Precisely."

"What was the nature of the questionable action that this colleague told you about?"

"I'm not prepared to answer that."

"In the best interests of your company?" Mills asks.

"Precisely."

"If you end up on the witness stand, you will most definitely have to answer these questions," Mills says.

Tribble proudly sweeps his arm across the powerful landscape of his office domain. "This is not a courtroom, Detective. And I think it's against your best interests to invoke the image of a deposition or interrogation."

The poker face yields to the fuck-you face.

"I am documenting everything that is being said in this meeting, just as any good lawyer would do," Tribble informs them.

"How did your argument end?"

"I suggested Davis speak to this person directly, to remove me as the middleman."

"Did he agree to that?"

"Yes. Ultimately."

"Was he still fuming?"

"He wasn't happy," Tribble says. "But you have to understand something about Davis. He could be raging at you one minute, and all is forgotten the next. He's a perfectionist. But he's also too busy to hold a grudge. I knew that we'd be back at work today and everything would be fine."

"But he's not, and it isn't," Powell reminds him.

"He had another blowout with another executive on Friday," Mills says. "Was Davis having a confrontation with that colleague you referred to?"

"I can't say. I wasn't in the room."

"Was it the chief human resources officer?" Powell asks. "We understand he chewed her out pretty good."

"You'll have to ask her," the man says. "I understand you'll be speaking to her next."

"Eventually we will want to talk with the head of your security team," Powell says. "Just to be sure Davis Klink was not facing any threats from individuals while traveling, or here at home."

"I assure you I would know about any such threats."

Powell shifts in her chair and leans in. "We will want to talk to the head of your security team."

"And the car service hired to chauffer Davis Klink around," Mills adds.

Peter Tribble, chief legal officer, stands, indicating the meeting has come to a close. "Speaking of cars, we'd like access to Davis's vehicle. Just to be sure there are no confidential or sensitive documents. Has it been recovered?"

"Yes, sir, but I'm afraid it's not possible to give you access to it now," Mills says, standing as well, their eyes locking. "The car is a crime scene."

"I thought Davis was found in a cemetery," the man says.

"He was. That's not necessarily where he was killed," Mills explains.

"There are often multiple crime scenes in cases like this," Powell says. "The scene of death is only one of many possible crime scenes. This whole office building could be deemed a crime scene. That would not be unusual."

The man turns pale, even for a Brit. His hands are shaking as he picks up the phone. "Stella," he says, "our guests are ready for their next meeting."

Tribble scratches his chin as he leads them to the hallway. Something worries him. It's all over his face.

"Is something wrong, Mr. Tribble?" Mills asks.

He shakes his head absently. "No," he replies. "But I think it's only appropriate that I sit in on your interview with Claire, if you don't mind."

"We don't," Mills says.

If you put Peter Tribble's office into a 3-D printer and hit "Copy Now," you would get Claire White's office. The only differences are the views (his looks east to Camelback; hers looks south to the Estrella range) and the art on the walls (his has none; hers has extravagant hangings, crazy abstract, almost mural-like spectacles).

"If you're admiring the art," the chief human resources officer says with a heavy brogue, "they're all originals."

"Wow," Powell says. "Extraordinary."

Claire White points to a large canvas to her left. "That's a Picasso."

"No way," Powell says.

"I'm Detective Alex Mills, Phoenix PD. My partner, Jan Powell."

"Claire White," she says, twirling a finger around a diamond necklace. "But you probably knew that."

"The accent?" Mills asks. "It doesn't sound as British as Mr. Tribble's."

"And it's not. It's Irish. Not even close, if I do say so myself."

Claire White asks them to have a seat on the sofa in her living room area. She sits opposite them, Tribble to her side. She's wearing what some would call a smart pantsuit, teal.

"I suspect you know why we're here," Mills says.

The scarf draped elegantly around her shoulders takes it cues from the wild abstracts on the wall.

"I do. We're shaken to the core. Davis's death is an unimaginable loss to us." She leans forward, rests her wrists on her knees, and peers at them through her thousand-dollar designer eyeglasses. She says, "It's my job, as chief human resources officer, to console sixty thousand employees, and that's exactly what I intend to do. Here at Illumilife we put *you* first, whether you are our customers, consumers, shareholders, or employees."

Mills leans forward to abbreviate the distance between them. "I notice you put employees last on that list," he says. "That's odd coming from the chief human resources officer, but I'm not judging."

"It's our credo. At Illumilife we put *you* first. You are all equal, no matter who you are," she chants. "That credo is written into everything we do. We are that kind of company. It is in the soul of everything we do. Now, what can I help you with?"

His mouth a contortion of snark and disbelief, Mills fears what will happen when he parts his lips. Anything could come out. He takes a deep breath and says, "You were one of the last colleagues, if not the last, to speak to Davis Klink on this property. We'd like to know more about that conversation."

Long tresses of chemical blond curls frame her face. She pulls some of them behind a shoulder and says, "I don't know how much I can tell you."

"Either tell us now or possibly at a deposition," Powell says with a saccharine in her voice so artificially sweet that Mills can taste it.

"Don't let them threaten you," Tribble tells the woman, who waves him off sharply, reflexively. No love lost there.

"It's not a threat," Mills says. "And I mean that. We're here seeking cooperation. We want to do what it's in the best interest of Davis Klink. Not this company, not the Phoenix PD. Davis Klink."

Claire White nods and allows herself a rueful smile. "That's admirable," she says. "I guess it's no secret that we argued before he stormed out of here."

"Was it serious?" Mills asks.

"I wouldn't qualify that," Tribble says.

"It was serious," the woman concedes. "I might have made a mistake. I went to him to make amends."

"Can you tell us about the mistake?" Mills asks.

She crosses her legs and, again, balances her wrists on her knees. Her bangles chime as they fall into place. "I might have sold some company stock during the blackout period."

"Is that like insider trading?" Mills asks.

"Don't answer that question," Tribble instructs the woman.

"If it was," White says, "it was an innocent mistake. I simply forgot we were in blackout, and I wanted the funds to finish remodeling my home."

"And that's a terminable offense?" Powell asks.

"It could be," White concedes.

Mills raps the edge of the table between them and says, "We don't want to take up any more of your time, so if you could describe for us how the argument with Davis Klink ended."

She nods, gathering her thoughts. But there's more in her eyes. There's an assessment of something, a reconciliation, maybe. Mills sure wishes Gus Parker were here in the room. Finally she says, "It ended with him saying that I was on my own with this, that the company would not support me if charges were filed."

"Did he threaten to report you?"

"He didn't say. He left it purposefully ambiguous."

"How do you know it was purposeful?" Powell asks.

"Because that's his style."

"Where were you Friday night?" Mills asks.

"At home," White replies.

"All night?"

"Yes."

"With?"

"Are you questioning her as a suspect?" Tribble wants to know.

"Everyone is a suspect," Mills reminds him, then to Claire, he asks, "Who was with you?"

"My daughters."

"Are you married?" Powell asks.

"Divorced."

"How old are your daughters?" Powell continues.

"Eleven and fifteen."

"None of you left the house at any time?" Mills asks.

"No," she says. "Not at all. Are we through?"

Mills stands to confirm that they are. "For now."

The others follow, a faint sigh from Peter Tribble as he rises, and bid farewell with handshakes.

As Shelly Newton escorts them out of the building, she reaches for Mills's arm and pulls him toward her. She whispers, but Mills can't hear her over the whining treadmills in the lobby where the security guards continue to channel their inner hamster.

"Come outside," he tells her, and she follows.

"Call me," she says. "I think I have some new information."

"You can't tell me now?"

She backs away. She shakes her head. "No. I'll get in trouble if they see us talking. I've been warned."

8

Gus Parker presses a button, and Mrs. Betty Freck comes sliding out on her tray, kind of like a CD ejected from a big, old computer. Her CT scan is complete. He asks if she needs help up from the platform. She nods. Gus reaches for her arm and lifts. At 150 pounds, Mrs. Betty Freck is not a massive undertaking, but she is heavy enough to strain Gus's back. He's out of shape, and he knows it. He needs to exercise more, especially since he's in his forties. Maybe he'll start climbing Camelback again instead of just adoring it for its beauty. Beatrice Vossenheimer says they should get back to doing yoga together, and they should. Mrs. Betty Freck is standing on her feet now, and she takes a deep breath.

"You all right?" he asks.

"I'm fine, I think. But I hate that machine. So noisy and cramped."

"Everybody hates it," he says. "You can get changed now."

He reminds her to stop by the front desk on her way out.

"The results?"

"The radiologist will read them in the next day or so," Gus replies. "What's today? Tuesday? So your doctor will have the results by Friday or Monday, latest."

She thanks him.

He goes back into the booth to double-check the images of Mrs. Betty Freck's sinuses. He types his code into the computer, but he doesn't recognize the page that pops up. Instead of displaying the woman's sinuses, the page displays somebody's neck. Somebody messed up. He hopes it wasn't him. Next, he types in "FRECK" and hits "Search." Her record appears, and he opens the file, finds the images. He scans them quickly to make sure they're readable, and they all look fine except for the last one, which is compromised by a blur across the top two quadrants. Mrs. Betty Freck must have moved her head during the very last shot. He magnifies the image, hoping that it might be readable with a good zoom. The blur does seem to disperse, and it gives way to this:

STAY AWAY FROM HER

Gus doesn't flinch. He studies the words with vocational interest, as if he's analyzing a simple technicality. He tilts his head to the right, then to the left, searching for a logical explanation. He scrunches up his mouth and squints at the words. "STAY AWAY FROM HER." Then he shakes his head and knows instinctively that the words aren't really on the screen. He doesn't have to ask anyone to confirm; he knows it's a vision. He doesn't always understand his visions, doesn't always know what to do with them, but he usually knows a vision when he sees one, and here he is staring at a vision that reads like a warning. It's either a message about Mrs. Betty Freck or a message about him. Likely him, he thinks. But he has no clue. His speculation goes nowhere. Until he thinks of the graveyard. He's back there, vividly, crawling on the ground. His hands rake the earth, sifting for an epiphany. And then, yes, a thud of recognition.

At the end of the day Gus dials Alex and tells him about the image.

"Could those words mean anything to the case?" he asks the detective. "'Stay away from her'?"

"They could," Alex replies. "But I don't know. We don't know enough to know either way."

"Could there be a mistress involved?"

"If you say there is, Gus, then I would guess your vision is reflecting that," Alex tells him. "Is that what you're seeing? A mistress?"

"I'm not sure. I'm absolutely seeing a warning. And the warning is about a woman. But I'm afraid this could be the psychic cart before the psychic horse."

"I don't believe in psychic horses," Alex says with a wry laugh. "Let me know when you have more."

He's off the phone with Alex for about two minutes when he gets a call from Billie.

"Do you miss me?" she asks.

"What do you think?"

"I think you miss me so much you'll want to fly out to Malibu and spend the weekend with me."

"Is that an invitation?"

"It's a summons," she says with a throaty laugh.

"I'll have to see if Beatrice can watch Ivy."

"Bring Ivy. Bring Beatrice. Just come to Malibu."

Gus tells her he'll think it over. So, he does some thinking after the call, and he does some more thinking during his twilight walk with Ivy as she happily skips along tugging at him. He searches the sky and absorbs all of its hues, really feels the colors shift across his face and pass through his skin. Washed clean from the day now, and the ointment of the night applied, Gus senses that the warning, "STAY AWAY FROM HER," was intended for him.

Mills has probably kept Shelly Newton waiting too long and hopes she hasn't entertained second thoughts in the meantime. It's been twenty-four hours, so anything's possible. Particularly now after the news from Preston and Myers: the Illumilife legal team will likely fight the subpoena for Davis Klink's phone records. In a letter to the court, the lawyers stated that records of Klink's calls could jeopardize trade secrets and other matters if it becomes public who called the company's CEO, when and for how long. There is a shitload of minutia in the letter, but the basic argument is that any number of incoming or outgoing calls to Klink's cell phone or to the company's switchboard could raise speculation about any part of the business. Say, for instance, the CEO of Coca-Cola called and spoke to Klink for an hour. Was he asking if Klink was thirsty? Or thirsty for a merger? Were they conspiring to take over Pepsi, or to sell off the toilet cleaner division of Illumilife to Procter & Gamble?

Fuck it and fuck them. It's a murder investigation. Mills and his squad will get the damn phone records. In the meantime, he dials Shelly Newton.

"Can you talk now?" he asks her.

"Yes," she says in a whisper. "Let me shut my door."

Her first words when she returns to the phone surprise him. "I like you, Detective Mills," she says. "I really do, and I want to help you."

"Okay . . ."

"Please leave my name out of this. I don't trust anyone in this building." She's still whispering even with the door closed.

"Before we continue, Ms. Newton, you should know that if someone at your company is implicated in the murder of Davis Klink, and your information leads to the apprehension of our suspect, you could be called to testify at trial," Mills explains. "I want you to know that before you say another word."

"I understand," she says. "And I'll deal with that when and if the time comes. But while you're digging around, please don't mention that you talked to me again."

"Agreed."

She speaks conspiratorially as she tells Mills what she's heard from Tracy Quibb, Claire White's executive assistant. Apparently, the executive assistants run their own information mafia where knowledge is the supreme currency. It's a higher form of gossip; it's organized gossip perpetuated by intrigue and laced with betrayal—all by necessity, all tacitly approved. This is how it sounds as Mills listens to Shelly's breathless account of Claire White's implosion. "She came rushing back to her office after the big blowout with Davis, nearly in tears! She screamed for Tracy to come in, shut the door, and then she picked up a paperweight and threw it against the wall and said, 'He threatened to fire me!' And I believe it, Detective Mills, because Davis was *that* upset. Her job was on the line. Until Davis was murdered, that is."

Mills certainly won't accuse Shelly Newton of being subtle.

"Plus," she continues, again in a conspiratorial whisper, "Stella, Peter Tribble's assistant, told Tracy that Peter was investigating Claire for misappropriation of funds. This is huge, Detective Mills. If true, it would not only be the end of Claire's job; it would be the end of her career."

"What kind of misappropriation of funds are we talking about?" he asks.

"I think it has something to do with Claire using money from the HR budget to fix up her house. She probably thought no one would miss a million or two."

"How big is her budget?" Mills asks.

"I can't say for sure, but we have fifty-four thousand employees in offices and factories around the world," Shelly says. "We're a Fortune 500 company. Claire always reminds people of that, you know, because she's all about flash and status. She loves for people to think she's loaded . . . and important."

"I take it you don't like her."

"She's not well liked," Shelly says. "Some people think she might be psychotic."

"Now that sounds like something I can use," Mills replies.

"No, no, please," she begs. "That's just an observation. She behaves strangely. She has temper tantrums. She's tightly wound. But it's not like we have a diagnosis. She could just be a total bitch, so please don't have her committed, okay?"

The nice thing about a phone call is you can roll your eyes and shake your head with impunity, which is exactly what Mills is doing now. "Don't worry," he tells her. "Claire White certainly takes the 'human' out of 'human resources,' but I don't have the authority to commit her. Is there anything else?"

"The acquisition of Portman Brands," she says. "There are a lot of people unhappy with it. Both at Illumilife and Portman."

"Anybody specific?"

"Executives who fear losing their positions once the companies are integrated."

"Names?"

"No. I don't have specific names. But I'll ask around."

He's sure she will.

"Killing Davis would stop the acquisition," she says.

"How so?"

"It's still pending approval, and my guess is that a dead CEO might cause shareholders of both companies to lose confidence in the deal."

"Is this your opinion or something you overheard?"

"Both."

"Whom did you overhear it from?"

"Peter Tribble."

"How many layoffs have happened under Davis Klink's leadership?"

"Thousands," Shelly says boldly. "It's business. In the last five years we've gone through three restructurings."

The math is as obvious as it is staggering: thousands of people had a motive to murder Davis Klink. Plus how many more who wanted to stop the acquisition. Plus his wife, his children, maybe a brother, a sister.

"But he was a brilliant businessman," Shelly insists. "Brilliant."

"Were you in love with him?" Mills asks.

"Oh. My. God," she says, just like that, heaving the words at Mills as if he deserves a few Molotov cocktails just for asking. "That's absurd! He was my boss. I ran his life. I saw all the blemishes. I respected and admired him, but I wasn't in love with him. That's appalling, Detective."

"Well, okay then, no offense intended," Mills says. "I'm going to ask you again if Davis Klink had a mistress."

She takes a deep breath, exhales. "It's none of my business."

"But?"

"But, if I had to guess, I would say of course he had a girlfriend or two over the years. Just based on his travel and expenses, alone."

"Did any of his affairs end badly?"

Silence. Then Shelly clears her throat and says, "I wouldn't know."

"No ugliness? No crazy phone calls? Threats?"

"I think you should talk to his security team."

"Speaking of phone calls, why did his daughter call through the company switchboard to reach him? Wouldn't she have called his cell phone directly?"

"No," the woman replies. "His children often called the switchboard and asked for me."

"Why?"

"Because Davis rarely answered his cell phone if it wasn't another exec calling," she replies. "The kids knew they could get to him through me."

"Sounds like business before family."

"It's business before everything," Shelly says. "Now I really must be going, Detective. I'll stay on the case, and we'll talk again soon."

She speaks with the thrill of a private citizen who thinks she has conjoined herself to the case. Mills thanks her, and because she "really must be going," he lets her go. He looks at his notes. Illumilife is a clusterfuck of rumor, suspicion, motive, innuendo, and ego.

The surveillance video from Safeway arrives Thursday morning. Myers, his shirt stained by ketchup or blood, had raced into Mills's office as soon as he had uploaded the file. Which explains why Myers's laptop is sitting in the center of the case agent's desk and why Myers is sitting in the case agent's chair instead of Mills. Mills flanks him on one side, Powell on the other. Preston hovers behind them. They watch every frame.

22:09:21: Vehicle enters alley.
22:09:28: Vehicle headlights go off, vehicle still in motion.
22:09:30: Glitch in videotape (four seconds).
22:09:34: Vehicle parks.
22:09:34–22:16:48: Vehicle parked. No activity.

Myers pauses the video and says, "So, he just sits there for seven minutes and doesn't do anything."

"We can count," Mills reminds him.

"And we can't assume he's not doing anything," Powell says. "Just because we can't see into the car doesn't mean nothing's happening in there."

> 22:16:48: Driver side door opens. Unknown individual exits vehicle.
>
> 22:16:51: Glitch in videotape (five seconds).
>
> 22:16:56: Unknown individual opens rear cargo door.

"I don't think that's Klink," Powell says.

"Hard to tell," Mills concedes. "Video's too grainy and dark. Hey, Myers, can you freeze this here, maybe zoom in?"

"I'll try," Myers says. Then he punches a few things into his keyboard and, using his fingers on the mouse pad, manipulates the picture on the screen, pulling the image closer. The unknown individual grows larger, much larger, but more distorted with every push inward of the zoom.

"Zoom out a bit," Mills says. "I can't make shit out of this."

Myers zooms out slowly.

"That's the sweet spot," Preston tells him. "Freeze it there."

The image is as close as it will come without the distortion. They all study the screen. Mills squints, trying to draw out a face, but the man is wearing a hat, the brim dipped coyly over his eyes. "He looks shorter than Klink. I think we have the CEO at six feet. This guy looks five-six, five-seven tops."

"Agreed," Powell says. "But he's dressed similar to our victim."

She's right. The suspect, and Mills is fairly sure he's looking at a suspect now, appears to be in a suit and tie, an ill-fitting one, but a business suit, no less.

"Play the video," Mills orders.

> 22:16:57: Rear cargo door is open. Suspect is speaking.

"Fuck, I wish these videos had audio," Mills snaps. "Anybody read lips?" "You'd have to be able to see the lips," Myers says.

Mills acknowledges the caveat with a quick nod, then, watching the suspect pulling at a shoe and the leg that follows, says, "What the fuck is he doing?"

22:17:07: Suspect is pulling Unknown Individual #2 by the ankles from cargo area. UI #2 emerges, hitting head on cargo door above. Suspect pulls UI #2 from vehicle.

"This could be Klink," Mills says. "But we can't get a good enough shot to confirm. He's dressed in a suit. He's towering over the other guy, so he's probably the right height for Klink."

"I think our suspect has a gun. Watch," Powell says.

22:17:55: Suspect spins UI #2 around. Both men walk from car, UI #2 slightly ahead.

"Either that's a gun under the suspect's coat, or he's got the world's biggest hard-on," Myers tells them.

"I'm going with a gun," Powell says.

Mills just shakes his head.

22:18:12: Suspect and UI #2 walk out of frame, UI #2 slightly ahead.

"That's it," Myers says. "End of video."

Mills leans against the wall and says, "Shit."

"We got crappy video with two individuals we can't positively identify, and it looks like one of them has a gun on the other," Preston says. "In other words, an outtake from *Law & Order*."

"But it's Klink's SUV," Myers reminds them.

"We get that, Morty," Mills says. "But now we have to believe that the killer marched Klink over to the graveyard on foot."

"And at gunpoint," Powell adds.

"It's within walking distance," Myers insists. "I told you, Preston and I did the walk. It's easy. No major roads to cross. A few neighborhood streets behind Safeway connect to Valley Vista."

"How long did it take?" Mills asks.

"We clocked it at nine minutes."

Mills shrugs. "And yet the victim, let's call him Klink, doesn't seem to resist. He obviously didn't resist if we're to believe they took a neighborly stroll to the cemetery and started digging."

"And where's the shovel?" Powell asks.

"I don't know," Myers replies. "Why are you asking me? I'm not saying what the video means. I just came in to show it to you."

Mills elbows the detective gently. "No one's putting you on the defensive, Morty. We're just thinking out loud. For example, I'm thinking about that stain on your shirt."

"I stopped at McDonald's for lunch. Got a Big Mac. A packet of ketchup exploded," Myers explains.

"Happens all the time," Powell says.

"And since we're thinking out loud, Mills," the ketchup-stained detective says, "I'm thinking maybe the killer placed the shovel at the graveyard beforehand."

"He would've had to do that under the cover of darkness, which could indicate two trips to the cemetery that night," Preston suggests.

Mills looks at both of his colleagues and nods. "I think we're good for now. I'm not so much concerned with the shovel as I am with the nearly seven-hour gap in Klink's whereabouts, assuming that's him," he says. "His secretary says he got that call at three in the afternoon. This video is time-stamped ten o'clock. What's he doing for seven hours instead of heading to the airport?"

"Assuming he knew his killer, maybe they had dinner and hung out for a few hours," Myers says. "And then, bam, it was a trap and the suspect takes him at gunpoint."

"Like I said, I think we're good for now," Mills tells them. "I'm not saying you're wrong, Morty. I'm saying we need to take a breath, stop speculating for a minute, and nail down where the fuck Klink went after leaving the office."

Mills stretches, then tries to stifle a yawn.

Powell and Preston take the hint and head for the door. As Myers leaves, Mills thanks him and says he's doing a great job.

On Friday comes the news that the judge, as expected, laughed at Illumilife's attempt to withhold Klink's cell phone records. The court ordered the wireless account be released to the cops for review. Which is exactly what Preston and Myers have been doing. It's late Friday afternoon before they have anything to tell Alex Mills. They're in his office now, disorderly stacks of papers in their hands. They apologize for not having gone through each and every call yet, or each and every signal to the towers.

"That wasn't my expectation," Mills assures them. "Actually, I'm surprised we have phone records this quickly."

"So are we," Preston says. "We obviously looked at the last ding first. It most likely came from the intersection of East Thomas and Sixteenth. Or somewhere on Sixteenth between Thomas and McDowell."

Mills knows the map of Phoenix. He knows the precincts blindfolded. Give him the cross streets and he can do a rough illustration. The neighborhood at Thomas and Sixteenth is unremarkable. Mixed use. Apartments, outdated ranch homes, businesses. All unadorned. Mostly run down.

"And then nothing?" he asks the men.

"Right. Not another signal after that," Myers says. "Eventually he lost his phone, ditched his phone, or the perp took his phone."

"I'm going with option two or three," Mills surmises. "But neither option tells us when Klink left that neighborhood and drove to Safeway."

"Or was driven," Preston says.

"All I know is the victim entered the neighborhood we identified around seventeen thirty," Myers says. "I have no idea when he left for the Valley Vista area."

"Obviously something went wrong between the last ping on Klink's phone at Thomas and Sixteenth and the first shot of him, assuming it's him, on the surveillance tape from Safeway," Mills says. "We're talking about two neighborhoods miles apart."

"We've only just started to review the cell tower data," Preston reminds him. "We want to see if the earlier pings tell us anything about where he might have been headed or what he might have been planning to do."

"Right," Mills says. "But from what we know so far, it does appear that something significant happened at Thomas and Sixteenth. I think it's worthy of a search there."

"Right now?" Myers gasps.

"No, Morty. Go home. Enjoy the weekend, and I'll try to do the same."

As he watches the two men shuffle out of his office, Mills can't help but have a nagging feeling. He knows it plays to a stereotype, but the fortunate, coddled Davis Klink is not someone who'd drive outside the boundaries of wealth just to see how the other half lives. Klink had no business in that neighborhood.

9

Gus is sitting on the deck, looking out at the ocean. Ivy rests beside him, her tail flapping against the wood. Waves crash hard, and the vibration rolls beneath them.

"You can tell it's a full moon," Billie says. "The surf is crazy." She and Beatrice are sitting at a large round table under the canopy, shaded from the sun.

Gus watches the crazy surf, and it all comes back to him, those days of rebellion, long days of surfing and late nights of partying; his life in Los Angeles swerved in and out of waves of glory and fear, freedom and despair. He was invincible, and he was broken. Banished by parents who considered themselves "too Christian" to indulge his psychic revelations, Gus recreated family here at the beach where everything and everyone was golden. He practiced his psychic visions on people who yearned for "inner truths." He wrote lousy poetry and smoked too much pot. But who didn't back then? He came to LA in his late teens and stayed until his midtwenties, supporting his lifestyle with the money people paid him to bring them closer to their destinies. It was strange. A friend knew a friend who knew a friend, leading to those late-night runs up Mulholland, or those early-morning sessions with that customer in Holmby Hills, a famous movie star who liked her visions told to her as the sun rose from the east. He remembers an all-night party at the Bel-Air home of a Warner Brothers executive where dozens of guests lined up for consultations, always offering him cocaine, which he declined, occasionally offering him a sexual favor (from the men, as well), which he also declined. He remembers returning to the beach at six in the morning, doing bong hits with the guys and sleeping until three in the afternoon. Some nights. Others were calm, deliriously peaceful. He listened to the music of Billie Welch back then, and he fell in love with her, as all boys did, unlike the way he loves her now. He might have even had a vibe about her back then, but he's not sure. Even if he had sensed their destinies would someday intertwine, he would have dismissed it as a by-product of his infatuation.

Today the temperature has hit the low seventies. Too cold for a swim. But the ocean is far from empty. Off to his right, farther north up the beach, surfers are in a line. An occasional wetsuit will pass on the beach below. Others stroll the shore in linen pants and sweatshirts. A few clusters of children unearth the beach to build sandcastles. He closes his eyes and lets the sun soak his face. For a few minutes he listens to the chattering of Billie and Beatrice. They're talking about saving the whales. And the elephants. Then Gus hears a backhoe. The noise erupts suddenly, roaring to life, the yearning arms of the machine screeching as they flex for the dig. Definitely not kids playing in the sand. He opens his eyes and sees, instead, two adults viciously shoveling out a hole. Not exactly a backhoe, but their strokes are fast, crazy, spastic. He blinks and they're gone. He blinks again and they're back. Again, and they're gone. He's somewhat inebriated by the sun, and feels himself slow on the uptake, so he turns to Billie and Beatrice and says, "Hey, ladies, someone's shoveling out a big hole right below us. You see it?"

Both women rise to their feet, drift to the railing, and look down. Beatrice has a glass of sangria in her hand.

"No, dear, I don't," she says.

"Billie?"

"Me either. Unless you mean the kids building their castle."

"Feels like I'm waking from an afternoon dream," Gus tells them.

"Oh, wow," Billie says. "You're seeing something, aren't you? A vision . . ."

"Yes," Beatrice tells her without waiting for Gus to answer. "He is."

Gus gets up and joins them at the railing. "I'm either seeing what happened to that CEO in Phoenix. Or I'm seeing another murder about to happen."

Beatrice rests her glass on the railing and grabs Gus's hand. "Can you concentrate on this, Gus?"

"I can," he says. "And I think it's the latter."

Billie just looks at him mesmerized, a wicked smile emerging on her face.

He nods, pulls out his phone, and sends a text to Alex Mills.

He waits, but Alex doesn't respond.

What does one dead man have to say about another? Anything? One dead man is quiet, so quiet, lying there in a cradle of dirt, invoking the Fifth. One dead man, his head bashed in, must have something to say about the other.

Alex Mills stares at the dead man.

The details of Davis Klink's murder had not leaked to the press, so this is not a copycat. But the similarities are obvious.

He looks again to the cardboard sign, the backside of a shipping box:

I should have guessed
It would come to this
That I would dig my own grave
That I would pay for my sins.
Here I rest. Never in Peace.

The call came in around eight thirty this morning. The sun is now tethered at noon. Mills guesses the death happened in the late evening prior. Cielo de Santos, a small, unadorned graveyard in a tract of Phoenix between Southern and Baseline, is swarming with cops. Patrol officers have set up a perimeter at East Twenty-Fourth and blocked surrounding streets to the west. The techs have combed and sifted while two photographers buzzed around them documenting the process, capturing the crime scene in its midday glare. The crude grave. The loosened dirt. The broken eyeglasses. The errant shoe.

From the looks of it, today's John Doe occupies a similar demographic as Davis Klink, the John Doe who came before him. White, late forties or early fifties, well-dressed. No wallet, no ID, but a gold watch and diamond ring have been left untouched by the killer; that all but rules out robbery as a motive. John Doe and Davis Klink blazed virtually the same trails to their deaths. They dug their own graves presumably with the same shovel used to bash in their skulls. This victim has lost the back of his head. All that's left is a hole the size of a cantaloupe and a lava flow of brain matter. But for all the similarities, one thing puzzles Alex Mills. Why here? This neighborhood is a pocket of authentic Mexico swept to the south of Phoenix mostly by prejudice and economics. A poorer neighborhood—fuck it, let's call it what it is, a barrio—that largely keeps to itself, its people are welcoming but reticent, trusting but hesitant. It's no secret some lawmakers in Arizona, shortsighted and handcuffed by their own bigotry, would enjoy deporting the entire village.

"Hey, Mills, look at this," a tech says to him. It's Roni Gates, kneeling on the ground opposite Mills, the grave between them. She's pointing at the victim's hand.

"I saw the ring," Mills tells her.

"No, no, no," the tech says, her words as spastic as her shaking head. "Not the ring. The dirt. Look, there's dirt under all of his fingernails, both hands. Can you see?"

Mills lowers himself to his knees and looks closer. "Yes," he says. "Indicating what, in your opinion?"

Crime scenes like this are what techs live for. Nearly salivating over the corpse, Roni, a collegiate-looking blond with ruddy cheeks, says, "I think it indicates that the victim was digging his grave with his own hands."

"Or trying to dig himself out," Mills suggests. "Maybe he was trying to escape before the final blows."

Either way it was a crappy way to die.

"But we got his prints," Roni assures him. "Sent them off about a half hour ago."

"Great."

This parcel of land sits on a full city block. The backside of a strip mall, the shape of a "C," surrounds it, holding the graveyard in the hug of the letter. It's entirely possible that a murder could take place here in the middle of the night without disturbing the neighbors. Mills gets up off his knees when he sees his scene investigator approach.

"The lady who looks after the place discovered the body when she was out this morning planting flowers," Powell tells him. "She says there's no money for cameras. And nobody in the community wants a gate."

A text message dings Mills's phone: "Interesting Vision. Maybe another murder. Call me."

He laughs and shows the message to Powell. "It's from Gus."

"Isn't he supposed to see things in the future?" she asks. "As in, your mother is going to be hit by a truck?"

"He does. But he also sees things in real time," Mills says. "And he can see things that have played out in the past."

She rolls her eyes.

"You know he can do it."

She just looks at him.

"You've seen him do it."

She kicks the ground and says, "Yeah, I guess. But it's such a leap for me sometimes. Are you going to call him?"

"Not now," Mills says. Within an instant his phone dings again and so does hers. They look at each other, spooked. A ding of an iPad echoes, and Roni looks up.

"There's a match," she announces.

The prints are back. Simultaneously they open their emails. Mills, even after all these years, gets a thrill from the anticipation. First he looks for the name. He'll read the report in a moment, but he has to have a name; he has to look at the corpse and give the wretched thing a name, and it's almost a "nice to meet you" moment when Mills can stare at the body and say, "We know who you are."

Nice to meet you, Barry L. Schultz.

We know who you are, Barry L. Schultz.

Turns out Barry L. Schultz's fingerprints showed up in two databases. He had recently applied to teach at U of A, and he had purchased a membership in the TSA PreCheck program. He had to provide a print for both.

"Damn, I love how fast the system works," Mills says to no one in particular.

He looks at the man's date of birth, then does the math; Barry L. Schultz is forty-six years old. His birthday is next month. Is. Was. Tenses don't matter at crime scenes. The report lists Schultz's current address: 2899 N. Palma Vista Circle, Scottsdale. Occupation: physician.

Mills pulls up Google on his phone and searches for "Dr. Barry Schultz Phoenix Scottsdale." Apparently the guy is a prominent plastic surgeon known for discount breast enlargements (Two for the Price of One!). Mills pulls up images of Barry Schultz, Breast Enlarger, and marches back to the grave. The Office of the Medical Examiner has arrived.

"You may be a doctor examining a doctor," Mills says.

"Huh?" says the man who pivots and looks up from where he's kneeling.

"Hey, Calvin!"

If one can have a favorite medical examiner, Calvin Cloke is Mills's. Cloke is a crazy fuck who bowls like a pro, plays guitar in a local metal band, and is built like a Humvee. He had one arm blown off in the first Gulf War and wears a permanent smile on his face.

"Good to see you, Mills," Cloke says when he gets to his feet.

The men shake. "Our John Doe, here, is a famous plastic surgeon in town. Barry Schultz. Ever hear of him?"

Cloke shakes his head, then points to the corpse. "I'd say a lot of my patients are good candidates for plastic surgery. Trouble is getting them to pay."

Mills nods and rewards Cloke with a laugh.

"As for me personally, you think I'd be looking for someone to fix this beautiful face?" the medical examiner asks, mugging.

The man has a big face, wide enough to accommodate that nearly psychotic smile. But beautiful? Probably not. His skin is a battlefield of acne trenches and roadside bombs. His face has been to war. It bears the scars. But the arresting blue of his eyes calms everything. They neutralize the territory, and Mills guesses that some women find the gentle warrior thing attractive, maybe sexy.

"Obviously blunt trauma," Cloke says, turning again to the dead man. "I haven't documented that, per se, but that's going to be my finding, unless you can tell me that the excavation of his skull has absolutely nothing to do with his death."

"I'm not going to tell you that," Mills says. "I'll let you get back to work."

"If you want to call it work," the man stage whispers, followed by a cackle of laughter.

Cloke is still laughing as Mills drifts away in search of the crime scene photographer. He finds the photographer at another corner of the graveyard and asks the guy to email him pictures of Schultz's ring and the watch. "The best close-ups you have," he says, then heads for his car, where he dials Scottsdale police and asks for help identifying next of kin. Mills heads out in that direction, toward Scottsdale, toward the doctor's address. He's on the highway for barely five minutes when one of Scottsdale's finest calls back and says he has a phone number for the wife.

Carla Schultz leans in to the door, clutching it, as if she hasn't the strength to stand on her own. Her eyes brim with tears. "As soon as you called, I knew you'd found Barry," she tells Mills.

"You figured he was missing?"

She studies him, confused by the question. "Well, yes. I called in a missing person's report last night. In the middle of the night."

She's not just the man's wife. She's obviously his patient. Her breasts are exhibit A and B, respectively. Her lips, a collision of two air bags, are exhibit C. Then there's the forehead, which refuses to budge. Otherwise, she's an attractive woman of forty feigning twenty. Make that *very* attractive. Her face is pure porcelain, or Botox, it doesn't really matter; it's a smooth sculpture blessed with emerald eyes that, while welling up, beckon Mills to ask for more. Her platinum hair surrounds her face and falls innocently just below her neck. She's wearing a tight T-shirt and, well south of the navel, jeans that make a statement of their own. She's the kind of woman who . . . but Mills never could, never would . . . so he never does. He can appreciate the beauty of another female, but there's only room for one on the pedestal.

"Would you like to come in?"

"I would."

He follows her into the sprawling ranch, a homestead influenced in style by Taos, New Mexico, Arizona's pueblo next door. There are roughened wood floors and adobe walls, earth tones and tiles, kiva ladders, mission tables, and leather so thick and fresh you'd think it was still alive.

They settle into a room that faces a wall of glass, like so many in the valley, looking out to a massive pool, an outdoor kitchen, a few canopies, some pergolas, you name it. Someone is killing wealthy men in the valley. So far that's the only connection between Davis Klink and Barry Schultz. "The missing person's report was not how we found him," Mills tells her.

"Are you sure it's him?" she asks, her voice trembling.

Mills is sitting on one of those well-nourished leather sofas framed with knotty wood. She's opposite him in a matching chair.

"Yes."

A sudden cascade of tears. She looks away, puts her face in her hands. Her body shudders. The appropriate reaction is for Mills to bow his head in protracted condolence, yielding to her private grief; the inappropriate reaction is to lunge forward, grab and hold her, and let her tears soak his shoulder. He chooses the appropriate reaction, but he's aware the other one is too tempting for his liking.

After a few moments she lifts her face, chokes back a final sob, and dries her eyes. "Do I have to identify the body?"

"No. We positively ID'd him through fingerprints."

She sighs heavily and says, "I didn't know you could fingerprint a dead person."

"We can."

"But I don't understand why you'd have Barry's fingerprints. He's never committed a crime in his life."

Mills smiles. "I'm sure he hasn't," he assures her. "And, actually, *we* don't have his prints. They're in the database because of TSA PreCheck and a teaching job at U of A."

"The medical school. They approached him about lecturing or something."

"That's a long commute."

"It was just going to be one day a week."

Mills opens a legal pad, then starts taking notes. "And I take it your husband traveled a lot," he says. "With the PreCheck membership?"

"We've been looking at beach property in Mexico," she tells him. "He's been down there a lot."

"Do you have children?"

"No."

Her reply is conspicuously void of emotion. It's a deposition reply.

"Was he worried about work, business, family? Did he mention anything or anyone suspicious to you?"

"No. I don't think so."

"Mrs. Schultz, I do have photographs of the watch and ring that your husband was wearing when we found him," Mills says. "Would seeing them help you digest this in any way?"

She looks at him coolly but nods. He hands her his phone. Her chin drops, leaving her mouth agape. She is still but for the gentle rising and falling of her chest.

"Ma'am?"

She doesn't answer.

"Mrs. Schultz?"

"Neither piece is custom-made," she says, her eyes not meeting his, staring instead into the distance of disbelief. "So, there are probably

thousands of men who have the same ring or the same watch, but"—
and now she begins to sob again—"how many would have both? What
is the chance that another man in Phoenix would be wearing exactly
the same ring and the same watch together?"

Again, he yields to her tears. The house is airtight. There's no
noise, not even white noise, save for her. It's a tomb. After the pause
runs its course, he says, "I think you're right, Mrs. Schultz. There's very
little chance of a coincidence like that. And, of course, we have the
fingerprints."

"My name is Carla, and can we please go outside so I can smoke?"
she asks, looking up from the lingering tears.

He thinks it an odd request coming from the wife of the doctor,
but, in her grief, who is he to question her nicotine habit? He simply
nods, and she leads him out to the pool, where she unzips a small,
woven pouch and withdraws a joint and a lighter.

Instinct overcomes sympathy, and Mills says, "You know I'm a
police officer. Right?"

She nods. "I do." Then she lights the joint and takes a massive toke.
She holds it in until it seems she's about to burst—her face red, her
neck clenched, her visitor concerned enough to pry her mouth open.
Before he does, she lets out, finally, a billowing cloud of herbal smoke.
"But it's practically legal everywhere now," she says.

"Not exactly."

"Are you going to arrest a widow?"

"No."

"Where did you find him?" she asks and takes another long hit off
the joint.

"We found the body in a shallow grave at a South Phoenix cemetery."

"South Phoenix? Why there?"

"We have no idea, Mrs. Schultz—Carla."

"But I don't understand," she says, a soft, childlike quality to her
voice now. "Someone buried him without telling me?"

Mills clasps his hands tightly, interlacing patience and mercy. "No
one found your husband and buried him. We believe the grave, as crude

as it was, was part of the MO. The grave and the homicide went hand in hand."

Carla Schultz offers him the joint. She actually offers him the joint! He shakes his head, doesn't know whether to laugh out loud or rip the thing out of her hand and toss it in the swimming pool. He chooses neither. Instead he says, "I'm going to ask you to stop smoking this in front of me. Is that okay?"

She nods. "I'm sorry." She stamps the joint out on the side of a firepit. "I'm fine now," she says. In other words, buzzed. Which is fine, really. Mills doesn't give a shit. That's not his job.

"Do you have any idea who would want to hurt your husband?"

By the look on her face he might as well have asked her to recite act 1 of *Hamlet*.

"I take that as a no."

"I can't think of anyone," she says.

"No disgruntled patients?" Mills asks. "Has he ever been sued for malpractice?"

"Yes," she replies. "But people don't kill you for a bad facelift."

"That we know of. . . ."

"He's had some disputes with some of the doctors in his practice."

"What kinds of disputes?"

"Money," she says. "Isn't it always over money?"

Mills tells her that he'll be speaking to the other doctors as part of his investigation. "Carla, do you know most of your husband's friends and acquaintances?"

"I'm not one of those hovering wives, but yes, I think I know who he golfed with, played poker with, that kind of thing."

"Did he know a man named Davis Klink?"

"Who?"

"Davis Klink. The CEO of Illumilife Industries. He was found dead about a week ago."

For a moment, the woman turns to the sky and lets the sun warm her face. It's only a moment, because Mills can see a sudden awareness in her eyes, the kind that connects the dots. "Right," she says. "I read about that."

"That's it? You read about it?"

"Yes. It was in the news. But I don't think Barry knew him. If he was buddies with some kind of CEO, I think I would know," she says. Again, there's acumen in her eyes. "You think the two of them were maybe murdered by the same person. . . ."

"Davis Klink was found in a shallow grave like your husband."

"I don't remember that part."

"We didn't release details of the crime scene to the press."

Without saying a word, she leads him back indoors. He's not sure if this is the end of the conversation, if maybe she's showing him out entirely, until she sits again in that room of leather and wood.

"I've never heard of Davis Klink before."

Mills nods. "It's very possible they didn't know one another. It could be that we have a killer targeting high rollers, so to speak. You know, successful men, but randomly selected."

"Unless this Davis Klink was a patient," Carla suggests. "That's the only thing I can think of."

"Tell me what happened last night."

Carla leans forward, wipes a tear away, and describes a night at home, the two of them in their home theater, watching *Beetlejuice*, when Barry's cell phone rang.

"It's one of his favorite movies, so he was a little pissed off about being interrupted," she says. "But he was obligated to take it."

"Why?"

"He was on call, and somebody's patient was freaking out."

"Not *his* patient?"

"No," she replies. "I thought we were just in for a quiet evening at home. I don't remember this being an on-call weekend, and we argued about it, but not long enough for a knockdown, drag-out fight, you know, because he had to call the patient back."

"And then he left the house?"

"Oh, yeah. Like superfast. The patient was frantic. She said her butt job was causing her ass to leak a cream-cheese-like substance. Pretty disgusting, but you get used to it when you're married to it. Anyway, I did think it sounded a little fishy, but he was out of here in a flash to go meet her at the hospital."

"What time was that?"

"About eight thirty," she replies. "I must've fallen asleep around ten. I woke up out of the blue around four o'clock this morning, and I noticed he wasn't here. Hadn't come home. I couldn't reach him on his cell. So I called the police."

"You said the call sounded fishy. What was fishy about it?"

"Come on, Detective! Cream cheese coming out of your butt?"

Mills tries to muster a serious look on his face. "I'm not familiar with your husband's work, ma' am."

"Well, I have never heard anything remotely related to cream cheese."

"Did you actually overhear the other end of the conversation?"

She shakes her head. "No, of course not. But Barry shared the highlights as he was flying out of here."

"And you never left the house after that?"

"No."

"You were home alone after he left?"

"Yes. Here. Alone."

Mills is still scribbling his notes in the pause that follows her answer. He senses in the static between them that she desperately wants him to get out of her house. It's a palpable shift in the energy. But he can't get up and leave. He hands her his legal pad instead.

"Please write down your husband's cell phone number and the name of his wireless carrier," he tells her. "Also, I need you to give me the make and model of his car. And his tag number if you have it."

She freezes, wide-eyed.

"Something wrong, Carla?"

She shakes her head. "No. Of course not."

A few minutes later she hands Mills the notepad.

"I'll have to get a search warrant for some other items," he says.

"No, no, no," she begs, "please don't search the house. My life is already turned upside down. I don't think I can take it. Please . . ."

She sinks deep into her chair and sobs. Mills gives her a few seconds and says, "We don't need to search the house. But I imagine your husband has a home computer."

"A laptop, sure."

"That kind of stuff," he says. He rises from the sofa and hands the woman his card. "Anything you can think of, even the smallest detail that might help us find who did this, please call me."

On the path to the front door, Carla trailing him, Mills tries to calm his brain from all the colliding question marks. It's one of those moments when he knows he has to silence the voices and nearly start from scratch to start at all. Clear the mind, then do the work. Remove the pieces, start again. He's almost successful, very close to a complete reset, when he hears the voice of Gus Parker. It's not a psychic thing. It's just a reminder, a nagging one, to get what he needs.

"Carla, if it's not too much trouble, I'd sure like to have some kind of object that belonged to your husband."

"You have his jewelry."

True. But Gus can't get near the man's jewelry. "I'm thinking about something that's not already in evidence that we can use, maybe to compare."

"Oh, you mean like DNA? That sort of thing?"

No, that's not what he means. "Yeah," he says, "something like that."

"How about a toothbrush? Or what about his beret? He wears the most stupid-looking beret when he golfs," she says. "Oh! And his golfing gloves!"

She returns from a brief scavenger hunt and hands Mills a tote presumably with the suggested objects inside. She's happy to help. It gives her some relief. He can read that on her face. He thanks her, then says he'll be in touch.

He's driving for about four minutes when he encounters his first red light. This gives him enough time to flip through his legal pad and send in a BOLO for Barry Schultz's vehicle. It's a white Maserati. Tag number: GR8LOOK. Mills shakes his head and scoffs out loud. "You can't make this shit up," he says to the dashboard, to the windshield, and to his snarky expression in the rearview mirror.

10

When Sergeant Jacob Woods enters a conference room rolling his eyes, those rolling eyes practically preceding him, the entrance means it's Monday morning, it's a debrief, things are getting messy and unfortunate, and nobody has the patience for lingering question marks, or unconnected dots, or murders with no leads. He stands at the head of the table, tosses his notebook in front of him, stares at the group (Mills, Powell, Myers, and Preston), and folds his arms across his breastplate.

"I know this is going to sound premature," he says, "but with two similar homicides on our hands, we should brace ourselves for the wrath of Hurley."

Scott Hurley is the beloved mayor of Phoenix who has built his reputation on reducing crime. He has a fucking coronary anytime a kid steals a Kit Kat from a 7-Eleven, never mind a homicide.

"Obviously the two cases are related," Mills tells the boss. "But we don't know yet if the victims have anything in common."

"Except their autopsies," the sergeant quips.

"We only discovered the second body yesterday," Mills reminds him. "We're comparing cell phone records, bank records, anything we can get our hands on. I sent out a BOLO for the doctor's Maserati. I'm assuming it'll stick out like a sore thumb and we'll have it soon. But for now, I want Preston and Myers to share what they're finding on Klink."

Preston swallows a swig of coffee and says the banks are complying with the subpoena, but it will be a few more days before they have anything to look at. He then gets up, walks over to the precinct map hanging on the wall, and points to a square of Phoenix. "This is where Klink's cell signal was last picked up."

He traces a finger from north to south and then reverse.

"This is Sixteenth Street, between McDowell and Thomas," Preston continues. "If we want to canvass the neighborhood, we'll need some support. Meanwhile, Myers, here, brought in the surveillance video from the Safeway where we found Klink's BMW. Not great quality, but it looks like Klink could have been taken at gunpoint to the cemetery. We can't verify the weapon, actually."

Preston looks to his colleague for a seamless segue, but Myers is face-first in love with a doughnut, white powder leaving chalk marks around the death of the man's diet. Preston sits, but that still doesn't prompt his colleague.

"Morty?" Mills says. "Take one more bite and then tell us what you've learned about Klink's automobile."

Morton Myers lets out a powdered sugar laugh and says, "Sorry! I haven't had breakfast. It's an SUV. A BMW. It was called in abandoned behind a Safeway not far from the cemetery."

Powell clears her throat and says, "It was towed from the scene. Still being processed by the lab."

"We went out to the Safeway, Preston and me," Myers says. "It's walking distance to Valley Vista."

"So, you think Klink met his killer at Safeway, dropped his car, and walked to his own grave?" Woods asks.

Myers rubs his chin. "That's not exactly what I think, Jake. But it's a possibility. The video and the timeline would suggest that, but we do lose his cell signal much earlier in the evening. Over at Thomas and Sixteenth."

"No chance he was killed at Thomas and Sixteenth and had his body dumped at Valley Vista?" Woods asks them.

Mills shakes his head. "I don't think so," he says. "First, the video suggests otherwise. He's alive at Safeway. He's walking. He's not far from the cemetery. Plus, we have a cardboard sign at the gravesite that he supposedly inscribed himself."

"Assuming we believe the killer," Powell interjects.

"I think we should go with that assumption," Mills tells the team. "Yesterday it was very clear from the dirt under Barry Schultz's fingernails that the guy either dug his grave by hand or tried to dig his way out."

"Unless his killer manipulated his corpse," Powell says.

"There's that," Mills concedes, "but I also think it's easier to make the kill right there in the cemetery rather than doing it elsewhere, transporting the body, unloading it, and dragging it to the hole in the ground. My gut tells me we should take the killer at his word."

"And what word is that?" Woods asks, the sarcastic inflection in his voice not for the weary.

"I think the perp has a reason for leaving the crime scenes just as they are. It's part of his narrative," Mills explains. "I think, at least for now, we should see what's in front of us before we go entertaining other theories. I have a hunch this guy isn't done."

"Is that your hunch, or a hunch from your psychic friend?" Woods asks. Myers laughs like a seventh grader at a Will Ferrell movie.

"It's my hunch," Mills replies.

"How long before you bring your psychic friend in?"

"He's in," Mills replies.

Woods's eyebrows go northward. "Oh?"

"He's in."

Woods says a magnanimous thank-you and leaves the conference room. Mills doesn't wait for the others to file out. He makes a beeline for the men's room, where he takes a world-record whiz. He's gushing like a friggin' fire hydrant when Preston enters and unzips beside him.

"Always a great way to start a Monday," he tells Mills.

"Peeing?"

"Woods."

Mills laughs. "Yeah, that, too."

"I'm working on a search warrant for Dr. Schultz's answering service," Preston tells him.

"Right," Mills says, "we need to know everyone who tried to reach the doctors' practice that night. You got the timeframe?"

"I do," Preston says, finishing up, shaking himself dry while Mills is still in midstream. "And you, over there, you got a bladder the size of Texas?"

"Guess so," he says. When he finishes, he washes, then follows Preston out of the restroom; they stand in the hallway. "While you're at it, we need a warrant for the doctor's office, too."

"HIPAA."

"Come on, Ken, you know HIPAA isn't such a huge obstacle. The courts have given us leeway in these kinds of cases, a shorter leash than normal, but still . . ."

Preston nods, then says he wants to regroup later.

Gus Parker is slowly waking up from a short nap aboard the Gulfstream. When she sees him stir, Ivy rushes to his side and rests her head on his knees. She loves flying. She bounced all over the place when they first got on the chartered jet in LA. Then, after takeoff, she settled in the seat behind Gus, her head at the window as if she were driving in the car with him, taking in the view. Gus promptly nodded off in the clouds, and here they are already descending quickly, smoothly into Phoenix. The pilot asks them to check their seat belts. Beatrice taps him on the shoulder.

"Wakey, wakey," she says from across the narrow aisle. "I sure could get used to this."

Normally, when Gus flies to the coast, he flies commercial. But when Ivy comes, Billie charters a flight because Ivy does not travel in the baggage hold. What's good for her dog, Glinda, is good for Ivy, Billie told Gus, and Gus agreed because he has never, and would never, check Ivy like a piece of luggage. She'd freak out. He'd freak out. There would be no Zen for anyone, and Gus equates flying with Zen, a certain departure from the tangibles of life, a kind of weightless floating and careless dismissal of inertia.

"I could get used to this, too."

A moment later they're gliding swiftly in final approach, and, with that familiar but ephemeral rush of adrenaline, they're zipping down the runway at Sky Harbor. As they taxi into the general aviation area, Gus spies the lineup of elegant Learjets and fellow Gulfstreams, all demurely awaiting those who are privileged enough to board. He doesn't fool himself—in fact he feels like a fool for traveling in such luxury—he has no business among these jets and among these people.

Just as the word "business" floats through his brain, the plane sidles up to a jet bearing the logo of Illumilife Industries. The hydraulics exhale, and Beatrice is up on her feet. "C'mon," she says to him.

"No, wait," he tells her, peering out the oval window. "I need to focus on that plane."

"Thinking of buying it?"

"No," he whispers. "I need to intuit something."

Quietly, she sits down, and Gus does a psychic zoom-in toward the logo:

ILLUMILIFE INDUSTRIES. PUTTING YOU FIRST.

Who could forget a name like that? Illumilife. It sounds like a cult. But it's the name of the victim's company. The CEO who Mills told him about. Gus remembers the guy's photo. And now his eyesight begins to blur. Through the blur, he sees the CEO walking down a deserted road, clouds of dust swirling around him, not another soul in sight. The man moves like a human mirage, shape-shifting, ghoulish, his image disappearing on the horizon, then reappearing anew. The man faces him now and smiles. "I have my whole life ahead of me," the CEO says. "My whole life." A Spanish song begins to play, and the desert fades away.

He shakes his head. He has no interpretation. And he has no time to mull it over because the pilot is standing over him. "Mr. Parker," the man says, "I'm sorry, but I have another charter. Can I help you with your things?"

Gus feels his face turn red.

"He spaces out like this all the time," Beatrice chirps. "Don't mind us. We'll be leaving now."

They take an Uber to Paradise Valley. Beatrice gets out first. They bicker over who'll pay the tip, but Beatrice insists. "Least I could do after you treated me to a weekend at the beach," she says. "Besides, I expect my advance next week."

Beatrice is on the second book of a two-book deal. *I Told You So: Memoir of a Psychic* is due out next year. Her first book climbed to number thirteen on the *New York Times* best-seller list. People now fly in from all over the world to consult with her, which is why there are so many overflow clients for Gus. He loves and hates her for this. Loves her, really.

It's noon. The security company told Gus their technicians would arrive between one and five o'clock to install new alarms for all of the perimeter walls around Billie's property. He calls Alex who answers with a growl.

"What's wrong with you?"

"Mondays with the sergeant."

"Is that like *Tuesdays with Morrie*?"

"No."

"I texted you yesterday, never heard back," Gus says.

"Oh, right. Sorry. We had another homicide."

"You mean like the first one?"

"That's what I mean."

"Hmm. That's sort of why I was texting you."

"It was a crazy day. You seeing things?" Mills asks.

"All kinds of things. Freaking me out a bit."

"I want to hear. Where are you?"

"At Billie's. Waiting for the alarm company."

"I'll swing by later," Mills says. "I have some things for you. Hope they tell you something."

Gus is intrigued but also hungry. After the call, he rummages through Billie's kitchen, searching for something edible. Billie's refrigerator offers the remains of a week-old pizza, a drawer of godforsaken vegetables, and some butter. The freezer yields a frozen lasagna, two bags of peas, and several ice packs for Billie's aching back. He's considering the lasagna, calculating how much time the microwave would need to infuse it with heat, when his rumination is interrupted by a voice behind him.

"May I help you?"

He freezes. An instant chill rushes his spine. He turns around slowly and, after a heavy breath, says, "Geez, you scared the crap out of me!"

The woman's face registers nothing. It's Della, one of Billie's housekeepers. She looks Gus over and mutters, "I'm sorry."

"That's okay," he replies.

"I'm shopping today," she says. "Make a list."

"I'm not staying here this week. And I don't know when Billie's coming back."

The woman, all five feet of her, gives him another dispassionate look and exits the kitchen.

Then he hears a loud bang. He thinks maybe Della threw a vacuum cleaner down the stairs to illustrate her current job satisfaction, but she had walked off in the opposite direction. A series of louder bangs comes next, shaking the house, and for a moment Gus thinks it's an earthquake, but he almost as instantly reminds himself that he's no longer in LA.

"Della?" he calls.

No answer.

"Della?"

Still no answer.

He tries to follow the trail of the banging to identify the source but finds himself walking in circles. "Della?" His voice is louder now, imploring, as he calls her name. He heads toward the studio and, on his way, hears the affirming sounds of a toilet flushing from a hallway powder room. "There you are!" he cries as she emerges.

"What in the world, Mr. Parker? Are you following me?"

"Sorry," he says. "But do you hear the banging?"

She raises one eyebrow, like a haughty cat, unflappable and theatrical. "You all right? There's no banging. And I'm going shopping!" Then she brushes past him and through the doorway that leads to the garage.

But the banging persists, and Gus realizes the sound is coming from outside, as if someone is shooting at the walls around the estate. Gunfire. He listens for the next shots. He hears firecrackers. He puts Ivy in the laundry room and shuts the door. His body already awash in sweat, Gus rushes out to the front driveway, sees nothing, sprints into the yard to the left, then to the patio and terrace to the right, inspects the walls, and finds nothing. He supposes this is something you call the cops for, but he fears it will be too late by the time help arrives.

He goes back inside, then cuts through the house and out to the pool where he skids to a dead stop. There, scrawled across the back wall of the property, the same wall the intruder had scaled, are four words in blood-red paint:

STAY AWAY FROM HER

But the banging, the shooting? Gus can't account for that. These words, though, have come to him twice now. He tries to catch his breath. He pulls his phone from his pocket, then snaps a few pictures of the vandalism. He can hear Ivy barking, but save for Ivy there isn't a sound now. The banging has stopped. The day is absolutely still. He sits on a poolside chaise, then inspects the photos. Something's wrong. One picture after another suggests that, in a stir of confusion or panic or both, he photographed the wrong wall. The words are missing. The wall in each photo is blank. Gus looks up from his phone and sees the discrepancy staring back at him.

STAY AWAY FROM HER

On the wall.

Not in the photos.

He gets up, walks to the wall. The words bloom larger as he approaches. He wants to touch the wall, feel the letters, but he hesitates. His hand shaking, he reaches for the "S." Just as he grazes the letter with the soft brush of his fingers, it slowly dissolves. He pulls his hand back. The remaining fragments of the "S" absorb into the wall, and the letter is gone. He touches the "T," and the same thing happens; the blood-red pigment of the letter fades, some of it dissolving into his hand. Gus examines his hand, like a doctor examining an X-ray, searching for the most elusive anomaly. There is nothing there but his hand. He feels his head turn, in slow motion, to the wall again, as if an autonomous force is tugging him. There are no words. The wall is blank. The letters are gone, without a trace.

11

Gus Parker can't really describe it, but there's something about playing Billie Welch music in Billie Welch's house that sounds as if Billie's soul is inhabiting the place. He would say it's surreal, but the word is overused and nothing in his world is ever surreal; there are no words for Gus's world, and if there are they're obviously embedded in some ancient text, hidden away in the basement of some ancient temple, hidden within a labyrinth of corridors and ever-descending stairways to a crypt far beyond the sunlight, far beyond the hands of curious excavators. There's no archeology for Gus's gift. In a faraway dream, his dead uncle once told him to look for a box the color of sea foam under the porch of his childhood home. Gus never did find the box but suspects that it contained the primordial code for his gift of visions, or the whispers of instructions, or the discovery of the one and only universal language that explains everything to every living soul, the elusive holy grail of communication. But there was no box, at least not under the porch, and ever since he's had to wing it.

The music plays in almost every room. The lushness of her voice is like a wandering spirit. With Billie's voice filling the home, he feels closer to her in a way that he sometimes doesn't in her presence. Her words envelop him, wrap around him like blankets. Her songs burn with longing.

"Uh, sir? We're done."

The alarm guys find Gus sitting, eyes closed, in Billie's inner sanctum, the interior room with the fireplace. He's on the floor, cushioned by the Kenya pillow, his feet resting on Malaysia.

"Sir?"

He opens his eyes, smiles. He likes where he's just been. "Awesome," he says. "That didn't take as long as I thought."

"We have some papers we need you to sign," the taller, older one says.

In the kitchen, Gus signs his name to a few documents, then shows the men to the front door.

"It's Fort Knox now," says the younger of the workers. "You'll have absolutely no trouble." He shakes Gus's hand and hops into their truck.

The other worker, Glenn, as his name tag indicates, hesitates. He turns to the truck, then turns back. "I'm sorry, Mr. Welch, but I kind of have a favor to ask."

"It's Parker. Gus Parker. What do you need?"

The guy stuffs his hands in his pockets, lowers his head. "Well, I've kind of been a fan, you know, of Billie Welch, like, my whole life." Then he finally looks up with a shy grin. "If this is out of line for me to ask, I'm sorry, but I brought one of her old albums with me and I'd like to frame it with her autograph. Do you think if I left it with you she'd mind signing it for me?"

Gus smiles widely, by proxy, for Billie. "Of course," he tells Glenn, the alarm guy. "She'd be happy to."

"Oh, my God! That is, like, so great," he says, his voice a few octaves higher. "When it's done just call me. Here's my card. You can leave it at the guard station out front, and I'll pick it up."

"No problem."

The man reaches into his truck, fetches the album, and gives it to Gus.

"You made my day," he says. "Maybe my year."

Gus waves as the men drive through the gate and almost collide with Detective Alex Mills who comes roaring up the driveway. After slamming on his squealing brakes, the detective throws the car door open and gets out. He's carrying a small box.

"Hey, man, your smile get any bigger, it'll break your face," Alex says. "You that happy to see me?"

"Just having a proud moment about Billie, that's all," he tells the detective.

Alex offers him a mocking "aw shucks" and follows him through the house and out to the pool, where they sit on a pair of chaises. Gus offers the detective something to drink. Alex, off duty now at five thirty, opts for a beer. Gus joins him. They sip.

"So tell me what you've been seeing," Alex says. "I'm curious."

"Don't know if it will be helpful quite yet," Gus tells him. "There are some things I can't interpret at this point. But let's get it on paper before I forget it all."

Alex pulls a small notepad and pen from his shoulder bag. "I doubt you'd forget, but go on, I'm ready."

First, Gus recounts what happened when he saw the Illumilife jet at Sky Harbor. "It was like a part of this guy's life was trying to tell me something," he tells Alex.

"Can you interpret that?"

Gus puts his head in his hands, closes his eyes. "When I see him in the desert, alone, walking that highway, and I hear him say, 'I have my whole life ahead of me,' obviously I'm seeing this CEO when he had nothing."

"Before he got rich?"

He opens his eyes and says, "Before anything, Alex. Not just the money, but the career. This was a voice of a guy who was just getting started."

"So, what does that tell you?"

Gus takes another sip of beer. "It tells me we need to look back at this guy's history, before he became the CEO of Illumilife, to know why he's dead."

Alex leans forward. "Are you saying his death has nothing to do with Illumilife? 'Cause there are plenty of people there with a motive."

"I'm not saying that. I'm saying this case warrants some history-gathering. Further back than you might have expected."

Alex shakes his head. "I don't know, Gus."

"Look, dude, it was my first experience with him, you know, just one vision. I could be completely wrong about it. It was vague, but I'm giving you my best hunch."

A hawk soars overhead, banking sharply in their direction.

"Shit, it looks like he's coming in for a landing," Alex says.

"He won't," Gus says. "He's just curious."

"So, now you're a bird whisperer?"

Gus shakes his head. "What's in the box?"

Alex digs into the box beside him. "Lots of shit from the second victim. But you probably know more about it than me."

"Why do you say that?"

"Didn't you see the murder happening?"

"I saw *a* murder happening," Gus corrects him. "I don't know if I saw *the* murder. Fill me in."

Alex tells him about the crime scene, about Barry Schultz, about the doctor's wife. He pushes the box toward Gus. "The wife gave us a bunch of stuff, like a hat, some gloves, the guy's water bottle."

Gus takes the box. "I don't think there's any emotion attached to this stuff."

Alex looks up squarely into Gus's face. "Right. You work with emotion."

"That's why I like to be at the crime scene."

"If there's nothing useful for you here, I can take you to the cemetery maybe tomorrow," Alex tells him. "What about the beret?"

Gus removes it from the box. He shrugs, then closes his eyes. "Did he wear this playing golf?"

"Man, that was quick."

Gus, eyes still closed, smiles. "No. That wasn't a vision. I figured the golfing gloves, the water bottle . . . Give me a minute."

"Take two."

Gus brushes his hands over the feltlike texture of the beret. The surface is, at once, a soft meadow and a worn, beaten path. His fingers create fleeting grooves of bending grass as they graze the material. He then goes underneath and lets the hat rest on the tips of two fingers. He amuses himself with the thought of touching the synapses of the doctor's brain, but that's a power far above his pay grade. Instead, he searches for a climactic memory, a pivotal moment in the doctor's life.

And nothing.

He pauses, takes a deep mental breath, and wills himself to see a door opening. The door is fully of his imagination, not a vision; it's a tool, a device he often uses when he can't break through the wall. He slides the door in from the left, pushes it across the horizon, lets it float to the right. He's like a stagehand in his mind's eye, setting the props where they need to go before the scene can begin. His doors usually open to a brilliantly blue sky and an invitation to probe the unfathomable. They usher in possibility, the arcanum of a psychic's power. Not so this one.

Beyond this door is a room of pulsing red light. He stands at the threshold, peering into the crimson haze. Then he sees the photographs. They're hanging from the ceiling, but Gus can't make out the images; he pokes his head in, sees the formulas in the tubs, smells the chemicals, and he realizes that the chamber in front of him is a photographer's darkroom from the old days. With that revelation comes the whirring and snapping sounds of old cameras, from the pre–digital age, and the flashing of bulbs that mitigates the blood redness of the lab. With a change of aperture, Gus can, indeed, make out the image in one of the hanging photographs: it's a man in scrubs donning a surgical mask, peering down into the lens of the camera, as if a patient on a gurney below is taking the shot. This has to be the doctor, Gus assumes, so he studies the photo with vigilance; he probes until the image comes to life, and when it does Gus sees the doctor at work. But the man is not so much performing surgery as he is impaling the patient. He's not making an incision. He's digging a hole. The patient, her insides splattering the walls, shrieks bloody murder.

Not of his own volition, Gus's eyes bolt open.

"You see a ghost?"

"Huh?"

"It looks like you saw a ghost," Alex says.

"I might have." Gus clenches his stomach, trying to divert a tsunami of nausea. "Look, I don't know really what I saw, but I did see the man digging."

"Which man?"

"A guy dressed like a doctor."

"So, he *did* dig his own grave," Alex concludes.

"He was digging something."

"You're sure?"

"I'm sure. I'm not often sure. But this I'm sure of," Gus says. "And I think there's something else."

Gus describes the darkroom.

"What do you think it means?" Alex asks.

"I don't have a precise message about it, but I have an interpretation. I think you need to gather photos."

"Photos?"

Gus takes a final swig of beer. "Yeah. I think you'll want to get photographs. Maybe old ones. This goes back to my hunch about the CEO's past."

"So you think the victims are connected?"

"Don't you?"

"Something's connected. Obviously."

"I'm getting a terribly deep sense about history," Gus says. "And photographs are your map to get there."

"So I need to ask the CEO's wife for family photos?" Alex asks. "That ought to warm her frigid heart."

"And you'll need to get some pictures from the doctor's family, as well," Gus tells him. "I'm suggesting that together, an album, of sorts, of your victims will help you in your investigation. Photos tell a story, Alex. The story will fall into place. Things will be revealed."

Alex's eyes bounce.

"You don't believe me?" Gus asks.

"I most certainly believe you," Alex replies. "I'm just psyched, you know, listening to my psychic. Get it?"

Gus looks at him deadpan. "You want another beer?"

"I do."

As Gus fetches the beer from the outdoor kitchen, his phone rings. He doesn't recognize the number, and when he answers he only hears music, Spanish music, playing in the distance.

12

A few nights later, back at his own place, Gus gets ready for Blaine Wrigley, his third client of the week. Washing his face, he's surprised to see how tired those eyes are staring back at him from the mirror, given the slow, nearly effortless shift at work today. But he's probably the only person he knows who sees crow's-feet and rejoices. He likes the affirmation of age. There's not one laugh line or one wisdom line he'd erase.

As he's toweling off his face, Billie calls. She'll be coming back to Phoenix tomorrow, and she says she's ready to be in her house now that the perimeter is fully alarmed. She says she misses him. He says the same. But there's something about the cadence of the conversation, the volley of dialogue, that suggests to Gus they're riding in a car and that he's seated behind her. When he says he has to go get ready for a client, Gus can viscerally feel the car pull to a stop to drop him at the curb.

Despite his misgivings about caffeine at seven o'clock in the evening, he brews a pot, and when Blaine Wrigley arrives about twenty-five minutes later, Gus Parker is in full throttle. "You're having problems with your ex," Gus says moments after he opens the door.

"How'd you know?" the man asks.

"I'm psychic," Gus says with a laugh. "Or it could be that you mentioned it last time."

The two of them settle in the office. "But now she wants to reconcile," Blaine tells him.

"Then you're not having a problem with your ex."

Blaine, baby-faced and muscle-bound for a guy of fifty, is nervous. His leg shakes. He looks away when he says, "No. It's not her. It's our son, rather her son from another marriage. He's the problem."

The first time Blaine had come to see Gus, the guy had been offered a chance to invest in a small chain of low-powered radio stations throughout Arizona. Gus had advised against the move, not based on a vision, specifically, but rather a hunch that Blaine had been bouncing from one bad investment to the next, without a real business plan for any of them; he was a low-grade get-rich-quick schemer, not the kind who causes injury to others—the kind who only causes injury to himself, repeatedly.

"How old is your stepson?"

"He's twenty-three and angry," the man replies. "He doesn't want us to get back together."

"Because?"

Blaine's voice goes MIA. He just sits there, says nothing, looks down.

"You were unfaithful," Gus says.

The man nods.

"And your stepson watched his mother fall apart."

The client lifts his head, locks eyes on Gus. "Damn, you're good."

Gus smiles. "That wasn't psychic. That was just a good guess."

"Well, I'm paying you to be psychic," Blaine reminds him. "So, if you wouldn't mind telling me what our future looks like . . ."

"Do you have a picture of her?"

The man digs out his wallet it, opens it, and hands a photo to Gus. The woman's neck is beautifully sculpted; that's the first thing Gus notices. Her hair is up, her eyes wide and ingratiating, and her skin flawless, as if she's just toweled off from a Dove commercial.

"Some sons will do almost anything to protect their mothers," Gus says. "That's what I'm seeing."

"Meaning what? How far will he go?"

"Has he threatened you?" Gus asks.

"More like a warning," Blaine says. "Every time I try to see my wife, this kid shows up and tells me to stay away from her. He always causes a scene, enough to get me to leave."

Gus's stomach rattles. He ignores the disruption and says, "First of all, I do see the two of you together."

"But Henry, that's her kid, is now calling me every day warning me to stay away from her."

Another rattle inside Gus. Then something falls down the stairs of his spine. "He says those exact words? 'Stay away from her'?" Gus asks.

Blaine thinks for a moment, then says, "Pretty much."

An affirmation of something. Maybe that explains Gus's recent visions. "Are you afraid of your stepson?"

"Not physically," the man replies. "I played football in college, and as you can probably tell, I'm not exactly a little guy like—"

"Like me?"

"No, man, I didn't mean that," Blaine says, a blush rising across his wide face. "You're kinda skinny, but you're not little. You're in good shape, you know, for someone your age."

Gus nods. "Thanks. I think."

"I'm just saying that I might be a lot bigger than my stepson, but size doesn't matter if the kid's got a gun."

Gus stares at the wall behind his client into his imaginary vortex of clues. "I don't think he has a gun."

"What makes you so sure?"

"It's just what I see," Gus tells him. "I see a very angry young guy. And he's not so much angry with you as he is with his biological father. His biological father died in some kind of accident, right?"

"You nailed it," Blaine says. "Small plane crash. Years ago."

Gus looks at the photo of the woman again. He grips it in his hands. "I have a strong feeling that you and your wife will reconcile. But it won't be here," he says. "I think your stepson is actually helping you, not in a good way, but he's helping."

"Like how?"

"You're going to have to leave Phoenix to get her back," Gus tells him. "That's what I'm seeing. This whole thing suggests a trip, maybe like a second honeymoon. If you can, invite her someplace special for a long weekend. Maybe Cabo, or Tahoe, or even Flagstaff. I think with the son out of the way, you and she can finally have those really important talks."

"He can't control where she goes."

"No. He can't."

"It's a great idea, Gus," the man says. "I should have thought of it myself."

"You were too focused on what to do about the son," Gus replies. "I focused on what to do without the son."

"Wow. Huge relief, man."

"Anything else?"

"Nah, that's it for now. Thanks for clearing my head," Blaine says. "I should send some of my buddies to see you. You'd blow 'em away."

Gus rises from his chair. "That's kind of you to offer. But I'm about as booked up as I can be now. I don't do this full-time."

Blaine says, "You should." Then he hands Gus his fee and leaves.

About an hour later, savoring some relief of his own, Gus returns to his office and sits on the floor to meditate. He chooses Tibetan chanting on his iPod and rests his noise-canceling headphones over his ears. At the moment, he's convinced the nefarious visions—those words on the CT scan, and again on the wall at Billie's house—were messages about his client, not about him. This kind of wholesale distribution of signs is not uncommon. He's soothed by the chanting. He's almost a sensory speck of nothing in the universe, when the quiet hum of Zen gives way to a flurry of static. Without surrendering his Zen completely, he feels for the wire that connects to his iPod, tries to give it a gentle twist; it's an instinctive move that requires no consciousness, but it doesn't work. The static grows louder, buzzing in Gus's ears like a brigade of mosquitoes out for blood. He catches himself shooing the noise away with his hand, and, as he does, the racket stops, giving way to a voice that is decidedly not Tibetan. "Stay away from her," it says. "Stay away from her." Gus comes barreling back to earth. It's a woman's voice. Not a stepson's voice.

"Stay away from her."

He rips the headphones off, then tosses them to the floor. He is a speck no longer but rather a full bundle of nerves.

"Stay away from her."

This woman's voice. It echoes in his head. It becomes a ghostly chant. He sits in a stupor. Then later, the chant follows him to bed, and, not helped in the least by the caffeine he had ingested earlier that evening, Gus Parker tosses and turns all night.

13

Perfect call to start the day. By "perfect," he means "worst."

Alex Mills just got off the phone with the mayor's press secretary, who was calling to remind Mills, in case he had forgotten, that there were two unsolved homicide cases without substantial leads and that the press was getting restless.

"Whatever we can do to help," said Nathan Hedges. "I've got a ton of resources I can throw at the press, including a spare public information officer who *speaks Spanish*."

As if, suddenly, Phoenix cares about Telemundo, or Latinos, in general.

"Grácias, but we have PIOs to handle the press," Mills told him. "But thanks for the offer."

Nathan Hedges doesn't give a shit about the press. Mayor Hurley doesn't give a shit about the press. The mayor's office cares about a quick, neat wrap-up of the cases, and that call was nothing more than an attempt by Hurley and friends to put on the pressure. Hurley wants his accolades, his crime-free accolades (which have a tendency to show up in national listicles of "Safest Places to Live" and "Top 10 Places to Raise Children" and "Best Mayors in America"). Hurley, ultimately, doesn't care about the press. Hurley cares about Hurley.

Sadly for Hurley, Mills doesn't care about Hurley.

He must be wearing his disgust on his face because when Preston and Myers file into his office a minute later, Preston says, "You have a hairball, Detective?"

Mills winces. "Good morning, gentlemen, to what do I owe the pleasure?"

"You want videotape from Thomas and Sixteenth?" Myers asks him.

"Sure. Why the fuck not?"

"There's a gas station at the intersection. Cameras everywhere as you might imagine," Preston says. "I doubt we'll need a search warrant or subpoena. You know, these businesses are usually real good with helping out."

"Usually," Mills says. "Get me video from the nights in question. It would make sense if the killer arranged to meet his victims there. Someplace random, unsuspicious."

"Will do," Preston says. "But while we're talking search warrants and subpoenas, I want to let you know the good doctor's colleagues aren't cooperating. So we'll need a warrant for the practice."

"Get one," Mills says. "Shouldn't be a big deal."

"They've already lawyered up," Preston informs him.

"Not surprised."

"We're not having any better luck with Schultz's answering service," Preston says.

"How so?"

"The company says it has grounds to fight the subpoena based on HIPAA laws, alone," Preston explains. "They say they have a duty to fight it."

Mills scoffs. "Jesus Christ, doesn't anyone want to know why Barry Schultz ended up dead?" he grouses. "Did you tell them that a homicide investigation supersedes HIPAA?"

"You might want to have a talk with their lawyer," Myers says.

Mills gets up. "Fuck that," he says. "Give me the address. It's time for me to pay a visit."

Physicians Messaging sits on the first floor of a generic office building in one of the generic office parks that have recently cropped up around

Broadway and Forty-Eighth. They're everywhere now, these concrete-and-glass barracks of business, killing the dreams of people who would rather be doing anything than pushing papers and answering phones and making copies and chasing spreadsheets and overusing PowerPoint. Mills knows Phoenix. He knows people. He can't imagine being most of them.

The office manager introduces herself, and Mills forgets her name as soon as she says it. She's as generic as the building in which she toils. Five-something, hairstyle-of-the moment, red lipstick, and a cross around her neck. "I don't think it's appropriate for me to discuss this, Detective," she says. "It's already gone to our Legal department."

"We don't need to talk on the record," he tells her.

He's standing in the reception area. Gray fabric climbs the walls, threatening to encase the whole office and its workers, yielding only to a display of inspirational posters that offer banalities like "Team-work Will Make You Soar!" with a murmuration of starlings against a harvest moon to illustrate the message.

"I'm sorry," the office manager says, shaking her head to accentuate her feigned sorrow. "But I'm prohibited from sharing information. We'll respond to the subpoena accordingly."

"Fine," Mills says. "But if you fail to provide the information we need, we can get a search warrant to turn this place upside down. I'd hate to do that."

The woman reddens but braces herself. Her jaw clenches, neck stiffens. "On what grounds, Detective? How could you possibly justify a search warrant?"

"I'm prohibited from sharing information at this point, ma'am," Mills says with as much snark as he can muster. "But let me just say in very layman terms that the doctor received a call from this answering service immediately before his disappearance. For all we know, an employee here could be implicated in the crime. Perhaps one of your operators lured the doctor to his death. We have to investigate all angles. And an inside job, which doesn't involve a patient, removes the hurdle of HIPAA that your lawyers are so fond of."

"Detective, please," the woman whispers. "You don't know what you're talking about."

Mills stares at her, his face instinctively hosting the are-you-fucking-crazy look as he considers her bold assertion. "Excuse me?"

"Not here," she says. "Please, can I speak to you in private?"

Mills doesn't answer. His face remains in its are-you-fucking-crazy pose; he adds a WTF shake of the head.

"Detective?" she whispers again. "Can you come with me?"

"Sure," Mills says, and follows her to a small, windowless conference room. It's an envelope of claustrophobia probably meant to intimidate the fuck out of employees who are dragged in here for a scolding. She asks him to sit opposite her.

"I mean no disrespect," she says.

"Just needed to show off in front of the employees?"

"No," she says, her smile collapsing. "I didn't want to cause a scene. I'm going to tell you something that I couldn't tell you out there." Her tone suggests she luxuriates in escalating anticipation, brokering information, wielding knowledge.

Mills has seen it all before. Flatly he says, "I'm all ears."

"First, you cannot attribute this to me. I never told you this."

"Right."

"I really wanted to share this, you know, to avoid all the legal wrangling. It would've saved you a lot of time, Detective. But I was scared of losing my job, to say the least."

"You could save me a lot of time right now, if you just spit it out, ma'am," he tells her. "And I mean no disrespect."

"The call did not come from here."

"What do you mean?"

Her smile returns triumphantly. "I mean that no one here paged or called Dr. Schultz that evening. Our records reflect that. There's nothing in our written logs. Our calls are computerized, as well. I've been through the data a dozen times. There are no incoming or outgoing calls associated with Dr. Schultz or his practice, for that matter."

Mills makes her wait a moment, then says, "All the more reason we need your records. If your intention by telling me this was to preempt the subpoena or a search warrant, you've actually done the opposite."

"But there's nothing to search for here. That's what I'm telling you."

"And I don't disbelieve you, ma'am. What you're telling me is critically important and, if true, warrants confirmation on our part. We need proof."

She rests her arms on the table in front of her and leans forward. "But you don't need proof from us," she says. "The fact is Dr. Schultz was not on call last weekend. All you have to do is ask the people who run his practice. There's your proof. Another physician was on call. Not him!"

Occasionally a theatrical witness does produce ovation-worthy information. It was worth sitting through her performance for this. "And you know this how?"

"First of all, we have the on-call schedules for all the practices we contract with," she replies. "Then, after going through all our logs and records from last weekend, just to be sure Dr. Schultz wasn't covering for someone else at the last minute, I just picked up the phone and called his office manager and asked. Imagine that!"

"Office manager to office manager," Mills says. "What a clandestine world you work in."

"Are you satisfied now, Detective Mills?"

"I believe I am," he says, rising. "I guess I owe you an apology. Or at least I need to tell you that I understand your concerns and appreciate what you've done."

She reaches for his hand. She doesn't shake. She just holds his hand in hers. "I know you do. I know you didn't mean to be a jerk."

He laughs.

"And I didn't mean to be a bitch," she adds. "But put yourself in my place. I'm not supposed to be saying a word to you, and, yet, I had this important information. Please, please don't bring my name into any of this."

"I won't," he says. "You have my word. And my sincere gratitude, Whitney," he says, suddenly remembering her name. If there ever was a Whitney, she's a Whitney. She's a portrait of Whitney.

Mills swings by headquarters, picks up Powell, and heads over to the home of Carla and Barry Schultz.

"You wanna call and see if she's home?" Powell asks.

"Nope," he replies. "That would prompt a conversation that I want to have with her in person."

"Makes sense. And if she's not home, I know a real good place out there for sushi."

"Just a warning," he tells his colleague, "she looks like the poster child for plastic surgery. Nip, tuck, boobs like nobody's business."

"I'm looking forward to it."

Is she? Mills is pretty sure she meant that sarcastically, but he'd never given much thought to whom Powell might be attracted. Surely not the plastic surgery type. At thirty-three, Powell's fairly attractive with an outdoorsy face and long, copper hair that, in her days as a patrol officer, she used to bleach blond. Freckles dust her cheeks lightly. Sometimes her face snarls up like a playground bully. Other times not so much. He musters a harmless question to her. "You think you'll ever settle down?"

"You sound like my mother," she says. "I will. When the right person comes along."

"Makes sense to me," he tells her.

"What doesn't make sense to me," she says, "is why we waited for Schultz's answering service to cough up the information, rather than talking directly to his practice."

"Because the practice isn't talking directly to us. I don't know why. I don't even know if they know why, now that lawyers are involved," Mills replies. "Besides, we were trying to track down the patient who called into the service that night. The service would have been the first point of contact. We had no reason to believe Schultz wasn't on call."

She nods. "So, no one called into the answering service?"

"There was no call for Barry Schultz," Mills replies. "Nor for anyone else in his practice that night."

"But the possibility remains that he could have been lured out that night by someone angry over a botched surgery," Powell says. "Someone who knew how to reach his cell."

"But, assuming the same person killed Schultz and Klink, how does a bad surgery fit into both motives?"

She turns to him, smiling. "Okay, I'm going out on a limb with this theory, but let's suppose Klink had a mistress and paid for her plastic surgery. The surgery was a disaster so she goes after both of them."

They're at a red light. He looks at her and says, "Actually you've snapped the limb."

"That bad?"

"No," he says. "It's mildly plausible if you think our killer is a woman."

"It could be," she says. "We don't have evidence either way. Do we even know what it would take, physically, for a man or a woman to carry out the murders?"

The light turns green. Mills accelerates and says, "Not yet. But do you really think a woman is going to get so angry over a surgery that she'd go out and commit murder?"

"Hell hath no fury like a woman scarred!"

Mills laughs. It's an unlikely scenario, and they both know it.

Carla Schultz's face betrays both exhaustion and despair but little else. Broken blood vessels, like red lightning bolts, pierce the corners of her eyes. She's done a lot of drinking or crying, probably both. She wears no makeup, and her skin is sallow. "Detective, I wasn't expecting you."

"I'm sorry," Mills says. "I should have called. But I was hoping you'd be home."

"Do you have news?"

He shakes his head. "Not really. We haven't made an arrest, but there's something I need to discuss with you."

She's hesitant at the door, moves to swing it open, then stops. "But look at me," she says. "I'm a mess."

"Mrs. Schultz," Powell says, "you're America's Next Top Model compared to most people we meet with."

"This is my colleague, Jan Powell," Mills tells her. The women share a light, polite handshake.

Carla Schultz invites them in. She leads them to the left of the foyer, past museum-quality art of the Desert Southwest, and up a stairway of Mexican tile and wrought iron. They sit in a loft overlooking the living room.

"Beautiful home," Powell tells her.

"Thank you," Carla says. "Barry's obsessed with the pueblo style, in case you didn't notice. He loves Taos. I mean 'loved.'" Her voice cracks. "God, I still find myself referring to him in the present tense."

"It's barely been a week," Powell says gently. "You may not adjust to this for a while. And no one will blame you."

"How are you holding up, otherwise?" Mills asks. "You have family and friends for support?"

Carla bites her lip. Mills can see her trembling chin. Tears brim, and she says, "I do. But at the end of the day this feels like something I have to go through alone. People tell me I'm wrong."

"I agree with those people," Mills tells her.

She shrugs and says, "What brings you here, Detective?"

"I need to ask you a question," he says. "Is there any way you were mistaken about your husband being on call last weekend?"

"Anything's possible," she replies. "Didn't I tell you I couldn't remember one way or another? The phone call surprised me. But Barry insisted."

"Right," Mills assures her. "I do have that in my notes."

"So, why do you ask?"

"Because we were trying to track the patient who called the answering service, and we discovered that your husband was never on call."

She looks at him with expectant eyes as if there must be more but says nothing.

"Can you think back to last weekend, Carla? May I call you Carla?" Powell asks her.

The woman nods.

"Okay," Powell continues, "think back to last weekend and ask yourself if anything happened that was not routine."

"It was a dull weekend as far as I can remember. Until I woke up and he was gone."

"But does your routine change at all when your husband's on call? And did it change last weekend?" Powell asks.

Carla slides her hands under her thighs and leans forward. "When he's on call—uh—was on call, we don't or didn't leave town," she says. "But that's it. We'd go out for dinner; he'd play golf. We might go on a short hike or to a gallery. As you can tell, we're collecting Native American art. Or we might cook, stay in, watch a movie. He could answer patients from anywhere as long as he was relatively close to home."

"I'm sorry to have to ask you this, Carla," Mills says, "but is there any reason your husband would have lied to you last weekend about being on call?"

Anger fills her eyes. "My husband did not lie," she insists. "I told you he got a call from the answering service about a patient with some post-surgery trauma, and then he called her right away. I don't know if he was technically on call or just covering for someone else who was. Okay?"

"But, Carla, there was no call from the answering service," Mills tells her. "There was no patient calling with post-surgery trauma. We checked."

Carla shakes her head as she speaks. "I don't understand. I remember he got a call from the service, hung up quickly. Then he called the patient and left the house. I don't know how I could have misunderstood that."

"Because you don't understand crime, Carla," Powell says. "And you're not supposed to. That's our job."

"Then someone was using that cream cheese butt story to lure him out," the widow muses.

"We don't think there was a medical emergency," Mills says. "He might have lied to you to get out of the house. Something to do with that call. But we don't know what. Do you think he was trying to get out of the house to go see someone in particular?"

She groans. "God no. I don't know. I hadn't even considered that possibility because he said he told the patient to meet him at the hospital. That's routine," she says. "But I know what you're implying."

"If you know what we're implying, is it possible he was going to see someone who he didn't want you to know about?" Powell asks.

"You mean a girlfriend?"

"Yes," Powell says.

"No."

"You're sure?" Mills asks. Without waiting for an answer, he says, "So Barry never left the home at odd hours or came up with odd reasons to take a drive?"

"Not unless he was actually on call or covering for someone," Carla says. "I don't control his every move, and he sure as hell doesn't have to sign in and sign out." She follows her remark with a hearty laugh, and that immediately sucks some of the tension out of the room. "But, my husband doesn't sneak around or make mysterious phone calls if that's what you're asking."

Mills leans in like a confidante. "Can you think of someone, anyone, who would have wanted to lure him out of the house last weekend? Anyone he might have argued with?"

She searches the wall behind them, as if a memory might be lingering there, or an epiphany waiting to strike. "I'm sorry," she says finally, tears inching down her face.

Mills hates the nagging question, hates having to ask it, but he'll hate the nagging question even more if he leaves the house without an answer. "I know you smoke dope, Carla," he says. "Is it possible your memory of last weekend is clouded? Were you high when your husband left the house?"

Her face is in her hands, and she screams. The muffled agony gives Mills a shiver. "Yes. I was high when he left the house," she says. "Yes, I get high when we're in for the evening just hanging out. Don't fucking tell me this is my fault."

Mills leans in. "No. Not at all. I'm sorry. I just wanted to establish your state of mind. What about your husband?"

She laughs bitterly. "Never high. Tolerated my smoking. Didn't judge and didn't partake. Okay?"

"Okay. Thank you, Carla," he says and then nimbly adds, "We've subpoenaed your husband's cell phone records, but we're also going to have to subpoena data from your landline here at the house to find out who's been calling him."

"Don't bother. I'll give them to you. I can get them off the computer."

"That would be fine, Carla," Powell says. "We may need to go through the subpoena process anyway with your phone company, just to keep it admissible, but feel free to provide us with whatever you can."

"And photos," Mills adds, suddenly remembering. "If you can dig up any old photos that you think might be helpful."

She wipes away a tear. "Photos of what?"

"Anything important to your husband. Your wedding. Your vacations," he tells her, trying to best articulate what Gus might need. "Any milestone in his life could give us a clue."

Still weeping, the widow nods. "Give me a few days," she says. "I'll pull together some photos and print out those phone records. I just need a few days."

Mills reaches for her hand and holds it. "Someone lured your husband to his death. We need to find out who and why. And we will. I promise you."

As soon as the car doors close with a solid thunk, Powell turns to him and says, "The doctor answers the phone in front of his wife, but he can't let her know who's on the line. So, he hangs up, goes into another room, and calls the person back. Then he leaves, and on the fly he just says, 'I gotta cover for Dr. Joe Blow.'"

"I have no problem with that theory," Mills says.

"So, Barry Schultz knows the person who's calling him, and he knows why he's getting the call," Powell adds. "This is not some mysterious stranger luring him out of the house. This has consequences. Like, say, Schultz owed someone money. Drugs, maybe. Gambling. Who knows?"

Mills's phone rings. "Hold that thought, Jan."

It's Ken Preston. "We got another grave," he tells Mills. "It's empty."

Mills takes the palm of his free hand and bangs it on his forehead. "Jesus."

"Where you at?" Preston asks.

"We're just leaving Carla Schultz, in Scottsdale," Mills replies. "I'm putting you on speaker so Powell can hear. Where's the grave?"

"Moon Valley. Desert Rose Memorial Park. Put it in your navigator."

Powell types the information into the navigator as Mills starts the car and pulls into the street.

"Are you on-site?" Mills asks.

"No," Preston replies. "We just got the call. Meet you out there?"

Mills takes a deep breath. "Yeah. But get me some techs and a photog."

"Done," the man says.

Mills ends the call and dials Gus Parker. "Detective Psycho," he says to voice mail, "it's a little after three. Meet me at Desert Rose Memorial Park in Moon Valley, if you're not at work. If you are, come by after. I think I'll be there a while."

Powell eyes him suspiciously as he puts the phone down.

"What?" he asks.

"Detective Psycho?"

"My name for Gus—sometimes."

"Does he just have indefinite clearance to work with you?"

"It's cool with Jake. Is it not cool with you?"

She scoffs. "I don't care. I like Gus. He's a bit out there, if you know what I mean, but he's cool."

"And he can be helpful," Mills says.

"And we did almost get him killed," she reminds him.

He doesn't need a reminder. The image of Gus trapped in a remote desert cave with that lunatic has yet to debit from his memory bank. Probably never will. Mills saved the psychic's life, but it never should have gotten that far. This case won't. It can't. And yet another grave awaits. A phantom draft of air comes from behind him now like the heavy, hissing breath of Mayor Hurley making its way down his neck.

The navigator tells him to exit here. Take a left.

14

Gus wishes he had a camera. He gets out of his car and steps into a portrait that would put most photographers out of business. How could they ever match the beauty? The cemetery absolutely glows under the dusky sky. Against the retina of the valley, the colors shift in silence, mostly unnoticed, from waning yellow to illustrious pink and to transcendent blue. He now, in this moment, understands that this is what people mean when they say "rest in peace." This is the "peace." Peace is an eternal dusk, a pastel state of bliss.

"It's like bedtime for dead people," he tells Detective Powell.

"What?"

She's sitting in Alex's car, working on her laptop. She looks up for only a second.

"Just the sky," he says to her. "The mood it brings."

"Right," she says back. "Mills is out there looking at the hole."

Gus nods. "Thanks."

"No problem," she says, her disinterest in him obvious.

Gus follows the sound of voices coming from a far corner of the graveyard and sees in the distance the silhouette of a crime scene—against the horizon, a small team hovers. As Gus gets closer, he spots Alex leaning against a boulder that is the only thing separating the detective from a drastic drop off a cliff. Not far from Alex, a photographer is kneeling and taking shots of the hole. "Hey, Alex," Gus calls. "Sorry I couldn't get here sooner. I worked a full shift."

"Wow. A full shift," Alex says, extending a hand. "You deserve a vacation."

Gus points to the cliff's edge and says, "Interesting place."

"No shit. If we ever get enough rain for a landslide, there's gonna be a lot of bones and bodies in the neighborhood below."

"I don't see that happening," Gus tells him.

The detective points to a cardboard sign staked into the ground. "You see *that*?"

Gus squints. "I can't read it from here."

Alex guides him closer until they're standing about ten feet behind the kneeling photographer. Here every letter of the sign comes into focus:

DIG YOUR GRAVE

"Again, we doubt a copycat, Gus," Alex says. "We haven't released details of the crime scenes to the public. We've shared information with surrounding departments, just in case something like this turns up elsewhere. But it's unlikely another jurisdiction would leak this."

"I'm going with the assumption that this is the work of the same person," Gus says. "I don't suppose I can touch the sign or hold it."

"Correct supposition."

"Honestly, the best thing for me would be to lie in the hole."

Laughter bursts from Alex's face. The photographer looks up similarly amused.

"I realize I can't do that," Gus says. "I'm just saying that the closer I can get to the suspect, the better. You know how this works."

Still laughing, Mills says, "Of course I do. I realize you're handicapped. But do the best you can."

"How close can I get?"

"You are as close as you can get."

Gus nods. He kneels, takes a good whiff of the crispy air, and feels the replenishment expand in his lungs. More quickly than usual, the stirrings of separation begin. His body stays behind while his mind explores with a greedy curiosity. It's the ultimate meditation, albeit at warp speed. Vast possibilities flash by in microseconds, not really visions of anything, more like random photos shaken loose from their albums; this is what the universe has to sort out, somehow, for every life, for every story. Until then, the photos are no more than abstracts and notions. So, Gus surfs onward. From the crest of a cosmic wave appears a dome. A white, official dome. Not an abstract, not a notion, this is a tangible place, and Gus can hear the shuffling of feet on marble. There's a vast, empty room, floor-to-ceiling books. In the distance, a man stands at a podium, reading from a stack of papers. He waves the documents in the air angrily, then slams them against the podium's surface. With that he vanishes. The room vanishes. Gus is outside. The street is leafy. It's springtime, and it's a city of wide avenues that run for miles. Gus arrives at a box of a building, a mansion, perhaps, or a museum. He's not sure. This is where his vision stops, right here—number twenty-five. An address?

He repeats the information to Alex.

"You do that with your eyes wide open?" the eavesdropping photographer asks him.

"Do what?"

"Your psychic thing," she says.

"Sometimes," he replies.

"I thought your eyes had to be closed so you could see stuff," she says.

"Sometimes they do."

Alex gives Gus's elbow a tug. "If you will excuse us, Donna. Gus is running short on time."

"Sure, sure. Didn't mean to pry."

Gus and Alex drift away. "She did mean to pry," Alex tells him. "Sorry."

Gus laughs. "No problem. I'm used to it."

"So, what do you think any of it means, if it means anything at all?" Alex asks.

Gus, leaning now against the massive boulder, searches the darkening horizon and says, "I can't tell you what it means for your investigation, but I interpret the setting as someplace official. I think that's obvious. I don't know about the man, but he seemed like a lawyer or maybe a government official."

"Government official?"

"Secretary of the treasury, maybe . . . or attorney general, that sort of thing."

"So, you just paid a visit to Washington, DC. Is that what you're saying?"

"I'm just guessing, but that could be it," Gus says. "Maybe those documents in his hand were actually ballots. Do you think we can tie the victims to election fraud?"

Alex utters a one-syllable laugh and says, "I don't see the connection, sorry."

"Or maybe we're dealing with a deadly whistleblower," Gus muses. "Maybe the CEO was up to some kind of financial fraud, and maybe the doctor was defrauding Medicare, I don't know, and there's a government whistleblower who actually kills instead of whistles."

A big smile from Alex Mills. "I mean no disrespect here, Gus, but the scenario seems farfetched. Very creative, but unlikely."

"Don't dismiss it."

"Oh, I don't dismiss anything entirely."

A slight breeze stirs. The neon of the valley comes alive, as if somebody flipped a switch, creating an incandescent grid under the darkening sky. "I should probably be going," Gus tells Alex. "I have to pick up Billie at the airport. She's flying in tonight."

"No limo?"

"We don't limo around Phoenix," Gus says, turning to leave.

"What about the address?" Alex asks.

Gus stops. "What address?"

"The one in your vision. Number twenty-five."

"Maybe it's the killer's address. Maybe it's the next victim's address. I don't even know if it is an address, but it's a significant number. I'll work on it."

He passes Detective Powell on the way back to his car. She's on a mission; he can see it in her face, in her determined gait. She's clutching her laptop.

"Good night, Detective," he says, but she either doesn't hear him or pretends she doesn't hear him, because she doesn't say a word.

"I saw your Detective Psycho leaving just now," Powell says. "Did he see anything?" Her eyes bulge mockingly.

Mills writes off the mockery to human nature; people often dismiss what they don't understand. She's dismissive, she's a skeptic, and she's a hard-ass. Powell is so by the book she'll get hired to write the second edition, and that's what makes her a brilliant scene investigator and thorough researcher.

"He saw some interesting images," Mills tells her. "Nothing conclusive yet. But stuff to think about."

"Well, I found some interesting images of my own," Powell says. "And I'm feeling fairly conclusive about them."

They step over to one of the monuments, and Powell sets her laptop on a flat surface (David Ludwig 1925–2005). In the absence of other options, Mills doesn't stop her. Her screen sheds a small field of light.

"Who are they?" Mills asks, pointing to the faces on the screen.

"You don't recognize them?"

"Could be our victims, I guess. Minus a few years, maybe."

"I've found one common tie between the doctor and the CEO," she tells him.

He lunges his face closer to the screen. "What? What kind of tie?"

She leans in to him. "After I talked to the caretaker, I sat in the car and pulled up Klink's bio from the Illumilife website and compared it to Schultz's bio from his practice's website," she explains. "Obviously they're in very different fields. But they have one thing in common. They graduated from the same college, University of Arizona."

He tilts his head back and forth. "U of A's a big school. Doesn't mean they knew each other."

"But they did," she replies. "I did a Google search for images with their names and 'U of A' in the search window, and sure enough, I found pictures of them drinking together at a class reunion."

"Is that what I'm looking at?"

"You are," she replies. "I'll email the pics to you. This one here is from their tenth reunion." She points to the picture on the left. "That one's from their fifteenth." She points to the one on the right.

"But there are a bunch of others in the shot, Jan," Mills says. "We can't tell how well they knew each other, or if they just happened to be in the same shot with friends of friends."

"All true," she concedes. "But at the very least, they're familiar with each other."

Mills examines the photo from the tenth reunion. The men are toasting, champagne glasses raised, it seems, to their own self-importance. "Wow," he says. "They are. And that's certainly more than we knew yesterday. Good work. If you're through here, so am I."

On the drive out of Moon Valley, Mills asks his colleague about the caretaker.

"He said they've been vandalized before, mostly by kids," she tells him. "But the empty grave was a first."

"Did he say why he didn't find the grave until the middle of the afternoon?"

"Said there were no funerals today, and since the hole was dug at the very back of the cemetery he didn't see it until he was finishing routine maintenance."

Mills nods, content with that explanation. "Assuming all that's true, then it's very possible our suspect was here overnight, and the thing went unnoticed for most of the day."

"Agreed," Powell says.

His phone rings. It's Kelly.

"Hey, babe," he says. "I'm with another woman."

"Good. Have her cook you dinner."

Mills laughs. "We're on the way back from Moon Valley. I'll drop Powell and see you at home in about thirty."

"I was thinking Mexican," she says. "Trevor aced his Spanish project."

"No fucking way! That's the best news all day. I'm in."

When he hangs up, he tells Powell about Trevor's project. "He's doing something about comparing Spanish dialects in Central American countries, like Mexico, Guatemala, Honduras, Costa Rica . . ."

"I know where Central America is," Powell says. "But that's great."

"We've been through some rough times with that kid."

"But look at you now," she says with a smile, "proud daddy!"

They're quiet as they enter the highway and the twinkling valley pours out in front of them. As usual, the mountains to the south are blacker than the night, their massive antennas blinking red like the pulsing eyes of aliens communicating in code. It's a dependable sight.

"So, I'm wondering," Powell says. "Why haven't you gone for a promotion? You've been doing this for years."

He shrugs. "Not interested."

"Mind if I ask why? You could do Jake's job in a second."

"I'm a guy for the streets, not for the office," he says. "I push around enough paperwork as it is. I don't want to do it twenty-four seven."

"So, no ambitions toward management."

He looks at her sharply. "No. Do you know who my father was?"

"Of course. The famous county attorney, Lyle Mills," she says with steroidal reverence.

"Exactly. The guy was so ambitious he worked himself to death at age fifty-eight," he tells her. "He was brilliant, but he was also stupid. He died too early. Heart attack. No thank you."

Mills craves the white noise of the highway right about now, the absence of both memory and anticipation, but Powell persists. "Did he push you to be more ambitious?"

"Yep. But I tuned him out. To a fault."

"He was your hero," she says.

"I don't believe in heroes. But yeah."

The small charter carrying Billie Welch lands at Sky Harbor. She steps off the plane, a small bag over one shoulder. Something about the orange light on the tarmac, the way it seeps inward to the vestibule where Gus waits alone, suggests a clandestine meeting or a forbidden love story or a midnight Hollywood rendezvous; it prickles him nicely and eerily at once. The experience at Desert Rose Memorial Park has given him one of his classic psychic hangovers; like a run-on sentence that won't quit, his imagination has run amok, and his brain buzzes with a landslide of words and images that connect and disconnect at the same time. This doesn't happen after every psychic vision. Only the ones that prove to be the most portentous, if history is any evidence.

She gives him a huge hug. Her lipstick is plum-colored, her face powder white. Her eyes, outlined in black, transmit a signal so instantly and fiercely loving that it almost throws Gus off-balance. Her face affects the seamless luxury of a Hollywood starlet rushing to a respite from stardom. Warmth overcomes him now.

"I am *so* glad to be back in Phoenix," she gushes.

Phoenix is the respite.

"You've only been here for five minutes," he says, deflated.

"You know what I mean."

He doesn't know anything.

For the entire drive to Paradise Valley, Billie assumes the role of run-on sentence, which is agreeable to him since it relieves him of his hangover. She serenades him with plans for a greatest hits album, a tour, maybe a live in concert DVD. This is all the result of meeting with "her people" in LA, where everybody has "people" and nobody, Gus has learned, has a soul to speak of. Which is why Billie's commute to and from the coast is so important. She does business there; she does life here. He gets it.

"My sister is helping me sequence the album. I'm going to record a few new songs for it," she says. "I'm also thinking it's time for me to write a book. I was supposed to write a book a couple of years ago with someone from *Rolling Stone*, but that sort of went off the rails. A memoir has never been a high priority, you know, because I've lived my life, and I'm not sure I want to relive all of the boring details. That would drive me crazy, so I'm not sure."

"The details are more fascinating than boring, Billie," he tells her. "You have a great life story to tell. I'd read it."

She grabs his arm and squeezes it, rests her head on his shoulder, and keeps it there until they swing into the security entrance to her community. Gus is about to glide through the residents' lane when the guard pops out of the booth and flags him down. Gus lowers his window. "What is it, Donald?"

Donald, the happy seventy-something bespectacled guard, hands him an envelope. "Someone dropped this off for you earlier today, Mr. Parker," he says.

"Okay, thanks."

Donald peers in the window. "I don't think I've seen either of you for a few days. Welcome back."

"Thanks, Donald," Billie says. "You doing okay?"

"I'm magnificent."

Billie giggles. "We know you are," she says.

He's driving through her property gate when Billie asks, "Who's the envelope from?"

"I have no idea."

And she doesn't mention it again, and he doesn't either as he follows her into the house. He resets the alarm. She announces she'd like a bath. He says he'll make it for her. But she says she'll make it and that all he needs to do is join her. That makes him smile and almost instantly erect with expectation. He laughs at himself, at his dick. A bath for two means a trip to Billie's home spa, a room at the back of the estate that might as well be in another house on the other side of the world. Inspired by a spa she visited in Indonesia, Billie designed the room and the hallway that leads there by summoning the bamboos and mists of a lush, jungle hideaway. You turn on a switch and the room is filled with exotic birdsong. You flip another and an entire wall becomes a waterfall, sheets of water cascading. Bamboo planks lead you to the sunken tub. "Hurry," Billie calls to him. "And bring a bottle of wine."

He goes to fetch the wine from the kitchen and is about to drop the envelope on a counter when he figures he should open it now before he forgets. The spa and anything that might, hopefully, happen in there could easily make him forget. He pulls a single sheet of paper from the envelope. He assumes it's a bill because that's all that seems to arrive these days. He tries to remember if he paid the alarm guys in person. He remembers signing forms, but that's about it. Gus unfolds the sheet, and his hand trembles.

What he's looking at is not a bill.

What he sees are four words, black on white, stoic block letters. Instinctively, he blinks his eyes to confirm the words are not a psychic vision. They're not.

STAY AWAY FROM HER

15

So much for that promising erection.

Gus stares at the threat and struggles to think what to think. But his mind is blank. He tries to intuit, to conjure, to visualize some kind of clue about the sender. Nothing happens. He picks up a landline in the kitchen and dials three digits. Donald answers.

"What can I do for you, Ms. Welch?"

"It's Gus. Just checking to see if you know who dropped off the letter for me."

Donald hesitates slightly. "I'm sorry, Mr. Parker. When I got on shift it was already here. It must have come in earlier today."

"Oh."

"Is something wrong?" the guard asks.

"Uh, no," Gus replies. "It's not signed, that's all."

"Tell you what I'll do, Mr. Parker. I'll leave a note for the other shifts, and I'll find out who took the letter for you."

"That's fine. Thank you." And he hangs up.

Shit.

Just shit.

Gus stashes the letter under his T-shirts in one of several drawers that have come to be known as his in the master closet. He catches his reflection in the mirror, and he looks haunted. He strips down. As he does, his cell rings atop the table where he left it. It's Billie.

"I'm in the tub," she says. "Come."

Alex Mills rises early for a Saturday. There's too much zipping through his brain. It's seven forty-five. He slips out of the bedroom and into the home office. There he logs on to his computer and finds the email from Powell with the images attached. It's almost as if he had been dreaming of these photographs. He hadn't, but he's obsessed now with the connection between Davis Klink and Barry Schultz, two men who graduated twenty-five years ago from the University of Arizona and, within a week of one another, were reunited in death after digging their own graves. That kept him tossing and turning all night.

Powell has sent him a handful of photos. They don't differ much. They're all college reunion shots, but just how well these men knew each other mystifies him. There isn't one photo of only the two of them posing together. In every shot they're joined by other alumni who, inferentially, are clutching various forms of alcohol. Powell also sent him the men's official bios. Davis Klink, according to the Illumilife website, received an MBA from the Wharton School of business after graduating from U of A. He worked at various conglomerates in various roles in various places all around the globe before joining Illumilife as CEO. His classmate Barry Schultz studied medicine, according to the website for Associated Surgeons at Better You Center (*Jesus Christ, Better You Center?*), at Northwestern University and did his residency at Beth Israel Chicago before returning to Arizona to practice in Phoenix. Both men are Arizona natives.

He flips a few pages back in his notes, then reaches for his phone. He dials Greta Klink. Voice mail answers. He dials again, and again he gets voice mail. Oh, what the hell, he thinks, and keeps dialing. Lucky number seven! On the seventh try, she picks up.

"Who *is* this?" she growls.

"Good morning, Mrs. Klink. It's Detective Alex Mills."

"Jesus Christ. Do you know what time it is?"

"It's eight ten," he replies.

"Isn't that a bit early for a Saturday morning?"

"I thought you would be up," he says, "and it's important. We're looking for the person who killed your husband."

He can hear the bedcovers rustling around her. "I'm not up," she replies. "I mean, I'm up *now*, but I wasn't up when you decided to call here twenty times."

"It was seven times, actually, ma'am."

"What can I do for you?" she asks, her voice still husky.

"I don't know if you saw it on the news, but we have another victim who seems to have been killed in the same manner as your husband."

She doesn't respond. It's a combative silence. Mills has heard it all before. "Anyway," he says, "we've come across some photos that suggest your husband and the other victim might have known each other."

"What's his name, Detective?"

"Barry Schultz, a plastic surgeon here in Phoenix."

"Never heard of him."

He's thinking, *With a face like yours?* But, instead, he asks, "Are you sure?"

"What did I just say?"

Mills stalls for a moment. "So your husband never mentioned him?"

"I said I never heard of him. I can get one of my maids to say it in Spanish if you still don't understand."

"What I don't understand is why you're so defensive. All we're trying to do is help."

He hears the very first squeak of a sob and that very first crackle of despair. And then, sniffling through her tears she says, "I am trying to plan a funeral, Detective. I want you to find his killer more than anyone else, but the thought of burying my husband with the whole world watching is crushing me."

"The whole world?"

"The media won't let up. They call all day. From all over the world, for Christ's sake!"

"If it's any consolation, I hate the media."

She offers him an abbreviated laugh. "And my kids, all of them, are assholes."

"My kid was an asshole for a while, too," Mills says. "But he's better now."

Again, a hesitant laugh, and then through a flood of tears she says, "If he knew the guy in college, I'm sure they lost touch. Davis was never in touch with anyone from those days."

"Anyone?"

She clears her throat. "Anyone," she says. "For him it's all about ambition and work. He doesn't have time for friends, old or new."

"But these photos are from a college reunion, and he looks as thick as thieves with these guys," Mills tells her. "And one of them is Dr. Schultz."

She delivers a massive sigh. "It doesn't mean they stayed in touch, Detective. After all, they call it a reunion for a reason."

"Right."

"If that will be all," she says, "I might as well get up and start my day."

"When is the funeral?" he asks.

"Tuesday. The *Republic* is running a glowing obituary tomorrow."

"Mrs. Klink, let me know if you need anything."

"Like what?"

"Whatever comes to mind," Mills says. "And I'll do my best to help."

"Fine," she says and hangs up.

So fucking cold, that woman. Mills suspects Greta Klink is either furious with her husband for getting himself killed or doesn't give a shit that he's dead.

He gets a similar response from Carla Schultz albeit not as acidic.

"I'm sorry I can't help you," she says. "Trust me, I want nothing more than to close this case. I can't sleep. I can't eat. My mother's staying with me because I keep thinking I see Barry's ghost haunting the house."

"I'm so sorry."

"He never talked about college friends," she tells Mills. "So it's unlikely he stayed in touch with any of them. Could you send me the photos?"

"Of course."

She gives him her email address. "I'm the second wife," she says, as if the fact had suddenly occurred to her, "so maybe all that stuff is ancient history. Besides, I think I would remember the name Davis Klink."

"I think you would," Mills says. "Thanks for your time and let me know if you need anything."

She didn't shed a tear during the call, but Mills could feel the molar mass of Carla Schultz's sadness landing on his chest. He stares at his notepad. Both men were raised in Phoenix. Both men ultimately landed back in Phoenix professionally. Why the fuck wouldn't they be in touch? Unless there's something their wives don't know. Or something these women are hiding.

16

Gus calls in sick Monday morning. He's not sick. He's dangerously distracted. Would probably screw up a CT scan, definitely an ultrasound. He'd take a picture of a fetus and hand the sonogram to the expectant parents who would wail in horror, "It's deformed!" He'd swipe the film back with equal horror and say, "No, it's not. It's a kidney. My mistake."

That would get him fired. Calling in sick will not.

Making love to Billie in her Indonesian spa challenged him in a way that sex never had and never should. With those four words "STAY AWAY FROM HER" rolling through the epicenter of his brain like a Pasadena tremor, he couldn't fully reconcile being in her. He went through the motions, and both of them climaxed, but he wasn't fully there. He finished the bottle of wine afterward and rediscovered, the following morning, the agony of a hangover the likes of which he had not endured since his twenties. He drinks too much when he's with her. She slept until noon and never mentioned the envelope. Often, earthly, pedestrian things don't occur to her. Especially now with the prospect of another album and another tour. He ruminated all weekend over the note, tried desperately to intuit, to search for some kind of psychic revelation, but nothing came. The psychic equivalent to shooting blanks, and for a psychic who actually shoots blanks (low sperm count, no children, a lot of regret), the weekend was a defeat.

Billie is sleeping in again this morning, so Gus slips out of the house and drives over to the Paradise Valley police station. An enormous saguaro greets him outside. A woman named Yvette with a huge smile and substantial overbite greets him inside. Her hair is a dark helmet of black. "How can I help *you*?" she asks, as if offering a personalized service.

He smiles back, aware that he's underachieving. "There were some officers who came out to my place last week," he says.

"Can you tell me their names?"

He shifts his weight from one foot to another. "That's the thing, I can't actually remember . . ."

"No problem," she gushes. "Let me get your address, and I'll see if I can find either the report or the dispatch for you."

He recites the address.

"Is the property in your name?"

"Billie Welch," he says. "Or, actually, it's under her company's name. . . ."

She looks up from her computer, gazing at him without blinking. "Oh. You must be Mr. Parker."

He hesitates and then says, "Yes. You must be psychic."

She erupts in giggles. Girlish for a woman probably in her fifties. "No, no, Mr. Parker. You're the famous boyfriend."

He winces. "Seriously?"

"Well, at least around here. Not much happens in PV. And Billie Welch . . . well, she's a living legend living right here in our neighborhood," she says. "It was Officers Thelan and Johnson. I don't even need to check. I remember they both came back pretty excited after being in her house!"

Gus gets an instant, interior signal. "Officer Thelan is off today, isn't he?"

"Ha! Now *you* must be psychic, Mr. Parker."

"That's what they tell me," he says. "What about Officer Johnson?"

"Patrick's in the back. I'll page him."

Patrick Johnson greets him affably and leads him through the secured door, past a small but bustling bullpen of uniformed officers both coming and going, and into a private office. Johnson closes the door, then gestures for Gus to sit, a desk between them. The man smells like a drugstore aftershave. Gus gets a good vibe, a clean vibe, and he's glad that Thelan is not on duty this morning. He shows Johnson the note that bears the words "STAY AWAY FROM HER."

The cop's eyes widen for a moment, predictably. He nods, then looks at Gus, exhaling in a manly kind of way. "Why didn't you call us Friday night?" he asks.

Gus fidgets. "I wasn't sure what the hell was going on."

"Not a good answer, Mr. Parker," the officer says with a smile. "You could have had one of us paged. Now it's three days later and we've lost time."

"Hey, I'm sorry."

"I'm not asking for an apology, Mr. Parker. I just want to be upfront so if we don't catch this guy you'll understand. Every second counts."

Gus nods. "Every second counts," he repeats. "I understand."

"Do you understand that maybe someone is stalking you, or Ms. Welch, or maybe both of you?"

"I would say I've considered that," he replies. He points to the note. "But, look, Billie doesn't know about this. Can we keep it that way, at least for now?"

The guy looks at Gus as if Gus is some kind of wilting flower. "Yes, Mr. Parker, we can do that for now," he says. "The security booth over there at Ms. Welch's community is outfitted with some great cameras. I'll see if I can have a look at the Friday footage."

"Awesome, man. Thanks. But won't that require some kind of court order or something?"

"You mean a subpoena?"

"That's what I mean."

Johnson laughs. "No," he says. "I know those guys in the booth really well. We'll just keep it off the record, so to speak, unless we find some kind of evidence."

"I hope you do."

"I'll get back to you," the man says, pushing himself away from the desk.

Detective Jan Powell swoops into Mills's office and announces, "Google is the greatest invention!"

Mills sits back to make room for her gusto. "Happy Monday to you, too," he says. "Did you uncover anything interesting?"

"Sure did," she says. "I think you should call the boys in for this."

He does. Preston and Myers arrive a few minutes later, Myers carrying a cup of yogurt. Mills manufactures an obvious double take on his face.

"What?" Myers asks.

"You know what."

"It's good for me."

"But you'd prefer a Twinkie."

"Of course I would," Myers concedes. "But you guys have to encourage me, support me. Today is the beginning of a whole new Morton Myers."

"You snuck out and saw your doctor last week?" Mills asks.

"I did," the detective confesses. "And he said the whole nation of France doesn't have as much cholesterol as me. The bad kind, too."

Mills asks them all to sit. "As I mentioned when I called you in here, Jan has some notes to share with us on her research."

"For those of you who don't know," Powell says, looking to the others, "I have photos of Davis Klink and Barry Schultz together."

Preston's eyes widen. "What?"

"Fuck me," says Myers.

"Yes, fuck you," Powell tells him. "Class reunion shots. They went to college together."

Powell and Mills briefly fill the others in on what they know and what they don't. "But here's the latest development," Powell tells the room of attentive faces. "I found another reunion photo late last night. Surprised the fuck out of me."

She removes an eight-by-ten sheet from a folder and passes it to Mills.

"Just printed it out," she says. "Tell me what you think."

Mills studies the photo first, lingering on the faces for a few moments, then hands off the picture to Preston and Myers. "I don't get it, Powell. There are five people in the shot, and you crossed out two of the faces," Preston says.

She grins. "Sure did. I'm only concerned right now with the native Arizona alums," she says. "One of the guys I crossed out is from Texas, the other's from Colorado. But don't you recognize the other guy posing with Klink and Schultz?"

Soberly Preston says, "I do."

"Lemme see that." Mills reaches across his desk and pulls the photo back from the others. "Oh, Jesus."

Myers, who's been picking at the yogurt like a child picks at spinach, looks up. The expression in his eyes is the equivalent of a drum roll. "That's the politician guy from the billboards, right? What's his name?"

"You're correct, Morty," Powell says. "US Congressman Al Torento. He's the only other guy from Arizona in the photo."

"'Your Pal Al'!" Myers cries. "That's what it says on the billboard!"

"Right again, Morty," Powell says. "Your Pal Al, representing the Sixth District of Arizona."

"You think he's next?" Myers asks, frenzy in his voice.

Powell looks at Mills. Mills greets her gaze plaintively and, without turning to the others, says, "Thanks, everyone, for stopping by. I want to discuss this with Jan for a moment. You all know what you're working on. Why don't we resume what we were doing and maybe regroup at the end of the day."

Preston and Myers file out, leaving silence in their wake. Mills can feel his left knee is bouncing out of control. A siren hurtles down the street. An airplane whines overhead. Finally, Mills says, "Fuck," and Powell indicates with a heavy sigh that she's thinking, more or less, the same thing.

"You think he's next?" she asks.

"Anyone could be next."

"Someone will be," she says. "According to the killer's plan."

He rubs his eyes. "But the killer hasn't told us what he wants. We don't understand what he's thinking. Does he have a grudge against the rich and powerful?"

"Yes."

"That was a rhetorical question, Jan," he says. "Is the grudge a general grudge, or is he targeting specific rich and powerful victims? And, if so, why? We don't have a clue to the guy's motive here."

She points to the photo. "That's our lead for now."

He studies the picture again. He infers a joyous arrogance from the faces but suspects the inference is a function of his own bias. But still. The joy of self-satisfaction clearly eclipses the joy of getting reacquainted. These men celebrate their success as if it were inevitable, as if they were entitled all along. He shifts his eyes to his computer and does a quick search for the congressman's district office. "I don't disagree with you, Jan," he says. "I think we need to call Al Torento and ask him what he knows about our victims. Whether or not he's a target, he must be wondering what the fuck is going on."

"My point exactly," she says. "Can I listen in?"

"Of course." He hits "Speaker" on the landline and dials.

Someone named Ashley, sounding about twenty-one, answers the call and, with the voice of a lollipop, tells them that the congressman is in Washington this week. "Would you like that number?"

"No," Mills tells her. "I have it."

"Can I ask who's calling?"

"Not necessary."

"I'm so sorry I couldn't help you, sir," Ashley says. "But thank you for your support!"

As he hangs up, Mills looks at Powell and rolls his eyes with a staggering concern for the next generation. He dials Washington.

"Thanks for calling the office of your pal Al, Congressman Al Torento, representing the Sixth Congressional District of Arizona. Our office hours are eight a.m. to five p.m., Monday through Friday. Due to the volume of calls received about the new immigration bill, we're unable to answer each—"

"Fuck this," Mills says, putting the receiver down. "I have a better idea."

Mrs. Al Torento opens the door to her Central Phoenix home and, after Mills and Powell introduce themselves, asks, "Is there something wrong?"

"We're trying to get in touch with your husband, Mrs. Torento," Mills replies.

"The name is Jennifer, and he's in Washington."

"We know," Mills says. "May we come in?"

"Of course." The woman opens the door completely and lets them pass. She's in her midthirties, probably, making her a younger bride for the congressman. Her hair is dark and wavy, shoulder-length. She's tanned and freckled and wearing a simple black dress and a stack of bracelets on each arm. "What's this about?" she asks as they gather in the foyer.

"We should probably speak to your husband directly," Mills tells her. "Can you give me a cell phone number for him?"

"Yes," she replies. "But I just tried to call him a minute ago and got his voice mail." She recites the phone number, and Mills dials. He, too, reaches Torento's recording. He leaves a benign message.

"Will there be anything else?" she asks them.

Mills hesitates, then figures what the fuck, and says, "We have a photograph. Could I ask you to look at it and, maybe, answer a few questions?"

She looks at Mills and Powell as if she's seen it all, done it all. "All right," she says. "Let's sit."

They follow her into a formal living room, where Mills and Powell sit in a pair of wingback chairs that evoke thoughts of great literature and English tea while Jennifer Torento assumes the full sofa opposite them for herself. The ceilings are high. Portraits adorn the walls. It's a symphony of a house, large and classical, so old in style in fact that it makes the woman across from them look like a child who's been left here all alone. Powell digs out a folder from her bag. She removes the photo and places it on the coffee table between them.

"Where did you get this?" Jennifer asks.

"It's from a class reunion. U of A. We found it online," Mills explains.

"Do you know any of the men posing with your husband in that picture?" Powell asks.

Jennifer lifts the photo from the table. "Including the ones you crossed out?"

"Whoever you recognize, Mrs. Torento," Powell replies.

"I don't know any of them," she says. "Who are they?"

"The faces not crossed out have been identified as Davis Klink and Barry Schultz," Mills tells her. "Obviously old classmates of your husband."

"Obviously," she says. "He'd probably know them, but I'm sorry I can't be more help. I'm his third wife, far removed from his college years, if you know what I mean."

"But if they were still close friends, you'd know it," Powell says.

"I'm not his social secretary, but yes, I'd think so," she concedes. "We have a very small circle of friends because my husband has no time, you know, when you consider how he commutes back and forth to our place in DC."

"When's he due back in Phoenix?" Powell asks.

"Well, Congress just went back into session," she says. "But he'll be back in a couple of weeks for a fundraiser."

"What kind of fundraiser?" Powell prods.

Jennifer sits up straight and pulls at her dress. "Look, I'm not going to answer any more questions until someone explains what's going on," she insists. "I guarantee the sooner you tell me, the sooner you'll hear from my husband. That's kind of the way it works around here."

"Those two men are dead," Mills says abruptly, pointing to the photo. "Maybe you heard about their murders."

She grasps at the cushions beside her. "Murders? I don't know what you're talking about."

"In the past two weeks both men were killed in similar fashion," Mills says. "It was on the news."

Her face doesn't move, but she parts her lips and says, "I don't watch the news. Unless my husband is on. Frankly, I don't keep track of crime in Phoenix. That's for Al to worry about if he wants to get reelected. I hardly ever have time to read the paper. I'm too busy with my own work."

"Which is?" Powell asks.

Jennifer crosses her legs and rests her cupped hands on her knee. "I teach at ASU. Professor of Spanish. Recently tenured."

"Congratulations," Powell says. "That's impressive."

The woman looks past them now, as if her knowledge of the world is mapped out on some distant wall. In a cold silence she seems to catalogue the accumulation of her degrees, the papers she's written, the theses she's defended, however it is that she's come to be smarter than the two cops sitting in front of her. This is what Mills infers from her repose, and he's not offended by the inference at all; the disclosure of her work changes his perception of her. These bias-busting moments are helpful, sometimes key to understanding people.

"Do you think my husband is involved?" she asks suddenly, still peering beyond them.

"Involved?" Mills asks.

She looks at him squarely now. "In those murders."

He does a double take of sorts. "We have no reason to believe that," he says. "That's not why we're here."

"Why *are* you here?"

"We need to talk to your husband," he says. "If he can tell us anything about these victims, maybe we can figure out who might've wanted them dead."

"And maybe we can prevent another one," Powell adds.

"Another murder?" she asks.

"If there's one thing we know about the killer," Mills says, "it's that he's not done."

She leans forward. "Al's in danger. That's what you're trying to tell me."

"We can't tell you that," Powell says. "Because we don't know."

Mills lifts himself to his feet and hands Jennifer his card. "Please have your husband call me."

Mills pulls the car around the corner, then parks at the side of the road. He wants to debrief before heading back. Otherwise, he'd be driving distracted by the maelstrom in his head. His brain is practically foaming at the mouth.

He turns to Powell. Their eyes meet like oncoming trains about to collide. Their first syllables are caught in midair when Powell says, "You go."

"No you."

"No, you're the boss."

"This is stupid," Mills says. "I'm thinking a million things, but first let's assume Toronto knows about the murders. His wife said he stays on top of crime in his district. . . ."

"Sounds fairly obvious," Powell says.

"So he knows about the murders, but did he know our victims well enough to remember them by name and recognize the connection? And if he recognizes the connection, don't you think he'd be freaking out that someone's out there hunting down U of A alums?"

Powell bristles and says, "If he's freaking out I think the wife would know."

"Maybe not."

"Either way, even if the men aren't still friends today, the coincidence has to be too close for comfort."

"Unless he's the one hunting down the alums."

Powell rests her elbow on the shoulder of Mills's seat. "You don't believe that."

"Anything's possible," he says. "The wife even asked if he was involved."

"That doesn't mean a thing, and you know that," Powell insists.

"It doesn't until it does," Mills says. "We don't know what's going on in that marriage, or what secrets she's had to keep. We don't know their history. Her question could have come from any number of psychological triggers."

"I don't get that vibe," Powell argues. "Besides, the same 'too close for comfort' factor that would spook him as a potential victim is the same 'too close for comfort' factor that would deter him from killing these guys. He's too easily associated with them."

A kid, maybe ten years old, glides by them on a bicycle, his mom on foot, walking briskly not too far behind. The mom, inserted snugly into yoga studio pants, smiles and waves. Mills waves back.

"We've been talking to a lot of wives lately," he says. "Second wives, third wives."

"I like Jennifer. She's not a cold, cunty one like Greta Klink," Powell tells him.

"Is that a word? Cunty?"

"It is if I say it is," Powell replies. "Either way, I bet it takes a special kind of woman to put up with a politician."

"Damn it. I wish we could get closer to Toronto," Mills grumbles. He looks at the neighborhood, not at Powell. "It would be great to tail him now."

"Know anybody in DC?"

Mills says yes, he does. "But no one who'll play, not yet. So, we better tail him the minute he lands in Phoenix."

"Unless we speak to him first."

"Even if we speak to him first."

"Right," Powell says.

Mills's cell rings. It's the boss. He shows the phone to Powell.

"Are you going to answer it?" she asks.

Reluctantly he does. "Hey there, Jake, what's up?"

"You tell me," the sergeant says. "You looking for a certain congressman?"

Mills mimes for Powell to keep silent and puts the call on speaker. "I am," he tells Woods.

"You wanna know how I know?" Woods asks. "The chief just paid me a visit."

"The chief?"

"Seems the chief got a call from Al Torento. The congressman says you were trying to reach him."

Mills catches his reflection in the rearview mirror and sees the disbelief rising on his face. "I was. About a half hour ago," he says. "So, instead of returning my call, Torento called the chief instead?"

"Seems that way."

"Why the hell didn't he just call me directly?"

"He's a congressman."

Dead silence.

Mills thinks, *Who the fuck cares?*

Powell looks out her window and shakes her head.

"Are you there, Detective?" Woods asks.

"I am," Mills says. "Not sure what the purpose of this call is, Jake, but since we're going through unusual channels, can you send the word up through the chief that we'd like to speak with the congressman?"

Woods laughs. "Your Pal Al doesn't want to talk to you. Says he's too busy. Doesn't have any useful information."

"So, the chief told him what I'm working on? 'Cause I didn't mention it in my message."

Woods laughs again. "Of course he did. It's not a secret."

"End of story? Or may I pursue Torento on my own?"

"You may do anything you think you need to do," Woods says. "I, for one, won't impede your investigation. But I, for one, don't need to hear every detail of it this morning."

"I don't think we have reason to suspect the congressman, if that's what he's worried about," Mills explains. "But we do have reason to suspect he might be in danger."

"Like I said, I don't need to hear every detail right now," Woods reminds him. "And say hello to Powell. Tell her she needs to learn to breathe softer. You both have a good day."

He's gone.

"He's kind of a prick today," Powell observes.

"Today?"

"Not very subtle," she says of Woods.

"I call it subtly overt."

"Whatever, Mills. I'm not a fan of the arrogant cronyism in this city."

"Compared to what city?"

She ignores the question and says, "I'm starving. You ready for lunch? That Spanish professor had me craving Mexican."

"Seems like Mexican is all I've been eating these days, but sure."

With one sniff, Gus Parker knows his home in Arcadia could use some freshening up. It's not a rancid smell, just the smell of airlessness and perhaps of microbes that might be multiplying on the kitchen counter, in the fridge, a toilet. Which is not to say those surfaces are vile, just defenseless. He wasn't planning a long stay at the house, only long enough to gather a few things for Ivy and to water the thirsty-looking plants, but he'll open the windows and let the place ventilate. While he waits for the air to exchange itself, he wanders outside to the mailbox. A voice calls to him. It's Elsa, a housekeeper for a family across the cul-de-sac.

"Hello, Mr. Gus," she says with a wave.

"Nice to see you, Elsa," he calls back.

She gets into a car and drives off, waving again from inside.

Gus gathers the small stack of mail, enters the house, and sorts the mail in the kitchen, which really does stink a bit, so he pours some dish soap down the drain and runs the suds through the disposal; he doesn't know if this actually helps, but it seems like the intuitive thing to do. He has a bill from the cable company, the electric company, his dentist, and his wireless carrier. The latter prompts him to pick up his phone from the counter and check in with Billie.

"You up?" he asks.

"Very much," she says, prematurely chipper for lunchtime. "Already did a call with my management team. Looks like the tour will open in Miami."

"Why Miami?"

"It's the first venue that can fit us in," she says. "Miranda's on her way over now to help with some planning."

"Cool, babe. Tell your sister hi. I'll be back a little later."

In a brief silence, Gus can hear her humming to herself. It's a familiar melody. Then she says, "You don't have to worry about me, Gus. I chose to come back here. You don't have to be a bodyguard."

From a woman who trademarked self-reliance, Gus is not surprised to hear that remark. He shrugs it off. Her independence is as much a part of her charmed life as her music. She's a good match for Gus, who's mostly a loner, mostly independent by default. When they're done with the call, Gus resumes with the mail. A few more bills. A flyer from "Your Pal Al," with an update of Congressman Al Torento's latest good deeds and initiatives. Wedged inside a circular from Safeway is a postcard featuring a picture of Billie on the front, like something from an old fan club. He loves the photo; she's sitting on the hood of an old muscle car, her guitar slung over her shoulder, her long, golden hair falling into her lap. It's a vintage shot. She's wearing blue jeans, a white gossamer blouse, and a necklace of turquoise beads that match the bracelets around her wrists. Pure flower child. Curious, he flips the card over to see who might have sent this. It could be Billie, after all, playing a joke, but as he reads the message scrawled across the postcard, he feels the blood drain from his face.

IF YOU DON'T STAY AWAY FROM HER,
I WON'T STAY AWAY FROM YOU

His next call is to Alex Mills.

17

When Alex arrives, the first thing he does is ask to use the bathroom.

"Had Mexican for lunch," the detective says.

Great, now I really am going to have to clean in there, Gus thinks. "Sure, go ahead."

Alex drops a folder on the hallway table and bolts.

Gus busies himself brushing down the pool outside while Alex busies himself with his business. The birds squawk extra loudly this afternoon, swooping from one tree to another, calling out for Ivy, no doubt, chagrined, it seems, at her erratic schedule now that she lives, at least part-time, in the luxury of Paradise Valley. Birds know these things. This particular flock, Gus is convinced, knows and loves Ivy like a best friend. They've come singing for her every morning since she was just a pup. "She'll be home soon," he tells them.

"Who are you talking to?" Alex asks as he steps through the sliders.

"The birds."

"Of course you are."

"Hey, man, thanks for coming over. You seem a little stressed," Gus says. "Are you okay?"

"If the rabbit hole is okay, then I'm fine," Alex replies.

"I'm not far behind you, I'm afraid," Gus says. "Come, I want to show you something."

Back inside, Gus shows Alex the postcard and tells him about the note left a few nights ago at Billie's guardhouse.

"Congratulations," Alex says soberly. "You have a stalker."

"But why would someone be stalking *me*? I'm not the celebrity. Billie is."

"Doesn't matter, Gus. Whoever this freak is, he's directed threats against you, not her. So, the legal system would view you as his victim, not Billie, if he's apprehended and charged."

"Okay, but—"

"Would you rather someone be stalking her directly?" Alex asks.

"No. Of course not. It just doesn't make sense."

They're sitting on the big brown couch in Gus's family room. "Sure it does," Alex says. "Obviously someone is stalking Billie once removed. He's trying to get you out of the way so he can get closer to her."

"By 'get me out of the way' do you think there's violence implied here?" he asks. "Because I do."

Alex weighs the question, nodding slowly. "I think there's potential, but I think right now he's saying if you stay away from her there will be no violence."

"So I'm just supposed to back off, obey his instructions, and everything will be fine?"

"I'm guessing that's the preliminary proposition," Alex says. "Aren't you picking up any psychic vibes from this? I'd think you would."

"Nothing. I've tried."

"The postcard came here to your house, right?"

"Yeah."

"So, it's really a Phoenix jurisdiction, but since you already went to PV with the other note, I think we should ask them to look at it all together," Alex says. "I'll make a call over there on your behalf. You said you spoke to an Officer Johnson?"

"Yeah."

"I'll take care of it, Gus."

"Thanks, man."

"Now, can you do something for me?"

"Sure."

"Give me a sec," Alex says as he goes to fetch his folder from the hallway. When he returns, he removes a photo, then hands it to Gus.

Gus lifts the photograph up, holds it in midair, and studies the image. As much as he tries, he can't quite penetrate it. He turns to Alex, and their eyes meet saliently.

"The guy in the middle is an Arizona congressman," Alex tells him. "I don't follow politics."

"Doesn't matter. It's an old photo. The two other faces that aren't crossed out are the two victims, Klink and Schultz."

"Hmm, they certainly all knew each other."

Alex moves closer. "But that's the thing. No one can confirm that. Two of them are dead, and no one else seems to know if these guys had any kind of relationship with each other beyond posing for these old reunion photos."

Gus shakes his head. Then his chin trembles as if he's bracing for a flood of tears. The tears are not his; he knows this. The tears are for a stranger by proxy. "No, Alex," he says. "They knew each other well. Their relationship continued well beyond a reunion or two. I sense it was a quiet relationship."

"Quiet?"

"Like they didn't have much to say to each other in recent years. I don't know. I sense they kept their distance. But they certainly knew each other."

"I see tears in your eyes, man. What's up with that?"

"I don't know," Gus replies. "But there's profound sadness at the core of this X-ray."

"X-ray?"

"Sorry. I mean photo."

A cranky chorus of birds bursts out of nowhere. Gus and Alex shift their attention to the back window, where a small flock does a graceful arc and twist over the pool and then flies away. Gus hears a car approach the cul-de-sac out front, and he knows it's Elsa. He can tell by her muffler—nothing obnoxious, just a minor rattle and snort. He can tell by the way she swerves into the neighbor's driveway and by the tinny sound of economy when she opens and closes her door. And then everything goes quiet. He suspects it's a proprietary silence, his alone.

In that silence his attention is pulled back to the photo and he utters an instant, "Wow. The congressman . . ."

"What? What about him?" Alex begs.

"It's him. He's the source of the Spanish music I've been hearing."

Alex laughs. "I love it. The congressman's wife is a Spanish professor."

"Oh," Gus says and then sheepishly adds, "Really?"

"You sound disappointed."

"No," he says. "I just thought it would be more significant than that."

"Maybe it is."

Gus returns the photo to the folder and hands it back to Alex. "Interesting that I can get a vibe about that stupid picture but nothing, totally a blank slate, when it comes to the notes from my stalker." He puts "stalker" in air quotes because it doesn't seem real.

"Not yet anyway."

"Though I did have visions about those words 'Stay away from her' before I actually got the note and the postcard," Gus says. "So I guess I was onto something."

"Hey, maybe you're too close to it because, you know, it's about you," Alex suggests. "Maybe your own anxiety around it is blocking you. I've seen that happen to you before."

"True."

"I'm thinking you should have your friend Beatrice take a look. She'll be more objective."

The detective rises from the couch. Gus follows. "Not a bad idea," Gus says. "Should have thought of it myself."

"I gotta head out," Alex tells him. "You working tomorrow morning?"

"No. Doing a half day," Gus replies. "I won't go in 'til one thirty."

They drift to the front door.

"Can I invite you to a funeral?"

Gus laughs. "I guess. Whose?"

"The CEO. Davis Klink."

"Absolutely," Gus says, swinging open the door.

"Ten a.m.," Alex tells him. "Garden of Peace Memorial Park. North Scottsdale. Look it up."

"Will do."

They do a brief shake, pat on the back, bro kind of thing. As the detective pulls out of the driveway, Gus spies Elsa's car parked in the one across the street. And though he's once again feeling haunted, Gus gives the car a big, affirmative smile, then heads back into the house where a bathroom is waiting to be disinfected.

The Garden of Peace Memorial Park rests in the shadows of the McDowell Mountains, not far from the home of Davis and Greta Klink. The cemetery backs right up to a soaring monolith, and it's almost as if you can imagine God looking down from the peak, commanding a kind of biblical awe among both the living and the dead below. The temperature is mild. There's a vague whirl of a breeze in the air. The sky could not be any bluer had Sherwin Williams had a stake in the morning forecast. In the dressiest show of fashion that Mills has ever seen from her, Powell is wearing a black blouse and black skirt. He's wearing the male equivalent: a black shirt and black slacks. He texted Gus earlier and told him to wear the same. They're waiting for him in the parking lot, just inside the arched gateway to the cemetery. Teeming bougainvillea climbs the arches and drapes the high white walls surrounding the lot. A steady chain of cars flows through the gateway in single file. A car full of kids rolls in, windows down, blasting rap music.

"I wish my badge worked here," he tells Powell. "I'd fuck with them."

"I'd join you," she says.

"Must be friends of his kids."

"Yeah," she says. "No class."

Mills recognizes the car coming in behind the rapping morons. It's Gus in his SUV. Mills flags him over.

"Good morning," the psychic says as he hops out. "Thanks for the wardrobe tip. Haven't been to a funeral since my mom's."

"We're not going to the funeral," Mills tells him.

"We're not?"

Mills can see the confusion pass across Gus's face. "We're going to act like visitors to a nearby gravesite. We've already located a spot, and we'll scope out the Klink funeral from there," he says.

"We're in camouflage, so to speak," Powell tells Gus. "And if you don't mind me saying, I'm a bit surprised you needed wardrobe tips for a funeral."

Gus offers her a dubious look, and then the expression on his face changes, or rather disappears. He becomes an ancient scroll without the words. His eyes darken as he looks the woman over. "I wouldn't be surprised if you fail the test."

"What test?" she asks defensively.

"Someone is putting you to the test," Gus says. "There's a man who wants you to meet his family. Am I right?"

Powell looks to Mills with hesitation in her eyes. "I'm not sure I like this."

"I can't help it," Gus tells her.

"Mills?" she begs.

"All right, come on, let's get moving," he says meekly, fully aware Gus has to do what Gus has to do. There's no interrupting a moment like this.

"He thinks if you agree to meet his family, then you're fully committed to him," Gus says to Powell. "If he hasn't told you that already, he will."

"Okay. Thank you," she says, cutting him off and turning away.

"Don't go," Gus calls to her. "I mean, don't go meet his family. You're not ready for that commitment. Not with him."

Powell keeps walking.

Mills turns to Gus. "Are we done for now?"

"Yes," Gus replies. "Sorry about that."

When Mills catches up to his colleague, she pulls him by his shirt and whispers in his ear. "That psychic dude is freaking me out. Is he in my head?"

"Not exactly. It's more like he's tuning into the energy around you. He means well. There's never any malice."

The Klink burial follows a private service at the family's church. Mills estimates the graveside crowd at 120. There are ten rows of ten chairs. About twenty people are standing. Greta Klink clutches a bouquet of roses. Her daughters, Mills assumes, sit to one side, her stepson to the other. Two Italian cypresses, one at each side of the entrance and perfectly groomed, guard the mausoleum that will house Davis Klink's body. From where Mills is standing with Powell and Gus, he can hear the pastor murmuring clichés in delicate but affirming tones.

"His achievements were massive, but so was his heart."

The son shakes his head and smirks.

"He left a mark on the world, but the most important mark was the one he made at home."

The daughters grab each other and shake. To the untrained eye the girls might seem to be writhing in tears. To Mills, they look like college airheads busting up over a twisted wad of toilet paper clinging to their professor's shoe. Greta Klink jabs one of them with her elbow.

Mills and his crew are watching from the more modest gravesite of Robert Bell (1929–2016, Beloved Husband of Nancy) about seven plots south of the Klink shindig. He scans the horizon for any outlier, the lone individual who creeps in the background to pay respects to his own murderous deed. It happens frequently enough for Mills to be here, to be scanning, but all he sees in the distance are lonely graves with their lonely residents, speechless mausoleums and headstones hardened to their fate. His gaze goes deep into the crowd. He recognizes Shelly Newton, the Legal guy Peter Tribble, and the HR woman Claire White from Ireland. The rest must be standard relatives, generic friends, and the enemies who Klink kept close. Mills scopes all the eyes he can see for signs of satisfaction, malice, or revenge.

"What about the guy with the blue bow tie?" Powell asks, breaking momentarily from her unconvincing façade of grief and tears.

Mills shakes his head. "No, he's just dressed like a douche."

"I don't like that chick in the big sunglasses," Powell says, determined.

"There are a lot of chicks with big sunglasses," Mills whispers.

"Well, I can't exactly point," his colleague says. "She's got blond hair."

"I'm counting about twenty blonds with sunglasses. It's a popular look today."

"Now you're just messing with me."

"Maybe."

"Six rows back. Two in from the right," Powell tells him.

Mills follows with his eyes. "Oh, her? What don't you like about her?"

"I don't know. I get a vibe."

Mills turns to her. "A vibe? That's why Gus is here. You stick to police work."

She responds with a burst of mock sobs. "I am doing police work," she cries. "The woman is wearing a scarf. I saw her adjust it, and when it slipped I could see a tattoo on her neck. This is not a tattoo-on-the-neck crowd."

Mills studies the woman, sees the scarf around her neck, one of those very thin ascot types like the kind you see on flight attendants, but he can't see the tattoo. "You're probably right, Jan. But these days tattoos are everywhere."

"I hear the Spanish music again," Gus says suddenly.

"Seriously?" Mills asks him.

"Seriously."

"I need you to concentrate on the words, Gus," Mills says. "I know you don't speak Spanish, but try to make out the words. Give me the words, and we can use a dictionary or something."

"Or introduce him to Toronto's wife," Powell interjects.

"That's right," Mills says. "Good catch."

Gus ignores them.

"But there's no sign of 'Your Pal Al' today," she says. "I'd expect he'd be here if he and Klink were close friends."

"He's in Washington."

"So what? Those guys in Congress look for any excuse to get out of work."

Mills laughs. "I think his wife would have told us if he was coming back to Phoenix for the funeral."

"All I'm saying is that Torento's absence makes it less likely they were close friends and less likely he can tell us anything useful."

"Unless he's our killer."

"He's way taller than the guy in the Safeway video," Powell says. "Plus, he has an alibi."

"Certainly not airtight," Mills says. "Now, if you don't mind, could you do a little more grieving over poor Mr. Robert Bell here?"

She puts a hand to her heart, sways back and forth, and sniffles. But her grief is short-lived. "Oh, look," she says suddenly. "Blondie's scarf is loose again. She's adjusting it. I can see part of the tattoo. Shit. I can't make out the image from here. Shit, shit, shit."

"I can't either," Mills says.

"She's obviously trying to hide it," Powell whispers.

Gus leans in. "I don't want to tell you two how to do your work, but let me just suggest you pull out your phones and discreetly take a picture of the woman."

"Damn it," Powell says. "I was so overcome with grief I wasn't thinking clearly."

"I'll do it," Mills says, removing his phone from his pocket.

But the woman doesn't adjust her scarf again, and Mills makes his disgust audible. Several minutes pass, and Gus says, "I think it was a butterfly."

"Did you see it?" Mills asks.

"No," Gus replies. "Just a hunch."

The service ends without major fuss or, for that matter, outburst of emotion. Greta Klink did a fair share of weeping, but few others joined in on the sadness. The crowd flows out silently, orderly, an army of black, like lines of type receding from the fleeting pages of Davis Klink's life. Mills searches the crowd for the woman with the scarf, but she might be that one guest who slipped out through the back. He doesn't have enough of a hunch to go after her. She nervously adjusted her scarf. So what? The tattoo, alone, proves nothing, means nothing, and certainly doesn't suggest she knows anything about Davis Klink's demise.

"Let's get out of here," he tells the others.

As they turn to leave, Gus says, "Wait. Look there. . . ."

Gus points to the entrance of Klink's mausoleum where Greta Klink is standing with the same young man Mills assumes to be her stepson. All the other mourners are gone. The man punches the air, narrowly missing Greta's face. She flinches and scowls, her own fists clenched. Their words are no louder than the hisses of territorial snakes until the young man hollers, "You fucking gold digger," and storms off.

Mills guides his crew away before the widow can see them.

18

They grabbed Japanese takeout on the way back to the station, and now Mills and Powell are eating lunch at his desk. Mills is plucking noodles and chicken from something called a Kyoto Bowl, which, he imagines, has nothing to do with Kyoto or any other city in Japan. But it's tasty, MSG-free, and a nice break from Mexican.

"I'm taking Toronto out of the killer column and putting him in the victim column," Powell says as she stabs at her sushi.

The columns are figurative at the moment, but Mills gets what she means. "Because?"

"Because let's assume he's next."

"Because?"

"C'mon, Alex, don't be a dick."

"Just because he's in a random photograph with the two victims doesn't mean he's next," Mills says. "Anyone could be next."

"We have to start somewhere."

"Here's what I want. I want columns," Mills tells her. "Go in the conference room after lunch with Preston and Myers and put our columns on the whiteboard. We're overdue. Just map out the players, and we'll make our lists. Victims, suspects, friends, family, lovers, liaisons, gold diggers, I don't care."

"Wow. You sound fucking enthused."

"I'm frustrated," he groans.

"But the food is good," she says.

"The food is good."

The food is almost gone when Preston comes barreling down the hallway and skids to a panting stop at the door, rattling the frame. Mills dabs the corners of his mouth with a napkin and says, "Hey, there, Ken, you need something?"

His face is the red siren of a heart attack. "This is huge," he announces, catching his breath. "Probably our biggest lead yet."

"Probably our only lead," Powell says.

"Come in, shut the door," Mills tells the man. Preston complies, takes a seat, and oozes not only manic excitement but also a kind of avuncular caring in his eyes. He's a solid veteran of the force, a smart man, who has somehow become smarter and quieter over the years instead of more cynical and brash. Preston tells them he has now acquired most, not all, of Davis Klink's banking records and that they offer a glimpse into what the CEO was doing in the hours after leaving his office and meeting his murderer.

"I don't think he was going to meet his sick daughter," Preston says. "On the Friday afternoon of his death, Klink withdrew half a million dollars in cash from two separate banks."

He says nothing more for the space of about ten seconds to let that sink in.

It sinks in like a cruise ship hitting an iceberg.

Mills breaks the silence and says, "Do banks actually have that kind of cash on hand?"

"They do at the kind of banks Klink does business with," Preston replies. "These banks cater to the ultra-wealthy. The records show the withdrawals. Videotape surveillance backs up Klink's physical presence at both banks about two hours apart."

"They just handed him over the money?" Powell asks.

Preston gives her a thoughtful nod. "They certainly weren't quick transactions, and not out in the open," he explains. "They take him into a private office, and he walks out about an hour and a half later with the cash."

"Don't the banks have to report big transactions like that to the government?" Powell asks.

Preston lets a smirk serve as his reply.

But Mills prods further. "Does the video show what happens in the private room?"

"No. We see him entering the bank, holding a briefcase, shaking hands, a short conversation, and then he's led into a private room. Same basic routine at both banks," Preston tells them. "I assume he would have security detail with him if the money had anything to do with Illumilife."

"Damn," Powell says, "sounds like he was paying off some kind of ransom."

"Or blackmail," Mills says. "Either way, I think it's time to go pay our condolences to Greta Klink."

The guards wave them through the gates of Miracle Canyon. This is Preston's first visit. He's in the back seat. "Jesus Lou-ee-zus," he cries when he sees the rambling estates. "This makes PV look like the slums."

They can't park anywhere near the Klink property because the surrounding streets are lined with the cars of genuine well-wishers who have beaten the cops to the after-party. The day has warmed since the cemetery service. The three of them—Mills, Powell, and Preston—hike on foot to the widow's front door. A butler-looking attendant greets them; he tells them Greta Klink is accepting visitors poolside.

"We remember the way," Mills tells him.

Out back at the pool, the cops join a line of maybe twelve people paying their condolences to the widow. A longer line forms at the buffet. An even longer line than that waits eagerly for refills of champagne.

At first her face registers unfamiliarity at the sight of Alex Mills. She narrows her eyes as if she knows him, not sure from where. He says, quietly, "Mrs. Klink, my colleagues and I would like to speak to you."

Then the bell goes off. "Oh, you! Oh, Detective!"

"That's right. Alex Mills." He takes her hand. She withdraws it almost instantly.

"I'm sure you can see I'm receiving guests right now," she says.

"We can wait," Mills tells her.

She shakes her head. "I just buried my husband this morning after two painful weeks, and you have the audacity to come to my house now. . . ."

"I'm so sorry," he says quietly, bending to where she sits. "But we thought you'd want to know about a possible lead in the case. . . ."

"Of course, but there *is* the sanctity of mourning," she reminds him.

Yes, he observes, a very catered sanctity with an open bar, a string quartet, and hundreds roaming the estate taking selfies.

"Ma'am," he whispers to her as discreetly as possible, "your husband withdrew half a million dollars on the afternoon of his death. We think that might be relevant to the case."

The color plummets from her face. But she does her very best not to melt. She tightens her chin. Elongates her neck. "Our lawyer is here," she whispers back. "He needs to hear this."

Greta Klink excuses herself from her guests, mutters something about checking with the caterer, and instructs a member of her staff to escort Mills and his crew to her office. It's the same office with the perfect furniture and the charm of an ice cube.

"Can I offer you something to drink?" the staff member asks them. It's a different maid from their first visit.

"No, thanks," Mills says.

"Feel free to take a seat," she says as she leaves them.

They don't. They remain standing and wait in silence. A few minutes later a man enters the office, his hand already extended as he walks through the door. He's the athletic, aggressive type—lean, fit, great hair, great tan, a Rolex, about fifty.

"Chad Pace," he says as he gives a hearty handshake all around. "Attorney for the Klink family."

Greta Klink drifts in behind him and all but swoons into the chair at her desk. "Please sit," she says.

"If you don't mind," Mills tells her, "we'll stand."

"What can we do for you?" the attorney asks.

"As we told Mrs. Klink, we have reviewed her husband's banking records and have identified some questionable withdrawals on the day of his murder," Mills replies.

"So she tells me," Pace says. "Again, I must ask, what can we do for you?"

"All we need is for Mrs. Klink to answer some simple questions."

"Ask away," the man says magnanimously, "but I reserve the right to counsel Mrs. Klink to refrain from answering any question that feels inappropriate."

Mills doesn't give Pace the satisfaction of a response. Instead, he turns immediately to Greta and asks, "Do you have any idea why your husband would withdraw all that money in one afternoon?"

"No."

"Did you discuss money matters with him?"

"Of course."

She's jittery, as if she's jonesing for nicotine.

"And he never indicated that he'd be withdrawing such a large sum on that Friday?"

"No."

"Was he anxious about anything?" Mills asks.

"I think I answered that question on your last visit," she says with an edge of resentment.

"I'm sorry," Mills says. "But I'm asking again because news of this cash withdrawal could prompt some different memories of his state of mind."

Chad Pace bristles (a courtroom bristle no doubt perfected in law school—Mills has seen his wife make the exact same gesture). "I don't understand the question," he says.

Mills nods studiously, pauses for effect, as he stares down Greta Klink, knowing whatever version of the truth he gets will be his burden to judge. "You know, blackmail, that sort of thing. Any reason someone would want to blackmail your husband?" he asks.

"I would advise Mrs. Klink not to answer that question," the attorney interjects.

"Fine," Mills says.

Greta lifts her hand. "No, I'll answer it," she says. "I cannot think of any reason in the world why someone would want to blackmail my husband."

"Would he discuss something like that with you?" Powell asks.

"Well, if he wouldn't, how would I know?" the widow replies with a smug smile.

"What about ransom or extortion?" Mills throws out there.

Pace steps forward, almost gets between the widow's desk and the standing cops. "I don't like that question. Too much speculation. I'm going to advise Greta not to answer."

Greta looks at the detectives stone-faced, as if she has every intention of taking her lawyer's advice this time.

"Fine, then," Mills says. "What was your husband's net worth?"

The woman replies with a gulp of laughter. "That's so gauche I can't even respond."

"We have other ways of finding out," Mills tells her.

"My client is not a suspect," Pace says.

Mills smiles, widely and purposefully. "She's not a person of interest, but it would be in her best interest to cooperate."

The widow slaps her hands on the desktop. "Well, I can't sit around and gab, folks. I have a flight to catch this evening. So, if you'll excuse me, I've got to wrap up things with my other guests and get ready."

"Where are you headed?" Preston asks.

"St. Bart's," she replies.

"So much for the sanctity of mourning," Mills says.

"Hey, my client doesn't have to listen to that," the man with the Rolex says.

Mills turns to him fully. "Well, listen to this. I can go before a judge within the hour and have her passport held so she can't leave the country."

The lawyer laughs. "Good luck with that. You have no grounds."

"Half a million dollars is missing from her husband's accounts," Preston reminds them.

Not a word. Instead, a pause that takes on all the awkwardness of silence in an echo chamber. Mills swears he can hear the hair implants sprouting from the lawyer's head. A maid ducks into the office, takes in the deep freeze, then withdraws with fear lodged in her eyes. That fear, alone, seems to empower the widow, who now sits up erect and regal and looks at the detectives as if she has a family crest in each eye. "His net worth is sixty million dollars," she says. "Half a million is a drop in the bucket, you see. I wouldn't leave the country for half a million dollars."

"Still," Mills says calmly, "it looks suspicious to us."

"Then I won't go to St. Bart's, goddamnit! I won't go!" she shrieks. "Now get out of my house."

Mills folds his arms across his chest and rocks a bit on his heels. "Before we leave so abruptly, may we have a minute with your daughter Jordan?"

Greta is steaming. It's all over her face. "What the hell for?"

"We'd like to ask her about the call she made to your husband before he left the office," Mills explains.

"She didn't make the call," Greta says.

"And you know this how?" Mills asks.

"I asked her."

"And you didn't think to tell us?" Mills persists. "That seems odd. Any chance we can speak to your other children?"

"This is not the time, not the place," she says.

"Are you suggesting that someone posing as your daughter made the call?"

The woman bolts to her feet. "That's exactly what I'm suggesting," she hisses. "And I'll ask you one more time to get out of my house, Detective. Get the fuck out!"

Mills assures the woman he'll be in touch with any developments and offers a nod. Then, with his colleagues trailing him, he gets the fuck out.

19

On his drive into work, Gus places a call to Officer Johnson at the Paradise Valley Police Department. It's been forty-eight hours since he showed the cop the note; he figures it can't hurt to give a nudge. But nothing's nudging this morning, not the parking lot of rush hour and not Officer Johnson. Johnson isn't available. Gus leaves a message.

He turns on the radio and listens to a breathy interview on NPR. Something about an effort in Kenya to remove wild elephants' tusks to make the endangered animals less attractive to ivory poachers. Gus admires NPR, its rigorous reporting with depth and relevance (he's very pro-elephant), but the satin-soft voices of the NPR announcers aren't well suited for waking people up on their morning commutes. He finds some Billie Welch music on his playlist and listens. The first song is "When We Collide," an aggressive, guitar-driven song about a love-hate relationship. It rocks, completely. Billie's anger in the song always surprises Gus. He's never seen her that angry. But her musical goodbye to her love-hate lover cuts deep like a knife. Every thrash of her guitar is a wound she leaves him. The tune gets stuck in his head. He can't release it. He doesn't want to be hearing her angry voice all morning, but he hears her angry voice all morning, through the MRI of Mrs. Sears's lower lumbar, through the MRI of Mr. Reilly's hip. He hears it when he drifts over to do an ultrasound of Louis Feldman's abdomen. He hums it during lunch outside in the courtyard.

The calls come after lunch. Gus can feel the phone vibrate several times between one and two o'clock. The only thing he sees on his screen is "UNKNOWN CALLER PARADISE VALLEY, AZ." He assumes it's Officer Johnson or someone from the Paradise Valley Police Department, but he has no choice but to let the calls go to voice mail. The calls persist, rapidly growing in frequency, increasingly distracting him. He loses his place during a mammogram. And again during Ethan and Mia Donaldson's fetal ultrasound.

Then, shortly after that near failure, he gets a text message: "Parker. PLEASE Respond. Officer Johnson."

With that Gus loses all focus on his work. He grabs another tech and asks him to cover for the next exam on the schedule. Then he steps outside and calls PV.

"Thelan."

"I'm looking for Officer Johnson. This is Gus P—"

"I know who you are, Mr. Parker," the cop snaps. "I'm the other officer who came out to Miss Welch's house that day."

"I remember."

"Your phone working okay?"

"Far as I can tell," Gus replies.

"'Cause, you know, we've been calling you all afternoon."

"I'm at work. In a medical setting, so I can't answer my phone."

The man scoffs. "Whatever. I'm going to transfer you to Johnson now, but just so you know you don't have to go running to Alex Mills if you're freaking out."

"Just so *you* know, I'm not freaking out. And Alex Mills is a friend," Gus replies. "And I live in Phoenix, not Paradise Valley. Are we clear?"

"Hold on."

A few seconds later Johnson picks up the line and, instead of challenging Gus for not calling sooner, simply says, "You should probably come down to the station, and you should probably bring Ms. Welch."

"Did you find something?"

"We did," the officer says. "But we need to talk in person. I don't want to do this over the phone."

"Just tell me, is Billie in any danger?"

"Not at this very moment," the man says, then clears his throat. "But I'd advise paying us a visit before we *are* talking a very real danger."

"I'll come down there first, myself, without Billie," Gus tells the officer. "But I won't get off work 'til five thirty."

Johnson says that won't be a problem, that he'll be happy to wait.

Stomach in knots, Gus arrives at the Paradise Valley police station at 6:05 p.m. Johnson escorts him to his office.

"We have a suspect," the cop says. "I reviewed the videotape from the security booth at Miss Welch's community." Johnson hands Gus a printout of a photo. "That's a screenshot of the guy. It's not great, but we know who he is."

"You do?"

Johnson says he searched the department's files for any crimes involving Billie Welch, and it turns out Billie had a stalker about twenty-five years ago and it wasn't just a fan. The man was dangerous.

"She was living here in PV, in a different house," Johnson says. "This guy broke in and was waiting for her to come home. Instead the maid shows up and he handcuffs her to one of the ladders in the swimming pool. If she had moved a few inches, she might have drowned, at least that's what the reports say. Miss Welch found her the next day, dehydrated from the sun and nearly unconscious. The guy was long gone. But he left Miss Welch a creepy note asking her to save a date for their wedding."

Gus can feel his eyes bulging from his skull. He tries to shake off the disbelief and says, "Billie's never said a word about this."

"Like I said, it goes back twenty-five years," Johnson reminds him. "Well before my time."

"I'm surprised she ever came back to live here."

"They caught the guy, Mr. Parker. The department investigated, and when they caught the guy they found evidence that he'd been following Miss Welch from city to city on one of her concert tours."

"Jesus," Gus whispers. He tries to imagine this. Was it a strange figure lingering outside each concert venue? Was he a lurking shadow, or had he been watching inside? Had he been in the front row? Had he been staking out the hotels on the tour? Gus can't conjure up any answers and realizes he's drifted off because he sees the young officer staring at him patiently. "I'm sorry," he says.

"No, I get it," the cop says. "It's kind of shocking."

"What's his name? The stalker's?" Gus asks.

"Richard Knight," Johnson replies. "The department did press charges, but they couldn't really charge him with stalking. There really weren't anti-stalking laws back then like there are now, but he was charged with criminal trespass, breaking and entering, reckless endangerment, assault, kidnapping, and he was found guilty on all counts. Sent away for a long time because he had violated his probation on an earlier conviction for assaulting his wife. I pulled all the court documents if you want to see them."

"Obviously the man is out of jail now," Gus says.

"He got out of prison after fourteen years, violated his probation again, and went back in," Johnson explains. "He's only been out again for three months. Obviously he's still in the area. Apparently, he's still obsessed with Billie Welch. I think there's a good chance we'll find him."

"I hope so."

The cop leans forward and gently says, "In the meantime, both of you are probably in a good bit of danger. One of our detectives wants to talk to you."

Gus only now begins to wonder what kind of conversation he's going to have with Billie. He closes his eyes for a second, just long enough to see a cord around his neck, his hands clawing at it as he's trying to break free. Then he's back, not sure whether that was a psychic vision or just a manifestation of pure human fear. A few seconds later the door opens and a man enters in street clothes, sporting a goatee and a pleasant face. He's wearing a fancy watch and, in his right ear, a diamond stud. "Detective Obershan," he says, extending a hand. "Pleasure to meet you, Mr. Parker."

"Gus will do."

"I'm sorry, Gus, that you're having to deal with this creep, but he's obviously still in the area and obviously not that bright, so I think it's a good bet we'll apprehend him," the man says.

"I don't gamble."

Obershan sits at the corner of Johnson's desk. "Then let's cut to the chase," he says. "Is your relationship with Billie Welch public?"

Gus does alternating tilts of his head. "Kind of, I guess," he replies. "I mean, we don't keep it a secret. We go out in public. But I don't think much has been written about us, except maybe in the tabloids."

"So, she hasn't mentioned you in interviews, and you haven't done any photo shoots together?"

Gus laughs. "Uh, no, I don't think anyone needs to see me. Billie's a very private person. She doesn't discuss her personal life all that much with reporters. She might have mentioned me once or twice in interviews, but that's all."

"That's enough for a man so obsessed with Billie Welch that he probably does a Google search for her five times a day, and now *you're* his target," Obershan explains, folding his hands in his lap. "In Richard Knight's deranged little mind, you're standing between him and his one and only true love. His plan is probably to eliminate you."

"That's encouraging," Gus says. "What am I supposed to do?"

"We have a better photo of him than what Johnson showed you. It comes from his release three months ago from prison," the detective explains. "I'll leave you a copy out front. If you recognize him and you think he's following you, please try to snap a picture. Don't approach him. But if he happens to be watching you from across the street or staking you out at work, get pictures or video. Any bit of evidence you gather is beneficial."

"Sounds kind of risky, but I'm good."

"You can file for a restraining order," the detective says. "But if you don't, you should probably mix up your routine if you have one. Make sure someone knows where you are at all times. And you have to be vigilant about knowing who's around you."

"Not easy for a guy like me whose head is normally in the clouds," Gus confesses.

"Alex Mills over in Phoenix tells us you're supposedly psychic," Obershan says. "Maybe that'll compensate for your head in the clouds."

"No guarantees."

The detective stands. So does Gus. "We'll be on the lookout for him. Don't worry," the man says. "We know a lot about this guy. We'll pick him up. Maybe not tonight, but soon. Again, I'm sorry he's out there bothering you."

"Me too."

"Do you own a gun?"

"No," Gus says.

"I think you should learn how to protect yourself," Obershan warns him. "It's the way of the world."

Gus doesn't say anything, just sees Johnson nodding affirmatively as the detective leaves the room.

On the way home Gus studies the photo Obershan had left for him. He can't take his eyes off it until, suddenly, he's at the edge of a stranger's bumper, avoiding a crash by maybe an inch. So, he pulls into a strip mall parking lot and searches Richard Knight's face. It's wide and framed by jowls. There's the scar of a frown, not inflicted by prison, Gus intuits, but by an entire life of disappointment. Richard Knight stares back at Gus with eyes that have known the warfare of mental illness, the deranged, unmedicated theater of battle. What a frenzied man! What a lost soul! How is Gus so lucky and this man so discarded? Just as he begins to feel a wave of sympathy for the guy, Gus feels the cord around his neck again. It tightens. He gasps. His fingers can't break the cord loose, can barely clutch at the space between the cord and the skin of his neck. His head snaps back. Mind over matter. He repeats this to himself like a mantra. *Mind over matter*. This is only fear. Only fear. *Mind over matter*. Richard Knight stares back at him from the rearview mirror.

"What do you want?" Gus begs.

"Her," the man says. "I want her."

"You cannot have her," he says to the mirror. "You will not have her."

The poor face of Richard Knight swells and vomits. The entire image explodes, instantly obliterating the man, and yet Gus sees everything in slow motion: the streams of blood and other fluids squirting like latent fireworks, body parts catapulting, teeth loosening one by one like shingles from a house during a violent storm. Whether in slow motion or fast motion or real motion, the images give Gus that cold vertigo of motion sickness. He grips the wheel to steady himself. When he looks again to the rearview mirror he's pleased to see Richard Knight is gone and that it's Gus staring back at Gus.

Mills is scrambling to pack it in for the day and to head home when his cell phone rattles on the desk. He eyes the mobile fucker with chagrin. To answer? To ignore? To hurl the phone across the wall? For some reason that escapes him, answering feels like the road of least resistance. "Mills," he groans.

"It's Carla Shultz, Detective. Barry Schultz's wife. Is this a bad time?"

"Uh, no. Not at all. What can I do for you, Carla?"

"I'm just checking to see how the investigation's going...."

Of course she is. He feels himself pausing a moment too long. "Well, I think we're making progress. We're learning more about common threads between Davis Klink and your husband. But I can't discuss details."

"I'm getting impatient, if you don't mind me saying," she says.

Fuck, she doesn't need to tell him about impatience. His impatience is impatient; his hindsight is already chiding him well before it has a right to. This case, most cases, are fucking snails in real time—every step forward, two steps back. What looks like a simple task on paper (canvass a neighborhood, locate a car, get a warrant) is most often a clusterfuck on the street.

"I understand, and I'm sorry. Sometimes, oftentimes, these things move slowly," he explains as a headache begins to clench. "We can't afford to make a mistake. I hope you understand."

No response for a moment. And then, weeping. Sniffles and tears. "Carla?"

"I've decided not to do a public funeral, just a private service," she says, as if that grounds her. "But I'm so tired. I don't know how . . ."

Her voice trails off, but she's still with him. He can hear her breathing. He gives her a respite and then says, "I know, Carla. I know what kind of toll this must take."

"I don't know what to do," she says, her voice shaking.

"About what?"

She begins to say something but stops. The hesitation sounds sketchy around the edges.

"Are you all right?" Mills asks, his head throbbing.

"I think so."

"Okay, then, I appreciate the call," Mills says, looking at his watch. "I'm sorry I don't have much of an update, but I'll be in touch if we find anything. I promise."

He's about to hang up, his migraine fully descending, when the woman cries, "Wait!" A bone-chilling moan follows. "Please meet me at my house, Detective Mills. I have something to confess."

Then the woman disconnects before Alex Mills can respond.

20

"I have a confession to make," Gus says when he walks through the doorway to Billie's home studio.

Billie doesn't blink, doesn't ask, just says, "I wasn't expecting to see you tonight, but so glad you showed up."

And there it is. The stripped-down, unvarnished treaty of no expectations. No schedule. No clock. No dependence. That should be fine for Gus, but something like a fist shook his heart. "Did you hear me?" he asks. "I have to confess something."

She strums a few more notes on the guitar, looks up again, and smiles. "You have a way of entering a room, Gus. What's on your mind?"

He has clearly interrupted her muse. He can tell this by the strum of her voice; she's there, but she's not. She's deep in the process of fusing words to melodies or melodies to words, and she can't be two places at once.

"We're being stalked," he says. He sits and describes the note that arrived at her security booth and the postcard that came to his house. He tells her about the surveillance video and his discussions with Detective Obershan. Billie's sudden crash from her creative retreat is palpable. Her moony eyes turn wide and fearful. She puts down the guitar and watches Gus intently. Seeing this, Gus reaches for her hand, holds it in his, and says, "They know it's Richard Knight."

She shakes her head back and forth; he has to squeeze her hand to make her stop. "No," she whispers. "I won't go through this again."

"I think I'm more the target than you," he says.

"How did this happen?"

"I don't know. He got out of prison, and now he's violating his parole. He must think of you as his full-time job, and he's returning to work."

She closes her eyes for a moment, then places a fist to her mouth as if she could cry or scream. Then, abruptly she gets up. "Okay, I'm out of here. I'll catch a flight to LA."

"What? You're flying to LA right now?"

She tilts her head toward the door. "Come on," she says. "I'm not staying here, and neither are you. You're coming with me."

"I can't."

"You must," she insists. "I'll charter a fucking plane, and we'll take the dogs, and we'll get the fuck out of here, Gus."

He follows her to the master bedroom, bargaining all the way. It's no use. She'll go. He says he'll fly out there for the weekend.

"You promise?" she asks.

"I promise."

Mills parks his car at the foot of Carla Schultz's driveway. There's no answer when he knocks at her door. He rings the bell. Then knocks again. The house is dark. He presses his ear to the door but hears nothing except a vacuum of air. A stoned person is not a reliable person. A stoned person forgets. Falls asleep. In the course of hunting criminals for a career, Mills has stood outside many dark, veiling homes, left to guess, to speculate. No matter how long he stands here, the stillness stays stiller than the night; the darkness hides whatever it hides, and he could be, in a split second, shot in the face, stabbed in the back, but awareness and worry are two different things in a career of hunting criminals. He doesn't worry. Awareness is enough. Fed up, he pulls out his phone and dials Carla Schultz. He hears three rings and then the screech of tires, followed almost instantly by a thundering and unfortunate collision of metal against metal, breaking glass, the creak of a car door. His heartbeat quickens. He rests his hand over his gun and moves down the path to the driveway. There, at the bottom, is Carla Schultz stumbling out of her Mercedes, which is impaled rather indecently on Alex Mills's bumper.

"Are you all right?" he shouts as he runs to her. "Are you drunk?"

With tears streaming down her face and her makeup trailing in rivers of black and blue, she shakes her head and says, "No. I'm not all right."

He grabs her. She falls into his arms like a fragile bird.

"I'm so sorry," she says, pointing to the collision.

"Don't worry about it," he tells her. "Your car took the brunt of it. We'll deal with it later."

"I'm not drunk," she says, looking up into his face like a lost child. "I'm tired. Haven't slept in days."

"You asked me to come by. I was worried when you didn't answer the door."

"Sorry, Detective. I had to run out to the pharmacy before it closed."

"Are you on something?"

"Klonopin," she says. "For anxiety."

He lets her go as she opens the front door and leads him in. He follows her into the kitchen, where they sit opposite each other at a curved counter area.

"You told me you have a confession to make," Mills says. "Do I need to read you your rights?"

She looks down to avert his gaze. "I don't know."

From somewhere comes a polite scuffle on the floor, a fast march of thumbtacks, and then a copper-colored Chihuahua launches itself into Carla Schultz's lap.

"Oh, Benny!" she cries. "Benny, meet Detective Mills."

Mills takes in the minor spectacle and says, "The pleasure is all mine."

The woman wipes the streaks of makeup from her face with a tissue. She talks baby talk to the animal. "Oh, you little baby, you little mischievous one, you little pooper with paws, you sweet girl, Mommy loves ya, boo-boo," she says. "I'm going to tell Detective Mills all about the tracking device on Barry's car. I think it's a crime, but I'm not sure, little poopy girl, little treasure."

A fucking tracking device?

Mills knocks twice on the granite island. "Hello? Mrs. Schultz? Can you direct the conversation to me? If you don't mind."

She looks up. She pats the Chihuahua's bum and sets it on the floor. "I'm sorry," she says. "I find this very hard to admit."

"That you put a device on your husband's car to track him?"

"Yes."

"Is that your confession?"

"Yes."

The migraine comes knocking again. "I'm not going to arrest you for that. The law is vague on this, but if both of your names are on the car, then it's definitely not illegal," he explains. "Frankly, 'Find my iPhone' would have been easier."

"It wasn't an iPhone," she says. "And he's too smart for that anyway. He was always checking his settings."

"Paranoid?"

"Maybe."

"I asked you about a possible affair, and you clearly rejected that notion."

"I know. It's embarrassing," she concedes. "I suspected he was screwing a drag queen."

Mills yanks on the stoic mask as quickly as he can. "Well, that's an interesting twist," he says.

"I don't have a lot of evidence. But he did spend a lot of time at drag shows. Late nights. Midweek. That sort of thing."

"I see. Well, there could be another explanation for that," he assures her. "But for now, let's get back to the tracking device. You know where your husband went the night he disappeared?"

She confesses with a hesitant nod.

"But you didn't tell us? You withheld the information."

"I thought you'd arrest me for the tracking device," she says quietly.

"It's probably more problematic that you withheld evidence."

"I know," she whimpers. "I know."

"You do realize that had you given me this information sooner, we might have a suspect in custody by now."

She lights a cigarette. Mills doesn't know which is more offensive—the fact that she smokes inside the house, or the fact that she smokes. He readies his eyes, nose, throat, and lungs for the noxious fumes. "Do you have an address?" he asks.

She exhales a column of smoke. "You mean, where he drove to that night?"

"That's what I mean."

"Yes," she says. "I have the basic area. I printed it out. That's why I called you."

"Okay," he says tentatively.

"Are you going to arrest me?" she asks, then takes another drag.

"I already told you no," he replies. "Give me the printout, and I can probably get some help knocking on doors tomorrow."

"I'll be right back."

She leaves the cigarette burning. He walks over and puts it out. When she returns with the tracking report, Mills scans it quickly and immediately recognizes one stop on the doctor's journey of death. The intersection of Thomas and Sixteenth. This is key. Both victims ended up in the same neighborhood before heading off to their respective graves. The tracking on Schultz's car seems to suggest a stop at the gas station there. There's not a big radius to work with, and that's good. But it's an area as unlikely for the good doctor as it was for Davis Klink. It's not an area synonymous with society and success, certainly not Maseratis. It appears, from Thomas and Sixteenth, that Schultz drove straight to his death. The tracking reveals his next stop was on a side street by the South Phoenix graveyard, where his body was found. But it wasn't the last stop. The car moved on an hour or so later, driven either by the killer, an accomplice, or by the ghost of Barry Schultz. Of course, Mills is convinced it was the killer driving, which makes what he sees next much more problematic. He sees that the killer did not go far, four miles or so, nine minutes of driving. He sees where the Maserati has been hiding all this time. And he can't fucking believe it. It makes sense. But it's a dead end. The trail goes fucking cold. The next and final stop after the cemetery, the killer presumably at the wheel, was Sky Harbor International Airport. A Maserati parked at the airport for almost a week would not necessarily raise suspicion. He's guessing it's in one of the parking structures and, save for some random admirers of its pedigree, that it's probably gone unnoticed. Fuck. Just an exponential fuck to the investigation. Away flies the killer. Perfect plan. Kill a couple of guys, then hop aboard a jetliner to execute the perfect Hollywood escape. There are some upsides to this, though Mills knows he could be kidding himself—every vehicle that enters a parking structure at Sky Harbor is photographed, and the earliest flight the killer could have made was probably 11:30 p.m. There can't be that many flights that leave at that hour of the night, if you eliminate the possibility that the suspect hunkered down somewhere out of sight until a morning flight. Fewer flights mean fewer manifests to comb through.

Wishful thinking.

But the alternative is a needle in a nationwide haystack. Or an international haystack. The guy could have flown to LA, connected to a flight bound for New Zealand where he's been happily fucking sheep for the past several days. It all goes to motive. Not the sheep thing. The murder thing and the subsequent escape plan.

The killer could've hopped on a private jet and soared into the clandestine beyond.

First things first. First they have to search the neighborhood at Thomas and Sixteenth.

"Detective? Does this stuff help at all?"

He snaps out of his stupor. He forgot she'd been standing there.

"Oh, yes. I'm sorry, ma'am. Yes, it does."

"I'm glad," she says.

"Better late than never," he says, pointing to the GPS printout.

"I'm so sorry," she concedes with a deep sigh, followed by sniffles.

"Sorry enough to give me a tour of the house?"

"A tour?"

"We're getting a search warrant," he reminds her. "It will list specific items of interest, but it will also give us latitude to seize other property."

"So you're going to search the house?"

He shakes his head. "I didn't say that. I said I wanted you to show me around, tell me about some of your husband's belongings."

"Okay, but please don't let them search the house," she begs. "I don't want strangers in here going through my things. It'll feel like a home invasion. This place will never be mine again."

"Again, we're looking for very specific items, unless you tell us differently," he says, his patience wafer-thin.

He follows her to a study, where he notes the computers and other electronics. She points out her husband's clothing closet, a giant walk-in matching hers, adjacent to the bedroom. She says he played the guitar, then shows Mills a small collection: three acoustics, one electric. Barry Schultz took a pottery class last year, but it turned out he was better at sculpting boobs than clay. That makes Mills laugh, and it finally lightens the air between them.

"Did your husband keep any old memorabilia? Anything from his childhood? From college? From his early days as a doctor?"

She rolls her eyes. "He has a bunch of shit in the attic. A lot of boxes and an old trunk that's been up there for years. It's locked, but you're welcome to break in."

It takes about a half hour for him to eyeball the attic, rummage through the stacks of boxes, remove several, and haul them down to the foyer. The trunk comes last. "I won't break into it here," he tells the widow. He explains that he'll have people come by tomorrow to pick everything up. "You'll need to sign some paperwork, acknowledging that you provided the items to us willingly."

"Of course," Carla says, then leads him to the front door.

"You're not omitting anything else?" he asks. "Nothing beyond the tracking device?"

She clears her throat, looking at him with a quivering chin. "No, Detective. I promise not to do anything else to impede your investigation."

There's something demure, if not flirtatious, in her affectation. And it is an affectation. Subtle enough for some to miss. But not a detective. "You'll need to come outside now," he instructs her. "To remove the teeth of your car from my bumper."

She's clearly too far down Klonopin Lane to be much help at this point, so he gets in her car, performs the necessary surgical maneuvers, and separates the vehicles. He mutters, "Good night," gets into his car, and drives away. He looks at his watch. Fuck, it's late. Like dinner-cold late. Like piss-off-Kelly late. But before he calls Kelly, he calls over to the precinct at Sky Harbor and reports the likely destination of the Maserati. He asks an officer there, Christina West, if someone can review videotape of cars entering the garages and lots there.

"All garages and lots?"

"Yes."

At first he's met with resistance, some moaning and groaning about hours and hours of videotape. But he's able to mollify the whiner with a specific date and a very specific time frame. One hour of review for five parking facilities. "There can't be that many vehicles entering between eleven p.m. and midnight," he tells her. "Once you see the plate go through, you'll know where the car's parked. A Maserati should stick out, you know, like a really expensive thumb."

Christina West exhales like an exhausted smoker and says, "No prob. But given the time, this might not happen till Monday."

"Unless I come in and do it myself." Which is exactly what he resolves to do.

21

The first thing Mills sees when he walks in the house is the look. The look, when it lands on Kelly's face, usurps everything. There's no kitchen, no dining room. There are no paintings on the wall. No windows. You have to look at the look. That's all.

"Oh shit, Kel, I meant to call," he says, his voice trudging its way to her. "I get it. Dinner's ruined. We'll have to go out. You get to choose the place. Fanciest place you want."

He watches as she, and her look, rises from her favorite chair by the fireplace, a chill all around her. "Dinner is the least of our concerns right now, Alex."

She's coming at him, her head shaking, so much tension in her face. "Then what's concerning us most?" he asks, trepidation roiling in his gut. "I told you I'd be late."

"Trevor," she says. "I got a call about twenty minutes ago from Dan Heathrow, Lily's dad. He's very upset. Apparently, he and his wife walked in on Trevor and Lily having sex."

Jaw on floor. Eyes out of their sockets. Tongue wagging as he stutters to respond. "What?" is all he can manage.

"You heard me," Kelly says, meeting him in the kitchen. "We have a situation. They're not letting him leave until we come over there to discuss."

Mills leans against the counter. "They can't just keep him there."

"They are," she says, grabbing her keys. "Let's go."

The surprise stutters their conversation as they drive. They keep looking at each other, like two living, breathing wow emojis. They take turns saying, "I can't believe it."

Then Kelly takes a breath so deep it makes Mills nervous. Finally she exhales and says, "But we can believe it, right? I mean, he's seventeen. I'm not making excuses for him, but it's not unusual for kids that age to experiment. I'd like this to not be happening, but . . ."

"I'm inclined to believe he was more than experimenting," he says. "I'm not shocked, but still, Trevor? Our Trevor? When did he get the kind of penis that does that kind of stuff?"

Kelly laughs. She explodes with laughter. Which prompts Mills to laugh. Soon they're both hysterical. Kelly almost runs a red light. She slams on the brakes and asks, "Is it bad that we're laughing? 'Cause I'm not happy about this."

Mills assures her it's an emotional necessity. Then he hears a sniffle, like a weepy sniffle, and he turns to her just in time to see her wipe a tear from her eye. "Hon, come on, it's not that bad. I'm not saying we throw a party, but this was bound to happen."

"That's not what I'm crying about."

"Then what?"

"I don't want to be old enough to have a kid who's having sex."

They arrive at the home of Trevor's girlfriend, ring the bell, and wait to walk the unhappy gauntlet. Dan Heathrow opens the door and guides them inside. He introduces them to his wife, Corinne. She looks like a younger version of Martha Stewart, and her house looks like a page out of a Martha Stewart magazine. Right down to the baseboards. Dan reminds Mills of a sitcom dad, with the sweater, the receding hairline, the hunched shoulders. "Your son is in our study," he says. "We wanted him to stay until you got here to resolve this. Let's sit, shall we?"

He leads them to the dining room table, where the four of them take a seat.

"We were on our way out of town, heading to Sedona, when I noticed the car was driving funny," Dan says. "Luckily we weren't that far, so we turned back. Not so lucky for your son. We came into the house and found him having sex with our daughter. In our bed! Pre-*marital* sex!"

"We know they're not married," Mills tells him.

"Don't be flip, Detective."

"Uh, you can call me Alex. I'm not here on police business," Mills says.

"Alex, I want your son to stay away from my daughter. Period. He's never to see her again."

"They go to school together," Kelly reminds him.

"I'm aware of that," Dan says. "But outside of school he better stay away from her."

"Fine," Mills says. "We'll advise him. If that will be all . . ."

"What?" the man thunders. "Are you kidding me? That's it? No punishment?"

Kelly sits up straight and in her courtroom voice says, "We think punishment is between Trevor and us, privately. I hope you understand."

Dan pounds his fist on the table. "Oh, no!" he yells. "No way! We want to know exactly what you're going to do to your pig of a son!"

"Would anyone like coffee?" Corinne asks. "I have a fresh pot."

Mills ignores her. "Did you just call my son a pig?"

"What would you call him?" the man asks, still frothing.

"I would call him a typical teen. And I'd call your daughter a typical teen, as well."

Dan roars with laughter. "Of course you do. Let me guess, you two are some kind of liberal Democrats who support Planned Parenthood and hate family values. Right?"

Kelly, calmly, says, "I don't think our politics are relevant here."

"Well, in this house they are," Dan insists. "We're a good Christian family raising good Christian children."

"We admire that," Kelly tells him. "But I think we need to deal with this privately as two separate families."

Dan rises, then slams his chair against the table. "You need to tell me right now what you're going to do to that kid. He's lucky my gun is locked up in the cabin."

"Honey," Corinne says tentatively, "that's not necessary."

"Nor is it advisable to discuss the threat of using weapons against my son," Mills adds. "How old is Lily?"

"She's seventeen," Corinne replies.

"So, they haven't done anything illegal," Mills says. "At least nothing I can think of."

"What happened here in my house may not be illegal, but it's immoral. Something tells me you people wouldn't know about that," Dan says. "But I know about your son, Mr. Mills. I read about the drug ring at the high school. I know he sold pot."

Kelly bristles. "That was a while ago, and the charges were dropped. And if you know so much about Trevor, you know that he and his teammates were being bullied and exploited by a coach."

Mills gets up. "I think we're done here." He yells for Trevor. He yells several times before his son ducks into the room, sheepishly, red marks on his face.

"Let's go," Mills tells his son.

"They took my keys, Dad."

"What happened to your face?" Kelly asks.

"Mr. Heathrow hit me," Trevor says flatly, as if he deserved it.

Mills rushes to Dan, grabbing him by the collar. "What the fuck, man? A good Christian dad with good Christian values couldn't resolve this without violence?"

"Looks like you're the violent one," Dan sputters. "I shouldn't have hit your boy. I'm sorry. It was an instant reaction."

"Let him go, Alex," Kelly shouts. "Come on, Trevor. We're leaving."

"But they took my keys," Trevor repeats.

"And we'll give them back when we know what your punishment is," Dan insists.

"Bullshit!" Mills roars, backing the man into the wall. "That's bullshit. Give us the keys now or I'll put your head through this fucking wall."

"Alex," Kelly warns.

"Tell me your punishment plan," Dan insists, turning his head to Kelly.

"None of your business," she says. "Give us the keys."

"Here," Corinne says. No one, certainly not Mills, had realized she slipped out of the room. "Take the keys. Take your son away from here. He's not welcome back."

They drive home, Trevor tailing them, Mills boiling. They say nothing. Not a word. They slip into the garage. Trevor enters the house a few steps behind them. "You're too old to be told to go to your room," Mills says to him. "But, please go to your room; we'll talk about this later."

He showers after Kelly, then lands in bed a few minutes later. She grabs his hand, stroking his arm. "And when we talk with him later, what are we going to say?"

"I have absolutely no clue," Mills says with a heavy sigh. "But I need to sleep on it, Kel. I really do."

The talk did not come the following morning. Or the morning after that. They dodged the idea of later, avoiding each other, and avoiding the subject, like some people who step over cracks in the sidewalk. Mills knows the dance is dysfunctional but his partners are willing.

Even now, on Saturday morning, at the beginning of what could become an intractable weekend, they hesitate. Breakfast is a convenient procrastination. So is the run to Safeway, the stop at the dry cleaners. Trevor needs a new pair of shoes. Mills needs to trim the Oleander. They accidentally convene around three o'clock, and there's no getting around the discussion.

"You have to be careful, Trevor," Mills says when they're all sitting in the living room. "I can't sit here and say what's wrong and what's right."

"Neither can I," Kelly says. "The fact is, part of becoming an adult is finding out what's wrong and what's right for yourself *and* facing any consequences of your decisions."

"Yeah, I know," Trevor says. "But everyone's doing it. You know, like everyone in high school is having sex."

Mills offers a chuckle. "Yeah, well, that doesn't seem like the basis for a good decision."

"You may be physically old enough to have sex, Trevor. But that doesn't mean you're emotionally mature enough," Kelly says. "Or Lily, for that matter. She may not know yet how emotional it can be to be so intimate with someone."

"But I'm sure you two weren't thinking at that level," Mills adds. "You were just having sex. Right?"

"Yeah. I guess," his son says. His face now sports a purple bruise from Lily's father.

"Were you using protection, Trevor?" Kelly asks. "Against pregnancy *and* STDs?"

"Yes."

"Good. But nothing is fail proof," Kelly says. "So you both need to be emotionally ready to handle unintended consequences. I'm not sure either of you are. Something to think about."

"I get it," he says.

"Okay, then," Mills interjects, "tell us what you were thinking having sex in Mr. and Mrs. Heathrow's bed?"

"It was Lily's idea. She hates her parents. They're so strict. They don't let her do anything."

"But it was stupid," Mills says. "Really stupid. And it was wrong. Don't you ever think of doing it in our bed, Trevor. Or you'll be sleeping out in the yard. No sex in this house."

"When we're home," Kelly adds.

Mills turns to her. "When we're home? No, I mean ever."

She shakes her head. "So he'll go have sex in a car and get arrested? No, thank you."

"When we're home," Mills says to his son. "Have some respect."

He then declares the meeting over. His head is throbbing. He needs a nap.

A nap, a vague memory of dinner, and a decent sleep later, it's Sunday and Mills calls over to the airport precinct to check in on the videotape.

The tapes have been pulled, but nobody has looked at them. Un-fucking-believable. He's all but wringing his hands. The precinct isn't overflowing with cops or support staff, but what the fuck else is going on over there? The thing is you never know. He doesn't know. His head throbs. He massages his temples. He drops a few more f-bombs. His tail between his legs, Mills shuffles over to his wife and delivers the bad news that he has to spend a few hours at Sky Harbor.

"Alex, this is probably one of those days you should be around your kid."

"I said it's only for a few hours."

"Nothing is for a few hours," she says. "Decide what's important."

"Hey, that's not fair."

She walks out of the room. He's too tired to follow and argue. Instead he yells, "Sorry, babe, tell him to vacuum the house while I'm gone."

She reappears, laughing. "Vacuum? Are you serious? Is that his punishment?"

"I'm not punishing him," he says. "I'm keeping him busy while I'm gone."

"Oh, I have plenty of chores for that," she assures him.

"There, then, it's settled." But he looks at her, and her face looks anything but settled. It looks pained still. Disappointed, disapproving. Her mood crawls under his skin. He calls Jan Powell, tells her about the Maserati, and asks if she'd mind meeting him at Sky Harbor.

"Because I have no life?" she asks.

"Never mind," he says. "I'll call Preston. I'm sure he has no life."

"Just messing with you. I'll meet you in the precinct office."

She gets there first and has a thin smile when she greets him. "How long do you think this will take?"

"Just fast-forward between cars," he tells her. "I doubt there's a lot of traffic going in at that hour. I'm betting we'll be done with the search in forty-five minutes. Give or take."

There are two computers in the corner of the office. She sits at one, he at the other. At a ninety degree angle apart from each other, he senses that vibe of camaraderie. It's just there. They slip in the thumb drives. He takes the West Economy lot and terminal 2 and terminal 3 garages; she takes the East Economy lot and terminal 4 garage. As he suspected, there's not much traffic and, thus, long durations of video where nothing happens. Not even a passing bird looking to park. So, it is, indeed, an exercise in shuttling the videotape from one car to the next: a Honda SUV ... eight minutes later a Honda Civic ... ten minutes later a Toyota Camry ... twenty-two minutes later a Ford Explorer. And so on.

"Anything over there?" he asks his colleague.

She coughs up a laugh. "A lot of shuttling. Not so many cars. But a very nice Porsche. And a guy with a bumper sticker that says, 'Honk if you *are* Jesus.'"

He leans back. "Close, but I think Schultz's would say, 'Honk if Jesus needs a facelift.'"

A patrol officer walks in. "Jesus needs a facelift? I was in church this morning. No one said a thing."

They laugh if only to break the monotony. The officer is a young guy named Sloane. Kevin Sloane. Mills has never met him. "I started walking the garages yesterday," the officer tells them. "Didn't see a Maserati, but I was only at it for maybe twenty minutes before I got called to deal with an unruly passenger."

"Unruly?" Powell asks him.

"He was pissed off about missing his flight. Wanted the airline to charter a plane for him."

"The airlines don't do that," Mills says. "That's ridiculous."

Mills is back at the computer screen searching. He's almost done with the garage structure.

"Not to mention," the officer says, "he was not just late for his flight; he was four hours late."

"Four hours? Where the hell was he?" Powell asks him.

"In one of the bars," Sloane replies. "Hammered."

"Fucking people," Mills mutters.

"Happens all the time," Sloane says. "I thought I'd get back to my Maserati search, if you'd like."

Mills turns to him. "Why don't you wait until we're done with the video? If we see the car, we'll know exactly where to search. We can go together."

Sloane nods, then retreats to another section of the office. Powell tells Mills that she's done with the garage at terminal 4 and is ready to screen the East Economy lot. "Cool," Mills says. "I just started West Economy."

Ford F-150 . . . eight minutes later Chevy Bolt . . . fifteen minutes later BMW 7 series . . . seven minutes later Nissan Pathfinder . . . thirteen minutes later Toyota Corolla . . . eleven minutes later Maserati.

White Maserati. He hits "Rewind." GR8LOOK.

"Got it," Mills says. "I fucking got it."

Powell rolls over to his side. "West Economy?"

"Yup." He's nearly salivating.

"What time?"

"Twelve eleven a.m." His skin's on fire.

"The killer was here," Powell says, rolling back to her desk.

"He was here. He might be long gone. Or this whole Sky Harbor thing could just be a smoke screen," he says. "Let's go."

Sloane jumps to his feet and offers to drive them over to West Economy. Mills rides shotgun, Powell in the back seat. Once they reach the parking lot, they begin a slow-motion reconnaissance mission to find the doctor's car. They drift up and down every row, scouting the vehicles on both sides. The rows are long and numerous. Every space, it seems, is taken. An hour later, they're only in row G, inching toward row H. Mills looks at his watch. Kelly is going to have a fucking fit. Up and down. Every row. He suspects a liver transplant would be faster than this operation.

"Maybe I should get out on foot," he tells the others in the car. "I'll take the far end of the lot while you guys continue this slow march of death."

"Oh, come on, Alex. It's not that bad," Powell says.

"You don't have a wife," he says.

She mutters something under her breath, and he says, "What was that?" And she says, "Never mind."

Sloane stops the car. "Go 'head, Detective. We'll meet up with you in a bit."

So, under a magnificent dome of blue, that warm desert breeze fluttering around him, Mills is on foot. There's engine noise all around and the confectionary smell of citrus trees bearing fruit. And jet fuel.

He duly notes every car he passes. His process moves faster than the crawling surveillance in Sloane's cruiser. He doesn't even glimpse at cars that aren't white. He can accelerate accordingly. White cars only. Maseratis only. One vanity plate. This is like finding a haystack in a needle. He reaches the back rows of the lot where they join together in the cove of a "U." Nothing here. So he works his way back toward the front, down the other side of the lot, still unexplored terrain. He's surprised to see so many white cars here. As if they're purposely goading him, mocking him. But that's not it, he knows. It's Kelly. He looks at his watch and realizes that if he doesn't make it home within the hour Kelly is going to be pissed. And when he looks back up, a white Maserati is staring back at him. Staring him down. Daring him to celebrate a victory. He freezes for a moment. Row L, space 111. He texts Powell, telling her to meet up there. Yes. Oh, yes. *You mother fucking Maserati.*

He snaps multiple pictures of the car. He approaches the vehicle, circles it. Confirms the ridiculous license plate. The gust of his sigh could change the wind direction. Powell and Sloane pull up and park in the middle of the lane.

"Nice work," Powell tells Mills when she gets out of the car. "I called to get some techs out here."

"Thanks. We're going to have to control the crime scene as best as we can with people coming and going from the lot," Mills says.

"I'd close the lot," Sloane says, "but Sunday is a big day for exits. And it basically would take a proclamation from the mayor to close anything."

Mills thinks about the crime scene in front of him, considers it possibly disturbed already by people who have come and gone since the killer abandoned the Maserati. "Or we just keep this in perspective," he tells the others. "Let's have the techs do basic processing here. It's far more important to get it back to the lab where we can get inside it. I want every inch of the interior under a microscope."

"Makes sense," Powell says. "Want me to call for a flatbed?"

"No, I'll handle that after the techs get here," Mills replies. "But I do have another call to make."

He wanders down the last row, no particular aim in sight, and settles arbitrarily against a Lexus. Leaning there, he dials Kelly and begs forgiveness. It doesn't come easily, only after he promises to build her a castle and do the dishes forever.

22

Within a half-mile radius of the PetroGo gas station at Thomas and Sixteenth, there are fifty-two residential homes, six apartment complexes, fourteen businesses, and eight empty storefronts. The report sitting in Alex Mills's email inbox Monday morning is unremarkable. Patrols had spent much of Thursday and Friday knocking on doors. They interviewed forty-six residents between the homes and the apartments, as well as eight business owners. Many of their knocks went unanswered. Mills scrolls down from page to page of the PDF attachment, mining for any morsel of truth, but there are no truths, at least none pertinent to the case. People often lie to cops in situations like this, not because they have something to hide about the case, more often because they have something to hide about their lives. Squatters, drug addicts, undocumented immigrants, whatever.

The report is mostly useless. Not one person interviewed by the patrols raises a red flag. No one reports anything suspicious or remembers seeing a vehicle matching the description of Davis Klink's or Barry Schultz's automobile. Maybe the BMW, several people told the officers, because those are more common. But certainly not the Maserati. Carl Thompson, owner of Fixit Fast, a computer and cell phone repair shop on Sixteenth, said there might have been an abandoned car or two at PetroGo across the street. A manager at PetroGo, Walt Hardy, disputed that, stating, "A BMW or Maserati wouldn't just sit here for days." Steven Ellis, a resident at 1568 East Glenridge, said a Maserati was up on blocks for about a week two doors down. Two doors down, Monica Crowning at 1566 East Glenridge offered a statement telling officers that Mr. Ellis is a meth addict who can't be trusted and that, at her wages as a Wal-Mart cashier, she could no more afford the front right tire of a Maserati than put up an entire car of that kind on blocks.

Okay, he's done. He knows the Maserati was in the neighborhood. And he knows where it ended up. Same for the BMW. He had hoped someone would have seen or heard an argument or, at the very least, seen if either vehicle visited a specific house or business. Both vehicles are now with the lab. He closes out of his email. Logs off the computer. Shakes his head in mild disgust at humanity. Then he calls Gus Parker. "Wakey, wakey," he says.

"What time is it?" Gus groans.

"Eight forty. Are you late for work?"

"Nah. Just sleeping in. Flew in late last night from LA."

"All right, jetsetter, go take a shower and meet me down here at headquarters. I think we should pay a visit to the doctor's office."

"Your doctor?"

Mills laughs. "Uh, no," he says. "Schultz. The dead guy. Thought you could conjure something up. If you have the time."

"I have to be at work at one," Gus says.

"Then I'd get a move on it," Mills tells him and hangs up.

Gus arrives in the lobby about forty-five minutes later, clutching a cup of coffee.

"You awake yet?" Mills asks.

"This is my first cup," Gus says, lifting his coffee as if he's making a toast.

They drive in Mills's car. On the ride out there, Gus tells him about Richard Knight and Billie's reaction. At her Malibu house over the weekend, she told Gus she was thinking of selling her Paradise Valley estate.

"She's that scared?" Mills asks.

"I think she's that fed up."

"Do you really think she'll sell?"

"I think once Billie puts her mind to something, it's pretty much a done deal."

Mills slows for a stoplight. "So, it sounds like a rather tense weekend in LA."

"Yeah," Gus says. "That's an adequate description."

"Well, fuck." It's all Mills can offer for the rest of the drive.

The five-story building that houses Associated Surgeons at Better You Center reminds Gus of a lavish spa. It's as if the doctors determined to build a façade worthy of the facelifts engineered inside. That is to say, a layer of beauty, beneath which hide the blood and guts. On the right side of the entryway, a wall of glass block symbolizes to Gus the distortion of the truth while a trough of gushing fountains to the left suggests to him the promise of timeless beauty. A fountain of youth.

"Are we going in?" Gus asks.

They're sitting in the front row of parking spaces with an unobstructed view of the nearly perfect patients going in for more perfection. This isn't what Gus had expected; he had expected much older people looking to turn back time, or heavier people hoping to trim their waistlines, lose their extra chins, and maybe lift their butts. And there are several of those, to be sure, but most of the women coming and going look like fashion models showing off the spring line of designer boobs.

"We're not going in," Alex tells him. "These people don't want to talk. Preston's been here a few times. They've completely lawyered up."

"You'd think they'd want to help find the doctor's killer."

"This place is all about image," Alex says. "They don't want the bad publicity."

An image flashes before Gus's eyes. Suits. An amoeba of suits displacing a corporate lobby. "You're right," he says. "It's the lawyers."

"And just to fuck with them we're going for a search warrant. I'll take extra delight in turning this place upside down." Alex snickers. "Even though Schultz probably didn't leave that night to see a patient, we can't rule out a link to his practice. But that's why I brought you here, to see what you can confirm . . . if anything."

Gus shifts in his seat. "So we're just going to sit in the parking lot?"

"You can get out and walk around," Alex tells him. "Count the Mercedes, the Porsches, the Jags, if you find that kind of thing fun."

Gus opens the door. "See you in a few," he says.

He walks the perimeter of the building. His assumption, more so than his clairvoyance, tells him that the patients inside are being pampered beyond belief and that every staff member has his or her own ingratiating gimmick to up-sell the desperately insecure on even more procedures. He stands at the south side of the building, and his attention is drawn to an upper floor. He fixates his gaze on a wall of glass up there. He doesn't see a vision as much as he senses some kind of trouble the higher his eyes climb. But the glass yields nothing. A Lexus glides into a space nearby. Its door opens, then closes with a cushioned thud. He moves to the east side of the office. The signs say, "Physicians Parking Only," and he inventories two Mercedes, a Tesla, and a Porsche Cayenne. The vehicles reveal nothing. He tries. He hyperfocuses. But nothing here. Nothing to suggest that Schultz's partners had any connection to his death. Gus wouldn't sign an affidavit absolving them of his murder, however; there's not enough here to be sure either way, just a strong feeling that Schultz's demise did not intersect with his working life. On the north side of the building the parking lot is deserted. There's a delivery entrance and a door to a mechanical room. He looks up five stories and sees a rooftop terrace capping the back end of the building. Just as his eyes rest at the pinnacle, he hears someone screaming.

He looks to his left, then to his right, then to the roof, again. The screams stop. He can't find the source. He closes his eyes, silently calls for a connection, and listens. First comes a howl, like a tornado storming across a deserted prairie. Then they begin again, the screams. They tumble at him, a cascade of screams, coming down the side of the building. He wants to open his eyes, to study this place more closely, but he keeps them shut and searches more deeply for a vision within. He really has to squeeze his eyes closed to concentrate. The screams persist for a few moments here, and then, like stones skipped from the water's edge, their echoes fade until the screams are just the plink of a teardrop.

Gus lifts his arms to the sky.

He doesn't know why, but his arms are pulled upward, stretching his muscles. He's not praising Jesus. This is not exaltation. And then, oh God, he's meant to catch something. Someone. He's meant to be the hands of deliverance. A power forces his eyes open into a blinding white light. And there, amid the white light, she falls from the terrace. She flies, she floats, and she falls. It happens in slow motion. Gus rushes for her. He scrambles to catch her. She cries and screams, but she doesn't make a sound. Gus can't hear her. The white light is too loud. The light is banging like drums, drowning her out. He can't catch her. She's an angel, she's a child, she's an apparition.

Gus can't catch his breath.

He watches her final moments as she whooshes, not to the ground, to his surprise, not to a bloody end on the pavement, but instead she falls, as if from a cliff, into the roiling ocean, the water closing all around her, and closing, and closing, until she is gone and the white light recedes.

"Excuse me, sir. Are you okay?"

Gus turns around. A woman stands at the delivery entrance. She's wearing scrubs.

"Sir? Do you need some help?"

It takes him a moment, as it often does, to come back. "Uh, no," he tells her. "I'm fine."

She gives him a dubious nod and disappears behind the door.

Back at Alex's car, Gus recreates the entire vision for the detective.

"I know you enough to know this means something," Alex says.

Even now, even after all these years since his estrangement from his family, those words for Gus carry more weight than gold. "Can we, maybe, analyze this a little later?" Gus asks. "I feel a little inside out. If you know what I mean."

"Like I said, I know you enough."

"It's like I fell from that building, too."

"I'm sure in a way you did," Alex says. "Let's head back to headquarters."

They drive in silence, but back at police headquarters, idling in the parking lot in a space beside Gus's SUV, Mills says, "My son got caught having sex with his girlfriend."

"Rite of passage."

"You think?" Mills asks.

"Yeah," Gus says. "But, you know, you can influence the passage. Talk to him. Give him a reality check about the consequences. He'll be fine, maybe even more responsible."

"We did. But I'm not sure whether anything we say will change his behavior."

"You can't control his choices," Gus says. "He's growing up now. You've been great parents. And no parents are perfect, trust me."

Mills takes that in for a second. Mulls it over. "Fine. I will," he says. "But now you trust me. Here's the plan to avoid your stalker: You need to stay at your house in Phoenix. I'll get PV to send me copies of their files, and I'll make a case to get you a 'special watch.'"

"What's that?"

"It means putting some extra patrols in your neighborhood," Mills explains. "I don't know what the cops in PV are willing to do for you, but if you stay in Phoenix I'll get you some coverage."

Gus nods, wide-eyed. "Thanks. Let me know when I can help you next." He opens the passenger door.

"Wait," Mills says, looking straight ahead. "I'd like you to reconsider carrying a gun."

Gus turns to him. "Wow, you too. The cops in PV think I should have a gun."

Mills taps the steering wheel with his hands. "They're right," he says. "Unless you're thinking of moving to Malibu full-time, you're in danger here."

Gus sighs heavily. "You really believe that?"

"Yup."

Gus seems to let that soak in for a minute, but then he says, "I don't do guns. I don't want one in my house."

"What about Billie? Does she carry?"

Gus laughs. "Absolutely not. She's even more of a pacifist than me."

"You say that like it's a good thing."

"It is, man. For some people." Then Gus offers him a handshake and hops out.

Mills knows he's not a psychic, himself, but deep in his gut, not his general gut, but that other place where he worries about the people he loves, he knows Gus should have a gun.

23

In the parking lot, Mills receives a text message from Powell: "We're in the conference room. Have stuff to show you."

They're practically salivating when he enters. Myers leaps from his chair. "We finished inventorying the Schultz stuff," he says.

Sure enough, they have. Pieces of Dr. Barry Schultz's memorabilia cover the entire table like a mosaic of his life. That's the thing that makes death the great equalizer; all the little pieces of your life, and the banalities that stitch them together, tell your entire story. The leftovers on the floor, the odds and ends poking out of boxes, deemed insignificant to the investigation, give proof to the banality. Mills finds himself staring into that proof for just a minute too long.

"We found three outdated passports," Myers gushes. "Tons of photographs. Old letters. Postcards. Travel souvenirs, by the looks of it."

Powell reaches to the center of the table and picks up a small stack of old photos. "These came from the trunk. We broke the lock. You need to see them."

Mills takes the stack from her. He shuffles through it. They're old photos from the doctor's childhood, high school, and college years—in no particular order. The doctor was a good-looking guy, light hair, blue eyes, a trim athletic build. He's on the tennis team. He's dressed for the prom. He poses with the family. With a girl. There he is on skis. He's on the chairlift. And there he is on the beach.

Powell puts a finger on the beach photo and stops Mills from sifting. "This is the money shot, so to speak."

It sure is. Mills sees it immediately. Schultz, hair wet and tousled, is flanked by two grinning buddies. Subtract twenty or thirty years and the faces of Al Torento and Davis Klink are smiling, somewhat smugly, back at you. They're posing with their backs to the ocean. Over their shoulders to the left, a mass of seaweed, like a washed-up lace dress, drapes a concrete jetty. Beyond that, in the very upper corner of the photo, a few buildings, presumably hotels, poke into frame, and a lonely pier farther up the shore sits against the horizon.

"That's not a reunion shot," Powell tells him.

"Clearly not. These guys are obviously still in college, here. You can just tell. They knew each other. They were friends," Mills says, his adrenaline surging. "This puts all three of them together. They obviously traveled together. Too bad I can't tell where this is."

"Yeah we've been trying to figure that out for the past hour," Preston says. "Could be Rocky Point."

Still studying the photo, Mills says, "Could be. Rocky Point was a very popular road trip from Phoenix back in the day." Then he laughs. "God knows I had quite a few weekends of debauchery down there, myself."

Myers picks up one of the old passports. "Maybe this will help."

"Only if these guys went out of the country," Mills says. "I don't think you needed a passport to cross the border into Rocky Point back then. I don't even think you needed it to fly into Mexico."

"For all we know it's a beach in San Diego," Preston interjects, "in which case a passport is irrelevant."

"Someone has to know where this is," Mills says. "Assuming the place still looks the same."

"Why is it so important? You know, where they are?" Myers asks.

"I think the important thing," Mills begins, "is that only a handful of photos were locked away in the trunk. You, yourself, said there was a ton of pictures. Am I right, Morty?"

"Yeah. We got easily a couple hundred."

"But only these were locked away," Mills says.

"And I stopped you about five photos from the bottom of the stack," Powell tells him. "The last five also all show the three men together, most likely from the same vacation."

Mills flips through them fast. They're night shots, shot with a flash to illuminate their sunburned faces, on the beach again, behind them a ring of teenagers around a bonfire. Still, no definitive characteristics that reveal geography. Just a deep, dark, sea.

"So," Mills says, "why were only these photos locked away?"

Preston clears his throat and says, "I think you're suggesting the photos are incriminating in some way. But if they are, why wouldn't have Schultz just destroyed them along with the negatives?"

"Proof of something," Powell tells him. "Proof that mattered to him."

"We just need to find out what that something was," Mills says.

"An alibi?" Powell suggests.

Mills lets the word resonate. "Maybe. Which is why it's important to establish where they were. It's the only place where we can put the three of them together, except for the reunions," he says.

The others nod back at him soberly. They all know this is equal parts fool's errand and investigative due diligence.

"Myers, scan the photos in. And let's blow 'em up to poster size," Mills says. "Maybe we'll see something we can't see now. It's a long shot, but I want it done."

"No prob," Myers assures him.

"What about the doctor's computer?" Mills asks.

Preston tells him that the computer is still with forensics. "No alarm bells so far. Nothing relevant to the case, but they're still working on the laptop and the other devices we seized."

Mills says he'll do the follow-up on his own. "In the meantime, everybody take a seat."

The squad shuffles about, dodges a few boxes, and sits.

"I know we took Toronto out of the killer column and put him back in the victim column," Mills says to the team. "But I want, just for a moment, to put him back under 'killer.' I have my reasons."

"Do share," Powell asks. "What's your scenario?"

"It goes like this," Mills begins. "Let's say 'Your Pal Al' was blackmailing Klink and Schultz. For what I don't know. But both men are dead. Klink tried to pay him half a million dollars, but Toronto killed him anyway so Klink wouldn't expose him. He probably needed the money for his reelection . . ."

"Or, Schultz, with all these photos locked away as some kind of insurance policy, was blackmailing the others for something," Powell suggests. "And Torento killed him instead of paying him off."

"But the congressman first killed Klink because Klink would be able to tie Torento to Schultz's murder?" Mills asks.

"I don't like the scenarios," Preston tells them. "If the killer's Torento, why would he choose such an outlandish MO? I mean, these ghoulish gravesites are not the MO of a person in the public eye who has everything to lose if he gets caught. If Torento killed, he wouldn't do it so sensationally."

"He's right," Mills says.

"Or not," Powell argues. "Perhaps we're dealing with an attempt at reverse psychology. You know, Torento kills this way precisely because we would never suspect him of doing something so public."

"I think it's a stretch," Mills insists. "I might have to retract my earlier theory."

"Plus, the guy has an alibi. He's been in Washington," Preston says.

"So we think. Who's to say he doesn't fly back here unannounced?" Powell asks. "He can insist he was in DC even if he wasn't."

"But he'd still need an alibi," Preston argues, "and he wouldn't have one."

Mills scoffs. "Come on, alibis in Washington can be bought and sold like blowjobs on McDowell."

Powell says, "Good one."

Mills says, "No. Sorry. That was inappropriate whether or not he has an alibi."

Myers says, "I don't get it."

Preston rolls his eyes.

"Wait a minute," Powell says. "The Maserati was left at Sky Harbor. So, let's just say Torento kills his old friend Barry. Then he drives the victim's Maserati to the airport, ditches the car, and takes off on a midnight flight to DC."

Mills shakes his head. "Nah, too conspicuous. Too easy to track his moves."

"You put in the request for flight manifests for that night?" she asks him.

"I put in a request for flight departures first," he says, pulling up an email from Sky Harbor Operations on his phone. "In the hours after Schultz's murder, between eleven thirty p.m. and five a.m., there were twelve commercial flights and five private flights departing the airport."

"He probably flew private," Preston says. "On a corporate jet of one of his donors."

"He'd have to disclose that," Myers reminds the team.

Everybody laughs. Even Myers.

The laughter settles quickly as an infectious dismay seems to spread around the table. Their eyes wander, avoiding contact. The fluorescent lights hum overhead, amplifying the room's anemia. "I was holding off on the manifests until we could confirm the Maserati was at the airport," Mills tells the group. "The precinct over there is reviewing surveillance cameras from the West Economy lot to see if they captured images of anyone parking the Maserati, getting out, walking in that area."

"We don't know if Schultz's killer got on any flight," Preston reminds them. "He could have taken a cab or an Uber from the airport and gone home."

"Anything's possible," Mills says. "But I'll be contacting the airlines for their manifests, and, who knows, maybe we'll recognize a name."

"You need help with that?" Powell asks.

"I'll share the data when I get it back. Then each of us will read through each passenger list and we'll compare what we find, if anything."

The others nod back at him again, and then Mills turns his attention to a stack of papers on the table and sifts. The pile contains Schultz's transcripts from college and medical school. If the subtraction in his head is correct, Mills figures the doctor graduated from U of A twenty-five years ago, medical school four years after that. If his grades are any indication, Schultz was a conscientious student, made the dean's list albeit inconsistently. He would not go on to cure cancer, but he'd hone his surgical craft and find a seemingly lucrative career preying on the vanity of the masses.

Finally a voice. "One thing I don't get," Powell says. "If we're talking blackmail, what's the blackmail?"

"There aren't a lot of varieties," Preston replies. "Sex, drugs, murder."

Mills drops the stack of papers on the table. "Where are we on the search warrant for Schultz's office?"

"I should have had it this morning," Preston says. "But I'm guessing tomorrow."

"Good," Mills says. "Because Schultz had access to all kinds of drugs. Doctors have closets full of samples. Not to mention an endless supply of prescription pads. For all we know Schultz was running a pill mill out of his practice."

Powell shakes her head. "I can maybe see a congressman involved in something like that, but not Klink. Klink's loaded. He doesn't need one-third of a pill mill to pay his mortgage."

"Doesn't really fit the Fortune 500 profile," Mills concedes, "unless Schultz somehow talked Klink into funding the operation."

"We've gone through most of Klink's financial records," Preston says. "The only thing that's really stood out were those big withdrawals on the day he died."

Mills gets up, then snags one of the photos of the men posing on the beach. "Enough for now," he says. "We all need to drill down, come up with some legit evidence that ties these guys together."

"Speaking of which," Powell interjects, "I've been waiting on forensic prelims from the Schultz scene to compare with Klink. I'll have 'em tonight if you want to look."

"I do," Mills replies.

He heads to his office, where he scans his notes for Torento's home phone number. He dials the landline, gets voice mail. He leaves another message with a cheery intern in the Washington office. Then he goes online and searches the website of Arizona State University. It's a clusterfuck of a navigation, a click marathon, but there she is, the last professor listed on the Spanish faculty page. He dials her office number, but she doesn't answer. He's getting nowhere fucking fast. Until he notices that under Jennifer Torento's short but impressive bio, her office hours are listed. She's available, it seems, Mondays 3:00 p.m.– 5:00 p.m., Wednesdays 10:00 a.m.–noon, and Thursdays 3:00 p.m.– 5:00 p.m.

It's 1:52 p.m. right now. Mills hasn't had lunch. He usually brings leftovers on Mondays, but Trevor ate like a pig over the weekend, his appetite apparently as strong as his libido. He calls Kelly.

"Hey, babe, I'm grabbing lunch in Tempe if you want to join me," he says when his wife answers.

"I had a salad at noon. Aren't you a little late?"

"How about we meet at the house for dessert?" he says with a lascivious snicker.

"Goodbye, Alex. I have a client in fifteen minutes."

"Your loss."

"You know I love you."

"I know you do."

And so, Alex Mills finds himself eating alone at Magic Café in Tempe, about two blocks from the ASU campus. There's nothing magic about the café, but they make the best Philly cheesesteak this side of Philly. He's the only one eating. Most of the patrons are sitting at the bar, sipping one of the ten thousand variations of organic coffee the café offers. They're all hipsters, the quiet, nerdy kind with their tablets and their laptops and their goatees and unkempt hair. They're mostly men, rail-thin like addicts or vegetarians or anorexics; it's hard to tell. Some of them sport minor tattoos. They're all dressed in black. He's surprised the place offers meat of any kind. These guys are so obviously vegan you can see the lentil beans coursing through their veins.

The cheesesteak is supposedly organic, too, whatever that means.

The waiter offers him dessert. "Fair Trade Certified and Ethically Sourced Cocoa soufflé on a quinoa and caramel puddle."

Mills smiles and says, "I'll pass." Then he walks over to campus and consults a posted map for the location of the Durham Language and Literature Building, the home of the School of International Letters and Cultures. Like most campuses, ASU is a bit of a jigsaw puzzle where visitors get reliably lost, but within ten minutes he finds himself outside the drab, rectangular building.

Her office is on the third floor. The door is closed. Mills leans in, lets his ear brush against it. He expects to hear muffled pretense and hubris. He went to college, and he knows what it sounds like. But he hears nothing. The office is empty, so he takes a seat on a bench across the hallway and waits. It's 3:06. Jennifer Torento is late. Three doors down, a woman sits behind a computer in a large, well-lit office. She's clacking on her keyboard, and she's wearing a pair of ogling, trendy eyeglasses. Mills can't read the sign on her door, but she looks to be the department secretary, or whatever they call them these days. He's about to get up and inquire with her when the sound of jangling keys stops him. He turns and sees Jennifer Torento walking briskly his way. Mills smiles and meets her eyes, but she disregards him and hurriedly opens her door. Mills can see her toss her keys on the desk. She stuffs a few things in a drawer and removes a stack of papers from her bag. He stands and lingers just outside her office. When she doesn't notice, Mills raps at the doorframe.

"Can I help you?" she says, half turning. Then recognizing him, she adds, "Oh. Hello. I don't know what you're doing here, but come in."

He enters.

"Close the door," she says. "Have a seat."

"I'm sorry to show up announced," he tells her. "But I tried calling."

"This is inappropriate, I would think," she says, as if she's chiding one of her students. "If a student comes by, you're going to have to leave. Now, what can I do for you?"

"I never heard back from your husband."

She provides a cold smile. "That's between you and him."

"I have another picture to show you," he says, opening his bag.

He hands her the photo. She looks at it, then at him, her eyes begging for context.

"You recognize your husband, don't you?"

"I do."

"Well, that's him again with my murder victims."

"You're kidding me," she says, her disgust palpable but not specific.

"It looks like they were all good friends back in college," he tells her. "Like they knew each other well, obviously traveled together. Are you sure you've never heard of Davis Klink or Barry Schultz? Never ran into them at parties? Had them over to dinner?"

"I think I would remember that."

"And your husband's never mentioned them? Even since we last spoke to you?"

She winces. "A conversation with one's spouse is privileged."

"Don't go lawyering up on me just yet, Mrs. Torento. I'm only trying to help."

"Help?"

He softens his voice. "We think your husband knows something about our victims. But we don't know because he won't talk to us. And he won't talk to us because either he's involved somehow or he's scared for his life."

"Haven't we been down this road?" she asks.

"Maybe. . . ."

"I'm sorry, but I don't know how to help you. If I knew Al back in his college days, I could certainly tell you something about these men, but I didn't. And I don't keep track of his social life now."

Mills leans in. "Isn't his social life your social life?"

"No," she replies. But her answer carries the weight of more than one syllable.

"You had told us he's coming back to town next week, I think, for an event."

"Next Friday. For a fundraiser."

"If you see anything suspicious, please call me. Could I ask you to do that?"

She laughs bitterly. "I'm not sure what you mean by 'suspicious.'"

He gets up. "I think you do, Professor," he says. "You're an educated woman."

"Can I keep the photo?" she asks.

"Actually, that's a great idea," he replies. "But this one's the original. You have a scanner?"

She says there's one in the staff assistant's office. "But I don't intend to bring the photo in there." She scribbles a few words on a piece of paper and hands it to Mills. "My email address. Send me a JPEG."

"Will do. And just so you know, my idea of suspicious in this particular case could come in the form of a mysterious phone call."

Jennifer Toronto laughs again. "My husband is a US congressman. He gets mysterious phone calls all the time. They're called lobbyists."

"The deaths of Davis Klink and Barry Schultz were both preceded by a suspicious phone call," he explains. "The call prompted Klink to leave his office immediately and Schultz to bolt abruptly from his house."

Now the chill of her smile melts to a patronizing grin. "I'll keep my ears to the ground," she says. "Have a good afternoon."

Walking back to his car, crossing a wide quadrangle of central-casting students and a generic campus distinguished only by the fanfare of sunshine, Mills realizes he's lost his way. With a groan and quiet tirade of cursing, he's off to find a map.

Forensics, as Powell lays them out for him, are at this point rather mundane. There's no aha moment here. It's good police work but no forensic epiphany. The team scratched up identical fibers (black, woolen fabric) from the dirt at both gravesites. The fibers are not consistent with clothing worn by either victim and, thus, are assumed to belong to a third party, presumably the killer. All that simply confirms what Mills already suspected; two murders, same murderer. The fibers appear under Davis Klink's fingernails, indicating that the CEO might have tried fighting off his assailant before assisting in the excavation of his own grave. By "assisting," the forensics show that both Klink and Schultz only dug briefly with their hands before a shovel was introduced into the activity. There's no sign of the shovel, but marks in the dirt suggest that hands, alone, were not responsible for the shallow graves. Blood-spatter analysis concludes both impact spatters and cast-off stains at both crime scenes. Blood samples from the lab confirm that the blood found at the two crime scenes was human blood, belonging to each victim respectively. No other blood evidence was found. Lab tests for toxins are forthcoming. Shoeprint impressions in the dirt appear to match shoes worn by the victims; a third impression was taken at both scenes, results to be determined. As for fingerprints, techs identified an individual Sharpie marker at or near each grave. Latent friction ridge prints found on each match the respective victims'. Identical prints appear on the cardboard signs used to mark the graves. At the Schultz scene a second pair of prints appears on the sign but does not match prints in the criminal database system. The second pair of prints will be preserved for matches with potential suspects.

Prelims from the autopsy show that both victims died from blunt force trauma to the head—blunt craniofacial trauma—with multiple fractures of the skull resulting in brain hemorrhages. Klink time of death was approximately 10:00 p.m. Schultz time of death was approximately 11:00 p.m. As indicated in forensics reports, lab tests for drugs, poisons, and/or other toxins are forthcoming.

"I didn't say it was going to knock your socks off," Powell concedes.

"That's okay. I wasn't expecting much."

Powell starts to gather the paperwork, but Mills asks her to wait. He tells her about his visit to Jennifer Torento. Describes the nuanced shift in her attitude. "Protective but bitter, I would say. Depleted."

"Depleted?"

"Like she's had enough."

"With us?"

"Not necessarily."

Powell smiles mischievously. "I'm just surprised you haven't heard from the sergeant already, all spastic because the chief is hounding him again 'cause you're hounding Torento."

"Technically, the day isn't over," Mills says with a laugh. "And maybe Mrs. Torento didn't alert her husband this time."

"Obviously not."

"I take that as a good sign."

"You do?"

"Yes."

A long fucking day segues into a long fucking night. Not by design. He blames his provocative imagination. He recognizes it. Comes with the turf. He knows this will be one of many sleepless nights ahead. After a few hours of tossing and turning and incurring the gentle but convincing wrath of his wife, Mills climbs out of bed and heads for the family room, where he contemplates an interview with Your Pal Al. It's one o'clock in the morning. An hour later, the imagined interview turns into an interrogation and every muscle from his neck to his ass is on fire. The congressman just sits there opposite him with an insufferable smirk on his face. Mills throws a magazine at him. Then a stray shoe. The shoe lands in the fireplace they never use. Then Mills stretches out on the sofa and closes his eyes. He refuses to sleep, or his subconscious refuses to let him sleep until he has that one stroke of genius that will unmask the killer. He laughs at himself. The stroke of genius doesn't come at two in the morning. It doesn't come at two thirty. It doesn't come at three. That's when he goes back into the bedroom and collapses beside Kelly, and he's sure it's her lovely scent, a secretion all her own, that puts him at last to sleep. Three hours later, three deeply slept hours later, his phone rings. And rings. He rakes his hand across the nightstand to find the damn thing and answer it. He knocks over *Bleak House* and a water bottle. It's 6:06 a.m.

"Hello?"

"Alex Mills?"

"Yup. Who's this?"

"It's Detective Ernesto Nevada with Avondale."

"Nevada? Like the state?"

"That's correct, sir," he replies. "Sorry to wake you up at this hour."

"No problem," Mills says. "My alarm's set for six thirty. What can I do for you?"

"Your department sent out an advisory last week, I think, and I got a crime scene here in Avondale that kind of matches the description of your cases. Somebody put me through to you."

"You got a body?"

"I do."

Mills tosses the covers back, throws his legs over the side of the bed, and his feet hit the floor squarely. "No shit," he whispers, suddenly aware the conversation might disturb Kelly. He drifts into the kitchen, then sits at the breakfast bar. "Crude grave?"

"Yeah. Red Creek Cemetery."

Mills tries to stifle a yawn but can't.

Nevada recites the cross streets. Mills tells him he's on the way.

24

Jan Powell hands him a cup of coffee. They've met up in the cemetery parking lot.

"You look like shit," she tells him.

"Thanks," he says. "I told you, three hours of sleep."

"Did you speak to Woods?"

"I called him on the way out here after I called you," Mills replies. "He's aware."

They find Detective Nevada toward the back of the cemetery, almost at the fence, and they make introductions. The makeshift grave is about twenty feet away. Nevada stands about five-five and wears a baseball cap emblazoned with the Avondale Police logo. The morning's attire consists of crisp khaki shorts and a polo shirt sporting the same logo as the hat. "Looks like our John Doe is not exactly a John Doe," Nevada tells them, hosting a smile on his face. "One of my officers recognizes him."

Mills can feel the whiplash on his face. "Well, it's my lucky day," he says.

"My officer has personally arrested this guy for DUI. Twice. That's just here in Avondale," Nevada says. "He had another drunk driving offense in Scottsdale last year. How he's kept his license I don't know."

Nevada guides them over to the open grave.

"Detectives, please say hello to Joseph Gaffing, age forty-five, resident of Avondale," he recites as he hands two photos to Mills. "I had his file pulled for you. As you can see from his mug shots, we have a very likely match."

Mills stares down at the partly bludgeoned man. There's enough left of the victim's face to get a decent look. He hands a mug shot to Powell so she, too, can compare. She nods affirmatively. The face is so swollen and purple, but thankfully the guy's got a deep scar on his left cheek that matches the scar in the mug shots.

"It's him," Mills says. "But you're getting his prints just to confirm?"

"Oh, yeah," Nevada says. "We also found an abandoned Mercedes parked illegally three blocks away. Confirmed it's leased to Gaffing. So we have at least two crime scenes if you want to take a look."

"You mind if I bring out some of my techs to work alongside yours?" Powell asks.

Nevada smiles widely. "I was waiting for you to ask," he says. "I'm sure it's going to end up in your hands anyway. Something else I want to show you . . ."

Mills and Powell follow the detective to a row of bushes where a cardboard sign is resting against the hedge, blank side up. Nevada pulls on his latex gloves and flips it over. "Pretty fucking weird," he says. "I mean, I saw your advisory and all but couldn't really picture it until I saw this."

As promised another grave
I'm sorry, so sorry
For the part I played
I'm a troublemaker and this is my penance
I deserved this. Love, Joe

Mills takes a picture with his phone. "I want our photog out here," he tells Powell, and then he turns to Nevada. "Why was the sign moved? If our perp's being consistent, the sign should be right beside the grave."

The man stuffs his hands in his pocket. "Sorry about that," he says. "The groundskeeper moved it. Said it would disturb people."

"Jesus," Mills whispers. "Is that the only contamination that you know of?"

"I'm confident the rest of the scene's intact," Nevada replies.

"The groundskeeper called this in?" Mills asks.

Nevada points to a lanky guy leaning against the fence. "That's him. Hey-Zoos Pacheco. Called us around five this morning. Says he starts his day early."

"You take a statement from him?" Mills asks.

"Yep."

"I'll go have a talk as well, if you don't mind," Mills says.

"I don't. But he only speaks Spanish."

"I have to learn," Mills concedes. "Can I get his statement translated?"

"Of course."

Mills returns to the body, then kneels to the ground. The victim died wearing a black T-shirt, black jeans, and a black leather blazer. As if he just came from some kind of hipster funeral. Forty-five trying to pass for thirty. There's dirt everywhere. All over his clothes, in his hair, caked in his silver watch, and yes, Mills notes, under his fingernails. This was, as the others were, a sadistic burial. He takes a close-up shot of the guy's face and verifies that he captured every groove of the scar. He gets up, then flips through the folder Nevada handed him. Joseph Gaffing, forty-five, was not, according to his record, an angel: cocaine possession (twice), writing bad checks, forgery, domestic battery (twice), and three DUIs. Mills doesn't need to know much more to understand that Joseph Gaffing had been a lifelong party boy who became an overage party boy who pissed someone off in the same way Klink and Schultz had pissed somebody off. But there's just something about the dead man staring back at him that lacks the pedigree of a CEO or a physician— assuming a dead man can have a pedigree at all. How this man had a connection to the other victims mystifies Mills. He looks for Gaffing's last known address, picks up the phone, calls Preston, and instructs him to go knocking. The Avondale detective approaches.

"Hey, I got press gathering at the entrance," Nevada tells him.

Mills scoffs. "They're going to be waiting for a while. Too early to make a statement of any kind."

"They just want the basics."

"It's your jurisdiction," Mills says. "I'd have your sergeant call my sergeant. Let them figure it out. For now, I think your officers should get the media off cemetery property."

"Just wanted to check in case there's any reason you want to talk to them."

Mills laughs. "Are you kidding? I want the opposite of that."

Nevada drifts toward the parking lot, and Mills rejoins Powell who's watching from a distance as the Avondale team does its measurements and samplings around the gravesite. "Are you getting our techs out here?" Mills asks her.

"Still waiting to hear," she replies. "Gonna be a long day."

"Can you look something up on your iPad for me?"

She nods.

"See if this dude has a LinkedIn profile."

She pulls out her device and taps in a series of entries. She scans the screen and scrolls. At first she shakes her head and grimaces, saying without saying that this is a dead end. "Maybe he's too highly employed like a CEO, which I doubt, to be bothered with a profile," Mills says. "Or maybe he's not employed highly enough. I'm guessing the latter."

"No, wait," she says. She stops, scrolls back, and clicks. "Here he is. Joseph Gaffing. 'Owner/President Student Blast Travel.'"

"Student Blast?"

She hands him the iPad. "Here. Take a look."

The man with the scar smiles back at him. His expression in the profile photo bears no resemblance to the expression on his face this morning, but it's the same guy. He's been with the company, holding various positions, for almost thirty years. According to Gaffing's profile, Student Blast is a "full-service travel agency with a specialty in chartered student tours."

"Hmpf."

"That's all you can say?" Powell asks.

"Impressive enough," Mills says. "I mean, that he held down a job for thirty years, considering his run-ins with the law. Never mind that he ended up running the company."

"And the connection to Klink and Schultz?"

"Hell if I know. Maybe he was their travel agent," Mills says with a laugh. Then it hits him. "Wait a minute. Our boys on the beach. They were somewhere on vacation, right? Maybe that *is* the connection to Gaffing. Think I'll pay a visit."

"To?"

"Student Blast, if I can find them. Might as well do something while we're waiting for Woods," he says. "I'll put Myers on social media. From what I know about Mr. Gaffing, I'm guessing he's a frequent user, with tons of friends, and tons of parties, and tons of selfies . . ."

"And probably a few dick pics on his phone," Powell says.

"And probably a few dick pics on his phone," he affirms. "Feel free to check if you locate a device. You're scene investigator once we hear from Woods. So stick around."

"I'm not going anywhere."

When he gets to the parking lot, Mills finds that a circus of reporters and photographers and cables and lights has converged on the first available square inch of public property outside the cemetery. A few reporters recognize Mills and fire questions.

"Detective, can you confirm that this case is tied to the murders in Phoenix?"

"I have no comment at the moment."

"Can you confirm that you have a body?"

"No comment means no comment," he says but then almost instantly recoils from his own dick-waving hubris and adds, "I cannot confirm anything at this time."

"Will anyone be making a statement?" a whiny reporter shouts.

"I'm sure someone will," he replies as he reaches his car.

"When?" another barks.

"I'm sorry. I really don't know," he tells them. "But you should plan on being here a while."

As he ducks into his car, he can hear a chorus of cursing and groaning from the antsy reporters and photographers, as if, once again, a murder has failed to cater to their deadlines. He drives off, then puts Student Blast Travel into his navigator. It pulls up a Central Phoenix address, and estimates his ride at twenty-six minutes. He heads back to the highway. Morning rush hour is just clearing. About six hundred feet from the on-ramp he pulls over, mindful of two cars in his rear-view mirror. The white unmarked van slips past him, accelerates hard, and continues straight ahead. The SUV sporting the decals of KPXT TV26 hits the curb and stops abruptly. Mills jumps out of his car, holds his hands high, and points to the driver. "Roll down the window," he says. "Where you headed?"

"Back to the station," the driver says nervously.

"Really?"

"Yeah."

"Is there something wrong?" asks the reporter riding shotgun. Her voice seems to suggest some kind of First Amendment umbrage.

"I just wanted to make sure that you or the other dude behind me weren't following me," Mills tells them.

"We weren't," the driver says sheepishly.

As a detective, Mills has been lied to so many times that he no longer has to filter the answers through the truth detectors in his brain; he just has a buzzer that goes off instantaneously. He imagines it blinks red. "Well, good," he tells the news crew, "because if you were following me to my next destination, I might have to arrest you for interfering with a police investigation."

"If truth be told, we have the freedom to travel anywhere open to the public," the reporter says with all the moxie of a made-for-TV judge. "We've never been pulled over for doing our jobs."

Her driver, a cameraman no doubt, turns to her, his eyes begging her to shut up.

Mills smiles. Nods. Leans in. "You certainly raise some good points, ma'am," he says. "I'm impressed with your argument. But be forewarned that if I have to pay attention to you in my rearview mirror, tailing me, instead of paying attention to where I need to be next, that could slow me down. Much like this conversation with you is slowing me down. And if you slow me down, you impede my investigation. This is not a game. Do not follow me onto the highway. Do not do that."

She shifts in her seat. Sweat runs down the driver's neck.

"If you want to cover the story that broke this morning, you should make a U-turn and go back to the cemetery," Mills adds. "Am I clear?"

"Yes," the driver says. "Of course."

The reporter says nothing, just looks ahead, feigning interest in something beyond the windshield.

"Ma'am? I asked you a question."

"No need to be condescending," she says.

He drums the roof of the car with his hands. "Yuh. Okay. I'm honestly not trying to be condescending. I just want to be sure that you are aware of the possible consequences of following me. So, let me ask one more time. Are we clear?"

"We are," she says, sneering.

He's probably just broken a thousand rules just now, but he doesn't give a shit.

He arrives, not followed, about twenty-five minutes later. Student Blast Travel occupies a one-story, low-slung yellowish building on Seventh Avenue, north of Osborn. If Gaffing worked at this place for almost thirty years, it's fair to say that in his tenure the cosmetics of the business never underwent a facelift. Even the posters in the window (Jamaica! Cabo! Puerto Plata! Cancun!) show signs of sun damage, fading, crackling, their corners curling. Mills walks in to find busy cubicles, about eight pods of four stations. The buzz of operators chanting, "It's the best spring break you'll ever have!" and "Would you like the beverage bracelet option?" sounds a lot to Mills like children singing rounds of "Row, Row, Row Your Boat."

He stands at the entrance, waiting to be noticed. When no one looks up he clears his throat. When no one hears him he raps his fist against a tabletop of brochures. That rouses a woman in the nearest pod who removes her headset and says, "Can I help you with something?"

"Is this business owned and operated by Joseph Gaffing?"

"Yes."

Others, still chatting with customers, turn and eye Mills curiously. "I need some information about the company," he tells the woman.

"Let me get Wanda, the supervisor."

Mills steps back, and, less than ten seconds later, he's rewarded for waiting by the appearance of a young woman who steps out from a far-corner office. She wears a tight blouse and a tight skirt and a pair of heels that give her tiny frame a six-inch lift. He introduces himself and flashes a badge at an angle that only she can appreciate, and she escorts him back to her office. It's a haphazard, low-budget version of a corner office, not much more than drywall and random windows that allow the occupant to spy on the minimum-wagers in the call center. There are two potted plants, fake.

"What has he done now?" Wanda wants to know, dread all over her face.

"I can't say," Mills replies. "But I need to get in touch with his nearest relative. I was hoping someone could help me do that."

Her expression changes. Dread becomes fear. "Is he okay? Did something happen to him?"

"Again, I can't say specifically," Mills replies. "But if something did, we'd sure want his family to be the first to know."

"We sort of are his family," she said, her lips turning inward.

"Is he married?"

"Divorced," she says, and the answer doesn't surprise Mills given Gaffing's rap sheet.

"What about kids?"

"No kids," she says. "His dad still comes by every so often, and he has a sister, but last I heard she's in rehab."

The woman diverts her attention to her computer screen and aggressively types away at her keyboard. Then she scribbles something on a notepad, rips the sheet, and hands it to Mills.

"Phone number and address for Mr. Gaffing," she tells him. "Joe's father."

He thanks her. "You said he comes by often? Does he work for Joe?"

She smiles. "No. It's sort of the other way around. Joe Senior owned this company for, like, twenty or thirty years," she says. "He handed it to his son a few years ago. But he still keeps tabs. He really doesn't want to let go, if you know what I mean."

"I don't blame him," Mills says vaguely and then adds, "The name of the company suggests you specialize in student travel."

"We're the number one charter company for spring break events in the country," she says proudly, her face brightening.

Mills turns around in his chair and surveys the call center; he turns back with doubt all over his face. "Out of here? The number one charter company is operated out of this small office?"

"Ninety percent of our business is completely automated online," she explains. "That's how we grew so fast. Joe Senior was responsible for putting us online. Years ago. We were the first to convert to a cyber platform."

"Joe Senior?" Mills asks. "Odd that the older Joe would be the cyber guy, not the son. . . ."

She shrugs. "Joe Senior knew how to grow the business like nobody else."

"So what exactly is Joe Junior's role?"

She giggles for a second and then self-corrects, sits up in her tight attire, and folds her hands on the desk. "He's the face of the company," she says deadpan. "And he's in charge of payroll and other human resources stuff."

Mills rises to his feet, extending a hand. "Thank you, Ms.—"

She gives him her card. "Melendez."

"Melendez," he repeats. "You've been an enormous help."

> Joe Gaffing Sr.
> 18602 West Laredo
> Glendale, AZ

First he texts Morty Myers: "When you're done w/social media, I need you to pull all Sec of State records on Student Blast Travel. AM."

Next he texts Ken Preston: "When you're done with the real estate, head out to Avondale, assist Powell. AM."

Then he calls Joseph Gaffing Sr. and reaches the man's voice mail. He enters the address into his navigator and drives. He drives in thoughtful silence. He's determined, of what he's not exactly sure. He just feels determined, and it's not only about solving the case; it's also about being at the top of his game, or at least returning to the top of his game, getting purposeful. He grips the wheel. He's too often distracted by the bumps in the road (people who don't answer the phone, who don't finish their jobs, who shun accountability, who let their dogs shit all over his yard—literally and metaphorically) that he forgets about the passion that fuels his engine. Objectively speaking (and he's imagining himself in front of an objective mirror here), he gives more shit about fighting crime than he can possibly count. He thrives on it, probably gives him the same satisfaction, if not the six-million-dollar bonus, as someone like Davis Klink signing a merger or acquisition deal. Every day is like a puzzle. Passion connects the dots, fills in the blanks, solves the crime. He lives for it. But the fucking clusterfuck of humanity and all its petty fucking grievances and bureaucratic bullshit and political fucking posturing and all the miserable people and their miserable lives—it's enough to burn a guy out. He's burnt out. He's known this for a while. The business with Trevor doesn't help. But now, here on this drive, gripping the wheel, he realizes it is he, alone, who can burn himself back in. So, surveying the clusterfuck of everything now is not an exercise in masochism; it's an exercise in liberation.

Joe Gaffing Sr. doesn't live in splendor. He doesn't even live in a McMansion. Odd for someone who runs/ran "the number one charter company for spring break events in the country." Joe Gaffing Sr. lives in a typical suburban, cookie-cutter stucco home with a faded red tile roof. The garage door is open. A car is parked in the driveway. Even a detective without a full tank of mojo would know those are signs that someone's home.

He rings the bell, and a dog barks. He hears the scuffle of feet, both human and canine. Someone says, "Stop your yapping." The door swings open, and standing at the threshold is an older man, easily seventy, in a T-shirt and shorts. He's taller than Mills, maybe by two inches, with shoulders that are wide but bowed with age. A basketball player in his day, Mills guesses. He wears white ankle socks, no shoes. His eyes are grayish. "Yes?"

"I'm Detective Alex Mills with the Phoenix Police Department."

"What do you want with me?"

"Are you Joe Gaffing Senior?"

The man says, "Yes," packing quite a bit of suspicion into one syllable.

"It's about your son."

The man looks down and shakes his head. "What has he done now?"

Mills senses a pattern. *What has he done now?* That might have made a more fitting inscription on the sign at Junior's grave.

"May I come in?"

Gaffing sways his head back and forth a bit, considering the request. "Yeah, I guess," he says. "But the place is very messy today. I hope you don't mind."

Mills offers a genuine smile. "I've seen everything in my line of work, sir. I'm sure your house is no messier than average."

The guy shrugs and leads him inside, through a living room, a dining room, a kitchen, and out to an all-season porch, proving Mills wrong one room at a time. The house is messier than average. Ghastly messier. A sink overflows with dishes. An avalanche of laundry pours off a recliner. Sticky floors throughout rival those of any movie theater. The screeching smell of incalculable dog urine just about takes his breath away.

Mills begins to sit, subtly inspecting the cushion upon which his ass will rest. A landfill of contamination, he assumes. He winces and says, "I'm sorry to have to tell you this, Mr. Gaffing, but I believe your son was the victim of a homicide. We found his body this morning."

The outbreak of confusion on the man's face is barely visible, but Mills can see it. He's seen it a million times. "I, uh, what?" Gaffing stutters.

"Do you know why anyone would want to harm your son, sir?"

The man sits there, his hand covering his mouth. He's shaking his head, and he won't stop shaking it as he stares off into nowhere; it's that nowhere that Mills is determined to visit. Joe Gaffing must be looking at his son's history, the good and the bad and the awful, must be reviewing life events, the ones that come flooding back at times like this.

"I don't know," Gaffing says.

"This is a shock, I realize that," Mills tells him. "But something is bound to come to you that will help us piece this thing together."

"I mean, I know my son has his problems, but . . . Are you sure it's him, Detective?"

Mills nods slowly. "We identified him by the scar on his cheek on one of his social media profiles. We'll likely get a fingerprint match in the database, considering his record," he explains. "And we found his car abandoned near the crime scene."

The man balls his fists. "Oh, my God," he moans. "He's all I have left."

Mills does an inquisitive tilt of his head. "I'm sorry. I thought you also had a daughter."

"She's been in and out of rehab for years. She doesn't talk to me. We're strangers."

"And your wife?"

"Died a year ago," he answers.

The man had all but given up. The state of his house can attest to that. "Is there anybody you can call?" Mills asks.

"Like who?"

"A relative? A friend?"

"I got distant cousins in Florida," he says. "My wife was the social butterfly. My best friend was always my business, she would say."

"From what I understand, you still run most of the business today."

Gaffing gets up with a sigh and crosses the porch as if he's leaving. At the entrance to the kitchen he turns back and offers Mills something to drink. He declines. Mills listens as ice cubes plummet into a glass, as liquid splashes over. When Gaffing returns he's carrying an amber liquid, like Scotch, in his glass. Mills doesn't need to ask, or to take a whiff. The piercing sting of the whiskey curls up his nose, displacing for a moment the baseline smell of dog piss. Gaffing sits, swirls the liquid.

"I handed off the business to Joe almost three years ago," he says. "I still own a share, and I have to keep an eye on the place, you know, to protect my interests."

"Considering your son's run-ins with the law, that's understandable," Mills replies. "I'm familiar with his record. You think maybe a victim of his forgery or bad checks was looking for revenge?"

"That was so long ago."

"Revenge can take a lifetime."

"I don't think so."

"What about the drugs?" Mills asks. "Do you know if he was in debt to support his drug habit?"

The man scoffs bitterly. "I wouldn't call it a drug habit, Detective. He was arrested a couple of times for possession. It's not like he was drugged up all the time. He never stole money from me, you know. He wasn't a lowlife. I want you to understand that. Despite his faults, he was a good kid."

Mills slides forward, then leans in. "Do the names Davis Klink and Barry Schultz mean anything to you?"

Gaffing ponders this. Eyes wide, searching. "No. They don't. Should they?"

Mills doesn't reply, instead offering two open palms, his hands lingering there like a bid for more.

"Who are they?" Gaffing asks.

"Klink and Schultz were killed, we believe, in a similar fashion to your son."

"You *believe*?"

"Yes," Mills says. "We would wait until all the forensics come back on your son before drawing a final conclusion. But preliminary observations would suggest that a similar weapon was used in all three cases and a nearly identical venue was chosen. The bodies were all found in cemeteries."

"Holy shit," the man cries. "Are you talking about those murders I saw in the news?"

"Unfortunately, yes."

Gaffing takes a full gulp of Scotch. "No way," he says after the swallow and the requisite airing of his throat. "There's just no way."

"You mean you have no knowledge that your son had any connection to Klink or Schultz?"

Another sip. "That's what I mean."

The man's eyes fill. The tears don't spill, but they gather like lenses of brimming grief, and that flood of pain is almost harder for Mills to watch. He studies the family photographs on the wall, looking for an anomaly, the aha image that might suggest how the younger Gaffing deviated from the normal path of family life. The four Gaffings pose happily for a family portrait. Judging from the clothes, the hair, and the younger faces, the happiness was captured, maybe, in the 1980s. There's no evidence of happiness beyond that era, since that family portrait seems to be the most recent one hanging on the wall. There's a photo of Joe Jr. swinging a bat. There's a photo of the daughter on horseback. She's probably sixteen, and she looks high even then. Thanks to the family business, Joe Sr. and his wife had plenty of places to flee. In a few photos they're posing on cruise ships. The next display is a collage of beaches, one at sunset, one at sunrise, two under a fierce blue sky, waves shimmering below. The overall effect of this collection of shots is to capture an average family doing average things and making average attempts to keep life uncomplicated and free of messes. The daughter, in cap and gown, graduates from high school and holds her diploma wide open; there's glee in her eyes, somewhere behind the dilated pupils. Joe Jr. graduates from high school, looks pissed off at something, clutching his diploma closed as if he has nothing to prove to anyone.

"Mr. Gaffing, did your son go on to college?" Mills asks. "Did he, by any chance, attend U of A?"

The man wipes his eyes on his sleeve and laughs. "My son didn't make it through his freshman year of community college," he says. "He came to work for me. It was the best thing for him."

"I'm told he was divorced."

"That's true," Gaffing says.

"And the ex-wife?"

"She'd never hurt him, Detective. She was an angel."

"What happened?"

"My son was not an angel, as his record clearly shows, and she got fed up."

"He beat her?"

"Like I said, his record clearly shows . . ."

Mills nods. "Were they in touch?"

The man shakes his head. "She lives in Montana, last I heard. I don't think they've spoken since the divorce was final fifteen, maybe twenty years ago."

Mills gets to his feet and hands the man his card. "If you have any questions, call me. If you think of anything that might help our investigation of your son's murder, do the same."

"I want to see my boy," Gaffing says, a solitary tear escaping the corner of his eye.

"You'll be contacted when his body is ready, sir."

In his car, Mills dials Jacob Woods. If a sneer could talk, it would sound like the sergeant's voice, aloof at its center, serrated around the edges. Avondale will yield, the sergeant confirms. "But, at this point, we might be better off handing the whole damn case over to our friends at the FBI."

The offhanded remark has the combined effect of an insult and a threat. This is Jacob Woods brandishing a short lease. Mills doesn't respond. He simply says, "I'll let my scene investigator know."

"While you're at it, tell Jan her resources are on the way."

And that's all Mills hears from his boss for the rest of the day.

25

Gus Parker slurps on a hearty soup at Beatrice Vossenheimer's dining room table. The evening had turned chilly, the temperature dipping to a mere sixty-three degrees. The fireplace is roaring, and the soup is hot, and it feels good. "A German specialty," she tells him.

A creamy broth surrounds dumplings, thick vegetables, and hunks of chicken.

"What's it called?"

"Geflügelsuppe Beatrice."

"What does that mean?"

"Beatrice's chicken soup."

Gus laughs. "I'm not supposed to be here."

"Because?"

"Because Alex said he could only protect me in Phoenix," Gus replies. "That's why I'm not staying at Billie's."

She stops, her spoon halfway to her mouth, and says, "So you'll spend an hour with me for dinner and go home. You can't be at your house every single minute you're not working."

"I have a client tonight anyway," Gus says. "Eight o'clock."

Beatrice blows on the puddle of soup in her spoon and swallows. She passes Gus a bowl of salad, then a plate of bread. She turns her face to the pink sky sitting outside her panoramic window. Gus follows her eyes to the view and instantly knows their intuitions are about to collide.

"Alex really thinks you're in danger," she says.

"I told you as much."

"He's right."

"Is it something that you see?" he asks.

"It's something that I feel."

"Fantastic."

"But no one's going to be pushing you off a roof, Gus."

He swallows a tomato. Bites his lip. "I never said anything about the woman falling."

"You saw a woman falling?"

"From a rooftop," he says. "I was going to fill you in on everything over coffee."

"And cake."

"And cake," he mutters absently. "But you're having hunches about my hunches."

"I'm having a hunch about your safety," she says. "I'd tell you to stay here, but Alex can't give you the protection here."

Over coffee and cake, mostly cake, Gus describes the visions he had at the doctor's office. "The Spanish music, the woman falling, falling from the roof, I don't know," he says. "I don't know how or why or where it fits into the context of these crimes."

"Not yet," she says. "I sense something is coming, gathering."

"Like what?"

She squeezes her eyes closed. She's chewing up another morsel of cake (German chocolate). She savors and swallows and says, "I don't know. Like a storm. A hurricane."

Gus laughs. "A hurricane? In Phoenix? That's crazy."

She opens her eyes and smiles. "I don't see it as much as I sense it. It's very convincing. Be prepared to evacuate."

"Well, I'm evacuating now, Beatrice. Gotta head home."

She gets up and grabs him by the arm. "You watch yourself. And open those eyes in the back of your head. Do not take Alex's warning lightly, my darling. Do not take it lightly."

With that sunny advice, Gus goes home and meets with his client. Barbara Rosenstein has to be one of the sunniest people who's ever walked into Gus's life. She wears it on her face, this warmth. She's a seventy-five-year-old woman, and she's been coming to see Gus once a month for the past year ever since her older sister passed away. Even in grief, Barbara Rosenstein refuses to be unhappy. Sometimes she just comes to talk, free of questions, free of concerns. Early on, Gus told her that he rarely, if ever, talks to dead people. He's not a medium like that. To which, she simply shrugged and said, "I already have one of those." She sits opposite him now with her blondish hair coiffed and her fingernails polished a shiny blood red. Her voice is from the old days when elocution was perfect and the accents favored a proper English, not like the British, more like the Boston Brahmins. "You're better than a therapist, Gus."

"I don't know about that."

"Trust me. I've tried a few."

"Give me your hands."

She complies, and he holds her dainty hands in his as if he's holding a tiny finch. He closes his eyes. He waits for those dark curtains to part and reveal. While he does, he feels the heat from her hands flow into his palms and tingle his wrists and radiate up his arms. She rises through his chest, and the curtains open, and there she is on the open sea, her face to the sun, her peace indelible. The ocean sparkles like a million jewels. She's laughing now in his vision, and she's truly free, there on the veranda of a majestic cruise ship, brilliant white on brilliant blue. He opens his eyes.

"I have to ask this question," he says. "I'm sorry if it feels inappropriate. But did you have your sister cremated?"

"Her children did," she replies. "We haven't done anything with the ashes."

"Right. I'm getting that."

"Go on!" she cries. "Go on, Gus."

"As sure as I'm holding your hands right now, I'm seeing something I'm profoundly sure of. It's in my bones," he says. "Have you thought about spreading them at sea?"

"Oh, Gus! That's exactly what she wanted."

"I know it probably sounds like a cliché or a likely guess," he concedes, "but I truly see you liberating yourself as you liberate her on the open ocean."

She squeezes his hands. "Amazing," she says. "We've been planning to do a cruise, the kids and I, and to bring her ashes along to be spread at sea, but we can't agree on the sea! Can you believe that? We're having a hard time picking the right body of water."

She laughs cheerfully at her own conundrum.

He wants to grab her by the shoulders and hug her tightly. Had he had a mother like Barbara Rosenstein he would have worshipped her. She would have mothered from a pedestal in the clouds. But he had not had such a parent. Not even close. Meg Parker did not believe in holding hands, did not believe in warmth, doled out affection even less than she doled out approval. She had been more tethered to the church than to her children. If he were to blame anyone or anything, and he really doesn't at this point in his life, he would blame the church for getting in the way of good parenting.

"Stay away from her. Stay away from her."

"What did you say, Gus?" Barbara asks.

"Huh?"

"You were talking about my sister's ashes."

"Stay away from her!"

"Gus! What are you saying?"

The desperation in her voice breaks his trance. "I don't know. I'm sorry."

"I'm so confused," she tells him.

"What did you hear me say?"

"You were telling me to stay away from her," she says, her voice shaking. "You said it a couple of times."

"No, no, no," he begs. He squeezes her hands tighter. "I'm so sorry. My visions got crossed. That had nothing to do with you."

He's tapping the floor, his knee bouncing. Jesus Christ, he gets it. Stay away from her. How many times does he need to be reminded? He's staying away from her. He's doing just what the stalker has asked. He closes his eyes tightly, wills away the malevolence. He gets it. He gets it. Enough. He stands in the rain. He's drenched, and then he's clean. He's wearing linen. He's perched at the stern of a ship. A valley of water spreads from the wake all the way to the horizon. The wind and the spray permeate. There are beaches out there, some with thick groves of palms. The lazy trees, bending low over the azure waters, glow in the golden fire of a late-afternoon sun. "I would say the Caribbean Sea, or the Mediterranean," he tells Barbara. "And I say this not necessarily because of their beauty."

He hears a tiny laugh. "Then why?" she asks.

"My sense is that the big oceans are too big," he replies. "I can tell how hard it is for you to let go. The Caribbean and the Mediterranean are big enough for her freedom but not so big that you won't be able to pinpoint. My hunch is that you'll want to pinpoint. You'll want to look at a map and say, 'See there she is.' I think the big oceans are too vast for you to do that, Barbara."

He opens his eyes.

"Oh, you're brilliant," she gushes. "Just the answer I needed to hear!"

She leans forward and kisses his cheek, and he sits there as it lands, letting it sink in.

Mills has homework. After dinner he's on his laptop and downloads the PDF Myers had attached containing the secretary of state records on Student Blast Travel. The company has filed its paperwork every year as required. The only significant change came three years ago when Joseph Sr. and Joseph Jr. swapped roles as president and vice president. Joseph Jr. is the owner of record and has been since the swap of titles. This corroborates with what Mills heard earlier in the day. He scrolls down. As far as the state is concerned, the company has had no meaningful events in almost fifteen years since it changed its name from Vacation Express & Student Escapes to Student Blast Travel. There's no explanation for the name change, and there wouldn't be in the state record; Joseph Sr. was president and owner of record at the time and had been since the company's inception. State records fail to excite Alex Mills, and these are no exception, so his next stop is Google, if for no other reason than pure entertainment. There's nothing like pulling the lever of a search engine and waiting for slots to fall into place. Mills remembers the days before the instant gratification of Google; research was real research, with phone calls, clandestine meetings (there are still clandestine meetings, but they're usually the by-product of finding someone on Google), and real fucking sweat.

He types, "Vacation Express & Student Escapes."

He knows it's a long shot since the name change dates back fifteen years, but he also knows that most newspapers have digitized their archives a lot further back, even if state agencies have not kept the exact pace. Still, the results are weedy. When he doesn't see an exact match word for word on the first page of results, he balks at the prospect of clicking secondary pages. He's not interested in a cyber goose chase. But then, what the hell, he clicks on page two. And then page three. And there on the third page is this headline:

PHOENIX GIRL DIES ON COLLEGE TRIP
LED BY LOCAL COMPANY

The archived story recounts the death of nineteen-year-old Rory Clarke, a sophomore at Northern Arizona University. The student had traveled to Mexico on a spring break trip led by Vacation Express & Student Escapes, a Phoenix-based travel agency. With one day left on the trip, the teenager died when two speedboats crashed in front of the Cancun resort where she had been staying as part of the chartered vacation. The boat in which she was riding splintered into a dozen pieces. Three other students were critically injured. Mills looks at the date of the article, does the math. The accident happened fifteen years ago and just six months before the Gaffings filed paperwork to change the name of their company. Alone in his office, just the dim glow of the desk lamp lighting the room, Mills feels a shadow of antipathy cover his face. It's the disgust and the sadness and the entire fucking dark hole of the human condition to which he too often permits occupancy in his head. Vacation Express & Student Escapes denied all culpability in the death of Rory Clarke. The company, according to the article, insisted that Clarke had booked the speedboat excursion independently and that the outing was not a tour-sponsored activity. Mills clicks on related articles and reads about the lawsuit filed by Rory Clarke's parents, claiming negligence and lack of supervision against Gaffing's company, a lawsuit that was settled out of court for an undisclosed amount.

After Googling "Student Blast Travel," Mills finds that the past fifteen years have been somewhat less eventful for the Gaffings, save for half a dozen lawsuits alleging the company cheated students and other customers out of money and one investigation, two years ago, by the state attorney general's office into (1) false and misleading advertising, (2) unfair and deceptive business practices, and (3) fraud.

In other words, a scam. The company paid a fine.

Mills logs off and heads to bed. He pulls Kelly close to him. Her damp, sweet nakedness makes him hard. But she's sleeping.

The irony of waking up to the sound of a woodpecker is not lost on him. The creature has been stalking the neighborhood for months, pecking at house trim, leaving clear evidence of his vandalism in the form of modest craters from one house to another. Looks like the aftermath of a drive-by shooting. Kelly is up. He hears the blow-dryer. Trevor knocks on the door. Mills tells him to enter.

"I need fifty bucks," his son announces.

"For what?"

"Senior day," Trevor replies.

"When is it?"

"Next month. The deadline's today."

"Well, it's a good thing you didn't put it off 'til the last minute."

The boy scoffs. "C'mon, Dad."

"What if I didn't have the cash today, Trevor?"

"I'd ask Mom, or follow you to the ATM."

Mills laughs. "You're hysterical, young man."

"Ask Mom what?" It's Kelly emerging from the bathroom.

Trevor repeats the request.

"That's a lot of money," she says.

"It includes everything. All meals, entertainment, the water park, everything."

Mills reaches for his wallet, then stops. "You think you're old enough to have sex, right? Then I think you're old enough to earn the money yourself."

"What do you mean?" Trevor asks.

"It means I have a garage that needs to be cleaned out. Our guest bath needs a paint job. And the windows! It's time to clean them inside and out. Could take days!"

"I see your point."

"Agreed, then?"

"Agreed."

When Trevor leaves the room, Kelly gives her husband a high five. And that's all he needs. That's enough to renew his vigor. So he showers, shaves, shoves breakfast in his mouth. His whole cadence is different. Add that to his new fuel for work and his footsteps have more bounce, less drudgery. His eyes are open. His brain, usually flatlining at this hour, has a pulse. His routine flies.

Only to come to a skidding, slamming, crashing thud when he and his team are summoned to Sergeant Jacob Woods's conference room and enter to find Mayor Scott Hurley sitting at the head of the table. Woods is next to him at the left-hand corner.

"Come in. Have a seat," the sergeant tells them. "Sorry to call you up on such short notice, but as you can see we have a guest."

Mills nods at his team, and they all sit. And all he can think is *Jesus fucking Christ. There's not enough caffeine in the world to face this douchebag first thing in the morning.* "Good morning, Mr. Mayor," he says with a straight face.

"Am I next?" Hurley asks.

"Huh?"

"Am I next?"

The man has always appeared to Mills as half human, half Donald Duck. He's not exactly sure what it is, the shape of the face, maybe, or the shape of the mouth, or the permanent craze in his eyes like two emblems of happy insanity, but the voters of Phoenix most certainly elected a leader with at least partial roots in cartoon lore.

"Maybe we haven't had enough coffee this morning," Mills tells the mayor. "But I don't think we follow you."

He dares to turn to the rest of his team who dare to uniformly shake their heads.

The mayor leans forward, resting his arms on the table in front of him. "Let me elaborate," he says, as if he's already articulated a meaningful reason for this meeting. "You keep finding signs that say, 'Who's Next?' and I want to know if I'm next."

"You mean next to be murdered?" Mills asks.

"That's what I mean."

"First of all," Mills begins, "we've only found one or two signs that say exactly that, and they've both been followed by dead bodies. So, all accounted for. The most recent sign was discovered Tuesday with Mr. Gaffing's body. It didn't suggest anyone would be next."

"So, are you just going to wait for another threatening sign to turn up before you do something?" Hurley asks.

"You mean another 'Who's Next?' sign?"

Hurley lets out a gust of air that imparts his disgust. "I hope you catch on faster when you're out there investigating, Detective."

"I assure you this has nothing to do with catching on," Mills says. "But I deal in certitudes, Mr. Mayor. And I'm, honestly, not at all certain why you would think you'd be our killer's next victim."

Mills can hear Powell try to stifle a laugh. He kicks her under the table.

"Because," the half man, half duck begins to answer, "it might as well be me. You got three victims so far. You don't have any solid leads. I might as well die right along with my city."

Mills looks directly at his sergeant. In his eyes, Mills is clearly but mutely begging his boss to explain why the fuck he was called up here to respond to such utter fucking nonsense. Woods looks down, feigning interest in his notes.

Fine, then.

"Well, come on, Scott," Mills says to the mayor. "You dying right along with your city? Don't you think that's a stretch?"

Woods coughs out loud. Powell stifles another laugh. Preston smiles.

"No, I don't think it's a stretch," the mayor says to the team. "The other victims are fairly prominent men in the valley. Why wouldn't I be next?"

Now it's Mills who must stifle a laugh. "Because, contrary to your assertion that we have no leads, we believe our victims knew one another. We're fairly certain they're connected," he explains. "So, if you had any personal relationships with Davis Klink, Barry Schultz, or Joe Gaffing, it would be in your best interests to tell us. Since you have not indicated that to us thus far in our investigation, Scott, we feel fairly confident that you are not on the killer's radar."

Nobody speaks.

Woods shuffles papers around as if he's actually looking for something.

An airplane roars overhead.

Morton Myers yawns unabashedly.

And then Preston says, "You know, Mr. Mayor, I've been sitting here listening to this whole meeting, and I'm still not sure what you're here to tell us."

The half man, half duck coughs so vigorously that his neck vibrates and his puffy cheeks shake at the force. "I'm here to tell you that I'm doing a press conference today." He emphasizes the word "today," and it lands with the intended thud. "And," the mayor continues, "I want all four of you there with your sergeant. I'll speak. The sergeant will speak. But we'll refer all questions to you, Detective Mills, and your squad. I think you all should go now and prepare. Fully prepare. Any questions?"

"No questions," Mills says.

"Good," the mayor says. "Because my office has been absolutely swamped with calls. This department has been too quiet. The public has a right to know. People are scared. This is no way to stay on the list of the ten best places to raise your kids!"

His pronouncements done, Scott Hurley gets up and briskly rubs his hands together as if he's washing them after the first mayoral shit of the day. When he's gone, the rest of them get up to file out, and, to Mills's surprise, Woods turns and says, "Good job, Alex."

There was no sarcasm. No snark.

The three-thirty press conference starts precisely at three fifty because the reporters and the photographers can't get out of each other's way. Radio reporters, television reporters, and newspaper reporters all jockey for the best seat in the house, particularly the front two rows, while the photographers scramble to run cables, erect tripods, and test microphones. Mills has seen it all before. He's watching from a window outside the community room. He can tell the TV reporters from the rest of them, in part because he recognizes some of them, but mostly because they're the highly coiffed ones, particularly the women in their tight, loudly colored pantsuits and luxury jewelry, their dubiously high but matching heels, and their heavily made-up faces (though there's no lack of makeup on the TV guys, either). The newspaper reporters make an effort to look presentable but lack the crispness and conspicuous indulgences of their television counterparts. The radio reporters mostly don't give a fuck as reflected in their pajama-quality attire, rumpled at best. They've come from all over today: the TV affiliates from Phoenix and Tucson, one all the way from Yuma, and newspapers and radio stations from cities and towns throughout the state. You'd think there'd been an outbreak of Ebola. Mills assumes Mayor Scott "Duckling" Hurley sent out a press release first thing this morning before he even met with the police department. But if the crowd is meant to pressure Mills, it doesn't. The mayor had ordered him and his team to prepare, and they did, not in any extraordinary fashion, just to the extent that they practiced what they would or would not say.

Mills enters the room last, following his team and the others. Josh Grady, one of the department's public information sergeants, opens the press conference with a polite explanation of the ground rules. "Both my sergeant, Jacob Woods, spelled just how it sounds, and the mayor will make prepared statements," he tells the group. "Then I will open it up for a limited number of questions to our detectives."

He identifies the detectives on Mills's squad and offers the proper spelling of their names. Then Grady introduces the mayor, who steps to the podium with a burst of energy in his feet and a burst of hubris on his face, as if he's accepting a fucking Nobel Prize. "Hello, everyone," Hurley says. "Thank you very much for being here. I know many of you came far. My first responsibility is to the people of Phoenix, and I want to tell them that our police professionals are following every lead to bring this killer to justice. We know many of you have been asking why city leaders haven't held a press conference lately, and we want to assure you that the investigation is the first and foremost priority. Revealing too much too soon could hinder the work of our detectives. But we also know that our residents are justifiably scared about their safety and the safety of their children. While it's true that we have not apprehended a suspect, we don't believe these murders are entirely random. Evidence at this stage suggests that they're not. I'll leave it to the sergeant to speak to the evidence, but let me just suggest to you today that that we don't see this as a widespread danger to the population at large. It should be business as usual in the great city of Phoenix, and living as usual, as well."

Half man, half duck makes a few more broad, cheery, Chamber of Commerce statements to the crowd and steps down from the podium. Next Grady introduces Sergeant Jacob Woods who, Mills knows, must tap dance around some of the mayor's misstatements and vague generalities, thus explaining the sergeant's less eager stride and less eager eyes when he faces the reporters. "It is accurate to say that we are following every lead in the case. At present we have three victims. All males. Davis Klink, forty-seven. Barry Schultz, forty-six, and Joseph Gaffing Junior, forty-five. Cause of death appears to be the same in each case, and I say 'appears' because final autopsy and toxicology results have not been returned. The killer's MO appears to be consistent. While we don't believe these murders are entirely random at this point, we're not concluding that. I appreciate the mayor's trust in me, however I will not speak to evidence at this time. You can ask evidence-related questions of my investigators, and they can determine if they want that information released. The three murders have happened in fairly rapid succession, and the department, consequently, is having its resources a bit stretched. We are confident, however, that we can get the job done with the resources we have. That said, while I agree with Mayor Hurley that activities in Phoenix should be business as usual, we'd like our residents to be highly aware of their surroundings. If you see something, say something. Call our tip line with reports of any suspicious activities. Thank you."

Grady asks Mills and his team to gather at the podium. Mills calls on a reporter from the Associated Press first. "With all due respect," the woman begins, which is never a good beginning, "what we have heard so far today doesn't really advance our understanding of the investigation. Can you tell us how close you are to naming a suspect?"

Mills thanks her for the question. "By better understanding who these victims are, we are a lot closer to identifying a suspect. We do believe we are dealing with one killer with virtually the same MO."

"So could someone please tell us what the mysterious MO actually is?" asks a radio reporter with a face full of boredom in the front row.

"Not entirely," Mills replies. "Most of you know that the bodies of our victims were found in makeshift graves at cemeteries throughout the valley. It appears they all suffered blunt force trauma to the head, which led to their deaths. I'm not going to elaborate on the MO any further at this point in order to protect the integrity of the investigation."

"What kind of evidence did you gather at the crime scenes?" asks a youngish TV reporter with purple lipstick.

"I'm not going to comment on specific evidence," Mills says.

Another TV reporter, not to be undone, yells out a question. "Are we talking about a serial killer?"

"That depends on your definition of a serial killer," Mills tells him.

The young man smirks. "Uh, how about one killer who kills many people?"

"That's not exactly the textbook definition," Mills informs him. "And here's our distinction: a serial killer is more likely to kill random victims or random individuals who fit a certain victim profile. A killer who kills victims known to him is less likely to be characterized as a serial killer. This doesn't hold true all the time, but it's a general guide. And, as the mayor indicated earlier, we don't think these murders were necessarily random."

"Why not?" asks Sally Tobin, the matriarch of Phoenix reporting. Mills guesses she's pushing sixty because she's been with the *Republic* for almost forty years.

"We're following leads that suggest the killer in these cases may have a singular motive to commit these murders," Mills tells her.

"And that motive is?" Sally continues.

Mills looks to Powell, who says, "We can't comment on that yet."

Sally shakes her head dismissively, not entirely disrespectfully, just an I'm-not-buying-it gesture from the old school when cops and reporters tangled over cold beers in dark bars rather than hot coffee in bright conference rooms. This is the new school where reporters half Sally's age dispatch a constant stream of press conference morsels in 280 characters or less. In a social media orgy, they feverishly poke at their smartphones while Sally writes longhand. The others need to be more like Sally.

Mills's phone vibrates. He looks quickly. It's a text message from Roni in the lab: "Done with Maserati. Impound?"

Discreetly he types, "Yes. Thanks."

Greer LaFountaine, a TV anchor in a pink pantsuit, heels to match, says, "Sources have told me that you have surveillance video of the first victim, Davis Klink, walking away from his car with the presumed suspect. Is that true, and, if so, will that video be released?"

"I can't comment on the existence of a video," Mills tells her.

"But my sources verified you have it," the TV anchor insists.

"We may," Mills advises her. At this point he's deadpan. "And if we do, it would not be in the best interests of the investigation to release it at this time."

"What if someone could identify the killer in the video?" Greer fires back.

"Are we having a debate?" Grady asks her. "Our case agent already answered your question."

Mills calls on an older, professorial-looking man. "I'm Earl Simons, from the *Apache Junction Times-Dispatch*," the man says. "Do you believe the killer is still in the area?"

"Yes, we believe the killer is in the area," Powell replies.

"But you can't tell us what evidence seems to indicate that?" Greer LaFountaine snipes at the detective.

That's all Mills needs to hear. "No, we can't tell you," he says directly to Greer. "I think that's going to do it for today, folks. We know you all have deadlines to meet and tweets to tweet, so thank you very much for coming. Any additional questions you can direct to Josh Grady, our PIO."

The press doesn't seem to recognize the end of the press conference, swept up as they are in a torrent of tweeting. When he and his squad are alone in the elevator heading upstairs, Mills turns to them and says, "That accomplished nothing. Trouble is our dimwitted mayor didn't see the shit show he was creating with that press conference. And he probably still doesn't."

"We didn't break any news, if that's what those reporters were looking for," Powell adds.

Mills says, "That's exactly what they were looking for. But we gave 'em a few tidbits, maybe a fresher perspective on things."

Powell scoffs. "It has to be obvious to them we don't have a motive yet. The waltz we did around that one was good enough for *Dancing with the Stars*."

"You think we did more harm than good?" Myers asks.

"I think it was a wash," Mills says.

Silence between the second and third floors.

"But we sounded good," Myers says as they ascend to the fourth floor.

Preston laughs. "We sounded exactly how Hurley wanted us to sound," he says. "Hung out to dry."

26

Mills has no idea how long the vehicles will sit in the impound lot before they're returned to the victims' families. Probably for a while. But he doesn't want to take the chance, so he's relieved when Gus is available on such short notice for a visit. Gus may live in his own remote corner of the universe, like a cliff dweller presiding over all of the oceans of the world, but the guy does have a schedule, and he hopes his psychic friend, who shows up in sandals and a worn, thin T-shirt, doesn't feel exploited. It's five thirty. They're in the impound lot. Mills thanks him so many times they're both embarrassed. He tells Gus it's okay to approach the victims' cars.

"Can I touch it?" Gus asks as he nears Davis Klink's BMW.

"It won't melt."

"No, I meant, like, would I destroy—"

"I know what you meant," Mills says. "Both cars are evidence. They've been completely processed. But I'd still like you to wear these. . . ."

Mills reaches into his back pocket, removes a pouch containing crime scene gloves, and gives it to Gus. Gus does a dopey exhibit of donning the gloves like a surgeon, his hands upward, snapping the latex into place at his wrists.

The psychic runs his gloved hands over the hood as if he's admiring the exquisite paint job and the sculpture of the body. Then he moves to the trunk, where he rubs the surface as though buffing a wax job. Then to the front windshield, where he glides a hand back and forth across the glass. He stands next to the driver's side window, then looks up at Mills. "Can I get in and hold the steering wheel?"

Mills nods.

He watches Gus climb in, and, through the windshield, he sees Gus clutch the wheel. After a few moments sitting still there, Gus shifts his body slightly from side to side and moves like that, his hands on the wheel, his body gently swaying, and Mills realizes the man is manifesting a ride. He observes in awe as Gus drives off somewhere but nowhere. The scene unfolding before him is so real that Mills can almost hear the tires chewing up the pavement, screeching around curves, as if the psychic power, itself, possesses its own velocity. Gus scans the horizon, and as he does he seems possessed, perhaps by the spirit of Davis Klink, perhaps by the sheer drive to find the truth; Mills can't tell. He can tell Gus's eyes are doing camera work, that he's committing the landscape to photographic memory. And then the ride stops. Gus sits back, taking his hands off the wheel. He slips out of the car and says, "Hey," to Mills.

"Hey?" Mills asks. "That's all you have to say?"

"No."

"Good. 'Cause it looked like you took a Sunday drive in there."

"I don't know what day of the week it was, but it was a drive."

"What did you see?"

Gus shields his eyes from the brilliant sun, removes a pair of Ray-Bans from a jacket pocket, and puts them on. "It was dark," he says. "I smelled salt air. The road was winding."

Mills looks at Gus with his hands open expectantly and his eyes begging for more.

"I don't know," Gus tells him. "I felt like I was on the road for an hour or two."

"An hour or two? You were in the car for about five minutes."

Gus bends to the driver's side front tire, touches it, and whips his hand back. "Ouch! That's hot."

Mills bends, as well, and brings two fingers to the tire. "Actually, it's as cold as a corpse."

"Not to me," Gus says as he rises. "Look, the power of what I'm seeing—and it is powerful—is not necessarily tied to this specific car.

In fact, I'm sure it's not. Which explains why the tire is hot to me and cold to you. Very simple."

"Simple?"

"I'm seeing some history here. I'm feeling a kind of escape, maybe, or somebody fleeing. I can't be sure. But you were right to bring me here. Davis Klink has been trying to escape something. He can't get away, though. Something indelible has happened. Spanish music was playing on the radio."

"Wait. Something indelible?"

"Something that can't be undone."

"His murder? *That* can't be undone," Mills says. "Maybe you're seeing the killer fleeing. Maybe it's the killer, not Klink, who can't escape."

"Interesting interpretation, Alex. Great intersection of our skills. But I'm pretty sure it's the CEO who's trying to flee."

Mills leads Gus away. "You do realize the car was off," he mentions. "You said you heard Spanish music on the radio. But the car was off. No keys."

"I know that, dude. The music was on while I was on the road. And I do know that I wasn't really on the road."

Mills nods. "I don't really understand how you do this."

Then Gus says, "I think you're getting closer."

They're standing in front of Barry Schultz's Maserati now. Gus performs basically the same ritual on this car as he did with the BMW. He inspects the exterior with his hands, gets in, grips the steering wheel, and, just as before, appears to take it for a drive. When the ride is over Gus hesitates before getting out, sitting there peering out the windshield at something. He scans the horizon, shakes his head, and opens the door.

Mills steps forward and recognizes his own rapid heartbeat. "Well?" he asks.

Gus lifts himself from the car, clutching the roof. "I went for another ride."

"I could tell. What did you see?"

"Nothing different."

"Nothing different. Are you kidding me?"

"I'm not kidding you," Gus says. "But that's the point. They were the exact same drives. I rode for about two hours again. The highway was pitch-black and winding. I smelled salt air. I heard Spanish music."

"No shit. . . ."

"No shit. And I did pick up a few more details. Nothing much. But I saw a road sign. It said, '105 km.' I think it also said, 'Playa Caribe.' C-a-r-i-b-e, but I'm not sure because I swear we flew by at, like, eighty miles an hour."

"We?"

"Huh?"

"You said 'we.'"

Gus scrunches up his face for a second. "Yeah. There were others in the car with me."

"Seriously?"

"Definitely. I could feel their presence and their fear. They were, like, all jangled."

"Did you see their faces?"

Gus shakes his head. "It was dark. Everything was dark. Inside the car was like soaking darkness. Enveloping."

Mills leans against the Maserati. He doesn't give a shit how much the car is worth at this point. "Is it fair to say Klink and Schultz were in the car together?"

"I don't know," Gus replies. "I think I can say for sure they took the same drive. Not sure if they went at the same time in the same car."

"I have a third victim," Mills says.

Gus just looks at him.

"Another homicide, Gus."

"Really? When?"

"Tuesday. Or very late Monday night. Body's with the OME."

"Damn. Similar crime scene?"

"Oh, yeah."

"Car?"

"Yep. But it's still with the lab," Mills says. "Guy's a travel agent. Joe Gaffing. Not exactly the same socioeconomic profile of the others."

Gus's pallor changes from ruddy to pasty white to greenish, one wave following the other. "You okay?" Mills asks.

"I think so," Gus answers slowly, as if he's not thoroughly convinced. "Maybe a little carsick. Ha-ha, get it?"

"You don't look good."

"I just think I'm done."

Mills nods. He's done, too. The day is crawling all over him. He needs a shower.

The shower doesn't work. The quiet dinner with Kelly, just the two of them, is a soft distraction. But he can't tune out. The residuals of the afternoon press conference, no doubt, aired on the evening news. But Mills doesn't watch. Still he's wired, and he can't unplug, not even later when he climbs into bed. It's not just the press conference—it's everything.

He tosses and turns and wrestles with his pillow. Poor Kelly. He doesn't know how she can stand it. She tries rubbing his back, then gives up and rolls over. Now she's mostly asleep, occasionally groaning at his restlessness. He zooms from one theory to the next, none of them congealing because his science, itself, has all the discipline of a pinball machine. Insomnia meets ADD. Everything collides, but nothing makes sense. And it won't stop. Eleven thirty.

Midnight.

One thirty in the morning.

They dig. They shovel. They die. They know each other.

Two o'clock.

They're on a beach. Salt air. The photos.

He swears he can smell a sunscreen of cloying coconut.

Then it hits him.

Playa Caribe. Gus could see a beach. A Caribbean beach. This has to be why he's awake—to inventory Gus's visions; they hover over his bed, taunting him, keeping him awake with a beckoning finger. He gets up. Goes to the living room. Turns on his laptop and searches "Playa Caribe." There are 499,000 results in .72 seconds. Damn.

Apparently, "Playa Caribe" is a popular name for hotels and resorts and beaches throughout (no surprise here) the Caribbean, particularly among Spanish-speaking destinations. Puerto Rico, the Dominican Republic, Cuba, Mexico, Costa Rica, Nicaragua, Honduras, Panama, and so forth. Needle in a Caribbean haystack. Mills rubs his eyes. As for hotels and resorts, there is no one single chain that has appropriated the "Playa Caribe" brand name, but there are at least a few dozen individual properties and locales throughout the enormous Caribbean region that use it:

Playa Caribe Hotel and Resort (Quintana Roo, Mexico)
Playa Caribe Parador (Mayaguez, Puerto Rico)
Playa Caribe Village (Guanica, Puerto Rico)
Playa Caribe del Sol (Puerto Viejo, Costa Rica)
Playa Caribe Hotel (La Ceiba, Honduras)
Playa Caribe Guesthouse (Ambergris Caye, San Pedro, Belize)
Playa Caribe, Isla Margarita, Venezuela
Playa Caribe, Santo Domingo

And on, and on, and it's 2:55 a.m.

He makes notes: Gus's "drives" in the impound lot lasted about two hours. He hears Spanish music. He sees a woman fall. He sees the number twenty-five. Klink, Schultz, and Toronto graduated from U of A twenty-five years ago. Photos on a beach, twenty-five years ago? Very likely, a Caribbean beach. Why not?

Mills needs to get some sleep.

He climbs back into bed. Kelly smells musky and delicious. He whispers, "I love you," twice, half hoping to wake her, half hoping her fine whispers of breath will continue to rise and fall undisturbed.

27

The residuals of the press conference were likely regurgitated on the news this morning. But, again, he avoids the televised reports. He does, however, fetch the morning paper (probably one of the last souls in the neighborhood to have a hard copy delivered), and he finds the headline written for Sally Tobin's story to be fairly optimistic.

POLICE CLOSE IN ON GRAVEYARD KILLER

While the press conference did not suggest as much, the headline is not technically untrue. Every day they investigate, they close in. He'll take it. What he won't take is the traffic jam this morning at the Starbuck's drive-through, so he ends up with a cup of police-department-issued coffee stew and a view of Morty Myer's double-wide behind as he's bent over the toaster oven, preparing his Pop-Tart.

Jan Powell intercepts the view. "Hey, I got a call from the lab," she says, entering his office. "Seems we got hair samples in Gaffing's fingernails. Not Gaffing's hair. Looks like he tried to fight off his assailant."

"Or pull his hair out, anyway."

"They match hair found in the victim's Mercedes. Longish blond hair."

"From what I recall, the guy on the Klink surveillance video was wearing a hat," Mills says. "Even the footage that Myers enhanced doesn't show the guy's hair color."

He pulls up the Safeway video on his computer and turns the screen toward Powell. They watch in silence for a moment as their suspect pulls Davis Klink from the SUV, and then Mills says, "See, you can't really tell what's under that hat."

He hits "Speakerphone" and calls Roni's extension in the lab. "You working the Gaffing Mercedes?" he asks her when she picks up.

"No," she replies. "But I can find out who is."

"Never mind," he says. "But I'd like a full analysis of the cars you sent to impound. I'm still waiting on those reports."

"Sorry. I'm at least two days behind. You'll get 'em today."

"Anything stand out from the minutia?"

He hears her cluck her tongue. "Well, I don't know if you noticed the position of the seats," she says.

Gus was in the cars; Mills wasn't. "No, I didn't."

"Our measurements suggest that the last person to drive the vehicles was quite a bit shorter than both men."

"That's consistent with other evidence we've seen," Powell tells her.

"Hey, Jan," Roni says. "Both seats were pulled too close to the steering wheel for either man to drive comfortably. And from what we measured, the seats were positioned at about the same distance in both cars."

"But no blond hairs?" Powell asks.

"No."

"Fingerprints?" Mills asks.

"We were able to match fingerprints in the Klink vehicle to Davis Klink. Likewise for Schultz in the Maserati," she tells them. "We found some partials elsewhere in the vehicle, but no other prints on the steering wheel except from the victims. I'm guessing your killer was wearing gloves."

"Blood or other fluids?" Mills asks.

"If there was blood, you would have known by now, Alex," she says, almost chiding. "And any other substances will be documented in the report. But nothing significant."

"All right, thanks," he says.

"We did collect several pot seeds on the passenger side of the Maserati," Roni adds.

Carla Schultz. He shakes his head. Powell smirks.

"Yeah," Mills says, "and a few joints, but you smoked those, right?"

"Goodbye, Alex. Goodbye, Jan."

The line goes dead, and Mills goes facedown on his desk, where he knocks his forehead a few times against the surface.

"Careful, Alex," Powell warns him. "Your brain isn't functioning all that well, as it is."

He lifts his head and hisses at her. "I'm fucking exhausted. This case just seems to be crawling. I'm not used to going at tortoise speed."

As if on cue, Myers enters Mills's office. He's clutching a Pop-Tart in one hand, a file folder in the other. "Can I interrupt?" he asks.

Mills gestures for him to pull up a chair. Myers places his breakfast at the edge of the desk and sits. "Joe Gaffing had cell service through Spectra Wireless," he says. "Well, I have a good friend at Spectra Wireless. He's been analyzing Gaffing's account, off the grid . . . if you catch my drift."

"I catch it, Morty, but your friend is probably breaking the law doing that without a warrant from us."

"I'm not saying we procure the information as evidence," Myers argues. "I just think when you hear what I have to say, you'll consider it an interesting lead."

"Okay, I'm listening. . . ."

"Turns out the last thing Gaffing used his phone for was to search directions on Google Maps."

"Directions to where, Morty? You need a drum roll?" Mills asks.

The man takes a bite of his toaster pastry, luxuriating no doubt in the heady mix of suspense and frosting. "He searched Google Maps for the address and directions to—" Another bite.

"Oh, for fuck's sake, Morty," Powell begs.

"A restaurant. Fiesta Taqueria," Myers announces, all puffed up.

"Thomas and Sixteenth?" Mills asks.

"Yup."

"Really?"

"Yup," Myers says. "It looks like Gaffing went into the alley behind the place, then parked down the block. It doesn't look, from his signal, that he actually went inside, but it's hard to tell. This shit ain't easy to find. My Spectra friend spent night and day on this."

Mills pauses, half consciously rubs his chin, and begins to think aloud. "So, Gaffing meets his killer in the same neighborhood as Schultz and Klink," he surmises. "Somehow, he gets separated from his cell phone because the next thing we know his car ends up in Avondale a few blocks from the cemetery."

Powell nods, pointing to the images on Mills's screen. "No different from what happened to Klink. They drove his BMW to Safeway, presumably from Thomas and Sixteenth, then walked a couple of blocks to Valley Vista."

"He takes away their phones so they can't call for help," Myers interjects.

Mills smiles. "Yes, Morty. I get that part. But I don't know. This doesn't feel cohesive."

Powell tilts her head, twists her mouth, and says, "Cohesive? What do you mean?"

"I mean the murders obviously look alike, but how these men came to meet their killer still seems murky to me," he replies. "Where's the cohesive motive on *their* part to walk right into the hands of a killer? Obviously they didn't think they'd end up dead. So what kind of meeting did they think they'd be having? Regardless of where they drove to or whether or not they had their phones with them, we're missing a bigger part of the story here."

Apparently, Powell and Myers don't disagree. But they don't say anything. They just look at him.

"And I think the Gaffing murder makes the flight manifests worthless to us," Mills adds. "They're starting to trickle in from the airlines, but why bother? Gaffing's murder means the killer didn't leave town after killing Schultz."

"Unless he flew out and flew back," Myers says.

"You mean a frequent-flying felon?" Mills asks. "Nah, too risky."

"Assuming it's one killer—and I think we continue to stick to that assumption—Alex is right," Powell says.

"I'll send out the manifests as I get them. But I don't want to waste too much time on them."

"So, now what?" Powell asks.

Mills leans forward, rubbing his chin. "I want to go back to that neighborhood and look around," he announces. "I'm not going to waste resources and bring out a bunch of patrols again. It'll just be Powell and me."

"We going door-to-door?" Powell asks.

"More or less," Mills replies.

"That's a lot of doors," Powell says.

"Don't worry. I've got something in mind. I'll let you know when we're confirmed to go."

As soon as he's alone in his office, Mills dials Gus Parker.

Gus Parker makes a quick detour around the mountain before heading to work. He stops at the Paradise Valley police station, hoping for an update on Richard Knight.

"I wish I had more to tell you," says Detective Obershan. "But right now he's evading us."

"If he's left the area that would be fine with me," Gus tells him.

"We got his last known address from his probation officer," Obershan says. "It's his parents' house in Glendale. We went. But the parents claim they haven't seen him in weeks."

"Does he check in regularly with his probation officer?"

"So far."

"So maybe you just grab him at the next appointment."

"If you want to wait that long."

"Do I have a choice?"

Obershan drifts toward the doorway. Gus takes the hint.

"We're doing all we can," the detective says as they reach the parking lot.

"Can you put out some kind of message for all law enforcement to look for this guy? Like in surrounding cities and towns?"

"We have," Obershan says. "Make sure you let us know if he contacts you again."

Gus nods and says, "I've been staying at my house in Phoenix."

"And Ms. Welch?"

"LA."

The detective grazes him with uninvited sympathy.

At some point during Gus's visit to the PVPD, a call came in from Alex Mills. The voice mail simply says, "Call me," so as soon as Gus is back in his car he dials. Alex wants him to go on a fishing expedition; those are his words.

"But it will be a fun expedition," the detective assures him. "I need you to walk a neighborhood with me and see if you come up with any vibes on my case."

"If that's your idea of fun, I'm in," Gus says. "But not today."

"Not today? I'm crushed, Mr. Parker."

"Come on, dude, I was just over at the impound lot last night taking your evidence for a test drive. I didn't know I was on retainer," he says. "Besides, I'm working all day. It'll have to be mañana."

Alex tells him that's fine. "Let's meet at eight. Goldberg's on Seventh. I'll buy breakfast."

28

The TV is on in the background. Gus is wearing boxers and brewing a cup of coffee. He has about thirty minutes before he has to meet up with Alex. All is quiet, save for CNN, in the soft unfolding of Gus's morning. The Dow is up. So is the S&P. He doesn't understand the S&P.

"The US lost nearly one hundred thousand retail jobs last year as a record number of consumers turned to online shopping," the newscaster says.

He never drank coffee regularly until he met Billie. On singing days she sips lemon tea. Otherwise, she'll drink coffee all day to push her through her crazy nights of musing and writing. He spoons Stevia into his cup.

"Several small earthquakes struck areas of Oklahoma overnight. Seismologists say this most recent outbreak brings the number of measurable tremors in the state to twenty-eight so far this year."

He has to admit the aroma is intoxicating, that full-bodied elixir to the yearning of the puffy-eyed masses. He pours, adds some almond milk, and turns to the bedroom. But something about Mexico catches his attention.

". . . on a spring break trip to Cancun, Mexico, and was never found. Her disappearance, never ruled a homicide, has become one . . ."

He hits "Rewind" on the remote.

"Next Friday marks the twenty-fifth anniversary of the disappearance of Kimberly Harrington. The Northern Arizona University student, who hailed from Michigan, went missing on a spring break trip to Cancun, Mexico, and was never found. Her disappearance, never ruled a homicide, has become one of the coldest cases known to US law enforcement officials. For years, Kimberly's parents have traveled . . ."

Ivy, who's already been walked, rises from the corner of the room and barks to the birds outside.

He looks at the clock. He still needs to shower. He's running late.

By eight o'clock, the breakfast crowd at Goldberg's has thinned. The wear and tear on the faces of the wait staff indicates it was another busy morning rush. So do the vapors of grease that swirl to the ceiling.

Mills easily finds a booth, lets Powell slide in.

"I hope they saved some grease for the bacon," he says.

She looks at her watch. "Where's your friend?"

"He'll be here."

A waitress offers coffee. This morning Powell drinks hers black.

"Maybe he's just a good guesser," she says.

"Who?"

"Gus Parker."

Mills shrugs. "Even if he is, you have to admit he does it better than anybody. It's a gift."

"I'm surprised a guy like you isn't more of a skeptic."

He laughs. "Yeah, I know. But I've spent a lot of time with Gus. I've watched him, and there's something, I don't know, almost religious about how he works."

"Religious? I doubt that," she says. Then she adds, "Well speak of the devil himself!"

A passing waitress yields to Gus who arrives sporting a ponytail and facial hair. He's in a loose-knit baggy sweater, sleeves rolled up.

"I didn't know Jesus was coming," Powell says.

"Isn't that a common assumption?" Gus asks. He sits and tells the waitress he'd prefer a cup of tea.

Powell snarls at him.

"What?" Gus asks. "I already had coffee. I don't need to be all jacked up to do my thing."

Mills withdraws a folder from his backpack and opens a small map of Central Phoenix. He points to the intersection of Thomas and Sixteenth. "We suspect all our victims were in this area, at or near the same gas station," he explains. "We're going to make a tight ring around the neighborhood, knock on a few doors."

"A few?" Gus asks.

"Or many," Mills replies. "That may depend on you. Maybe you get a strong vibe about a certain street or a house. We'll start at a restaurant and then go to addresses we missed the first time around. You know, people who weren't home, didn't answer their doors."

They order breakfast. Mills and Powell both choose the All-American (a mixed platter of fat and cholesterol), and Gus predictably asks for yogurt, fruit, and granola. He runs his fingers through his newly sprouting beard.

"You growing it out?" Mills asks.

"I don't know," Gus says with a withering shrug.

The waitress returns with coffee refills. Gus reminds her he's drinking tea. She rests her hand on his shoulder. "Anything for you, darling," she says and drifts away.

Powell whistles lasciviously. "The old broad likes the hipster look."

"It's not a hipster look," Gus tells her. "And I don't think she'd like being called an old broad."

"And I don't think I like being lectured about being PC," Powell says.

"Uh, Jan," Mills interjects. "Why don't you lay off Gus for now. He's here to help us, and he's been under a lot of stress lately."

"I'm being stalked," Gus says.

"So I've heard," she admits. "That must suck."

Gus offers a few details. The food arrives, and, as she's chomping on a piece of rye toast, Powell says, "Amazing how Billie Welch never gets old."

"She never gets old to me," Gus assures them.

"I mean physically," Powell says. "She looks like she stopped aging. What's her secret?"

Gus, intently studying the yogurt, says, "She only thinks of love and beauty. Nothing else crosses her threshold, you know, in her mind."

A burst of laughter from Powell. Mills and Gus look at her, say nothing else. They silently finish eating. When they're done Mills pays the bill, letting Powell slide out. "Bladder," she says. "Meet you two outside."

Gus leaves his car at Goldberg's and gets in with Mills. Powell follows them, then parks behind them on East Glenridge, about four houses in from Sixteenth. A few high clouds scatter across the sky, no doubt chased away by the rising sun and the slight desert wind. Another month or so and it will be fry-an-egg-on-the-sidewalk weather.

They start at Fiesta Taqueria on Sixteenth. The waft of chili pepper hits them in the face. The place smells like heaven if heaven is Mexico on a hot, lazy day with fajitas sizzling, tortillas frying, margaritas flowing, and a cerulean blue sky that hangs like a partition between here and anywhere else. Mills needs a vacation. Fiesta Taqueria is virtually empty, but it's very early. Mills counts four customers among the twenty or so tables and the bar. They talk to the proprietor, Jimmy Jimenez, and show him the victims' photographs.

"Hey, yeah, I think I recognize that guy," the man says. He's pointing to the photo of Davis Klink.

"You think he's been in here?" Powell asks.

"I do."

"Can you maybe remember the last time you saw him here?" Mills asks.

The guy scrunches up his face, then shakes his head. "Nah, I don't know," he says. "Maybe a month ago. He wasn't a regular or anything."

"Do you remember seeing him in here alone?" Mills asks.

"I think so," the owner says. "But I'm not sure. He might have been in here with a woman. What happened to him?"

"He's dead," Mills replies.

"Aw, shit. That's too bad," Jimmy Jimenez says. "If I can remember anything, I'll let you know. Okay?"

"Sure," Mills tells him. "But what about this guy?" He holds up the photo of Joe Gaffing. "Could you look again?"

The guy shrugs. "I'm sorry. I don't recognize him."

"That's okay," Mills says. "We thought we might have tracked him here. You think your employees could have a look?"

"Sure. My main staff won't be in for a bit, but, yeah, maybe you could send me copies."

"I can. And you can call me if anybody recognizes these guys."

Mills knows it's a long shot.

"No problem." Jimenez recites his email address, and Mills hands him his card. The men shake hands, a hearty and heartfelt handshake.

"Wish I could be more helpful today," Jimenez says, "but while you're here, can I get you something? I know it's still early for lunch, but anything you want, it's on me. It's the least I can do to support our cops."

The offer brings a smile to Mills's face, the placid smile of that hot, lazy afternoon in Mexico, not a phone, or a uniform, or a sergeant in sight. "We really appreciate the offer, but we're a bit behind schedule," he says. "But thanks."

The guy offers a rain check. Mills gladly accepts.

Now they're off to the residential area off Sixteenth, and if the first house, where no one comes to the door, is any indication, it's going to be a long day. They get no answer at the second house either. Mills asks Gus to go ahead of them and stroll both sides of the street. He hands the psychic photos of the three victims. "I'm just giving you these to hopefully prompt a vibe or something," he tells Gus. "Don't approach anyone."

At the third house, Mills and Powell knock and hear a woman speaking from behind the door. "I don't open the door to strangers," she says. "Who is it?"

"Phoenix Police," Mills replies.

"Police?"

"Yes, ma'am."

"You'll have to put your identification up to the peephole, please." Her voice is oldish, alarmed.

Mills holds out his badge and his picture ID.

The door opens slowly, revealing a little sparrow of a woman. She could be one hundred years old, standing there in her housecoat and with her wisps of white hair. Mills can't imagine how she reached the peephole. "Sorry to bother you, ma'am," he tells her. "I'm Detective Alex Mills, and this is Detective Jan Powell. We're just canvassing the area to see if anyone can identify a few men for us."

"I live alone," she says, and it sounds like a preemptive strike.

"That's okay," Powell replies. "We just want to know if you've seen any of these men coming or going from the neighborhood."

"I keep to myself," the woman insists. Her eyes are moist.

Mills offers her a beaming smile. "We understand." He pulls out the photos. She studies them, one hand to her face. Then she shakes her head.

"No. I'm sorry," she says. "I really don't watch the neighborhood. Maybe I should."

Their knocking goes unanswered at the next two homes. He and Powell cross the street. He eyes a house painted baby blue with white trim. He thinks color reveals a lot about personality. Anomalies in color often suggest anomalies elsewhere. He's staring at a street of mostly dusty brown homes, one fading into the other. Blue sticks out. They go to the blue. A springy redhead answers the door. She says her name is Lucy Drill. "Like the dentist!"

Lucy Drill, like the dentist, studies the photos but doesn't recognize the faces.

"I'm sorry," she says. "I hate to spoil a real live episode of *Law & Order.*"

Powell gives the woman a once-over and says, "That's okay. Thanks for looking."

They cross Lucy Drill's lawn and meet Gus in the middle of the street.

"I got nothing here," he tells them. "Didn't pick up a thing, so I went around the block and across Sixteenth. I think you should hit a few places over there. Something's askew."

"Askew?" Powell asks, her sarcasm not well concealed.

"What he means is that everything is what it is—until it's not," Mills says. "Isn't that right, Gus?"

Gus laughs and says, "Something like that."

"It's not that different from how we investigate cases," he explains to Powell. "We look at all the pieces, and we focus on the pieces that don't fit. That's what Gus does."

She looks at him squarely. "So, we're skipping the rest of Glenridge? Is that what you're saying?"

"That's what I'm saying," Mills replies and turns around.

Gus directs them to East Paloma, where he points to a nearly dilapidated ranch house, its windows shielded by bedsheets. The wounded home is desperately in need of a paint job, maybe a wrecking ball. Mills rings the bell, thinking this book by its cover suggests a meth lab, but you never know. A shirtless teenage boy answers the door. "What?" he asks. He's bronzed-skinned with a bundle of black curls on his head. He should probably be in school. His eyes are mean. Mills goes through the introductions.

"You police?"

"That's what I said."

"Sheee-it, no," the kid says and bolts. He pushes right between Mills and Powell and zips across the rocky yard.

"Hey, wait, buddy," Mills calls to him. "We're not . . ."

Then, from inside the house, Mills hears the bellowing voice of a woman coming toward them. "Who's out there, Eddie? I *told* you not to answer the door, *coño!*"

She's short and thickset and pushes the detectives aside.

"Eddie! Get back here! Where the hell do you think you're going?" she screams. "Now! *Pendejo!*"

"Excuse me, ma'am," Powell says.

She turns to them, fire in her eyes. "Who are you?" she asks.

"We're detectives, ma'am," Mills says. "We didn't mean to disturb the house."

She throws him the shadiest shade. "Right. You just hold on a minute while I drag my kid's sorry ass back in here."

She marches down the lawn and starts screaming in Spanish, returning just about a minute later, dragging her son by his ear.

"Hey, kid," Mills says, "whatever you did is somebody else's problem. I'm not here for you."

The woman shoves her kid through the door. "Get back in bed," she orders. Then, to the detectives, she says, "He's home sick from school today. Something's going around."

"Again, we're sorry to disturb," Powell says, "but we're canvassing the neighborhood, looking for some information about a few men."

Mills reveals the photos.

"A lot of people 'round here, they got that no-snitch thing going on," the lady says. "Not me. I see something, I say something."

She has a Spanish accent, more likely from the Bronx than from Mexico.

"Then maybe your son is hiding something from you," Mills says. "If he's scared of us."

"No, he ain't hiding anything. He smokes pot sometimes, and when I catch him I bring him down to the precinct where the cops give him a good lecture. I don't want him to get arrested, but I don't want to ignore it, you know?"

Mills laughs. "Yes. In fact I do. Personally."

She shrugs and eyeballs the photos again. "Yeah, this guy, I think," she says, pointing to Davis Klink. "I think I've seen him at work."

"At work?" Powell asks.

"Yeah, I work most nights around the corner at the taco place," she says.

"Fiesta Taqueria?" Mills asks.

"You know it?"

"We were just there," Mills tells her.

She smiles. "The real good stuff. You meet Jimmy?"

"Yes," Mills says. "He recognized this guy, too. But didn't remember much about it."

She nods. "I'm sure I waited on his table before."

"How long ago?"

She shakes her head. "I couldn't say. Maybe January."

"Did he come in alone?" Powell asks.

"I think so," the woman says. "But, hold on, I think he might have been in a couple of times with a woman. A blond or a redhead, maybe."

"Can you remember anything else about her?" Powell asks.

"Like what?"

"Like the color of her eyes," Mills tells her. "Or the way she dressed. Or if she had an accent, or a tattoo . . ."

"Yes!" the woman cries. "I think she had a tattoo. I'm not sure, but I think she did, and I remember thinking that this very elegant man was kind of mismatched with this tattooed woman. But, hey, who am I to judge?"

"Do you remember how old she might have been?" Powell asks.

"No. But she wasn't young. She wasn't, you know, his younger woman."

"Got it," Powell says. "Do you remember the placement of the tattoo?"

"I don't think so. Maybe her shoulder or her arm. I think she'd come in wearing something without sleeves. She had pretty eyes."

The lumbering trucks and screeching buses on Sixteenth are making it hard to hear. Mills leans in closer. "Do you recall how they behaved with each other? Affectionate? Angry?"

"I'm so sorry," the woman says. "I think I'd remember if they were fighting, but they were just two customers out of hundreds, you understand?"

"Of course we do," Mills replies. "Thank you for your time."

"I don't recognize the two other guys," she says.

Mills points to the picture of Gaffing. "We think he may have been at the Taqueria even more recently."

She peers, does a subtle shake of the head. "No. I don't recognize him."

"That's fine," Mills assures her. "You've been a great help. Really."
They meet Gus down at the bottom of the driveway.

"You must be onto something," Mills tells him. "You've connected a couple of dots already. That woman? She works at the taco place. Recognized Klink."

They're barely on the sidewalk when Gus abruptly stops and waves his hands in the air. "Wait. Wait. Wait," he says. "Just wait."

Powell rolls her eyes. Mills pretends not to notice. Instead he says, "What is it, Guster?"

"Speaking of Mexico . . ." Gus begins.

"Who's speaking of Mexico?" Powell asks.

Gus points emphatically to Sixteenth Street. "The Taqueria! Did either of you see the story about that girl who went missing in Cancun?"

Powell shakes her head. Mills tries to think but reluctantly mimics Powell's response.

"Yeah, it's the anniversary of her disappearance," Gus tells them. "She was on spring break."

"And this has what to do with us?" Powell asks.

"Nothing, necessarily," Gus replies. "But I've been getting a vibe about Spanish stuff all along."

"Piñatas?" Powell asks.

"Jan . . ."

"Never mind," Gus says. "Her name was Kimberly Harrington. Google it."

"Don't mind if I do," Powell says.

The name is familiar to Mills. He thinks it was one of those famous cases. There have been more than a few of them. Pretty girl vanishes. Unsolved for years. Haunting. It's coming back to him.

"'Next Friday will mark the twenty-fifth anniversary of Kimberly Harrington's disappearance in Mexico,'" Powell reads from her phone. "'The Northern Arizona University student, who hailed from Michigan, went missing on a spring break trip to Cancun and was never found. Her disappearance, never ruled a homicide, has become one of the coldest cases known to US law enforcement officials.'"

"Of course," Mills says. "Huge case. Kimberly Harrington. It was all over the news, you know. Especially here 'cause she went to NAU. They thought she was kidnapped, maybe sold into the sex trade, or something."

"Oh, right," Powell says, as if a bell just went off in her head. "I remember that. I was barely a teenager when it happened, and it scared the shit out of me."

"Just gone without a trace?" Gus asks. "No witnesses? No body ever found?"

"Correct," Mills tells him. "You don't remember hearing about it? It was all over the news. There were even shows about it, like *Dateline* and *20/20*."

Gus doesn't answer. He tilts his head, squints, and shudders from the shoulders down.

"What is it?" Mills asks.

"I don't know," Gus says. "Just one of those chills."

"And there's another connection to Arizona besides NAU," Powell tells them, and then again reads from her phone. "'The tour operator, Go Go Mexico, a Phoenix-based travel agency, tells the FBI that while it organized the trip and had personnel on the ground in Cancun, it did not consider itself a chaperone to monitor or supervise student activities after-hours.'"

"I think they were sued anyway," Mills tells them. "Let me see." Powell hands him her phone. He reads for a few moments and says, "Yes, they were. Doesn't say much about the suit here, but wow, I can't believe it's been twenty-five years. I'm getting so fucking old."

Gus gives him a throaty laugh of commiseration.

"Wait," he says. "A quote from my father!"

Powell puts a hand on his shoulder, perching herself to read along.

"Damn," Mills says, his mind drifting back. "I think I remember him doing interviews with the media about this. "'I can't confirm or deny any local investigation into Go Go Mexico, but my office would be interested in any activity by any persons locally that might suggest conspiracy or premeditation in the woman's disappearance," said County

Attorney Lyle Mills. However, Mills said he had no cause to believe at this time that any activity of that nature took place.'"

"Wow," Gus says. "A voice from the past."

A ghost. The voice of a ghost has crept inward, become one with his skin, with his blood. Exhumed from the grave, Lyle Mills stands larger than life and, as always, casts a shadow. In an instant, Mills sees every room of his childhood home and hears his father calling his name, down the hallway, the voice disembodied. *Alex.*

"You got your tablet?" he asks Powell.

"In the car," she says. "Where's yours?"

"Same, with no juice." They share an eye roll. He picks up his phone, then sends a text to Myers: "Pull Sec State Report: Go Go Mexico."

"You're connecting the dots," Gus says, staring off into nowhere.

"What's that?" Mills asks.

"Connecting the dots."

"Is that a suggestion or an observation?" Mills asks.

"It's both."

Gus then directs Mills and Powell to two more homes on East Paloma, but their knocks go unanswered.

"How about we go north of Thomas?" Gus asks. "I mean, since we're doing this randomly."

They get in their cars and ride two blocks north of the PetroGo gas station and turn left on East Mountain Shadow. There the whole process begins again. Mills and Powell knock on a few doors; Gus patrols the area for a vibe. Mills and Powell get a series of guarded residents who don't know anything or won't say anything.

Gus leads them to the other side of East Mountain Shadow, across Sixteenth. There at the corner sits a real estate office (Cohn and Drake Desert Realty), and Gus suggests the detectives go in and inquire while he continues to wander the neighborhood. On the way inside, Mills feels his phone vibrate. He looks at the screen. It's an email from Myers. Subject: "Sec State Report Go Go Mexico." A woman says, "Hello. How can I help you today?" Mills looks up and sees an attractive blond sitting behind a reception desk. The office looks like it's auditioning for *Architectural Digest*. Mills knows pretense when he sees it. A spiral staircase here, subway tile there. Furniture that makes a statement ("We're beautiful and expensive, but murder on your ass"), and accessories that hail from the exotic land of HomeGoods. The reception desk is a circle in the middle of everything. Above it hangs a doughnut-shaped chandelier, lights dripping from the hole and illuminating a path to the woman's cleavage. Mills does the introductions, explains the reason for the visit, and says he'd like to pass around a few photos. The receptionist gives him a double take. "Let me see if I can get one of the owners out here."

About a minute later, a well-coiffed man emerges from one of the larger glassed-in rooms at the back. The guy's probably six feet tall, and his abusively tight dress shirt suggests he knows the way to the gym. His face is smooth and tanned, and he seems astutely aware of that. He wears a diamond pinkie ring. Mills tells him why they've stopped by. The man, Josh Drake of Cohn and Drake, bids them to follow. "Nice place you got here," Powell says.

"Thank you." He leads them into his office.

"Looks kind of staged," Mills tells him. "You know, like you stage a house."

The man laughs and exposes a mouthful of Beverly Hills teeth. "Very observant, Detective. We think our office should reflect the perfection of the homes and estates we sell. You said you have photos?"

"Yes," Mills says, withdrawing them from his bag. He hands the photos to Josh Drake.

"And you think we would recognize them, why?"

"Because these men were in the area shortly before their deaths," Mills replies.

"Can't say I recognize any of them," the man says. "If you want me to scan them in, I can show them to Warren when he gets back."

"Warren?" Mills asks.

"My husband. The Cohn of Cohn and Drake."

"Gotcha," Mills says. "You have mostly upscale clientele?"

"Mostly," he says with too much pride.

"Is it possible that one of these men could have been your husband's client without you knowing?" Mills asks.

"Possible, but unlikely. We tag team mostly."

"Go on and scan the photos," Powell says. "It can't hurt to have your husband look."

It takes Drake less than five minutes, the small talk about real estate notwithstanding, to scan the photos and hand them back to Mills. "I'll let you know if Warren recognizes any of them," he says. "But honestly, the only crime we've seen around here is when someone stole all our cardboard boxes out back. Not exactly something you call the cops for." He mock winces. Then he laughs.

"Someone stole your boxes?" Powell asks.

"Not the end of the world, Detective. No need to write up a report!" Another laugh, so satisfied with his own wit. "We bought a new refrigerator for the break room—we call it a café—and we stuck the box out back with a few others to recycle. And then the next morning, all gone!" His eyes are wide and theatrical.

"Could it be that the recycler came to get them?" Mills inquires.

"No. It was a Monday. Recycling doesn't come 'til Thursdays. But, whatever, we just hope someone put them to good use, or had the good sense to recycle them for us! End of caper!"

Mills smiles politely. "Yes. End of caper, indeed."

"I've been pushing Warren to put surveillance video out in the alley in case someone tries to steal our cars," the man says. "I thought the great cardboard heist would convince him, but it didn't. Nice to meet you both." He extends a hand. Both Mills and Powell shake it.

Out on the sidewalk, Mills ruminates. He feels his lower teeth grazing the uppers. He turns to Powell and says, "Our killer stole the cardboard to make those graveyard signs. I'm almost sure of it."

"Good call," she says.

He laughs.

"I have no idea why I'm laughing," he tells her.

"All we have to do is have Mr. Drake or his husband identify the cardboard we took in as evidence and, bingo, a lead," Powell says.

Mills is still laughing. "This is so stupid to me. A fucking refrigerator box? I mean, it's stupid, but it's a break, but it's stupid. I just don't know why."

"We'll take what we can get," Powell says. "At least we know why your psychic sent us into that office."

"So, now you believe in Gus Parker?"

She smirks. "If we get a positive ID on the refrigerator carton, then yes." Now she's laughing, too.

"Did I hear my name?"

They turn and see Gus approaching.

"Anything interesting?" the psychic asks.

Mills starts to laugh again but wills himself to stop. "Yeah," he says. "We might have found the source of those signs left at the graves."

"You think the realtors were in on it?" Gus asks.

"No, no. But we think the killer might have used some of their refuse to make his grave markers."

Gus tells them that he's identified a few more homes. One on East Mangrove and two on East Iris.

The person who answers the door on East Mangrove says his name is Bernard Williamson. "I swear I didn't do it, Officers," he says with a big laugh. What is it with everyone trying to be a fucking comic today? Mills ignores him. Bernard Williamson is Mills's height. He's dressed in silk pajamas. His eyes float lazily behind shockingly green contact lenses.

"It looks like we might have disturbed your sleep," Mills says and then gives a brief explanation for their visit. "We have photos of the victims. Would you mind looking?"

He studies the photos and smiles. "I know that one for sure," he says, pointing to the face of Barry Schultz. "He used to come by the club all the time."

"What club?" Powell asks.

"Style 11," he replies. "I perform drag there on weekends, and the doctor, I don't remember his name, he'd come by and try to sell us all on cosmetic procedures."

"You're kidding," Powell says.

"I am not kidding," the man insists. "A few of the girls got Botox, nose jobs, and some other surgery to, you know, soften their faces. He did great work. I can tell you that. But not for me."

"What do you do for a day job?"

"I'm an accountant," the man says. "In fact, I have to slip into some business clothes. I have a client due here any minute."

"Sure," Mills says. "But before we leave you, can you remember ever seeing the doctor behave oddly or suspiciously?"

Bernard lets out peals of laughter. "Oh, honey, everyone in that club behaves oddly! But I can't say I ever saw him do anything suspicious, though I do think he once got punched out in the parking lot for grabbing Feline Dion's ass. Feline's boyfriend mistook it for a sexual advance, but it wasn't. The doctor just wanted to show her how she'd look with a plumper behind."

"How long ago was that?" Mills asks, keeping a straight face.

"Maybe a year and a half, two years ago," he says. "I can't believe he's one of the victims. That's tragic!"

"Yes, quite," Mills says. "Any chance he was involved with one of the performers at the club?"

"Involved?" Bernard asks, an eyebrow arched. "You mean romantically? Sexually?"

"Yes."

"I don't know," he says. "I never heard anything, but mostly I mind my own business."

"Are you sure it's the same doctor who came by the club?" Mills asks.

"Yes."

"And the doctor never came to this house?"

Bernard Williamson clasps his hands to his heart. "Goodness! Does this make me a witness? Will I have to take the stand?"

"No. And no," Powell tells him. "Just answer the question. Did the doctor ever come to this house?"

"He did not," he says with an indignant flourish. "I don't intend to go under the knife as long as my natural beauty holds out. What's your excuse?"

Mills taps Powell on the arm, indicating they should begin their retreat. He thanks the man, then hands him his card. "If you think of anything else, please call."

"Will do," he says with a wink. "And if the two of you ever stop by Style 11 for a show, you ask for Gigi Poodleskirt."

"Who's that?" Mills asks.

"Me."

They meet up with Gus on the street, and Mills pats him on the back. "I wouldn't call it a lead, brother," he says, "but you continue to connect the dots. Nice job. There's a connection here to Barry Schultz."

Gus stares at him intently and says, "I think it's a coincidence, not a connection."

"Well it bears some further exploration on our end," Mills insists.

Gus says they need to go south of Thomas again. Powell sighs loudly and impatiently. But Mills says, "That's why we're out here. If he gets a vibe, we follow that vibe."

They get in their cars and backtrack. Gus indicates East Iris, to the west of Sixteenth. He tells Mills to park a few houses in. Out on the street, Gus points to a house—its exterior is illustrated with cartoon images of children at play, bunnies, lollipops, and happy faces. Mills regards the place dubiously. "It's a daycare center," he says, reading the words scrawled across two of the windows.

"In this hood?" Powell asks.

"Poor people have babies, too," Mills says.

A woman answers the door. Her name is Lee Leighton. She spells it for them. "What can I do for you, Detectives?"

Mills explains why they're in the neighborhood. The woman, a late-fortyish brunette, says she's heard about the murders on the news. "Really scary," she says, "but why would you be looking around here?" She's wearing linen pants and a simple cotton blouse mostly covered by a light, but oversized, zippered sweatshirt. "Weren't these men all rich and successful? This isn't exactly that kind of neighborhood."

"We believe they visited this area shortly before they died," Mills explains.

Her eyes widen, and she puffs out a breath. She says something, but, again, the heavy traffic on Sixteenth makes it hard to hear. Mills, frustrated, says, "Can you repeat that?"

"I said it's upsetting. Crime is closing in."

"It can feel like that sometimes," Mills concedes.

"I've been doing home daycare for a long time, and I worry about every child who comes through my door," she says. "I confess I'm a big worrier. Now more than ever. The world is changing."

"Isn't this place awfully quiet for a daycare center?" Powell asks.

The woman smiles. "Oh, they're out back playing in the yard with a couple of my assistants. Would you like to take a peek?"

"No, that's okay," Mills replies. He brandishes the photos. "You recognize any of these men?"

She stares at each one of the faces with great sorrow in her eyes. "How awful," she says. "For their families. But, no, no, I don't recognize them. I saw their pictures on the news, but they're not familiar to me."

"Thank you, ma'am," Mills says.

Again, a truck rumbles by on Sixteenth. The woman smiles and nods, then retreats into her house.

"A lot of empathy," Mills tells Gus when they regroup. "But a misfire."

"My misfire?" Gus asks.

"Just a misfire."

Gus points to the final house. It's a few doors down. They knock, but no one comes to the door. "You want me to keep wandering?" Gus asks.

"No I think that's enough for one morning," Mills says. "We have a few things to follow up on, most notably the cardboard."

"Can I keep these photos of the victims?" Gus asks.

"Sure. Go crazy."

As they walk back to retrieve their cars, Mills opens Myers's email.

Alex,
   Looks like the company shut down 25 yrs ago. But you'll see a familiar name. PDF attached.
   MM.

The attachment downloads in about six seconds. "I think I need reading glasses," he tells the others. Powell laughs. Mills leans against his car and holds the phone far enough away so he can decipher the small print.

"Why don't you just fire up the tablet?" Powell asks.

"I told you, no juice."

He doesn't need a tablet to see that Go Go Mexico dissolved twenty-five years ago, coinciding with the disappearance of that college student. Nor does he need a tablet to see that the company had been in business for eleven years before its demise, or that its owner and president was Lester Gaffing. . . . Its owner and president was Lester Gaffing? Who the fuck? Gaffing! The next line reveals exactly what Mills expects it to reveal:

Joseph Gaffing Sr. Vice President / Treasurer

There's a dawning all over his face. He can feel it.

"What?" Powell begs.

He describes the information in the secretary of state's report.

"No shit," Powell says. "Gaffing."

"We gotta go," he tells them. He pulls up Gaffing's address, then shares it with Powell. "Meet me there."

"What about him?" she asks, pointing to Gus.

"Right. I forgot. I'll swing by Goldberg's first and drop him back at his car."

"I can Uber," Gus says.

"Fuck Uber. Let's go."

As soon as Gus is discharged at the diner, a round of thank-yous and you're welcomes in the vault, Mills peels out for Glendale, nearly swiping a City of Phoenix garbage truck as he exits the parking lot. While exceeding every posted speed limit, he dials Preston and asks him to find out who at the FBI investigated the Kimberly Harrington case.

29

Joe Gaffing's appearance at the front door is, once again, preceded by the yipping and barking of a dog inside. The man swings the door open and says, "Back so soon?"

"Who's Lester Gaffing?" Mills asks.

The man seems to deflate, even hisses like a balloon losing air. "My brother," he says.

"So the two of you ran Go Go Mexico? You served as vice president?"

"You've been doing your homework," the man says.

"This is my colleague, Jan Powell," Mills tells him. "May we come in and have a chat?"

Joe Gaffing shakes his head slowly, then shrugs. "Yeah. Sure. I got nothing to hide."

"Yet you chose not to tell me about Go Go Mexico," Mills says.

"You didn't ask."

He leads them to the same back porch where he first spoke with Mills, passing on the way new (or old) piles of laundry, the teetering mountain of dishes in the sink, and a redistribution of food containers and boxes on the kitchen counters. They sit on the porch. Ashtrays brimming with half-smoked cigarettes surround them. Powell coughs incessantly. When you add the stale smoke to the wind tunnel of dog piss, you have the makings of an upper respiratory catastrophe.

"I'm so sorry about the loss of your son," Powell says, calming her cough.

Gaffing nods, smiling. "Thank you."

The moment is genuine, peaceful, and it also provides a lull before the detectives launch into their questions.

"So, you took over Go Go Mexico and changed the name to Vacation Express and Student Escapes shortly after the disappearance of Kimberly Harrington?" Mills asks him.

"For business reasons."

"Like you did again fifteen years ago after that girl died in the boating accident," Mills says.

"For business reasons."

"What happened to your brother after he sold you the business?" Mills asks.

"Moved to California, took a job doing sales for a cruise line," Gaffing replies. He narrows his eyes, then turns his palms up. "And this has *what* to do with my son's murder?"

"Not sure," Mills says tentatively, knowing that a small dose of uncertainty on his part projects something human. "But Kimberly Harrington was on one of your tours when she disappeared."

"That's no secret," the man tells them. "It was our darkest day. We cooperated with the investigation as best as we could." He says the word "investigation" as if it's in air quotes.

"You sound like you didn't have much faith in the investigators," Powell says.

Gaffing eyes her. She's probably his daughter's age. Something registers on his face, then almost as quickly disappears. "The Mexican authorities were not the most sophisticated at the time. And, frankly, not that interested at first. I've said all along they lost precious time."

The source of the animal urine jumps up on its owner's lap, licks its owner's face, and turns to Mills with a what-the-fuck-you-looking-at expression. The man pats the dog's head.

"Maybe so, Mr. Gaffing, but the FBI was on the case, as well," Mills says.

"We were pretty much out of the picture by then. Though they did question us, of course," Gaffing replies. "Mind if I smoke?"

Reflexively, falsely, Mills says, "Detective Powell has asthma. So, if you wouldn't mind . . ."

The man nods, but his hands tremble.

"Were you there at the time?" Powell asks. "When the girl disappeared?"

"Different members of my team took turns going back and forth to Cancun during the spring break season," he says. "We had staff on the ground to manage logistics, complaints, any activities we sponsored."

"Were you or your son in Cancun when Kimberly Harrington went missing?" she persists.

"We both were," Gaffing replies. "It was awful. Joey was young and immature, and he didn't know how to handle it."

"How old was he?" Mills asks.

"Early twenties. We sent him home. He was getting in the way more than anything."

"Like how?" Powell asks.

"You know, acting like he was smarter than the police, like an amateur sleuth, like somehow he was going to find the girl and become a hero."

The man lowers his head into his hands. He begins to quietly sob and sniffle. Mills catches Powell rolling her eyes as if the man's misery is worthy of ridicule. Her dismissive reaction reminds him how new she is to Homicide, perhaps immature for the work. She's tough, and that's great. She's thorough. Also, great. But Mills has seen many like her, people who recoil from humanity not because they're jaded but because they're hiding from pain. He'll lecture her later. Maybe.

Joe Gaffing reaches for a tissue from the box beside him. It's not a new box. "I still don't see how any of this has any connection to what happened to my boy, Detectives."

"It might not have any connection, sir," Mills says. "But when this little bit of history came to our attention, we thought we would investigate further."

The man sits up, puffing out his chest. "It wasn't like we chaperoned the trip. We never made any promises to provide supervision. We just made all the arrangements. We hosted a few activities, you know, beach stuff, dances, a few parties, but we didn't set curfews. Nobody had to sign in or out. These were adults."

Powell leans forward and says, "I'm sure you provided a complete list of people on that trip to authorities. . . ."

"At the time, of course. I think we provided lists for all our tours in Cancun that week. But there were probably two or three other companies offering spring break packages at the same time as ours."

"I don't suppose you'd still have those lists," Powell asks.

He hesitates. "Jeez, that was twenty-five years ago. I don't know that we have records going back that far. Things weren't as fully computerized as they are now. You know what I mean?"

Mills stands. "Sir, I'd appreciate it if you could check," he says. "Maybe at the office. Or in storage. Wherever. It would be easier than having us come in with a search warrant to turn everything upside down."

Mills was careful, in the leveling of his tone, to not make that sound like a threat. It wasn't a threat. It was a practicality. Junior's death, alone, is enough to secure the warrant.

Gaffing gets out of his chair. "I'll do what I can. But I wouldn't be surprised if we destroyed records that old."

"Even records that noteworthy?" Powell asks.

"Like I said, I'll do what I can."

Out front Powell asks Mills if she can go meet her boyfriend for lunch. He tells her sure, go ahead, whatever. He gets in his car, but sitting there, before he starts the engine, he has a crack of an uneasy feeling. Something. He rests his face on a closed fist and surveys a fill-in-the-blank proposition. Nothing. Then he gazes at himself in the rearview mirror, his eyes searching, and, for no conscious reason, it hits him. A photograph. A photograph hanging on the wall. He jumps out of his car. He sprints to Gaffing's front door and presses the bell as if he's calling for a nurse in the ICU.

He hears the man approaching from inside. "What is it? I'm coming for Christ's sake."

The door swings open.

"I'm so sorry, Mr. Gaffing," Mills says. "But I need to see one of the photographs on your wall. Back on the porch."

"What for?"

"May I? Please?"

Gaffing steps aside, then follows Mills, who heads into the house. On the porch, Mills sees it immediately: a picture of Gaffing and his late wife posing on a beach, behind them a stone jetty strewn with seaweed, in the distance a pier. Surely there are a million backdrops like that in the world, but this can't be a coincidence; maybe it's the angle at which Gaffing and his wife are standing—that's it, it's the angle. Replace Gaffing and his wife with Klink, Schultz, and Toronto, and it's the same exact beach in the same exact place. Mills points. "That photo. Where was it taken?"

Gaffing looks at him cautiously. "Cancun."

"The same year Kimberly Harrington disappeared?"

"Of course not," he says. "I wouldn't want that memory hanging in my den. It was several years later."

"Same hotel?" Mills asks. "Same hotel where Kimberly's tour group stayed?"

"Actually that spot is right between the hotel we used for tours and another, much fancier place."

"What hotel did you use for tours?"

"It was called the Playa Grande Resort," Gaffing replies. "But it's changed hands a few times since. Been totally renovated. I think it's now the Playa Caribe Excelsior."

Playa Caribe. The words roll over his chest like a truck. He quickly recovers from the impact and asks, "Does your company still use the property?"

"As far as I know. But as I told you, I'm not really into the day-to-day."

"Right," Mills says. "I don't know why I didn't notice this the first time I came here, but I have a photo of two of our victims standing, I believe, in the exact same place as you and the Mrs."

Again, the man eyes Mills suspiciously. "Do you think I did it? Are you trying to build some kind of case against me?"

The question, like a reckless driver, makes Mills suddenly swerve. "What? No. No. Do you think that's why I'm here?"

"I don't know why you're here. But you've been here twice. Or three times if you want to count this little stunt with the photograph."

"Just doing diligence, Mr. Gaffing."

He slams his fist into a wall. "I did not kill my son!"

Mills faces him, eases his stance, and says, "I'm sure you didn't, sir. But we do want to find the person who did. That's our number one concern, right now. That's the only reason I'm here."

"Can you go now, please?" the man begs.

"Of course," Mills says. "I'd like to take the photo with me if possible."

Offense is taken. It's in Gaffing's eyes. "Are you serious? That's my favorite picture of me and my wife. You can't have it. You can't."

Mills nods. "I understand," he says. "But again, I'm doing anything and everything I can to find your son's killer."

"No. You can't have the photograph."

"When will you be in the Student Blast office again?"

"I don't know."

"Unless you can do it here, could you maybe go into the office and scan the photo to me?" Mills asks. "My email address is on the card I gave you."

The man says he can do that. Mills is not convinced he actually will.

They have a quiet dinner. The kind of dinner when the whir of the AC dominates the conversation. They chew, sip, and there's nothing particularly wrong, just an unspoken agreement to decompress. Kelly smiles at both of them. Mills nods. Soon, though, Trevor is up, clearing his dishes, offering to clear theirs. Like most teenagers, he's Pavlovian for a Friday night. "Should we be grounding him?" Mills asks his wife.

"Dad!"

"The chores, Alex. You gave him endless chores."

"But where are you going tonight?" he asks his son. "You're not seeing Lily, are you?"

Trevor snickers. "Of course not."

"Better not."

"We haven't broken up," Trevor says. "If that's what you're asking." He's nearly at the front door, keys jangling, when the doorbell rings. "I'll get it," he yells to his parents.

Kelly looks at Mills, but he shrugs. He hears a hushed conversation out front, then Trevor calling, "Mom, Dad, we have visitors."

They head to the door, where they find a dour Mr. and Mrs. Heathrow standing there. "Is everything all right?" Kelly asks them. "Please come in."

She leads them to the front room, where she asks them to sit. "We'll stand," Dan says. "We won't be long. We're sorry to drop in unannounced. But this is about Trevor. We thought you'd like to hear it from us first."

Mills closes his eyes for a second as the chill goes right to his skin, the hair on his arms standing on end.

"What about me?" Trevor asks Dan.

"Relax," Mills tells his son. And then he turns to Dan. "We're all ears."

The man, his bowling-ball head as red as a ripe tomato, clears his throat and says, "We're thinking of pressing charges against Trevor."

Mills takes it in the gut. So much so he can't speak.

"What?" Trevor screams. "What the fuck!"

"Trevor, please," Kelly says, her eyes storming. Then she turns to Lily's parents and says, "You had better explain."

"There's really nothing to explain," Dan says. "Your son forced himself on Lily."

"Bullshit! Total bullshit," Trevor cries. "That did not happen."

"In Lily's version of things, it did," Dan says. "And we believe our daughter."

"That's bullshit. I would never do that. Ever. Mom? Dad?"

"Trevor, why don't you hang out in the office while your mom and I sort this out?"

"I'm not leaving until this bullshit—"

"Trevor, do what I said. I still make the rules around here."

When Trevor retreats, Kelly steps closer to Dan and his wife and says, "You better know what you're doing."

"The more I hear how your kid behaves, the more I believe he forced himself on Lily," Dan says.

Mills shakes his head. "It's a 'he said, she said' situation."

"Typical denial," Dan says. "A good parent wouldn't try to cover up for his kid."

"Get the fuck out of my house, Dan!" Mills howls.

"No, wait," Kelly says. "Let me just prepare the Heathrows for the very real scenario of fighting this out in court. You'll be asked to put your daughter in a courtroom to claim Trevor did what? Rape her? Sexually assault her? If we had any inkling our son was capable of that, we'd be right there with you. But we all know that didn't happen. Don't we?"

"My daughter doesn't lie," Corinne squeaks from the corner of the room.

"I suggest you call the cops and file a complaint against Trevor," Mills says. "It's your right. Go ahead. We don't fear the truth."

"Wait," Kelly insists. "Can't we all take a deep breath? I'd rather we agree to an intermediary step before we end up in court. It makes much more sense. I know some great private mediators who the court uses from time to time. I've sent my clients to plenty of them. Would you consider that?"

"Yeah, right, so you can handpick one of your liberal shrinks or somebody to decide what really happened? I don't think so," the bowling ball mutters.

Kelly laughs a bitter laugh. "No," she says. "Not at all. In fact, we'll let you pick the mediator."

Corinne starts to say something, but her husband interrupts her. "What about our priest?"

"That would hardly be an impartial mediator," Mills says.

Corinne steps forward and says, "We'll find someone."

"But if we're not happy, we're pressing charges," Dan says with a poke to Mills's chest. "And your son can kiss his football scholarship goodbye."

Mills wants so desperately to take that squirrely, little finger and twist it until it breaks. But instead he says, "Okay, now, will you get the fuck out of my house?"

"No wonder your kid's a thug."

Trevor appears from the hallway, having ignored his parents' instructions to sit it out in the office. "I did not force myself on her, Mr. and Mrs. Heathrow," he says. "In fact, it was her idea to have sex in your bed. Her idea."

Corinne whispers, "Oh, my God. . . ."

"Trevor," Mills warns him.

"No," the kid says. "Ask her about that. And ask her why."

Lily's parents slam the door shut behind them as they leave.

Mills is shaking.

30

The case of Kimberly Harrington's disappearance involved several FBI agents over the course of the investigation. The Mexican authorities led the investigation, of course, but they were assisted by Special Agents Jeremy Hicks and Henderson Garcia, both legal attachés assigned to the US Embassy in Mexico City. Hicks retired six years ago. Garcia is still based in Mexico.

"So, I talked to Garcia, and he knows the case well, says the files are accessible, given that the case was never closed and they regularly get tips, although most of them are lousy," Preston explains. "He's sending me a PDF of the lists of people they interviewed in Cancun. But he said it will take a while to actually get me all their statements because there are numerous files and they take forever to upload. He was, shall we say, very curious about our interest."

"Of course he is," Mills says. "Did you fill him in?"

"Yeah. He's even more curious now."

They're standing at the coffee maker outside Mills's office. It's 11:20 a.m. Monday morning.

"Good. Just start with what you have and go from there."

Preston takes that as his cue to leave.

By three o'clock in the afternoon, Mills still hasn't heard from Joe Gaffing. He picks up his phone, dials. The man picks up on the fourth ring.

"What?" is all Gaffing says.

"Mr. Gaffing, this is Alex Mills with the Phoenix PD."

"What is it?"

"I thought you were going to scan a copy of that photo for me."

"I am," the man says. "I'm just finishing up at the office now."

"Good. So I suppose you've had a chance to check on those customer records for me."

"Right. We have no records from that far back, like I warned you."

"So, let's say I get a search warrant for your computers and whatever other records you have in the office, we won't find a manifest for the tour Kimberly Harrington was on?"

"Are you threatening me?"

"No," Mills says. "Just clarifying."

"You will not find a manifest."

"What about in storage? Would you have it in a storage locker somewhere?"

The man exhales a puff of disgust. "Jesus, do you know how many boxes of shit I have in storage? You just asked me about this on Friday. There's no way in hell I'd get through all that crap in three days."

"I can send a team to help you sift through the boxes, sir."

"Not necessary."

"Do you have any reason to believe that any of my victims, excluding your son because we already know he was there, was in Mexico on the same tour as Kimberly Harrington?"

"It's possible," the man says. "But let me tell you this. The FBI must have the manifest in their file. Every single student who was on my tour with her was interviewed by them as potential witnesses. I remember that. Most of the students were hysterical."

"I bet."

"But, you realize, those boys didn't have to be on my tour to be in Mexico that week. It was a popular week. And, like I told you, other companies ran trips there, as well."

The man's patience is obviously frayed, his last nerve on its last nerve.

"But the groups mingled?" Mills asks.

"If you're asking if the kids were confined to their own tour groups, the answer is no."

"That's what I'm asking."

"So checking for every student on my tour would not necessarily get you what you're looking for."

"Gotcha," Mills says. "I'll be waiting for that photograph. Thank you, Mr. Gaffing."

Gaffing is gone without another word.

The photograph arrives about thirty minutes later. Mills chalks up the delay to an old man with a scanner. He finds the photo of Torento, Schultz, and Klink posing on the beach. He lines the two images up side by side on his screen. There's no mistaking it. He prints them out and summons his squad to the conference room. Powell and Myers show up together, and Powell says, "What's with the goofball smile, Alex?"

Ignoring her, Mills tapes the photos to the whiteboard, then dials Preston from the console on the table. "You coming?" he asks.

"Oh, sorry, man. I just got the first PDF from Mexico City. Can I just listen in while I go through it?"

"Sure. No problem. How's it look?"

"Massive, when you consider there's another PDF to come, and these are just lists," Preston says. "I think I could use some help."

"You can borrow Myers or Powell tomorrow," Mills replies. "Just listen in as best you can for now."

"All ears."

Mills points to the photos. "We're looking at two photos most likely taken in the exact same place on the exact same beach. It's a beach in front of the hotel where Kimberly Harrington went missing during her spring break trip twenty-five years ago this week."

Myers whistles.

"We know this," Mills continues, "because the tour company that operated that spring break trip has confirmed as much."

"But that doesn't mean Torento and our victims were in Cancun at the same time or even the same year the girl went missing," Powell says.

"True," Mills concedes. "But let's say our victims were on the same tour as Kimberly Harrington; they would have been interviewed by the FBI, according to what the tour company tells me. So, I'd rather be eyeballing those lists instead of flight manifests at this point."

"I'm eyeballing as we speak," Preston says.

"Can you find out if agents interviewed students who were on other tours, as well?" Mills asks him. "Our victims could have gone there through another company. It might be hard to place them."

"And if we do place them, what exactly does that tell us?" Powell asks. She's leaning back in her chair, her arms folded across her chest, not easily impressed this afternoon.

"It tells us," Mills begins patiently, "that we need to look deeper into their backgrounds, further back than the occasional reunion, back to this beachside photo and whether or not the guys encountered Kimberly Harrington in Cancun. Wouldn't it be interesting if they were all on the same notorious trip as the missing college student, and now they're dead?"

Preston scoffs. "It's twenty-five years later."

"Never too late for shit to happen," Mills says.

"But our congressman's in the photo, and he isn't dead," Powell reminds them.

"Not yet," Mills says. Then he tells them all to have a good evening, grabs the photos, and walks out.

31

That night, while Mills is in bed, nothing happens. He pulls Kelly close, he strokes her back, and she makes a purring sound as if she's happy with his touch, but when he moves his hand around and brushes her torso and then her breasts, she inches away. Those mere inches might as well be miles. He leans in, kisses her neck, his mouth lingering just long enough to taste a tear that rolls off her cheek. "Kelly? Babe, what's wrong?"

He gets up on his side, partly balancing on an elbow, and he pulls her toward him until she's on her back, and then he runs his hand lightly across her face and finds the rest of her tears. She's weeping. He reaches back to his nightstand and flips on a light. "Kelly, what's going on?"

She stares at the ceiling. "I'm sorry," she says. "I'm just not in the mood anymore."

"I've noticed. Is it me? Is it all the stress about Trev?"

"It's not you, and it's not him."

"Then who is it?" he asks, for a split second genuinely worried it's another man.

"It's nobody. It's me."

"But we've always been so good," he says. "Probably better than most couples—and more often."

"We're perfect together," she assures him. "But I'm not perfect right now."

He lies flat, then pulls her close so she can rest her head on his chest. He strokes her hair as she drapes an arm across him. They lie there for a moment, still and quiet. "What's not perfect about you, babe?"

"I went to the doctor last week. . . ."

His stomach twists. The blood seems to drain from his face. He never could have pretended to be ready for a moment like this. "What is it?"

"I'm menopausal."

"What? Are we that old?"

"Wrong response."

He lifts her face, then plants a kiss firmly on her lips. "Sorry. You know I don't mean that."

"So we're looking at hot flashes, moodiness, a change in libido, and who knows for how long," she says. "I'm kind of young for 'the change,' but I suspected it all along. And now the doctor's confirmed it."

"Well, it could be a lot worse, Kelly," he says. "You could be sick. And you're not sick."

She begins to weep again. "I know that. But I feel like my life is over."

"C'mon, that's a bit much," he says. "You can feel sorry for yourself if you want to. I support that, hon. But I don't support the doom or the gloom about life. We've got a great life, you know, aside from this bullshit with Trev."

She wipes her tears and smiles. "I know."

"Do you?"

"Yup."

"Next time you find out something at the doctor, don't wait a week to tell me," he says.

"Just be ready for a lot of changes," she warns him. "And I want to apologize now for any temperamental episodes in the future. And for running the air conditioner at twenty below zero."

"Apology accepted."

"You and Trevor might want to go buy flannel."

"Hard to find in the desert."

"And I'll probably won't be doing as much cooking," she says cheerfully. "Or other household chores."

"Wait a minute! I don't think that's a symptom of menopause."

"It is if I say it is," she insists with a hearty laugh.

"Good night, Kelly."

He flips off the light and holds her until the rhythm of her body and her breathing changes and she's drifted off to sleep. But he can't sleep. He stares into the black fabric of night, and through the seams he finds slivers of their memories. The very first day they met, how she walked over to him, confidently, her hand extended, and how she smiled and her eyes gleamed when she said, "As a law student I just want to say how much I admire your father. Lyle Mills is an inspiration." That did not endear her to him; it didn't turn him off, either, but he would not have considered dating a woman whose first attraction to him was an attraction by proxy. He would tease her about her "come-on" line for years. And next he sees her coming toward him down the aisle. She was illuminated. And the joy and the beauty and the grace on her face said everything. Maybe too much. Trevor's birth. Fear, love, panic, love. Their first house. The road trips. Birthdays. Holidays. This is a kaleidoscope of everything they've ever been and how impossibly lucky they are. They've never forgotten that. They remind each other constantly, even now, all of these years later. Sometimes the only reaction to all of this love and all of this good fortune over these years is to weep. And he has wept openly with her, and it has made them stronger.

He's fully awake. He starts to balance their checkbook in his head. Do their taxes. Worry about Trevor. Worry about work. About the FBI report. About the congressman. About everything. He gets up, goes to the living room, and powers up his laptop. He emails Sergeant Jacob Woods: "Imperative that we talk in the morning." He emails his squad: "Myers, work with Preston on FBI files; Powell, follow up with realtor's office re: cardboard, Meeting @ 3 p.m. All hands on deck." Then he sends an email to Gus Parker and attaches the two photos of the beach: "Let me know if you see anything here. One shot is the travel agent's dad and mom, the other is the congressman with two of the victims. Same beach. Thanks, A."

It's almost midnight.

Alex goes on Google and searches for "menopause."

There are 160,000,000 results in 0.74 seconds.

What, 160,000,000 results? That completely overwhelms him. Maybe knowledge is not the antidote to Kelly's menopause. Maybe vacation is. He goes into the kitchen, pours himself a glass of wine, returns to his computer, and Googles "Hawaii."

Somewhere between Maui and Kauai he passes out on the couch. He sleeps until six thirty when Kelly tugs at his hand.

"Was it the smell of my menopause that chased you from the room?"

"Huh?"

"Why don't you crawl into bed for another half hour? You look like you could use it."

He yawns broadly, then sits up. "Jesus. What the fuck . . ."

"Either get back in bed or join me for coffee."

"Coffee," he says.

On his way into work, his phone dings with Woods's reply. "I'm in my office," it reads. "Stop by when you're ready."

Gus and Ivy stroll the neighborhood for a morning walk. She's been a lot peppier since she and Gus have been more predictably at his house in Arcadia. The birds are singing, and she responds with her typical leaps in the air when she spots them in the trees. This neighborhood, the sound of the valley whirring to life, people with their pets and their kids and their jobs, this is the real world. When he's with Billie, whether behind the gates in Paradise Valley, or looking out to the sea in Malibu, he's not fully in the real world. He can't quite put his finger on it, but sometimes it's as if he's left his life when he leaves his home and goes to hers. Ivy, her eyes studious, looks at him as if she can read his mind.

"No, I'm not having second thoughts," he tells her. "I'm just happy to be home with you. Okay?"

That seems to satisfy her, and she prances on. He doesn't want to tell her that the indulgences have started to wear on him.

"Race you home?"

That's all Ivy needs to hear, and she's off like a bullet. He runs behind her, yelling at her to stop when they need to cross a street, resuming the chase on the other side. She's yipping at the air. At home he bathes her and cooks up some human food for her. She dries off in the sun by the window, sleeping on the warming tile floor. Gus opens his email, sees the message from Alex Mills, and downloads the photos. He doesn't have to be at work until eleven.

Mills is not fully seated when Woods says, "So, what's up?"

"Good morning, Jake."

"I think your word was 'imperative.' Imperative that we speak."

"Right. It was. Because it's imperative that we interview the congressman."

Mills braces for an eye roll or a dismissive wave of the hand. Neither happens. Woods just sits there waiting for his subordinate to tap dance. But Mills smiles because the sergeant is not going to fuck with his newly reclaimed mojo. The days of his mojo getting fucked with are over. "I know it's not a popular decision, but it has to happen," he tells Woods. "You remember the Kimberly Harrington case?"

"Of course I do."

"The twenty-fifth anniversary of her disappearance is this Friday."

"Wow, twenty-five years," Woods says. "But what does this have to do with Al Torento?"

"That photo I keep telling you about . . . of those guys . . . it was taken in front of the same hotel where the girl was staying."

"At the same time?"

"We don't know," Mills replies. "That's what we want to ask the congressman. We can't ask anyone else because the other two guys in the photo are dead."

"Gotcha. Well, I'm not going to stand in your way."

"And if he circumvents me again? If he goes to the chief or the mayor?"

Woods leans forward, cupping his chin in his left hand. "I'll back you. I'll recommend that Toronto help us out."

"Recommend?"

"Come on, Alex, we can't force the guy to submit to questioning," Woods says. "We have no grounds."

Mills gets up. "He knows his two old buddies are dead. Apparently he has no fear, our invincible congressman."

"Or he doesn't want his name dragged into this during an election year."

"Yeah, yeah, we've been down this road."

"I'm not saying it's a good excuse, but it's all about PR when you're trying to stay in office. You just can't have your name associated with a case like this."

Mills drifts to the door. "You don't think his stonewalling looks suspicious?"

"I didn't say that. I think he's freaking out because he's afraid he might be next, or he's freaking out because he knows something."

"Thanks, Jake."

The sergeant nods but says nothing as Mills backs out the door.

Gus studies the people posing in the photos. They're on the same stretch of beach, the sea spreading out behind them. The man and woman are happy but not without troubles. The three guys are happy but not without mischief. He sees from one photo to the other a vivid entitlement in their eyes, as if, of course, they deserve this vacation, of course they will indulge, of course they will act as if they own the world as they reign over this corner of Mexico. Of course they will break the rules. He sees this specifically in the young men. The husband and wife feel entitled to be here, too, but they don't want trouble. They have enough of that at home. She'll allow herself more liquor than usual because, Lord knows, she needs it. The guys, though, they'll make noise about their desires. They'll grunt and whistle and ogle at the females on the beach and in the bars, and to them it will be all about "getting lucky," because this vacation will be a complete disaster, and a waste of money, if they don't all get laid at least once. Better be more than once.

Yes!

This is where the Spanish music plays. This is where it's been playing all along. It's a mariachi band on the beach. All day. All night. The tempo races, and Gus can see a frenzy of people dancing in the sand, in the water, on the terrace overlooking the beach. People spill out from everywhere in reverie. A constant beat. Horns blasting. Gus can almost smell danger in the sultry mix of salt air and alcohol, in the cocktail of perfume and cologne. Something fearsome stalks these people. Maybe he's projecting—considering what he knows about the two dead guys in the photo—but the fear feels linked to that specific beach at that specific time, not to crudely dug graves twenty-five years later in Phoenix. He closes his eyes and tries searching for answers about the missing girl. He repeats her name several times. Waiting. On the sixth try, he finds her shrieking with joy as she splashes in the water, as she dances to the music, as she clinks margaritas with her girl-friends and they toast their fortunate lives. On this beach. In this par-adise. Under the sun. Under the moon. It's so dark now. He opens his eyes, and he's compelled to look at the man in the middle. He can't look away. It's the congressman Alex has been talking about. There's a gun. The congressman is in a room, and the blinds are closed. Gus sees the gun, but he can't hear what's happening. Too much noise from the street, too much traffic.

Ivy barks.

He turns to her and realizes she's the only sound for miles. He looks at the clock on his screen. He'll have to leave in a half hour.

Mills puts a call into Al Torento's office in DC. A staffer answers and tells Mills that Torento is unavailable. Mills has no patience for unavailable. Really no patience. Without revealing too much, he stresses the importance of Torento taking the call. The staffer audibly balks, which makes Mills want to reach into the phone and grab the guy's throat and squeeze his voice box 'til all that's left in Washington, DC, is the squeak of a cornered mouse. Instead, he closes his eyes, warding off a migraine, and listens as the man tells him to call the district office and ask for Cal Whitmore, the congressman's chief of staff.

"Thanks for calling your pal Al's Phoenix office! This is Paisley. How can I help you this morning?"

The woman's voice is the equivalent of two hundred milligrams of caffeine surging through the bloodstream of a sixteen-year-old cheerleader.

"Yes, this is Detective Alex Mills calling from the Phoenix Police Department. I need to speak to Cal Whitmore."

"Your call is super important to us, sir. Can I put you on hold?"

"Sure."

While on hold Mills listens as Al Torento narrates an exuberant list of his phenomenal accomplishments. His inflection has the same effect as riding in the car with Grandpa Mills, whose idea of driving was gas-brake-gas-brake-gas-brake. "I introduced legislation to protect Arizona's water. I voted yes on fair trade, no on raising taxes, yes on education reform. I cosponsored a bill to protect our borders from illegal aliens and terrorists." Then the prerecorded narration segues into a rendition of "The Star Spangled Banner" sung by Glen Campbell, who makes it as far as the "perilous fight" before Paisley interrupts.

"Thank you for holding, sir," she says. "I appreciate your patience. I checked, and Cal's in a meeting."

Jesus effing Christ, Mills thinks. *It took you that long to determine he's in a meeting?* He shakes his head and says, "Please put me through to his voice mail."

Mills leaves a message.

When his phone rings about five minutes later, he knows instinctively that it's not Cal Whitmore returning his call, or Al Torento coming out of hiding. And he's not wrong. It's Gus Parker reporting for duty.

"So I observed the two photos you sent. Very vivid. Very active. They took me right back to that spring break in Mexico."

"They did?"

"Oh, yeah. Those guys were there, for sure. On spring break. And I think I saw that girl, the one who went missing."

"You think?"

"I can't be sure. It's possible that the power of suggestion influenced the vibe," he explains. "But the most important vision I had was the gun. There was a gun."

"Okay . . ."

"I'm not sure what was happening, but I saw the congressman in a dark room, and there was a gun."

"Who was holding the gun?"

"I don't know."

"C'mon, Gus."

"I don't know if anyone was holding it. I just saw a gun."

"Was this in Mexico?"

"I have no idea. But I don't think so. In my vision, the congressman looks more like the guy on the billboards, older, you know, not a college student."

Mills enjoys this. Always enjoys this. "Could you tell what was happening, Gus?"

"Well, all I could see was the congressman in this dark room, a bare room, no furniture really, except a chair, I think," Gus says. "And I really don't know what was going on, but the expression on his face was so—what's the right word here?—potent. Yeah, he was either furious or terrorized. Like he wanted to kill someone, or like he was about to be killed. I couldn't hear what was going on because of all the traffic noise outside the room."

"Wow."

"Is that enough?"

"No," Mills says with a laugh. "There's no such thing as enough. But it's great stuff. Let me know if anything else comes to mind."

"If I have a chance later today, I'll try to get back to that room. See what else it reveals."

"Sounds good."

"Have you considered a woman?" Gus asks. "As the killer. There seemed to be a feminine kind of vibe in that room with the congressman. Just a fraction of a vibe, really, but I thought I'd ask."

"A feminine vibe," Mills repeats. "Hmm. I don't know."

"I think I'm seeing a woman with blond hair. But I might be getting mixed up by that girl who went missing. I told you she came to me in a vision. She was splashing around in the water—"

"We found evidence of blond hair in our third victim's car."

"It's a woman's hair," Gus says emphatically.

"But not necessarily the killer's."

"Not necessarily," Gus concedes. "But worth considering."

Mills pauses while he tries to fit a feminine piece into the puzzle. "Doesn't exactly fit the profile," he tells Gus. "She'd have to be strong, stronger than your average female to somehow overpower these guys."

"We don't know they've been overpowered."

"They're dead, Gus."

Gus laughs. "Right. And I'm not telling you that your suspect is a woman. I'm just asking if you've ruled that out."

"I have not."

"Good. Gotta get to work, man."

Fascinating shit, Mills thinks as he ends the call and goes to seek his second cup of coffee of the morning. But there's a balance. Always a balance with Gus Parker. A balance between how much is real and how much Gus's revelations play like hippie poetry or those artsy movies with subtitles and symbols. For such a fan of classic literature, he rarely gets the pathos of those movies. And while he often doesn't get Gus, he likes having a hippie brother.

Preston sends a text, asking if Mills can push the meeting back until three thirty. As Mills is typing, "Fine," he sees a text from Kelly. He sends the one to Preston, then reads what Kelly sent him.

"Got a call from Corinne Heathrow," the text reads.

"Lucky you," Mills texts back.

"Mediation scheduled for Thurs afternoon in Chandler. Can u do that?"

"This Thurs?"

"Yup. Problem?"

"No I'll make it work, babe."

"I checked out the person they hired. All good."

"ok, love you."

"XO."

And then his phone goes quiet. All his phones go quiet. His personal cell, his work cell, his landline. Crickets. Until he gets an email from the chief's assistant, saying the chief would like to meet with Mills. Today, if possible. The chief? Pressure directly from the chief is unusual, but, of course, Mills had reached out to Toronto this morning, which probably prompted the man-baby congressman to go running to the chief once again. Knowing he can push this off for at least a few days, Mills replies to the email, saying today won't work. Maybe tomorrow. *Maybe never.* Meanwhile, no one from Congressman Toronto's office has returned his calls, not from DC, not from Phoenix, least of all not from Toronto himself. Mills dials the man's wife. She's not overjoyed to hear from him—not rude, just not inviting. She's tired, worn, weary. That's how she sounds.

"Are you on campus?" Mills asks.

"I was just about to head to a meeting," she says.

"I really need to speak to your husband. It's important."

"I've told you I'm not his secretary."

"I don't want to cause him any trouble, I promise you, but we think he may be the missing link here. Please, if you could just reach out to him . . ."

She sighs. "He left last night on a trade mission to Brazil. Like I told you before, he'll be back in Phoenix on Friday for a fundraiser. Goodbye, Detective."

Holy fuckstick.

At 3:37 p.m., Preston, with Myers like a puppy at his heels, enters the conference room, carrying his laptop and files and a grin on his face. Powell, who's already told Mills about a big score, is seated by Mills. "What's with the big smile, Ken?" Mills asks. "You got good news?"

"I wouldn't say 'good' news," Preston begins, "but we're accomplishing a lot and learning stuff."

"Like?"

"Those guys were not on the same tour as Kimberly Harrington," Preston replies. "We've reviewed the list of students provided by Go Go Mexico to the FBI legal attachés. There were four lists, one from the Kimberly Harrington trip, and the three manifests from other Go Go Mexico trips that overlapped at the same time. We don't see their names on *any* list."

"The congressman?" Mills asks.

"No. The agents also made a list of all guests staying at the Playa Grande hotel on the day that Kimberly Harrington disappeared," Preston says. "It was a huge list, but of the guests staying at Playa Grande who weren't affiliated with a spring break package, none matched the names of our victims."

"That doesn't mean they weren't there," Powell says. "Staying at a different hotel. These kids are known to cross-pollinate on spring break trips. I know I did."

"Literally," Mills teases.

The others laugh. Even Powell.

"Garcia, in Mexico City, has also started sending me abstracts from the investigation that include narrative," Preston begins, deferring to his laptop. "This was reported on the news early in the case: 'Mexican authorities believed they found evidence of foul play on the Playa Grande property.' Apparently there were some bushes that were almost destroyed, some forensic evidence, too."

"And what then? They couldn't connect this to the girl's disappearance?" Mills asks. "Instead, they're content with the mystery?"

Preston shakes his head. "It's not that simple. They found some hairs, a few shreds of clothing, and some blood in the bushes. But according to Garcia, hotel workers had trampled all over the scene in an effort to clean it up and consequently contaminated most of the evidence. The Mexican investigators, apparently, were not all that careful, themselves. The evidence would never prove reliable."

Then it occurs to him. Gus Parker has been seeing a woman falling. He's been seeing that image all along. She's falling. There's Spanish music.

"Could it have been evidence of a bad landing?" Mills asks. "From a balcony."

Preston and Myers look at each other.

"Like she was pushed or fell," Mills persists.

"We know what you mean, Alex," Preston says. "We still have more of the report to go through, a lot more. But there *is* mention of a possible fall."

"Right. But they searched the hotel and never found conclusive evidence of a fall from any of the balconies above the scene," Myers says.

"Besides," Mills speculates, "if she fell off the balcony, how did she survive and where in hell did she go?"

"Remember, she disappeared," Myers says. "There's no evidence that she's dead."

"Unless someone moved her body," Mills says. "Any DNA from the scene that wasn't contaminated?"

Preston opens a file, then reads a few lines to himself. "Not from the suspicious scene in the bushes. But it looks like the investigators were able to gather some DNA that matched Kimberly Harrington. From her hotel room, apparently. There isn't much detail here. But I have to believe that with all the attention the case has gotten over the years, that they've preserved it if they ever had it. Or they would have gotten it from her parents."

"Find out," Mills tells him.

"Will do."

"I want to compare that DNA to the DNA on the hairs we got from Gaffing's car and fingernails," Mills says.

"What? You think she's come back from the dead to kill these men?" Powell asks.

"Like Morty said, she disappeared. There's no evidence that she's dead," Mills replies.

"That would certainly be a sensational ending to a sensational case," Powell says. "But unlikely."

Mills shrugs. Ironically, sometimes the most sensational is often the most obvious, and nobody pays attention because it's too sensational too believe. He turns to her and says, "Powell has a big break to announce. I forced it out of her while we were waiting for you two to show up."

Preston and Myers both react with similar faces, slight pouts, a bit deflated, as if Powell is about to upstage them. Suddenly, she's all businesslike, her hands clasped in front of her. "We have traced the cardboard grave markers conclusively to a real estate firm on Sixteenth," she says. "The owners positively identified two of the items in evidence. They had just purchased a Whirlpool refrigerator and put the carton in the alley behind their office for recycling. The timing checks out."

Preston squints at her, cocks his head, and says, "But I'm sure they weren't the only ones buying Whirlpool refrigerators in Phoenix."

She clenches her jaw, and, on the back end of a sneer, she says, "No shit, Sherlock. They identified another item, too. The cardboard sign left at the empty gravesite came from a computer monitor they ordered off Amazon. The box went in the alley along with the Whirlpool carton."

"Wow," Myers says.

"Yeah, wow," Powell repeats. She holds up a document stapled at its corner. "Signed affidavits by the owners of the firm."

"So where does this bring us?" Preston asks. "How does it advance the case?"

"Don't be an ass," Powell tells him.

"I'm not challenging you," he says. "This is great work. But I'm thinking strategy."

Mills clears his throat if for no other reason than to remind the room that he's in charge. "This confirms that the neighborhood we've been focusing on is central to the investigation. Our victims can be tracked there. The signs can be tracked there. I'm not going out on a limb to say our killer lives or works there."

"Exactly. I doubt he'd go far to rummage up his cardboard scraps. He lives there or works there and knows what kind of crap people leave in the alleys. That is, if it's a *he*," Powell says, a hint of histrionics in her voice. "Let's not forget that the woman at the realty office is a blond. She had easy access to the cardboard."

Mills asks, "What woman?"

"The receptionist," Powell reminds him. "With the ample chest."

"Yes, okay. She's blond. Good to know."

He dismisses the meeting, asking Powell to stay behind for a minute. "I'm stuck on Al Torento," he admits to her.

"I think we all are," she says.

"I know. But here's the thing: He supposedly left last night on a trade mission to Brazil. When I called his office this morning, no one said a word about it. I know it's been a long day, but I'd like you to do some digging around. Quietly. He can't know we're digging. Just make sure it's a legitimate trade mission."

"As opposed to?"

"Make sure he's not fleeing the country."

32

I t's a long day for Gus Parker. One exam after another. This must be the season for malady in the Valley of the Sun, because he's never seen such an assembly line of patients walking in the door, a kind of conveyor belt of aches and pains and breasts. His shift started later, and his shift will end later.

He goes to take a leak. He looks at himself in the bathroom mirror, and he's covered in sweat. The sight shocks him. He doesn't sweat like this unless he's running with Ivy or doing a strenuous hike. He closes his eyes and meditates for a moment, calms the conveyor belt of images and voices and notions in his brain. There's only an endless sea, still as glass, and breathing. A passing thought of Richard Knight ripples the water. *Shut up*, he tells the thought. Gus and Billie dip their toes in, wade to their ankles. *Shh. Take me to my shut-up place.* No voices. No images. Nothing. Yes. Gus is there now. He's sailing now. The middle-aged man and the sea. *Shut up, Hemingway. Really, shh!* He's floating. There's not a sound. He's weightless, improved. A crisp breeze cools him, dries his sweat. Gus opens his eyes. His reflection affirms him, says, "Man, that meditation was a good idea." But as he turns to the door, something forces him to look back. It's a sudden wave that rises from his gut. He can't make out what he sees in the mirror now. It's not his face. He sees a smile of missing teeth. He sees eyes that are red and fierce. Gus tries, just for a moment, to return to the sea of glass, to the calm, but he can't get there. He just can't. Now he's probably late for his next exam, and something isn't right.

Stephen Kline, sixty-seven, five-ten, 190 pounds, allergic to penicillin, has been suffering dizzy spells. He's pale, slow-moving, his pace subdued by the vertigo, no doubt, but also by a latent sadness that Gus intuits. "Have you ever had a CT scan of the brain?" he asks the man.

"No."

"Well, it's not as obnoxious as an MRI," Gus says, smiling.

"My doctor says that's next if the CT scan shows nothing."

Gus guides the patient to the machine. "Have you been tested for inner ear problems?"

"Of course," the man grumbles. "The inner ears are fine."

After Stephen Kline's CT scan, Gus walks him to the changing room and offers to stay if he's not steady on his feet. The man declines. Gus has three more exams, including his next patient, Veronica Gomez, who looks like Sandra Bullock and is having trouble with her sinuses. "I can't breathe," she says. "And the pain, oh, my God."

She's forty-six but talks like a millennial on social media. She's pleasant, calm through the procedure, punctuating her visit with Gus with jokes about her postnasal drip and morning phlegm.

Gus is done at seven thirty. He shuffles through the closing ritual and is out the door just before eight as the creep of nightfall is all but complete. There's still a glow of dusk in the sky, but just a sliver on the western horizon. The streetlights are on, as are the store signs in the strip mall across the street. There's no salvaging the day at this point. He climbs in his SUV and heads home. Something still nags at him, though. Casts doubt. There was something in that bathroom mirror he should have seen. He's tired, spent. Sweaty again. The drive feels like an out-of-body kind of thing, as if he's too self-aware for his own vessel. Could be he's on the brink of a psychic breakthrough. Or he's having an anxiety attack. Gus wouldn't know. He's never had one. Camelback at night, a silhouette in the distance, beckons. He's happy to follow, to be beckoned. But he suddenly feels crowded in. He hears a faint rustling, like Ivy rising from sleep in the back seat. She can't be in the back seat, but, instinctively, Gus turns to check anyway. That's when a hand grabs his neck, crushing his Adam's apple, squeezing his windpipe. He swerves. A car honks. His tires squeal. The grip around his neck won't release.

"Gus, do not react. I have a gun."

It's a man's voice, but kind of light and pudgy like a child.

"You're going to keep driving, and I'm going to navigate, and you're going to listen to my instructions."

The man's voice climbs up Gus's spine. His sweat has turned cold. He glances in the rearview mirror, but he can't make out a face. All he can see, besides his own, are fierce, bloodshot eyes that don't blink. This is not a vision. In his gut, Gus knows the man's name, but, shuddering, he grips the wheel, steadies himself, and asks, "Who are you?"

"Shut the fuck up and drive," the man says, loosening the grip on Gus's neck.

Gus catches his breath, considers his options, his eyes darting from left to right as if he can alert a passing car. Sweat trickles down his back.

"Take the Hohokam to Forty-Fourth. Then Forty-Fourth up to Tatum," the man instructs him.

"To Paradise Valley?"

"You're taking me to Billie's house."

When Gus attempts to turn his head and get a look, the man slugs him in the face. Absorbing the sting, Gus looks in the rearview mirror again and says, "You can't hide from me. I know you're Richard Knight."

"How the fuck do you know my name?"

"The police in PV are on to you."

"Shut up. Take me to Billie's," the man says, still in the voice of a pouty child. "You want to see my gun?"

The man raises a pistol in the back seat. It's visible for a flash, and then it's gone.

"It's loaded," the passenger says. "Now give me your phone."

"My phone?"

"Hand it over."

Gus fidgets, then does a show of looking for his phone. "Damn. I must have left it at work."

A hand grabs his shoulder and squeezes. "You fucking liar. You think I'm stupid? Give it to me now, or I blow your brains out the second we stop."

Gus doesn't see that happening, but then the man lunges forward from behind and grabs the steering wheel, jolting it sharply to the right. The car squeals as it careens into the next lane, narrowly missing an airport shuttle bus; drivers all around lean on their horns, and Gus, fighting for the wheel, whips back into his original lane, where, with all of the force he can muster, he brings an elbow down on the arm of Richard Knight, jabbing the man so hard Knight loses his grip on the wheel and withdraws. Gus estimates he swerved a full ampersand before he finally regained control of his car.

"Jesus Christ," Gus says with a massive sigh. "You almost got us killed."

"That was my point," Knight says. "Now give me your phone."

Gus relents, handing the nutcase his phone. He doesn't know what's going on in the back seat, but he can hear the man rummaging through a bag or a box. He can hear metal against metal and the chirps of a few phone keys. "What are you doing, Richard?"

"A little trick I learned in prison recently," the man replies. "I'm scrambling your phone to be sure no one can track it. Just to be sure it pinged its last ping."

"Oh, come on, man. . . ."

"Just shut up and let me concentrate."

And then, as he gets on the Hohokam Expressway, Gus suddenly goes calm. He sinks back, breathes normally, and takes in the view of Camelback, now tinged by the urban glow. He's okay. He contemplates bolting from the car when they hit a red light on the surface streets. He considers speeding excessively until a cop pulls him over. But both outcomes are uncertain.

"You're going to wave to the guards, and you're going to drive through the residents' gate when we get there," Knight says. "You understand?"

"I do," Gus replies. "Would you like to stop somewhere for dinner?"

"Are you fucking kidding me? Huh? You think I'm stupid?"

"No, of course not, Richard. I think you might be hungry. I know I am."

"You can cook up a feast at Billie's. Okay?"

Gus says that's fine and drives. They hit Tatum, and the city light recedes. All is black and quiet. He rolls down his window, and the warm desert air soothes him, this night air pungent with citrus, blowing past him, the light winds lulling. As instructed he waves to the guard booth, but there's no guard in sight, and he drives through the residents' gate, then through Billie's private gate. Knight tells Gus to park in the garage. Gus considers telling the man he doesn't have a remote, but the remote is clipped to his visor. He also considers saying all four bays are full but can't calculate the consequences if the stalker discovers that three bays are empty. So in they go. Knight gets out of the car first, comes around, and points the gun at Gus's window. "You can get out," Knight tells him. "Don't put your hands up. Just get out."

Gus complies, and the man's weapon is at his neck. "Where's the circuit breaker?" Knight asks.

"The circuit breaker?"

"Yeah," the man says, tapping Gus with the weapon. "The circuit breaker. Don't play dumb. It's probably here in the garage."

"Probably," Gus says, but he doesn't know for sure. The overhead bulb is still on, but its glow is feeble at best. Seconds later, the far wall in front of them lights up. Gus turns and discovers Knight holding a flashlight.

The nutjob fans the flashlight back and forth, searching all four corners of the cavernous garage until it sweeps back and illuminates a box hanging from the wall by the doorway to the main house. "There," he says. "Go on."

When Gus reaches the box, Knight orders him to open it. Once the box is opened, Knight's flashlight inspects a mini keyboard of breakers—for what Gus hasn't a clue. But when Knight stops the cone of light on the breaker labeled "GATE," Gus gets it. "Turn it off," the man orders him.

"I don't think that's a good idea."

"I didn't ask you if it's a good idea. Turn it off. We don't want any interruptions."

"What if there's an emergency or something?" Gus asks.

"I am the emergency or something."

Gus shakes his head and flips the heavy switch. Then he lowers his hand to the wall switch by the door and hits that, flooding the whole garage with light. "What exactly do you want, Richard? I mean, what's the plan here?"

"I'm going to take your place. You know that, right? Billie loves me. Now come on, I want to see my new house."

Knight bears all the features of an aging bully, his adolescent sneer slightly morphed by desperation. He's a stocky guy, his head shaven to a buzz. He must imagine himself military, given the haircut, the army jacket, the camo pants, and the boots. His face carries the vestiges of acne, each pockmark a battle scar of a troubled youth. Gus doesn't have to ask about that, won't ask; he just knows. Richard Knight stands about three full inches shorter than Gus, but he's thick, almost bulbous in places, his gut hanging over his pants. Knight orders Gus to let him in the house. Gus unlocks the door that leads in from the garage. Just inside the vestibule, Gus notices Knight eyeing the keypad for the house alarm. "Disarm it," the intruder says. "Disarm it right now. If it goes off, I'll shoot you dead, right here, instantly. Your body will be cold before the cops get here."

Gus's body is cold now, but he's not going to argue. He punches in the code. Then he feels the gun at his back, pushing him onward.

"Oh, my God!" the gunman cries as Gus leads him down the short hallway to the left. "Is this what she smells like? It's beautiful. It's delicious. What is it?"

Gus turns around, and the pistol is in his face. He stumbles backward, steadies himself, and, as they reach the front of the house, he says, "She lights a lot of incense. But there's nothing burning now."

"Then it must be the remnants of her!" Waving his gun overhead, Knight turns 360 degrees, taking in the high-hanging tapestries of the grand foyer. His mouth gapes open with wonder. Then he stops his spin, and with a clownish smile from ear to ear, he looks at Gus and says, "I want a tour. And I want it now."

"A tour."

Knight points his gun. "Get moving."

Gus runs a hand across his forehead, trying to collect a cogent thought. How to handle a madman? This isn't a first for Gus. Last time something like this happened, it was a serial killer, a lunatic involved with the Phoenix Police Department. But it happened while working on a case with Alex; it didn't invade his private life. It threatened his life but not his life here—inside the walls that were built to keep strangers out. "C'mon," he says to Knight. "Let's start in the studio."

He leads the stalker down the winding hallway, adorned with Billie's gold and platinum records. He hears the man whimper at each display. They enter the studio, and Knight leaps past him and says, "This is where she writes her music. She always talks about this room in interviews."

"That's right, Richard. This is where the magic happens."

The man narrows his eyes and scowls. "Don't you stand there acting like you know her better than me."

Gus suspects it's a bad idea to rationalize with him, or correct his grammar, however he feels compelled to say, "I've been with her for over a year, Richard. We're a couple."

The stalker points his gun at the far wall, the only bare one in the room, and fires. The blast sends a shock wave from Gus's head to his toes. Yes, it was a bad idea to rationalize. A bad idea, indeed. The wall took a bruise.

"I told you it was loaded," Knight says.

"I realize that."

Knight paces the room, stopping at each of the six guitar stands, admiring the guitars as if they're museum treasures on exhibit. Which, to him, Gus figures, they probably are. The man sits on a stool, removes a guitar, and cradles it on his lap. He strokes it with his hand, caresses it to his chest. Swaying in the chair, Knight hums softly. Gus recognizes the melody; it's a Billie Welch song, of course, and the madman treats it with love and devotion, sitting there in his incantation, the movement of his lips like soft kisses for Billie. Gus has to be careful with what he says, here, so he braces himself and holds his breath; no harm can come to these priceless instruments. No bullet holes. No smashed guitars.

"Can we move on?" Gus asks.

"You're really kind to do this, Mr. Parker," Knight says. "You know she's in love with me. You're being what they call very gracious."

"She's in love with you?"

The man winces. "Yes. Sorry you have to hear it from me."

"Did she tell you she loves you, Richard?"

The man laughs. "Haven't you listened to her music, Gus? It's all over her lyrics."

"What is?"

"Her love for me," he replies. "She's singing to me. Directly to me."

"Oh."

"You didn't get that, Gus?"

"I'm sorry, no. I didn't."

The man shakes his head, then looks to the floor, almost ashamed. "I don't know what to say. We didn't mean for you to find out this way."

Gus turns his head so the man can't see the terror in his eyes. He's not afraid of the gun, for some disquieting reason; he's afraid of the insanity. And he has no clue what to do. He can't calculate the right move, the right response, and he's been deep in calculation since the man's eyes first appeared in the rearview mirror. The challenge is to calculate and act at the same time. "Let's go, Richard," he says, hoping the man will follow without resistance. The man not only follows, but he also follows quietly, not another word from him until they reach the round room with the fireplace. Gus stands aside at the entrance, making way for his stalker. Knight walks past him, surveys the architecture, then turns around and asks, "Why so many pillows?"

"Billie collects them from all over the world."

"So, she just sits on the floor?"

"That's the point," Gus says. "But sometimes she sits on one of the chaises."

Then the gun is in his face. "Do you and Billie fuck in here?"

Gus doesn't answer. He just stares at the man in utter disbelief.

"Do you? Do you fuck in here?"

"No," Gus replies falsely. "We don't make love in here."

The man scoffs. "I didn't ask if you made love. I asked if you fucked. Because I know you don't make love to her, Gus. No one does. She's waiting for me."

"Yes," Gus says.

His gun still pointed at Gus, Knight says, "Sit down. We need to talk."

Gus nods and sits, as does the stalker, several pillows away.

"I need to plan," Knight says. "I need to know what Billie likes. I've been trying to prepare for our life together, but do you know how hard it is to find information about someone as reclusive as Billie Welch?"

"She's not nearly as reclusive as she used to be, Richard."

The guy's face lights up. "That's good news! What's her favorite food?"

"Italian," Gus says falsely. Instantly, falsifications become his tactic. Knight will not invade Billie's life. Gus will protect the inner sanctum of Billie. He will not hand over the keys and betray the fortress. This is good. It feels better. His stomach unknots.

"What's her favorite color?"

"Red." She hates red.

"Her favorite TV show?"

"She doesn't watch a lot of TV, but I would say old reruns of *Friends*." She always hated *Friends*.

"I'm talking about a current show."

"Oh. Then it would have to be . . . hmm . . . probably *Funny Melania*."

The man cocks his head. "I've never heard of that."

Neither has Gus. "I think it's about a First Lady who's trying to escape the White House," he says. "It's on Netflix." No, it's not.

"I don't get Netflix," Knight says. "And I don't appreciate humor at the expense of our government."

Gus nods emphatically. "And neither do I. But apparently, Billie does."

"I believe in serving your country," the man says. He then goes quiet, pensive. Doesn't say a word. Gus, meanwhile, listens to the white noise of the house. Ordinarily so peaceful, the white noise sounds barbed with danger. He closes his eyes, expecting to see Billie there, expecting her arms to wrap around him, expecting her to tell him what to do with a few simple words of wisdom. Instead, he sees a beach. He sees that same beach from Alex's photos. But this time he sees himself on the shoreline. He's in Mexico. Alex is with him. The water is a lazy tide of sapphire gems, the waves splashing gently at their ankles. They turn away from the surf and gaze upward at the hotel, at the beehive towers and the balconies stacked from bottom to top. He's never actually seen the hotel, but here it is; he knows in his gut, he just knows, Alex Mills is contemplating this place right now, right now as Gus sits here opposite the gunman. He doesn't have to check, but he does anyway. The souvenir pillow on which Gus sits is the pillow from Mexico. He wants to laugh right now here in this United Nations of cushions. He wants to bust out laughing, but he doesn't, because he doesn't trust the temperament of Richard Knight. Instead, he smiles crazily.

"You okay, Gus?"

"I'm fine."

"Did you fall asleep?"

"No."

"I thought for a minute you really trusted me with this gun," Knight tells him. "I thought you trusted me enough to go to sleep."

"This has nothing to do with trust. I was daydreaming."

"Get up. Show me more."

Gus guides the man through the dining room, the kitchen, four of the guest rooms, the office, and the family room that looks out to the pool. He makes a conscious decision to avoid the master bedroom. There's no way in hell he's bringing this lunatic into Billie's most private space, no way in hell he'd leave the footprints of Richard Knight in there. When Knight asks about the master bedroom, Gus has it all figured out. He tells Knight that the room is being renovated, the floor is already gone, and the place is being chemically treated to remove defective Chinese drywall. So damn clever, Gus thinks. So freaking resourceful for a hostage.

"So where does she sleep?" the man asks.

"In one of the guest rooms I showed you."

"Which one?"

"Uh, the one near the spa."

"Take me back there."

"Seriously?"

Again, the gun is in his face. "Yes."

"Did I mention I'm hungry for dinner?" Gus asks.

"Fuck dinner. You'll eat later."

In the guest room, Knight climbs onto the bed. He lies on his back, running his hands all over the ornate spread. "She sleeps in this bed?"

"Yes."

He pulls the pillows to his face, four of them, and whiffs each one. He inhales deeply the fictitious scent of Billie Welch. Then he sits up, nearly delirious. "Oh, my God! This is sweeter than I imagined. So much sweeter."

"You're not going to cry, Richard, are you?"

The man's eyes flood with rage. "I'm a real man. Not like you."

"Actually, Billie likes a man who knows his emotions."

"Fuck you." The stalker points his gun at the closets. "Her clothes in there?"

"Some of them," Gus replies. "She has clothes all over the house."

Knight hops off the bed. "I want to see."

"Go crazy," Gus says, regretting the words just as they escape his mouth.

The man swings the closet doors open and stands there with his arms stretching wide, as if one of the dresses will leap from its hanger and hug him tightly. Then he enters. He meanders through the hanging clothes, his face full of Christmas morning wonder. Gus watches, fascinated, a bit frightened, aware now that there is nothing he can do or say to balance this unbalanced person. The man is too far gone into madness.

Knight is dancing like a giddy toddler with one of Billie's stage cos-
tumes when the phone on the nightstand rings. Like an alarm, the shrill
ring pierces the air, and Gus jumps ever so slightly out of his skin.

"Don't answer it," the gunman orders.

"But—"

"I said don't answer it." He emerges from the closet, the gun aimed
at Gus.

"Okay, but what if it's Billie?"

"Get in here," Knight says, waving his weapon. "Don't answer the
phone and get in here."

"You want me in the closet?"

"What the fuck did I just say, Gus Parker? Get in the fucking closet
and sit down!" The man raises his gun. His fingers tease the trigger.
"Now!"

His nerves going haywire, Gus reluctantly enters and sits. He stares
into the barrel of the gun, down its dark, hostile tunnel, figuring that's
it, he's done for.

33

Joseph Gaffing answers the phone on the third ring, the scar of a dozen cigarettes lodged in just the word "Hello."

"It's Alex Mills from Phoenix PD."

Gaffing responds by not responding.

"Mr. Gaffing?"

"Yeah. What is it?"

"Just calling to check on funeral arrangements for Joe Junior . . ."

"You're late."

"Late?"

"Yeah," the man growls. "As soon as the body was released, I had him cremated. Why do you ask?"

Mills hesitates, his plan preempted. "We sometimes will go to a victim's funeral to scope the crowd for potential suspects."

"Well, sorry, but Joey's up in smoke."

Mills lets that sink in: the death of a son, the ashes and the resignation, unresolved issues up in smoke. There's a lesson here. Mills is lucky to see it and sad to see it. "I'm sorry," he tells Gaffing.

"There was no service," the man says. "Just a few people from work. My brother flew in from Los Angeles."

Mills senses someone in the doorway. He looks up and sees the chief standing there. *Jesus.* "I'm sorry I bothered you," Mills tells the bereaved father.

"Your next call will be to tell me you've caught the guy who did this. Right?"

"Of course," Mills says. "Until then, take care."

He's not off the phone for two seconds before the chief says, "May I come in?"

"Of course. Take a seat."

The chief remains standing, because of course he does.

"What's up?" Mills asks.

"I understand you have a mediation session tomorrow," the chief says.

This knocks Mills off-balance, even though he's sitting. "Oh," he says. "That's what you wanted to see me about?"

Mills's personal cell rings. He doesn't recognize the incoming number, so he ignores it. Not that he has a choice.

"Yes," the chief says. "I've been waiting for you to get back to me. Was there something else?"

"I thought you wanted an update on the case."

"I can get that from Jake," the chief says. "But what's this business with your son? I heard from a Dan Heathrow who claims his daughter—"

"I know what he's claiming," Mills interrupts. "I'm confident this is a misunderstanding."

"Are you?"

Mills stands. "I just said I was. I know my son. He's not a perfect kid. He can be a stubborn, bullheaded shit, but I don't think he's capable of doing what the Heathrows think he's done. He's always shown respect to women. Of all ages. He has a great relationship with his mother."

The chief looks unconvinced. Neutral, like a judge. "You have your hands full, Alex. But hopefully this matter can be worked out in mediation."

"I think it will."

His cell rings again. Same number. He sends it to voice mail.

"You're a popular guy," the chief says.

"Apparently."

"You know you can't afford a family distraction now," the chief says. "I don't have to tell you that."

But you just did. "You don't."

"And the department can't afford the distraction either. Make this go away."

"Consider it done, sir."

The chief turns on his heels, like a soldier, and leaves, nearly colliding with Jan Powell in the doorway.

Can I not get five fucking minutes?

"There really is a trade mission to Brazil," Powell announces.

It takes him a second to comprehend. "Oh. And Torento is on it?"

"Yes."

"You found proof."

"There's a photo in the online edition of the *Republic*. He's shaking hands with some dignitaries at the Sao Paolo airport."

"Great," Mills says. "Now the question is . . . will he ever come home?"

Powell laughs at first, then looks at him with doubt all over her face. "You serious?"

"Think about it," he says. His personal phone rings again. Same number. He sends it to voice mail. "Torento knows we're still pursuing him."

"I don't see a congressman as a fugitive, but crazier things have happened," she concedes, then steps out the door.

About ten minutes after she's gone, his phone rings again. Immersed, distracted, call it what you will, Mills's train of thought has derailed. It's a pileup. A clusterfuck. And, shit, now it dawns on him: the same unfamiliar number could be another train wreck of parenting calling. *I have a kid, and he could be in even more fucking trouble.*

"Hello?"

"Alex?"

"Yes. Who's calling?"

"It's Billie. Billie Welch."

He does a double take. Her name and her voice are as unexpected as a desert rain. But his muscles relax. Trevor's fine. "Hi, Billie. What a surprise. Everything okay?"

"I can't reach Gus," she says. "I'm worried."

"Oh? I talked to him yesterday morning. Seemed fine to me."

"I tried calling him several times last night, and he never picked up," she explains. "It's not like him to not return calls. I'm a bit frazzled."

She is. Mills hears the tremors in her voice. His job right now is to calm her, not to freak out. Still, an electric current torques his spine as if he's touched a high-voltage fence. Deflecting, he says, "I'm sure he's okay, Billie. It would not be unlike him to forget to charge his phone."

"But I've been trying him again all day today," she says. "And nothing. My assistant called his work, and they said he didn't show up. Again, not like him. Really, Alex. We know there's a stalker out there. . . ."

The zaps spread from his spine to his shoulders, down his arms, to his hands. "He didn't show up for work?"

"No," she replies, her voice cracking as if tears aren't far behind. "Can you help us?"

"Of course. Of course I will," he says. "I'll head over to his house now and see what's up."

"Oh, God, Alex, that would be so great. My sister's here with me in LA or I'd ask her to go do it. I know you're busy, but if you could please go over there and call me back, I promise I'll make it up to you. I really will."

Mills looks at his watch. It's 5:30 p.m. He reaches in the top drawer for his keys. "No problem, Billie. I'm on my way."

"I asked the police in Paradise Valley to do it, but they said they couldn't because Gus doesn't live in their jurisdiction. I only called them because I kept getting your voice mail."

He's not about to tell her this sounds like trouble or just feels bad in his gut, which it does. "Go get lost in your music. Let me worry about the Guster."

"Actually, I got to catch a flight, Alex. And I'm, like, panicking. I just booked a session in Nashville this weekend. But I'll call as soon as I land."

"Don't panic. Like I said, go get lost in your music."

"Maybe I should just come home."

"Is that what Gus would want?"

She says, under the circumstances, she doesn't care what Gus would want. And Mills believes her. "Billie, pardon me for sounding—I don't know—a bit crass about this, but aren't you one of those types who has the means to be wherever you want whenever you want?"

"I guess . . ."

"Then go to Nashville. And if anything happens here, turn around your plane and come back."

She agrees. She thanks him, her voice still trembling, and hangs up.

On his way to Arcadia, he pulls Beatrice Vossenheimer's phone number from a county database and dials. She answers on the third ring and flatly says, "You're calling about Gus."

"Wow, Beatrice, has anyone ever told you you're psychic?"

She doesn't laugh. "I know you're calling about Gus because Billie contacted me a few hours ago."

"Oh. So I assume you haven't heard from him."

"Not in this dimension," she says with a curious chirp.

"Okay . . . care to elaborate?"

Beatrice goes quiet. He can hear her breathing. He imagines her summoning. And then she says, "I think he's close by. I can feel it. I went looking for him, psychically speaking, and I think he's here."

Her words are simple, factual, and without emotion.

"Here?" Mills asks. "Where is here?"

"Paradise Valley. My gut tells me he's down the street at Billie's house. I don't know what's going on there. I got mixed messages that he's fine but also that he's not fine."

"But I told him to stay at his own place," Mills says. "I'm heading to his house now."

"Shall I stop by Billie's?" she asks. "It's only a few doors down."

"No, Beatrice. Please don't go near there. Just don't," he warns her. "Thanks for the hunch. My next call is to PV Police. I'll be in touch."

They're in the kitchen. Water boils on the stove. Gus fetches pasta from the pantry and pours it into the pot. "I've served you three meals already. What happens when we run out of food?" he asks Richard Knight. "You're going to take me to Safeway at gunpoint?"

"No," the stalker says, sitting there at the massive island in the middle of the kitchen, the pistol following Gus's every move. "This is the last supper, Gus."

Gus can't put his finger on this particular brand of derangement, but there's something cinematic about the insanity that's unfolded over the past twenty-four hours. It's believable because it's happening, but it's also fantastical because the breakdown of the human mind he's watching has a kind of time-lapse quality to it, its own metamorphic arc. He has watched his captor climb a staircase of emotions, a winding staircase for sure, where each step incites a different mood in Richard Knight. There's no particular order to the anger, the glee, the despair, or the ecstasy, and at each step the crescendo of every mood takes Gus by surprise. He can feel it in his nerve endings. "The last supper?" he asks.

"You either do as I say or I'm going to kill you and leave your body here in Billie's house."

"I thought you were going to kill me either way," Gus says as he rinses lettuce in the sink. "And for the record, it bothers me when you call her by her first name."

Gus hears the man violently push his chair from the island. He hears the man whip over to the sink. He feels the cold metal barrel of the gun probing his neck. "Fuck you! Shut up!" the man howls in his ear. And then, in a perverse whisper, he says, "We're going to eat, Gus. And I'm going to tell you my plan. It's very easy. In the morning it will be over. You'll do what I say, and then you'll be a free man."

Richard lowers the gun.

Gus moves to the stove, where he stirs the pasta, his stomach as knotted as the bow ties floating in the pot. He tends to swallow his fear to keep his exterior calm, to keep his mind clean and agile, but like all things he swallows, the fear goes to his stomach, and in there it boils like the cauldron on the stove.

"Just tell me what you want," he says to Richard.

The gunman has returned to his seat at the island. "I want to eat dinner. That's what I want. So, let's eat, Gus. Then we can talk."

On the way to Gus's house, Mills puts in a call to the PVPD, where everyone, apparently, has left for the day. He gets as high up as he can get in the rather stunted hierarchy before someone forwards his call to Randy Obershan's cell phone. The detective answers, says he heard from Billie Welch, as well, and that he knows she's looking for Gus. "Just talked to one of the guards over there, and he says he thought he saw Gus drive in last night. Wasn't one hundred percent positive, but said he's fairly sure Gus went in through the residents' gate."

"No cameras?" Mills asks.

"Only on the visitors' lane," Obershan says. "I'm actually on the way to the Welch house now. I got a couple of officers meeting me there."

"Good. Glad to hear it."

"We'll ring at the gate to her driveway," the detective tells him. "If Gus Parker is in there, he'll hear us."

"He may hear you, but what if Richard Knight has him holed up in there?"

"I'm not going to crash her gate, if that's what you're asking," Obershan replies. "I have nothing to go on."

"Call Billie Welch," he says. "I guarantee she'll authorize the destruction of her property. She can afford it."

"If it comes to that."

"Let me know what you find as soon as you get there," Mills says. He recites his phone number. "Even if it's nothing, man."

Over at Gus's house, Mills hears the dog barking inside. He knocks on the front door. Puts his ear to the wood. He only hears the dog, otherwise just the hum of an empty house. No footsteps. No Gus. He opens the gate to the side yard and peers into each window, each one framing, in a way, a still life of purgatory. Nothing has changed in there; it has simply stopped. Mills has done this a million times, but never, or hardly ever, in search for somebody as close to him as Gus. For the third time, easily, he dials Gus's number, just on the off chance. Again, the call goes to voice mail. He's in the backyard now, by the pool. He puts his face against the expansive slider and sees Gus's kitchen as he had left it, and the family room, disturbed by mere living, but undisturbed by the day itself. Suddenly the dog, Ivy, comes bounding to the glass, yelping and pawing. Her barks turn to cries, then whimpers. She scratches for Mills. He bends down, touching the glass. "Hey there, girl," he says. "Everything's going to be okay. Don't worry, girl. . . ." Gus could be in there but not the way Mills would hope to find him. There was no sign of forced entry at the front door, no sign back here either. As Mills turns to check the other side of the house, Ivy jumps at the glass, and she's on her hind legs nearly pounding at him. She's barking again, howling like a wolf, and he can hear her all the way to the front yard and even out in the driveway, where he sees a diminutive woman standing by his car.

"Hello," she says. Her eyes are curious.

"Hello. Are you one of Gus's clients?" he asks.

"No."

"Oh, you live in the neighborhood?"

"I work for the family across the street," the woman says, pointing to a house on the other side of the cul-de-sac. "I do cleaning for Gus sometimes."

She speaks with a heavy accent, a Spanish accent. He flashes his badge. "Have you seen him today?"

"No. Not today," she replies. "Is Gus okay?"

He nods. "Oh, yeah. I was just looking for him. That's all. And he hasn't returned my calls. We're friends. It's not really police business."

"You want to go inside? I have a key," she says, removing it from her pocket.

He nods and gestures for her to come forward.

"My name is Elsa," she tells him as she opens the door.

"Alex Mills."

The dog rushes at them, then leaps at Mills.

"Down, girl," he says. "Stay down."

His commands prove ineffective, but all Elsa has to do is say, "Ivy," and the animal sits in silence.

"Nice touch," Mills tells the woman as he kneels to the floor and puts his arms around the dog's neck and hugs. "It's going to be all right, Ivy. You're a good girl. Gus will be home soon."

He searches the house, both Elsa and Ivy at his heels. The house has that gone-to-work kind of vacancy. Nothing seems trespassed. There's no sign of a struggle. Gus's office is meticulous. The kitchen anticipates another meal, maybe, or still digests the last one, but it, too, is clean. A few magazines litter the couch. A blanket sits there in a ball.

"Since you clean the house, Elsa, can you tell me if anything's missing?"

"Gus is missing," she says. "But everything else is here."

The guest room is undisturbed. The only disheveled room in the house is Gus's bedroom. Mills sees shoes scattered on the floor and clothes piled on the chair and the unmade bed, and he thinks this aspiring mess is nothing more than Gus's signature, certainly not any kind of home invasion. Back in the living room they find that Ivy has left a mess by the sliders. "I'll clean it up," Elsa says.

"Thanks. I think I'll take Ivy home with me until Gus gets back."

She nods and smiles. "That's nice of you. I'll lock up when I leave."

He finds the dog's leash hanging from a hook in the kitchen. Ivy hears it jangling, and she's immediately at Mills's side. He and the dog are at the front door when Elsa calls to him. "You think you'll find him?"

"I will," he replies. "For all we know he flew home to Seattle and left his phone with the TSA. People do it all the time."

He knows that's not what happened. Gus is no more inclined to fly home to Seattle than he is to fly home to Pyongyang. Mills stuffs the dog in the back seat and, because he hasn't heard from the cops in PV, makes a beeline for Billie's house.

"Sounds like we have a guest," Gus says to Richard Knight.

It's the bell ringing from the driveway gate. The ring mimics a deep doorbell chime, and it repeatedly fills the house like a pipe organ with hiccups. Gus can tell the chime is sending shivers up the stalker's spine every time the person out there presses the button.

"Don't let them in," Richard says. "Don't talk to them on the intercom."

"Can I go see who it is?"

"You can't open the front door."

"But I can see from the foyer balcony. Let's go."

They climb the stairs, the bell still chiming, and when they reach the top Gus peers out the window and is not surprised to see three cruisers from the Paradise Valley Police Department. He thinks maybe he should hit a light switch, blink the lights to send a signal, but he has a gun at his back. Gus really has to wonder if Richard Knight would pull the trigger. His gut says no, but his mild spasms of anxiety say yes. "It's the police," he tells his captor.

"I can see that, Gus."

"They've come here looking for me."

"Of course they have, Gus. But as long as you don't answer the bell, they'll figure you're not here. I don't think they're going to jump the gate. Do you?"

"I doubt it, Richard," Gus replies. "It's a very tall gate."

The landline rings.

"Who's that?" the stalker asks.

"I don't know," Gus says. "It's Billie's house phone."

"Will it go to voice mail?"

"Eventually."

In the meantime, there's a manic orchestra with no conductor. The bell chimes; the phone rings. The sounds overlap, clash, and ricochet off one another. "I'm going to find that phone and rip it out of the fucking wall, Gus. Come on!"

They return to the first floor. Twice the phone has stopped ringing and started again like the insistent calls of a jilted lover. The driveway bell persists. True to his word, Richard finds one of the landline phones in the kitchen, picks up the base, rips it from the wall, then, almost foaming at the mouth, snatches the cordless handset from the counter and smashes it on the floor. It crumbles to smithereens under his foot.

A few minutes later the bell goes quiet. The cops have given up. They probably came by as a courtesy check, found no one home, and left. Or maybe they'll be back. Certainly Billie is looking for him. And she's made a career, and maybe a relationship, out of refusing to take no for an answer. That had to be her calling the house last night and again today. Or maybe it was the cops. Or Beatrice. Or maybe God. His thoughts, as fruitless as they are, are now interrupted by the sight of dangling ropes.

Richard, awash in sweat, his hands wringing, has removed the rope from his bag of supplies. Last night with his hands bound tightly, Gus had been taken to the pillow room and told to sleep. But Gus discovered that he doesn't sleep so well with a crazed gunman in the house, or with rope binding his wrists. And now it looks as if Gus is in for the same deprivation tonight.

"You think maybe I could sleep in a real bed this time?" he asks.

"I don't see why not," Richard says. "This could be your last night to dream. It's up to you, Gus."

Mills counts three marked cruisers and one unmarked flanking the gates at Billie Welch's driveway. He cracks a window to give Ivy air and gets out of his car. Obershan turns and sees him. "Nothing," he says. "We were just about to leave."

"Leave? You sure he's not in there?"

"As sure as we can be without bulldozing the gate."

"What about the emergency code? PV requires that, right?"

"Of course," Obershan says. "But it's not working. It won't open."

His stomach churns. "What does that tell you?"

"It tells me either Ms. Welch disabled her security code or the alarm installers somehow messed up the circuitry to the gate."

Mills has to be careful here not to tread. But still. Can this dude be that stupid? "With all due respect, Billie didn't disable the security code. Richard Knight did."

"You make it sound like that didn't occur to us," the detective says, his voice deep with offense.

"No. You made it sound that way," Mills tells him. "We don't need any more proof that Gus is in there with that lunatic."

"Actually we do if we're thinking of storming the place," Obershan argues. "Besides, Richard Knight would have had to get inside to mess with the gate. The codes are set from the house. The circuitry is all inside. There's really no way he could have gotten in now that the property is really a fortress, Alex."

"You try the bullhorn?"

"Uh, no. We rang the bell at the gate about a dozen times."

"Try the bullhorn."

"And say what?"

"Oh, I don't know. How about, 'Knight, we know you're in there and we have you surrounded'? Something like that?"

"If this was your jurisdiction, you sure as hell wouldn't do it, Alex. We have no probable cause to disturb the peace. And in this neighborhood bullhorns aren't appreciated."

Mills offers a wicked scoff. "Are you fucking kidding me? Of course you have cause. You afraid of wounding the delicate ears of the elite?"

Obershan puffs out his chest and squares his jaw. "Enough, Alex."

Ivy barks. Mills turns to his car and sees the dog flouncing in the back seat. She's pacing from one window to another, yelping.

"You call that a K-9 patrol?" Obershan quips.

"I call that Gus's dog, smartass. And, by the looks of it, she can detect her owner inside."

"Or maybe she just needs to take a dump, Alex. It's your car. You decide."

The decision has nothing to do with Ivy's bowels. The decision has everything to do with staying or leaving. It's not an informed decision to make.

"Look, we want to help you find your friend," Obershan assures him. "But we've got nothing to go on. I don't think Knight would be stupid enough to come back here. And neither one of us is going to get a SWAT team out here based on a guess. If we can get clear evidence that Gus is in the house, we might consider storming the place. But you know the downside, Alex. An assault like that could trigger something crazy in our suspect. Knight might do something stupid, and Gus could get hurt."

"Obviously nobody wants that," Mills concedes.

"But if it comes to that, we'd still need consent from Ms. Welch. If we can get a hold of her, that is."

"*If?*"

"We can't reach her . . ."

"Right," Mills says. "She's on a flight to Nashville to do some recording or something. Maybe you should try her in an hour or two."

Mills is the last one left. After all the others are gone, he stands there, his eyes locked on the house. He considers camping out here all night, watching the house, watching for a light to come on, or one to go off, anything, any sign of life. He eyes the gate. The bottom half is solid wood, framed in steel; the top is a crown of wrought iron with spike deterrents. The gate is connected to the walls at either side. He might be able to stand on his hood, reach the juncture of the gate and the wall, climb over the wrought iron south of the spikes, and slide down the other side. He moves his car. He hears himself say, "Here goes nothing." Then Mills takes a leap to the metal brace connecting the wall and gate, goes flying, but instantly falls on his ass on the car. The hood seems to crumple, but he's certain it's his ass. Of course, there's a gradient from the wall to the street, and the slope keeps the car lower against the wall than it looks. *Fuck it.* He tries again, recalculating the velocity it will take, the running start he'll need to leverage this time to make it. He doesn't have a lot of room to play with. He starts back at the windshield. Ivy barks at him, as if she's begging him to stop, as if he's making her nervous. Then Mills picks up a few running steps down the hood and up he goes, and goes, and he reaches, and his hand slaps against the top of the wall, and he plants a foot. He looks up. Still a ways to go, but at least he's made contact. Mills pulls himself up, one leg scaling the wall, the other scaling the gate. After a few measly steps he loses his footing and chides himself. *This is no fucking way to be a superhero.* His legs scramble as he tries to replant his feet. It takes a minute, but he regains his climb and is able to pull himself onto the lowest branch of iron. He sees it won't be as easy as it had looked from below to topple over this thing; from this perspective, Mills can see the iron spreads rounder and higher than he had thought. Somehow he thought this would be as easy as flying horizontal over a high jump. Somehow he thought he was the track-and-field athlete who does this all the time. He's never done it. He's watched others do it. And they sure make it look easy. "Fuck," he groans. He really thought he could do it by simply appropriating the skills of others. "Fuck this."

Just as he utters the second of the two "fucks," he loses his footing again. Both feet. He's dangling now, kicking at the wall and the gate. The more violently he kicks, the more he causes vibration in the wrought iron. With the vibration comes the tremors that bounce his hand on and off the iron; each time he narrowly catches himself, until ultimately he misses, losing his grip. No grip, no footing, he flails, then plummets. *This Spider-Man thing is overrated.* It feels like slow motion, but it's a hard landing on his ass at the very front edge of the hood. He struggles to his feet and considers himself lucky that this hood did not add insult to injury by having an ornament.

"Gus," he roars. He knows it will do no good. But, he's beyond logic. "Gus!"

The adrenaline. The thumping in his chest. The labored breath, panting.

"Gus! Come on, Gus!"

He drifts to the front seat, slips in, then collapses behind the steering wheel. He's not the praying type; that is to say it's unlike him, as a very lapsed Catholic, to ask God to intervene in a tough situation. Instead, he mutters, "Please take care of yourself, buddy," and takes off. Worn out from the commotion, Ivy is asleep now in the back seat. He doesn't wake her when they arrive. Instead, he scoops her heavy mass in his arms and carries her inside. "Hi, honey," he says to Kelly. "We have a guest. And I broke my ass."

Lightning strikes in violet flashes. But it doesn't make a sound. It just lights the night with its benign signature, white on purple. Gus can see it through the bedroom window. He likens the condition of the sky to his own fate. Not a word, not a soul, nothing. Outside it doesn't rain; it's a dry lightning, heat lightning. Richard Knight has left him here in one of the guest bedrooms, lying on top of the bed, his wrists bound. If not for the electricity outside, he'd be in complete darkness, so there's something merciful about the languid storm, if you can call it a storm. He doesn't know what to call it. He's blind, or he *feels* blind. Except he did have some kind of vision or vibe about Alex. He thinks Alex was nearby, maybe down the road at Beatrice's house. Alex was close. They have to know Gus is here. They have to know time is running out. Richard Knight doesn't have long before he completely cracks. Gus is certain of it. He doesn't know what the crack will look like, whether it will be sudden, whether it will be jagged, whether it will hurt, whether there will be blood, but this can't go another day.

Kelly draws the line when Ivy hops on the bed. "I love her, too, Alex. And it's not like I care about the linens," she says with a laugh. "But I'm allergic. I can tell."

Mills gives her a pout. "Fine." He calls Ivy to come to his side of the bed and points to the floor. Obediently, she lies down and snorts, wagging her tail. He can tell why she's Gus's child. For the third time since he's come home, he texts Obershan and inquires about Gus's cell phone. Surely they've been able to track it by now. He had requested a signal retrieval from his own department, but he was told there was some kind of issue with the cell tower. A coincidence? Or had Richard Knight somehow scrambled Gus's signal? He had called Billie and left her an update on her voice mail.

"You're obsessing," his wife says. "I know that look on your face."

"Hon, Gus is missing. The longer he's gone, the more serious this gets."

"I understand," she says. "But I also know there's only so much you can do."

"No. I swear there's something I'm missing. . . ."

"Sleep," she says. "We have a big day ahead of us tomorrow."

He turns to her. "We do?"

She turns to him, hell in her eyes. "Uh, yes, we do, Alex. The mediation."

"Oh, fuck. Oh, Jesus Christ. Right."

She rolls over.

34

Mills wakes up to a bark and a growl, and it startles him, paralyzes him, in his sleepy stupor for a second before he looks to his side and sees the dog's head resting on the edge of the bed. "Oh, girl," he says. "You scared the shit out of me."

Ivy shakes her head and barks again. That's her cue to go outside. So, Mills jumps into a pair of sweats and a T-shirt and goes for a walk with his friend's best friend at his side. Kelly is already out of the shower when they get back. She moves about her morning, distracted, carrying a heavy weight, it seems. Mills reaches for her and says, "It's going to be fine, Kel. We both know Trevor didn't do what those people said he did."

"Do you believe a mediator will believe that?" She has that look, that clenched jaw, the gnashing teeth, her eyes gnashing too, if that's possible.

"The mediation was your idea," he reminds her. "Because you knew it was the best option. Because you trusted it would settle this thing without harming Trevor. No reason to second-guess now."

She doesn't say much else before she drifts out of the house.

Now, as he leaves for headquarters, he finally gets a text from Obershan.

"Sorry, Mills. We've been trying. Problem with the towers," the text reads.

"Sabotage?" Mills texts back.

"Don't think so. We think it's a provider issue."

"Cell service is fine."

"Don't know, Alex. We're still working on it."

"Keep me posted."

"K."

Oh. Obershan's one of those with the "K."

Mills backs the car out of the driveway and heads to work. He swerves and nearly hits someone on the highway, his thoughts completely elsewhere on the map. He takes a detour and drives over to Gus's house. He does a walk around, then peers in through the windows, looking for any change since yesterday, any noticeable alteration in appearances. Through every window, not a sign of life. He puts his ear up against the glass sliders in the back. Just a hum. The static hum of yesterday. But in that hum, Mills hears his own voice. He's interrogating the rhetorical witness. "When did you last see him? Where was he? Where was he going? When did he say he'd be back?"

If he could, he'd go AWOL and hike the forbidding terrain behind Billie's house and climb the wall. If Richard Knight could do it, surely so could Mills. And so what if it sets off the alarm? The more commotion, the merrier. He'd need tools. And rope. And his hiking boots. Water, too. Maybe a search party. At least one other person to help him navigate. Powell would probably do it. Then he shakes his head. *Stop it*, he tells himself. *It's a fucking fool's errand*. As is removing his phone from his pocket and dialing Gus. But he does it anyway. Because, why not?

"Hey there. It's Gus. Leave a message." *Beep.*

Mills hangs up.

He's about to self-flagellate when an idea intervenes by mere seconds. The idea has a name. It's Calvin Cloke. The insanely happy medical examiner who is also, and this is the best part, a drone enthusiast. Or an expert. Or both. It doesn't matter; Mills remembers Cal telling him he bought a "really state-of-the-art" drone a few months ago. He remembers Cal saying, "Man, you got to come fly this thing with me." Today's the day to take the happy ME up on his offer. And Mills knows just the flight plan.

Cloke is as groggy as a drunk pillow when Mills calls. "Yuh?"

"I hope I woke you up."

"Why? And who the f-nut is this?"

"Mills. Reporting for drone duty. If you're sleeping it means you're off today. . . ."

"Shit, Alex. I'm working nights, so I'm sleeping in for a reason," Cloke says. "What the hell can I do for you?"

Mills explains. Suddenly, Cloke is wide awake, as chipper as that thing that decimates wood and, sometimes, bodies. "I'm in," he tells Mills. "I can meet you in thirty, maybe forty."

They agree to meet at the Circle K at Forty-Fourth and Camelback. Meanwhile, Mills texts his squad: "Be in later. Working on something."

No one responds. Which is the best response of all. He grabs a mocha at Hava Java, then heads east to the Circle K, where he waits ten minutes or so for Cloke to show up. At the gate to Billie Welch's community, Mills flashes his badge and says, "The guy in the Humvee's with me."

In front of Billie's gate, Cloke readies the mission from the back of the Humvee. Incredible how much this guy can do with one arm. Perched under the back hatch, Cloke fires up a laptop, and then from a built-in compartment, he withdraws an enormous carton that Mills helps him lower to the ground. Cloke pulls out, from the carton, a species of drone the likes of which Mills has never seen. It's as if Star Wars had sex with Big Brother's sister. A six-legged metal spider, it's fucking monstrous.

"How many cameras does that thing carry?"

"I can switch between four cameras. Live."

"No shit. As we watch?"

"As we watch. Mostly as you watch. I'll be flying this thing."

"Zoom?"

"Yes," Cloke replies. "But I've yet to penetrate too far inside a structure. Besides, that's illegal."

Mills snickers. Cloke flips some switches on the drone, adjusts some wires, then presses a remote. The drone lifts—seemingly by magic—from the ground and hovers about two feet, then three before Cloke brings it down again. "Just a test," he tells Mills. "Don't look so mesmerized."

Mills laughs. "I'm about five years or so behind technology."

Cloke types some codes into his laptop. A screen comes up, all blue, then separates into four quadrants. "Your cameras," Cloke says. "You'll monitor all four screens."

Then Mills watches with the glee of a ten-year-old as Calvin Cloke hits the remote again and the drone takes flight. "You want a full circle around the house?"

"At least one, Cal. Low, high, as close to the windows as you can get."

And off it goes, rising and rising, against the perfect dome of blue sky, higher than Billie's gate, then over the gate, into the grand entryway and courtyard. Mills realizes his eyes should be on the laptop, so he veers his attention to the screen, where he can see live video of the garage, the façade of the house, each window. Cloke maneuvers the thing slowly and sweeps back and forth. "You tell me if you want a zoom, a higher or lower shot."

"Can you try to shoot through a window?"

"I'll try, but there's a lot of glare with the sun," Cloke says. "Arizona is not always drone-friendly that way."

Today is no different. The drone treats Mills to beautiful shots of a beautiful home, to the roof lines, to the exquisite camouflage of a desert mansion and the succulent gardens that surround it, a home that by design disappears into the mountains, a burnt-clay exterior, a red tile roof, panoramic windows. There are fountains and waterfalls, not gaudy, just quiet and lulling. He feels like an intruder here, spying, but he knows Billie would be all for it.

But he can't fucking see Gus.

"I don't suppose you have speakers mounted on that thing," he says to Cloke.

"No. Sorry. Everything but," Cloke says. "Were you planning on broadcasting to the kidnapper in there?"

"I'd like to."

The drone has now done a full swing around the estate, providing various shots at various angles. "Around again?" Cloke asks.

"Yes."

This time Cloke operates the drone to circle the house in the opposite direction. He finds a shaded area, like an inner courtyard, a few small tables, and another fountain. Cloke lowers the device and zooms through a window. Mills recognizes the studio immediately. He remembers the first time Billie and Gus gave him a tour of the house. "That's where she writes most of her music," he tells Cloke.

"Sweet. I like my rock 'n' roll a little harder than Billie Welch," he says. "But she's still the queen."

"I need to see shadier areas like this," Gus tells him. "The rest of the windows have too much glare."

"You'll have to bring that up with the sun."

"Okay, here, Cal. Here at the pool, there are all those doors that should give us a good view into the house. If you can get under the covered area, start from the left, go to the right."

"Dude, I can get under the covered area, but I don't know if I can get out. A bit risky."

"Do the best you can."

Cloke pilots the thing close, does a low sweep, just outside the covered area, and hovers from one door to the next. The zoom works well. There's no glare. But there's also no sign of life in there. Nothing stirs. "Fuck," Mills says. "Great video, but we got nothing."

"Sorry."

"Not your fault. It's a huge house. He could be anywhere. Lots of interior space."

"Should I bring this thing in?"

"Yeah. Sure."

Mills can taste the bitterness of his frustration. This was such a good idea, and yet it failed. He failed. What the fuck must Gus be thinking now? That is if Gus isn't dead. Mills hasn't entertained that outcome, and yet it loiters in the dark corners of his consciousness; of course it does. If it didn't, why would Mills be here trying to penetrate Billie Welch's private fortress? Why would he be haunted by the thought that leaving here, right now, is equivalent to signing Gus's death warrant?

The whirring of a flying beast interrupts his morbid thoughts. He looks to the sky and follows the slow approach of the drone as it swings into view from the left side of the house, skimming the tops of vegetation, and dipping over the wall. It totters for a moment, then begins its descent, as if pushed and pulled by invisible hydraulics, to the ground. A perfect landing.

An imperfect mission.

He woke up to a constellation of acne. Or rather the dying stars of acne. Richard Knight's scarred face hovered over Gus. "Rise and shine," the lunatic said.

Gus uttered a grunt.

"Sleep well?"

"About twenty minutes here and there," Gus said. "Thanks for asking. Now how about untying my wrists?"

The man laughed. "Uncomfortable?"

Gus gave up trying to move around midnight. First his muscles seized up. He couldn't twist. He couldn't turn. Then came the throbbing in his bones from his shoulders to his knees. "Dude, just untie me."

"Of course I'm going to untie you. You have to make me breakfast."

"Can I take a shower? Please?"

"Yup, you smell. But I don't know . . ."

"What don't you know?"

Richard surveyed the bedroom and the adjoining bathroom. "I'll be sitting on this bed, Gus Parker. Don't you dare try to crawl out a window."

Gus struggled to sit up. "There's no window in there big enough to climb out of. Untie me, please."

Gus took his time in the shower. He turned the room into a steam bath and cleansed himself of Richard Knight's residue. He watched the water swirl into the drain and wished that were his way out, too. He'd have liked to go with the water, that kind of escape, as if he were surfing to freedom, as if the drain led straight to the ocean. He was obviously lost in thought because all of a sudden he heard the voice of Richard Knight roaring, "Get the fuck out of there already! It's been twenty minutes!"

Gus had not noticed the man entering the bathroom. He didn't think it had been twenty minutes, but he wasn't going to argue. "Okay, Richard. Just get out of here so I can dry off. I don't need an audience."

"I make the rules. Remember?"

"Richard, I am not getting out of this shower until you leave the bathroom. We can stand here all day at an impasse, but I'm not moving. And I don't think you're going to shoot me over this. You need me."

"Do I?" the man asked with a snicker.

Their voices were hollower in here, bouncing off the bathroom tile with a dull echo. "Oh, yes, you do. I'm your bargaining chip. Billie will never come to you if she knows you killed me just for stalling in the shower. They call it a shower stall for a reason."

"You expect me to laugh? Or don't you know how serious this is?"

Before Gus had a chance to answer, he was startled by the sound of shattered glass. He poked his head out, craned his neck, and saw a crack in the mirror over one of the sinks, pieces of glass and pottery in an angry pattern on the floor. "What the hell, Richard?"

"I'm mad."

"Yeah. I can see that."

Richard had removed a plant from its pot and had thrown the giant clay vessel at the mirror. "We're wasting time, and I'm hungry."

"Then get out of the bathroom and I'll dry myself off and get dressed."

"Five minutes. I want my breakfast."

Ten minutes later, Gus emerged, refreshed but wary. The steam should have loosened his muscles, but it didn't.

Now, it's 10:35 a.m. And Gus is cooking egg whites with spinach and provolone at gunpoint. He fries up turkey bacon. Every move aches. He brews a fraudulent pot of coffee as he did yesterday. He tells Richard the coffee's regular, but it's really decaf because there's no way in hell he'd give that nutcase caffeine. Gus doesn't know how this is going to end. But just as he did last night, Gus has a dread in his gut, a sickening dread that there's no turning back for Richard Knight, that today's the day. So, Gus has to will himself to stay rational, steel himself to stay calm.

He does this by watching from the audience's perspective. Gus is an observer of the terror, but he won't be terrified. He watches frightful scenes unfold, but he won't be frightened. This is how he suppresses the fear. It's only a movie. *Only a movie.* He's watching a movie, and sometimes it's tragicomedy. Sometimes he can actually laugh, like right now, watching his captor spread cream cheese on a bagel.

After breakfast, Richard, with the gun to his hostage's head, forces Gus toward the game room. On the way, Gus thinks he sees a flash, something outside the family room overlooking the pool. It's like a giant bird, or the shadow of a bird, diving toward the French doors. It's here and gone in an instant, so it could be his imagination, but he sure wishes whatever it was would strike hard and fast, and crash through the glass. That would cause a distraction. But the instant is over the instant Richard shoves him into the game room.

Billie never uses the game room. It's just here for parties. Two pinball machines. A pool table. A small bowling lane and a bar. "We're going to throw our engagement party in here," the man says. "But it's going to be a surprise. We won't tell any of the guests why they're invited, and then once everyone is here Billie will make the big announcement."

Gus is sitting on a stool at the bar. Richard leans on a pinball machine across the room. Gus regards him with a rational nod.

"Cat got your tongue?" the stalker asks.

"No."

"Then say something, goddamnit!"

"Like what?"

"What do you think of our plans?"

Again, he wants to laugh, but he can't. He hears those erratic echoes of psychosis in the man's voice that sound like a teetering desperation. "I think this is a great room for a party, Richard."

"Good! Now do you want to know the plan for today?"

"I suppose."

"It's easy, Gus. Just a phone call and an email, and you could be a free man!"

"To whom?"

The man comes forward, then takes a seat at the bar next to Gus. He smiles. "To Billie. Come on, Gus, keep up. You have to call Billie today and break it off with her."

Gus cocks his head. "Really?"

"Really! How will she ever feel free to be with me unless you let her off the hook?"

"I don't know if she'll go for it, Richard."

The man balls up his face, and it turns red. His eyes emit fury. "Of course she'll go for it," he cries, slamming the gun against the bar. "I've been planning this forever. It's destiny. I just can't believe you're so stupid that you didn't understand my plan from the start. Stupid. Stupid. God! You're so stupid!"

Gus offers nothing but silence. He sits there, an elbow on the bar, his hand supporting his head. Too early to order a drink. He closes his eyes, knowing that Richard is staring at every inch of him. He tries to hum his way into a meditation, aware his murmurs will only exasperate his captor. But fine. It's all fine. There are so many rooms and doors in this house Gus will find an escape. He'll have to come up with a plan of his own. Then his arm collapses. Richard has knocked his elbow off the bar, and Gus's head almost crashes against the surface.

"Don't fall asleep on me," the man warns.

"But, Richard, I haven't slept for two nights. I mean, really . . ."

"You have things to do for me. You need to call Billie and break it off. Then you're gonna send her an email so she knows you're serious."

Gus eyes the gun resting on the bar top. "What if I don't?"

He raises the gun. "Then I kill you," he says. "You can cooperate with me and get out of here alive, or I'll shoot you dead for getting in my way. You decide."

"You're going to have to give me a few hours," Gus tells him. "Billie doesn't wake up before noon."

Then the man smacks him in the face. Gus reels back. The stool slides out from under him, and he tumbles to the floor. "Jesus, what was that for?"

"You're stalling!" Richard cries, slamming the gun on the bar again.

"What? I'm not stalling," Gus insists. "She doesn't get up before noon. And I should know."

Richard is on top of him now, his hand around Gus's neck. "You should know, huh? You should know because you fuck her? Because you fuck her every morning?"

The man squeezes at his windpipe. Gus's voice is barely a squeak when he says, "Get off of me. I can't breathe."

"Billie will cleanse herself of you! She will detox her body of your contamination! And then she'll be mine."

Gus struggles for a breath. Fighting is not in his nature. But neither is dying. So he attempts to roll away out from under the man who's now drooling in his face. The man is probably twice his weight. Gus can't roll. Richard takes his free hand, the one not squeezing Gus's neck, and pins Gus's right shoulder. Gus knows nothing about wrestling but instinctively he shoots his right arm upward and curls it around Richard's restraining arm at the elbow and yanks as hard as he can. It's a fast move and a good move because it pulls Richard off-balance, and that's enough to knock the man's hand from Gus's neck. Richard rolls to the floor with a thud. Gus gets to his knees. He grabs the fallen bar stool, raises it over his head, and brings it down on the man's chest. Richard lets out an "oomph," and Gus slams him with the stool again. And then once more. There's another "oomph," but this time the stalker grabs at the barstool. He rips it from Gus's hands and, sitting up, starts to swing. Gus dodges the first try, jumps to his feet, and gets it on the shins on Richard's second try. The impact stings, sends shooting pain up his legs, but doesn't immobilize him. From the corner of his eye, he can see the gun sitting on the bar. The barrel is pointed at him like a sober reminder. In the other direction, the door. Damn, damn, damn. He has to make a choice. Make a run for it or grab the gun. The door leads to the hallway, which leads to the family room that overlooks the pool. He could get out there, run down the side yard to the front. But, then what? He can't jump in his car and take off because he doesn't have his keys. Now the barstool goes flying across the room. Richard is on his feet, and he's between Gus and the doorway. It's too late. Gus has hesitated just a few seconds too long. He's nearly hyperventilating as he lunges for the bar and grabs the gun. He's about to lift it and turn when both of Richard's hands come down on his. Gus and Richard try to push each other off-balance. Without surrendering the gun, Gus lands a good hip check, but it bounces off the man's fleshy middle. Richard pulls Gus with his heft, their hands sliding down the counter as their arms wrestle for control. Gus is out of his weight class. The sheer physics of his stalker's size and force handicap him. His wrists are about to snap. One more drastic pull and his shoulders will come out of their sockets. He tries to elbow the man in the chest. He makes contact but not with enough impact. The man lifts Gus's hands now, the gun still cupped within. The whole struggle remains in the air for a moment before Richard forces their hands back to the bar with a crash. Repeatedly the guy smashes their entwined ball of fists against the bar. The metal of the gun digs into Gus's flesh. He can count the bones about to break in his hands. But Richard keeps lifting and smashing until the pistol comes loose. Gus didn't let it go. It had to be friction, alone. However it happened, the gun is no longer in Gus's hands. And then it goes off.

It turns out the FBI did preserve DNA samples from Kimberly Harrington's hotel room. The bureau can now test the DNA against the hairs found in Gaffing's car and entwined under his fingernails. That's the word from Ken Preston.

"I'll have our lab send the samples over," Mills says. "It's a long shot, but come on, can you imagine if that woman is still alive, hiding out, exacting revenge on the anniversary of her disappearance . . . ?"

His squad gazes at him uninspired. It's noon, and not one of them looks awake. They're all sitting in the conference room, and Mills watches as his colleagues yawn in relay around the table. "Late night?" he asks them.

"Karaoke," Powell says.

"Seriously? I wouldn't have figured you for karaoke. What about the boys?"

"Karaoke," Myers says. "And beer."

Preston nods. "Guilty as charged."

"What? All of you together?" Mills asks.

"Oh, yeah," Powell says. "You should see us."

"What do you mean? This wasn't the first time?"

"No," she replies. "We've been doing it for a few months."

He looks at Preston in disbelief. "I wouldn't have figured you for karaoke either."

"Because I'm over the hill?"

"Yes," he says. "But thanks for the invite, everyone."

"Would you have come?" Powell asks.

"Probably not."

"There you have it. You're not social," she tells him.

"Right," Myers says. "So what's your excuse for not sleeping?"

"Who said I didn't sleep?"

"Have you looked at yourself in the mirror?" Powell asks.

"I'm taking care of a friend's dog. She snores."

Powell leans in with a big smile. "I know how fascinated you are by Kimberly Harrington's DNA," she says, "but you really did miss something last night at the karaoke bar."

"Oh?"

"Yeah. Mrs. Al Torento," she says.

"Jennifer Torento does karaoke? I definitely can't picture that."

"It wasn't *that* Mrs. Torento," Preston says.

"It was Your Pal Al's second wife," Powell explains. "And she had a few interesting things to say about her ex."

Mills can't believe what he's hearing. "You just met her at a bar and started talking about the case?"

"Of course not," Powell tells him. "I met her in the ladies' room. She wanted to borrow some lip gloss."

"You wear lip gloss?"

"Anyway, we were standing there and we got to talking about stuff, and she asked what I did for a living, and she asked if I was married, and I kind of thought she was hitting on me, but she wasn't. She told me she was divorced and never remarried, and I said something like, 'One of my friends with me is like a little boy and the other is a much older man,' and she said either one would be better than her ex-husband. And then, you know, one thing leads to another and I find out that her ex is Al Torento!"

Mills can feel his face light up. A smile emerges. "No shit," he says. "I love it."

"So, she tells me the guy's a bit of an asshole. I think 'bit' was probably an understatement. Of course, it's an ex talking, but still, she described him as overly ambitious and extremely narcissistic. And occasionally violent."

"With her?"

"Yeah, but she won't go on the record. She signed some kind of nondisclosure agreement in the divorce."

"Won't prevent her from being deposed," Mills reminds them. "What about the first wife? Should we be looking at that?"

"If you'd like to visit a cemetery in San Diego," Powell says. "She died of breast cancer not long after the divorce. He divorced her as she was getting sick. . . ."

"This is according to Mrs. Torento number two?"

"Yes," Powell says, "and she said he had a habit of shoving, sometimes punching, when things didn't go his way."

"Good to know," Mills says. "Not entirely surprised."

"He gave her a black eye once," Powell explains. "She heard he was more violent with his first wife."

"Well, I can't see the current Mrs. Torento standing for that crap," Mills says. "But, speaking of the congressman, we know he left the country for a trade mission on Monday, and there hasn't been another body since. Interesting, huh? No activity the whole time Al Torento's been away. Supposedly he's back tomorrow."

Preston arches an eyebrow. "Harass him 'til he talks," the older detective says.

Powell rests her hand against her chin and nods emphatically. Myers yawns. It's a huge yawn, one that threatens to suck up all of the air in the room. Mills takes that as his cue to dismiss the meeting. He stops into the restroom and catches a glimpse of himself in the mirror. There's worry all over his face. Not so much about the case. More so about Gus. His gut tells him Gus is probably at Billie's, despite the failure of the drone mission, but his gut also knows that Gus could be anywhere. Anywhere people vanish.

On the way back to his desk, his phone rings. It's his personal cell, and it's Billie Welch calling again. She's panicked, her words rushing out. "I'm coming back there. PV says there's no sign of him at my house. I've tried calling him. Beatrice has tried calling him. You've tried calling him. What the hell's going on, Alex? He can't just disappear into thin air."

"Catch your breath, Billie," he tells her. "You know Gus can take care of himself, right?"

"Unless he's already dead. Unless Richard Knight—I don't know—took him out to the middle of the desert and shot him in the head. . . ."

"I think Richard Knight is a very disturbed man. I don't think he's a killer."

"What makes you so sure?"

"From what I know of how he stalked you," Mills says. "He wants *you*, Billie. He doesn't want to kill anyone."

"If he wants me badly enough . . ."

"We don't even know if Gus is with him."

"Where else would he be?"

What can Mills reasonably say? He won't tell her about the failed drone mission; that would just make her more distressed. He decides he's not going to tell her about the malfunction of her driveway gate; that would just panic her. Storming it would not necessarily yield the favorable result, anyway. In fact, it could prove lethal for Gus. This isn't good. He notices his fingers drumming the desk, his temples throbbing to the beat.

"I'd think Gus, as a psychic, would be one step ahead of trouble," he says.

He's met by silence. A kind of disdaining silence. He thinks he hears in the vapor of a whisper, "Oh, my God, this is fucked."

"Billie?"

"You know he's in trouble, Alex. Psychic or not."

"I'm calling over to PV now," he says.

"Why can't you people track him on his cell phone?"

"We're working on it."

"I'm cutting Nashville short. I'll leave for the airport in an hour," she growls. "Call you when I get to Phoenix."

He stares at the phone for a few seconds after the call ends. He's about to pick it back up and dial Obershan when it dings with a reminder. Shit. He has to go. The mediation session begins in forty-five minutes. It'll take at least half an hour to get there. He dashes out stealthily, avoiding curious eyes. He dials Obershan once he hits the I-10 curve on the way to Chandler. After an exchange of the mandatory minimum pleasantries, Mills asks, "What's your follow-up today with Gus?"

"Given the fact that Knight made direct threats against your friend, this *is* our top priority."

"Maybe Knight has him somewhere not so obvious, after all."

"Maybe," Obershan says. "We're talking to his parents again today. Also, his probation officer. We're looking to see if there are surveillance cameras anywhere near Gus's job. The timing suggests Knight could have met up with him shortly after Gus left work. That coincides with the last ding from his phone."

"What about his phone? Any progress there?"

"Contrary to what we thought, it's not the cell towers. It's not the service. Everything's operating fine," Obershan tells him. "It's like Knight grabbed Gus's phone and tossed it into Tempe Town Lake."

Of course. No different than what the graveyard killer likely did with his victims' phones. A lake, a riverbed, a wash, a dumpster, all the same when criminals are tech savvy enough to elude police. "Well, shit," Mills says. "That's a dead end."

"Probably," Obershan concedes. "But we'll chase down whatever we can today. I'll keep you posted."

Then he's gone.

When Mills steps into the office of Bernice Goodman ten minutes later, everyone is there waiting: Kelly, Trevor, the Heathrows.

"Am I late?" he asks.

Kelly says, "No. Sit down."

Mills can't bring himself to acknowledge the other family, so he doesn't. The lobby is playing Gus Parker's kind of music—strange vibrations from India, rain falling, beads rattling, voices chanting. A woman comes through a door. "Hello, everyone, I'm Dr. Goodman. For those of you who don't know, I'm a child psychologist, family counselor, and professional mediator. So, let me tell you how this will work."

She's probably five-two. As lithe as a sparrow. She's easily seventy, under that pleasantly styled dome of gray hair, her skin free of cosmetics, her eyes blue. "I will speak to each child individually, first. Then I'll speak to them together. We will resolve this here, but it could take a few hours. Parents, you're free to leave and come back."

"We'll stay," Dan Heathrow announces in a gust of testosterone.

Mills squeezes Kelly's hand. He's going to go out of his mind.

"Fine, then," Bernice Goodman says. "Let's start with Lily."

One shot rang out. One bullet pierced the air. Gus went deaf for a second or two. He picks his head up off the bar, and it feels as if a metal Frisbee is lodged in his skull, rattling in there, as if he suffered a concussion. He checks for blood. There's no blood. When Richard Knight tore the gun from his hands, the man fired it merely an inch from Gus's ear. The room convulsed. Gus felt a river of blood pouring from his nostrils, from both ears, too. It was vivid seepage. But it was only phantom seepage. He looks around. He sees the remains of Angel's Envy, an eighty-proof explosion that also knocked Stoli and several glasses off the bar shelves. Shards rained into the sink, flew onto the bar. He picks a few pieces out of his hair. He supposes he's lucky none of it pierced his skin. Richard Knight stands at the doorway.

"Get up," the man says. He waves the pistol. "We have a call to make."

He moves Gus into the kitchen, and Gus says, "Now what?"

"Call her. Break it off."

"You're going to plug the landline back into the wall, Richard?"

The man snarls. "You think I'm stupid? I know they'll trace the call and find us. You're going to use one of my burner phones, Gus."

"You came prepared."

Sputtering, Richard says, "Of course I did. There's never been more at stake for me. For Billie. For you. Call her!"

As Gus is about to dial, he considers dialing 911 instead of Billie. But figuring Richard is even marginally intelligent, the three taps of 9-1-1 on the screen might be a fatal giveaway. "Come on, Gus. Make the call!" the man insists. "I know how much this must hurt you, but the sooner you get it over with, the better. Like ripping a Band-Aid. Just do it! Call Billie. Now!"

Gus scrambles to remember Alex's phone number, a memory problem for the technology age when everyone's phone number is a stored contact.

"Hello, you've reached the law office of Weissman, Antonelli, and Darymple, please hold for an operator—"

Wrong number. Gus hangs up. "What happened?" Richard barks.

"I got her voice mail."

"Try again."

He does.

"Mitzi's Dance Studio . . . We're in a class, but your call is imp—"

He hangs up again. "Jesus Christ, why won't she pick up, Gus?" Richard cries. "Did you two have a fight? I bet you had a fight. You treat her like shit, don't you? Man, I am so glad to come to the rescue. Now more than ever."

"Would you shut up, Richard? Would you?"

Richard lifts a lavender-scented Yankee Candle from the counter and hurls it at Gus. It grazes Gus's head and crashes to the floor behind him. In that split second, a numerical epiphany surges to Gus's memory in ten perfect digits: Alex's phone number. Maybe it's the impact against his skull or maybe it's sheer will; who knows and who cares? He dials Alex.

His phone rings. The others look at him with low-grade disgust. Dan Heathrow points to the sign that says, "Please Silence Your Phones in the Waiting Room."

Mills looks to his wife. She nods. He picks up.

"Hi, it's Gus."

His eyes practically bounce out of his head. Gus Parker!

"Gus fucking Parker!" Mills jumps to his feet.

"I'm calling to break up with you, Billie."

"Billie?" Mills asks. "What the fuck, Gus?"

"I'm sorry Billie, but I have to break up with you. Check your email."

"Gus? Where are you? Are you okay?"

"Not really."

Mills goes as calm as a hostage negotiator, but his insides are a storm. "So, you're calling to break up with Billie. But you're not. You're with that stalker. He has you."

"Yes. I am. I'm serious."

Mills hears things crashing on Gus's end. "What's that noise? Tell me where you are, Gus, and I'll get help."

A pause, then, "I can't do that, Billie."

"Are you at your house? I checked there, and you weren't home."

"No. I'm sorry."

"You're not blindfolded, are you?"

Another pause, and then Gus says, "No, I'm sorry."

Mills can hear a man cackling in the background. "Are you at her house? Just tell me. Yes or no."

"Yes, yes, yes. You're better off with Richard."

Then the line goes dead. There was no caller ID. For a few sickening seconds, Mills stares at his phone as if it should tell him what to do. "Fuck!"

"Have some respect and take it outside," Dan Heathrow hisses.

Mills ignores him. He dials the Paradise Valley Police and tells them to get out to Billie's place. He then turns to his wife, who looks at him shell-shocked.

"Thank God," she says. "What a relief."

"A relief? A relief? It's not a relief until someone gets there and gets him out."

"You called Paradise Valley."

He rubs his temples. "I gotta go, hon. I'm jumping out of my skin."

"Go."

"What about Trevor?"

"Let me worry about Trevor."

"But how do you think it'll look?" he whispers.

"Don't worry about them," she whispers back.

"How do you think it'll look to Trev?"

Trevor gets up, then leans in to his parents. "You guys don't know how to whisper. Don't worry about me, Dad. I'm fine."

The room tilts. The lights go fuzzy. His throat tightens. A strangling at his neck.

"Dad? I haven't even been called in yet. And then there's a joint session after that."

"I'll be back," Mills says as he steadies himself. "I'll be back within an hour, no matter what happens to Gus. I promise."

Kelly grabs his arm. "If you don't go, I will," she says, her voice quivering. "It's Gus. He's family. Get going. My stomach's in knots."

Mills can't untangle his own intestines. As he moves past them, Corinne Heathrow looks away. Dan smirks and rolls his eyes. Mills doesn't give a fuck. His blood runs cold.

His hands shake just a bit too much as he grabs the steering wheel and whips into traffic, still not giving a fuck as he drives, the whole world a gauzy make-believe, all the way to Paradise Valley.

35

Gus is mighty proud of his ruse when he hears the approaching sirens, though he's not entirely relieved because Richard Knight can hear the sirens, too, and the man has turned to fury and panic, wildly racing from one end of the house to the other, his arms extended over his head, clasping the gun. Gus uses Richard's sprawling mania as an opportunity to sprint into the garage, where he flips the circuit breaker for the driveway gate to On. On his way back in, he hits the panic button on the alarm system, and now the house is quaking with sirens, itself, which adds to the confusion and to the gunman's implosion. He wails, Richard does, like a man who's lost his only love, not because she's left him but because they're being torn apart by a dark and evil enemy. Gus figures this loss must be very real to Richard, as disturbed as the man is, and feels just a little bit of sympathy for him. Even as he roars. Even as he throws over more furniture. Gus makes for the front of the house. He inches open the front door and steps out onto the driveway courtyard and sees the first cruisers barreling toward the gate.

He has only a glimmer of relief before he's hooked by the neck. Richard presses the gun against his head, just above his left temple. "Come back inside," his captor says. "Don't make a fuss for me, Gus. Not now."

The man drags Gus into the house by the clavicle, but, as he does, Gus reaches for the button to open the gate. He nearly misses it with his flailing hand but slaps it on the second try. Knight apparently doesn't notice and continues to drag him across the foyer, through the family room, knocking over a few tables in there, and out the French doors to the pool. Just then, Gus can hear the stampede of cops crash into the house, a whole army of feet advancing, expanding, and then pouring out the doors to the back of the estate, to the pool, as well.

Richard, his arm still around Gus's neck, fires a shot into the air to warn them.

The cops shout at him. "Drop your weapon! Drop it, Richard." But Richard doesn't flinch. Gus pulls at the arm around his neck. Richard tightens it. Gus tries an elbow to the man's stomach. Richard barely buckles, but in the one instant that Richard shifts on his feet, Gus throws his hands up and wrestles for the gun. The two of them twist into each other like coiling human rope, and in the intertwining of friction and frayed nerves, muscle and madness, Gus is unsure who's coiling whom. They struggle and grunt, and a cop yells, "Gus, don't do that." It's Detective Obershan. But Gus doesn't listen. At this point he's pissed. And he's done. This nutcase has done enough damage. Gus knees the guy in the stomach, then the groin, doesn't care if he's fighting dirty. Richard Knight flips backward, losing his grip on Gus. But the gun is still in Richard's hand, and he fires into the air again.

Obershan yells, "Gus, get back. Get back!" This time Gus complies, retreating from the standoff, moving behind the line of cops, who stand there with their guns drawn. The cornered man scrambles to his feet, waves the gun, and spins a 360 as if looking for Gus. That's when Obershan shoots. He strikes the stalker in the butt, and Richard rolls into the pool—knees, then ass, then head, an almost slow-motion quality to the tumble—where he lands facedown in the water. The sound reverberates. A firecracker, a growl, a splash. The pool becomes a small pond of blood. The sight turns Gus's stomach, so much so he assesses a proper place to vomit (a potted plant, maybe). Then there's a hand on his shoulder. A firm hand that shakes him, and for a split second the ground spins and Gus sways. He turns.

"You okay?" Mills asks him.

"Hey, Alex . . ."

"C'mon, let's get out of the way."

Gus looks back, reflexively, just to confirm he has seen the end. As he does, he sees the suspect being fished out of the pool like an injured beluga. Mills leads Gus inside. Gus glides in disbelief through the crime scene and then out the front door to the driveway, where the glare of freedom hits him. Beatrice is standing there. She opens her arms. She shuffles toward him, pulling him into an embrace.

"Oh, Gus!" she cries. "Oh, my Gus!"

"He's a little dazed," Mills tells her.

"I'm fine," Gus says.

"PV will want a statement from you," Mills tells him.

"They can talk to him at my house," Beatrice says. "I'm taking him away from here."

Mills shakes his head. "They're probably going to need him to do a walk-through, you know, room to room to describe what happened over the past few days."

Beatrice narrows her eyes, then puts her hands on her hips.

"Oh, fuck it," Mills says. "Just go. I'll handle things."

As Gus and Beatrice turn toward her house, an ambulance barrels past them up the driveway to take the criminal away.

36

ills zips back to Chandler, again breaking every speed limit in the book. He had promised to be back within an hour. He's ten minutes late. He's relieved about Gus, but he can't think about Gus. He shouldn't have left Trevor, but he had to leave Trevor. There was no good option. His muscles ache, now, his whole body clenched. But when he arrives at Bernice Goodman's office he's happy to see that the session is ongoing. In fact, it's about another twenty minutes before the mediator steps out into the lobby. She sits in a wicker chair opposite them. The kids remain in her office.

Dan Heathrow protests. "I don't want my daughter alone with that boy."

Bernice folds her hands in her lap. "I don't believe he's a threat to her," she says softly.

Mills takes that as a good sign. Dan laughs an acidic laugh but says nothing in return. The doctor smiles. "As you know," she continues, "I've spoken to each child individually, and also in joint session. I've listened very carefully and have used my skills to draw out the truth. I'm confident I've reached the truth."

"We're all ears, ma'am," Dan says.

She clears her throat and says, "There was no forceful act here."

Kelly exhales a sigh of relief that fills the room.

"This is something the Heathrows will have to deal with as a family," the mediator continues. "Lily was afraid of how you, Mr. and Mrs. Heathrow, would regard her unless you thought the sex was forced upon her. She was terrified of being ostracized in her own home. She also thought the punishment would be far less severe if you thought the sex was not consensual."

"That's nuts," Dan says.

"Whatever it is," the woman says patiently, "it was not Lily's idea to lie." She turns directly to Mills and Kelly. It's an oh-shit moment like no other. "It was Trevor's idea."

"What?" Kelly begs.

"Trevor didn't want Lily to get in trouble. So he told her, persuaded her rather, to lie to her parents. To make it his fault entirely. Neither he nor Lily ever thought it would lead to the threat of pressing charges. They were naïve, misguided. But considering their age, not unusual."

"Which is why they shouldn't be having sex in the first place!" Dan erupts. "What they did is wrong."

"That's not for me to judge," the mediator says. "But I can tell you it's normal. I encourage both families to talk it out. It's a family matter. Trevor and Lily both made serious mistakes."

She excuses herself and returns with Trevor and Lily. Trevor is about to hug his mother when Dan gets up and cuts him off. That's Mills's cue to intervene. "What do you think you're doing, Dan?"

"I'm gonna tell your kid that even though we won't be pressing charges, he better keep away from my daughter. Do you hear me?" he yells at Trevor, the man's face purple with fury. "In God's name, stay away from her."

"Done," Mills says. "Let's all go home."

Trevor rides shotgun with him. Kelly is behind them in the rear-view mirror. His son's lack of judgment stuns him, but Mills will have that conversation with Trev at another time. For now, he lets some of the relief sink in.

Gus sleeps. Through the day, through the night. He wakes up at Beatrice's the following morning.

"Richard Knight is in custody," she tells him. "They sewed up his butt in the ER and took him to jail. He's staying there 'til his arraignment."

"And probably a very long time after that," he says. "Was it on the news?"

"All over the news. But the nice thing about living here is that news crews can't get past the security booth. They do have choppers, though," she reminds him. "But look at you, my dear, you have a black eye! Your hands are swollen. We need to get you to the hospital."

He shakes his head. "I'm fine. No hospitals."

She cooks breakfast.

He takes a shower, scrubs like crazy. When he gets out, Billie is there waiting. She's sitting on the bed and rises when she sees him. Her eyes fill with tears. He pulls her close against his damp body. She runs her hands down the length of his back. She won't let him go. His towel almost comes undone. "I flew in yesterday," she tells him, "but I didn't want to wake you."

"That's okay," he says.

"Honey, you're all bruised," she says, choking up. "I insist you come to LA."

He shakes his head. "I don't know. I don't know."

"What do you mean you don't know?" she asks, stepping back from the embrace. "After what happened here yesterday, I will never live in that house again. Never. It was my dream home. And that's gone."

Gus knows somehow, someway, and at sometime, the loss will find its way into her music. She'll write a song about it. "I understand," he replies.

"I'm selling it," she says. "LA will be home full-time."

"I don't know that I can say the same for myself."

"What's keeping you here?"

He looks at her as if she'll never understand. Because she probably won't. "My job. My clients. My life, Billie," he says. "I've planted roots here for many years. After all the years of touring, you're used to uprooting yourself. I'm not."

"I don't want to let you go," she tells him.

"I don't want to let you go either."

"Same old story," she says. "I can never seem to have a man in my life because of my life."

He grabs her hands. "How about we don't figure this all out now?" She nods.

"I'm supposed to go give a statement to the cops," he says.

"Beatrice said you did that yesterday."

"I did. But I have to meet them at your house to do a walk-through of the crime scene."

"Oh, Jesus." She gulps. "Well, I'm coming with you, Gus."

"No," he says. "I don't think you should. I'll meet you afterward."

"I'm staying at my sister's."

He kisses her lips and holds her face to his.

POLICE SHOOT ALLEGED STALKER
AT HOME OF BILLIE WELCH, HOSTAGE FREED

Mills is just about done reading the *Arizona Republic*'s account of Gus Parker's ordeal when he gets a call from the station lobby.

"You have a guest down here."

"Who is it?"

"Man says his name is Robby Downs."

"I don't have any appointments."

"He says he wants to talk to you about Joe Gaffing in Mexico."

Robby Downs is probably the same age as Gaffing, looks midforties, with hazel eyes and male-pattern baldness. He has a firm, athletic handshake when Mills greets him.

"I heard you were asking about the registration list for the Kimberly Harrington group," the man says.

"Why don't we go up to my office and talk?"

Upstairs, Mills offers his guest a cup of coffee and Robby Downs accepts. Then Mills leads him into his office and shuts the door behind them. Downs sits and says, "I'm not sure if I can help you with your investigation, but Joe's dad wanted me to try."

"Mr. Gaffing?"

"Joe Senior, yes," the man confirms. "I roomed with his son at the hotel in Mexico."

"It was a long time ago," Mills says. "Do you remember much about the trip?"

"It's hard to forget," Downs replies. "It might have been just an ordinary trip, but then Kimberly disappeared. You always remember something like that."

"So do you remember anything unusual?"

"Not really. But Joe Senior told me you were asking about three guys who weren't on our tour, and it got me thinking. . . ."

"About?"

"About the night Kimberly disappeared," Downs says. "There were three guys who showed up in our room that night. I didn't know who the hell they were, but Joey said he met them at a bar down the road. They were all going out to party some more, but I was sick. Had too much sun and booze at the beach all day. I was already throwing up, so I wasn't about to go out and start drinking again."

"And?"

"And, you know, Joey called me a big pussy, but I was like, 'Fuck you, I'm not moving from this bed unless I have to puke again.' And then they left. I was either half asleep or dreaming, but I think maybe Joey came back once, then left again. Anyway, I woke up the next morning, and he was lying in the next bed snoring his brains out."

"What time was that?"

"I think it was almost eleven. It was late. Past breakfast."

"No sign of the other three guys."

"No."

"Did you get their names?"

The man shakes his head. "Sorry. I remember being introduced, but I don't remember their names. They said they weren't with a tour group. I remember that because it was odd, you know. In those days, anyway, all the kids were with a tour group. But these guys said they were on their own. Rich kids, I think."

"And they were staying at a different hotel?"

"Yeah. I don't remember where, but yeah, not at our hotel."

"Do you think you'd recognize them if I showed you a picture?"

"Maybe."

Mills turns to his computer, guides the mouse, and opens the "Mexico" folder. He clicks on "beachphoto1.jpg" and turns the screen to his guest. "Is that them?" he asks.

He watches as Robby Downs peers at the photo and studies the smiling young men, their backs to the water, the jetty behind them. Downs begins to nod slowly, absorbing a memory, it seems. He squints at the men one last time and says, "That's them. That has to be them."

"Has to be?"

"It's their stupid, drunken smiles," Downs tells him. "The same stupid, drunken smiles that barged into my room that night."

"But you were drunk, as well. Which could make your memory unreliable."

Downs shakes his head. "No. I was drunk during the day. It had to be eleven o'clock that night when they showed up. I was still puking out the alcohol, but I was sober. Sober enough to know to stay in."

Mills turns the screen back. Then he stares at the man, trying to assess veracity of character. The guy has a plain face, not homely, just plain and unburdened. Not a twitch in his eyes. Not a smile, not a frown, not a passing regret. "You gave a statement to the feds when they got down there?"

"Oh, yeah," Downs replies. "But all they asked was what I was doing that night, where I was, who I was with."

"Did they ask about your roommate?"

"Yep, but all I could tell them was that he went out with some guys. That's it," he says. "I still don't know if there's any connection. I kind of doubt it."

"You do?"

"I've been working with Joe Junior ever since. Until, you know . . ."

"His death."

"Right. And he did have a reputation as a partier, even as an adult, but I never got the feeling he was hiding anything. Except maybe his drug habit. All I can tell you is that those guys were in Cancun. They came to my room. And Joey left with them. I don't know if that helps, but Joey's dad wanted me to try."

Mills is still skeptical of Downs's twenty-five-year-old memory, but that's enough for Mills. He shakes the guy's hand, then escorts him back to the lobby. When he returns to his desk, Mills goes to the congressman's website and checks Toronto's public calendar for tonight's event. Called the Dick and Jane Ball, it's a fundraiser for childhood literacy. It starts at seven o'clock at the Phoenician. Semi-formal attire. Mills suspects this is one of those bashes given by the well-heeled who tend to care more about being seen at bashes than the causes the bashes benefit. Childhood literacy, hunger and homelessness, juvenile diabetes—what's the difference? There will be a five-course meal, an open bar, and a silent auction. There will be dancing. Mills guesses there will be plenty of Dicks on hand. Maybe not so many Janes. But plenty of Suzies and Buffys, the socialites of greater Phoenix who practically wet themselves at the opportunity to buy a new evening gown. Their selfies will shut down the internet. Your Pal Al is a keynote speaker. Mills can't help but smile. The look on Toronto's face. It's going to be priceless. He sends out an email to Preston, Powell, and Myers.

> Reminder: We're going undercover tonight at Toronto's fundraiser. Meet in Phoenician lobby at 6:30. Dress swanky. That means a suit, Morty.

He picks up his phone and dials his wife. Asks if she can meet for lunch. It's the least he can do for screwing up her Friday night. For once, she says yes. Again, a smile consumes his face. But this time there's no malice. It's just fucking joy for Kelly Mills.

Miranda, Billie's sister, serves them lunch in the courtyard of her modest Phoenix home. Billie paid for the place, so it's certainly not average, but it's also not palatial. It's a large L-shape ranch with a pool in the back and a courtyard just steps from the kitchen. A typical bougainvillea with no self-control blooms on the property wall, shedding its flowers everywhere, including the breakfast table. A pink flower lands in Gus's spinach omelet. He's tempted to eat it because, why not? "Sorry about that," Miranda says.

Beatrice plucks the flower from Gus's plate and places it atop her ample bun.

Billie and her pup are staying here while her assistant arranges for the PV house to go on the market and for things to be shipped to LA or to storage. It's happening. Gus senses the inevitability, but he's still unsure where within the inevitability he fits. And he's not melancholy. Just unsure. "I know you can't stay," Gus tells her. "I understand why."

She's picking mindlessly at a plate of fruit, a bowl of granola. "And I know you can't leave," Billie says. "But I'm going to change your mind."

Miranda reaches for both of their hands. "Stop it, the two of you," she chides them. "Don't make rules. Don't break rules. Can't your boundaries overlap? Billie, you've got enough money to fly Gus to LA every week!"

"That's if he wants to be flown," Billie says. "I can understand if he doesn't."

"I'm right here," Gus reminds them. "Being flown is fine. I wish I could finance such a luxury myself, but I can't."

"And you don't have to," Billie says with dispassion. "And it doesn't matter."

"Does that mean I get to babysit Ivy every week?" Miranda asks.

Gus shakes his head. "Probably not. I think Ivy needs to go where I go."

Beatrice raises her Bloody Mary. "Look at that! A decision made by committee! Let's toast."

They clink a variation of water (Gus), tea (Miranda), and Bloody Mary (Billie and Beatrice).

"To Gus and Billie," Beatrice declares. "May their boundaries overlap forever."

On his second trip into the kitchen during cleanup, Gus becomes aware of a television set murmuring in the adjacent family room, and, as he finely tunes his ear, he recognizes the typical inflections of a newscast (the strange sound effects, the roller-coaster narrations of a news anchor, the chitchat, all that). He leans over the kitchen counter and looks. It's CNN.

"A strong line of tornadoes is expected to hit the central plains over the weekend," the news anchor reports, *"while flooding continues to plague the Southeast. We'll be monitoring both situations closely."*

Billie's arms come from behind. She grabs his waist and pulls him close. "You're an amazing man," she whispers in his ear. "I don't tell you that enough. I assume you already know. But in case you don't, you amaze me."

He places his hands over hers, creating a sort of belt buckle of hands at his waist. Then he laughs. "Is it cliché to say the feeling is mutual?"

"Only if you're writing a song," she says, kissing his neck softly before drifting back to the courtyard.

"And today is the twenty-fifth anniversary of Kimberly Harrington's disappearance. Harrington was the Arizona college student who vanished on a spring break trip to Mexico. A vigil will be held tonight in her hometown of Dearborn, Michigan. Her parents, who have never given up hope, will join us live in our next hour."

Gus gets a vague stirring in his gut. He tries to infer, but this sudden alert fails to visualize, fails to fully articulate. The only thing he understands is that today is no coincidence.

37

Kelly convinced him to pack it in early. Lunch was perfect. They stopped at Whole Foods and grabbed a portable smorgasbord from the buffet, drove to Papago Park, and ate under a flawless sky with the kind of breezes the Chamber of Commerce should charge for. She complained of fatigue, but once he got her laughing she came alive and he pulled her close. He held her in his arms even while she ate. She had a good feeling about one of her cases. She believed in her client's innocence, and she had a revelation about how she must argue in front of the jury. Mills cheered her on. They kissed long and hard out there surrounded by the prehistoric landscape, a world closer to Mars than Earth, the red buttes obviously the secret lodging for visiting extraterrestrials. She said, "Come home early. We can continue this make-out session before your stakeout tonight."

That's all he needed to hear.

Back at the station, he confirms with his team, suggests they go home around three, get some rest, and grab an early dinner. The response is unanimously happy and obliging. Mills assembles what he needs—some files and photos—stuffs the case material into his bag, and he's out the door at three thirty. The drive home, itself, is charged with adrenaline. At home he checks his closet for the suit he'll wear tonight. Not too much lint.

"Are you there to observe?" Kelly asks. "Or are you going to confront him?"

"Confront," he replies. "Politely, calmly, as graciously as possible. Though he deserves none of the above."

"Maybe he truly knows nothing."

"Then why not just say so? We've reached out to him a million times."

"He's trying to avoid the spotlight," Kelly says.

"He doesn't get to decide where the spotlight lands."

"He's going to think you're there to arrest him."

"We don't have enough to arrest him," Mills replies. "You seem worried."

She shakes her head, then shrugs. "Oh. I don't know. Something just feels odd to me."

"How about that make-out session you promised?"

She rolls onto the bed. "How about a nap first?"

He laughs. "Both sound equally seductive," he says, lying down beside her. He sets his alarm and then pulls her close. She falls asleep first. It's only a matter of minutes before Mills slips away and joins her. He's in a deep, cave-like, almost mortuary sleep when his phone rings about an hour and a half later.

"Jesus," he groans, groggy and disoriented.

"Ditto that," Kelly whispers.

He reaches to the nightstand but knocks the phone to the floor. He lunges almost upside down from the side of the bed to retrieve it. "Hello?"

"Detective Mills?"

"Speaking."

"It's Jennifer Torento. The congressman's wife."

Her voice is almost breathless.

"Is something wrong?" Mills asks.

"Yes," she says. "I think so."

He hears passing traffic and the wind-tunnel effect of a Bluetooth car connection. "Don't you have a fundraiser to get ready for?" he asks.

"That's just the thing," the woman says. "We do. But Al took a call a few minutes ago, wouldn't tell me who it was, said it was classified. Then he stormed out of here."

"And where are you right now?"

"I'm following him."

"You're following him? Right now?"

"Yes, goddamnit, I'm following him. Is that a problem? Something just isn't right, and I thought you'd like to know."

Mills swings his legs over the bed, then jumps into a pair of jeans. "Uh, yes, of course. Don't hang up, Mrs. Torento. I appreciate the call."

He pulls on a shirt. He has no time for a suit. In his race to get out the door, he can't even stop to explain to Kelly. But he does scribble a note: "I have to go—Emergency." She follows him to the driveway and blows him a kiss.

"Classified, my ass. I'm going to get to the bottom of this," Jennifer Torento tells him. "Didn't you say I should be on alert for strange phone calls?"

He climbs into his car. It's a few minutes after five o'clock. "Yes. I did."

"Oh, my God," she cries. "You were right."

"We don't know that, Mrs. Torento. Not yet. I need you to tell me where you're driving right now."

"I'm heading east on Camelback. Almost at Twelfth Street. I had to run a few lights."

"How close are you to him?"

"He's four cars ahead of me," she says.

"Call him right now."

"I've tried. He won't pick up," she says. "This damn fundraiser starts in two hours! This is some bullshit, Detective. I'm going to kill him if someone doesn't do it first."

He listens to her fire off what sounds like a Spanish tirade of curses. But he can't be sure. It's not the Spanish music Gus has been hearing; that's for certain.

"Where are you now?" he asks.

"Turning right on Sixteenth Street. Heading south."

It's a guess, but it's not a guess. It's a fair estimation that Torento is driving to the same neighborhood off Sixteenth associated with the whereabouts of Klink, Schultz, and Gaffing. Mysterious phone call, abrupt departure, unlikely neighborhood.

"Do not hang up," he tells her. "I have to make another call, but don't hang up."

He picks up his personal cell and dials Powell, tells her there's a change of plans, and instructs her to rouse the others and get them to the PetroGo station at Thomas and Sixteenth. "Immediately," he orders.

This is a shitty time of day to be on the freeway, but he's heading down the Squaw Peak and luckily most of the commute is heading in the opposite direction, so his general speed is eighty. He occasionally has to slam on the brakes because assholes don't know how to drive and there's always a bottleneck at this hour the closer you get to I-10 and the 202.

"Mrs. Torento, are you still there?"

"Yes."

"Where are you?"

"Still driving south on Sixteenth. Not moving fast, you know, with the traffic."

"Okay, stay calm," he tells her because she sounds anything but. He can almost hear her frothing at the mouth, a mixture of anger and panic in her voice. A bad combination. "Can you see him?"

"He's a ways ahead of me," she replies. "Looks like he's turning now."

"Okay, keep your dist—"

"Oh, shit! I think I lost him."

Mills sees trouble ahead on the Squaw, then exits at Indian School. "Don't worry, ma'am. Please remain calm. If you can find him, great. If not, I'll come meet you somewhere. I'm not far from you now."

"No. There he is," she says. "We're sort of driving through a residential area. I have to slow down or he's going to see me." Then she adds, "What? Now he's turning back on Sixteenth. I have no idea what this man's doing."

"What direction is he driving?"

"South again. We're at a red light. About to cross Thomas."

Mills heads west on Indian School toward Sixteenth. Fuck, fuck, fuckety-fuck (that's how his rapid breathing sounds to him). The faintest beads of sweat line up across his forehead. There's a pressure, like a fist, inside his gut. "That neighborhood is familiar to us," he tells the woman.

"I see him turning. He's taking a right turn now."

"Tell me the street. Can you see the street sign?"

"Yes. Iris. East Iris," she says. "I think we're on a residential street again."

East Iris rings a bell but not a specific bell. "Fine. Don't get too close to him. I do not want you to confront him. I'll be there in just a minute."

"He's pulling over in front of a house."

"Stay back," he says. "Let me make another call."

He dials Powell and tells her to move the crew to East Iris once they get to PetroGo. He's on Sixteenth heading south, now, almost at Thomas. Mills reminds the congressman's wife that he's only moments away.

"He's getting out of his car," she tells him. "I'm so pissed I want to run him over."

"Not a good idea, ma'am. Please, just park your car. Wait."

"Where's he going?" she mutters, perhaps to Mills, perhaps to herself. "He's crossing the street and walking over to . . . what's that place? A school? A daycare center? Why—"

That rings a very specific bell. "Did you say daycare center?" Mills asks.

"Yes," the woman replies. "Why the fuck, if you'll excuse my language, would he be dropping by a daycare— Oh, my God!"

"What?"

"If he has a child with another woman somewhere, I swear you'll be arresting *me* tonight."

He crosses Thomas. "Don't jump to conclusions, Mrs. Torento. We don't know what's going on. He could be in danger," he reminds her. "In which case he's going to need you to be as calm and rational as possible."

She's bawling now. Sobs are flooding Mills's ears. "He's going into the house," she says.

"Do not get out of your car."

"What should I do?"

"Just wait for me. I'm seconds away. I promise."

"I need to know what's going on in there," she barks.

"I'm telling you, do not approach that house."

"Oh, dear. Oh, no. He's in. The door's closed," she narrates in panic. And then a pivot, as if her voice is suddenly a slamming door, and she says, "What the hell's been going on behind my back?"

Mills thinks this would be a lot easier, actually, if it were just a mistress and a baby. He can't rule anything out. "Calm and rational. That's all I ask," he tells her. "And please don't budge from your car."

He's almost at Iris. It pops into view on his GPS.

38

It's early yet for sunset. The sky morphs from blue to gold but will stave off twilight for a while; it's a protracted dusk that Mills has always found in his favor—more light to expose the truth, that sort of thing. He sees Powell's car parked half a block down from the daycare center. In front of her is a white Volvo SUV. He pulls beside it, looks in, and recognizes the congressman's wife. "Mrs. Torento, I'm parking ahead of you now," he tells her after they've mutually lowered their windows. "Thank you for staying put."

"We're never going to make it to the fucking ball," she says, as if that's the easiest consequence she can contemplate. The swing from fear to anger to panic has apparently left the woman dazed.

"My team will go to the house and investigate," he says. "I'll need you to remain in your car."

Mills parks, checks his file, and pulls out his notes about this neighborhood. He and Powell had interviewed a woman named Lee Leighton at this address but found nothing significant.

Preston rounds the corner, and Mills waves him forward, farther down the street. Mills follows on foot, gathering his squad along the way. "It's reasonable to assume Torento is the fourth of four men to be lured to this area for the same reason," Mills says as they convene. "It's reasonable to assume he's in danger. But if true to pattern, his killer needs to get him out of here first. They'd have to make a trip to a cemetery. We're not going to let that happen."

Myers appears last, his tires squealing as they hit the curb.

"Is that the right address?" he asks, pointing to the daycare center down the street.

"Yes," Mills replies.

"Is it a real daycare center?"

"I don't know. But if anyone spots a child, guns down. You hear me?"

Nods all around.

Mills instructs Preston and Myers to knock on the front door. "Just tell her you're looking for the congressman. Judge her temperament. Get inside. But remember, if this woman's done something wrong, she might have accomplices in there with her."

"The first thing we ask is if she's alone in the house," Morty says. "Whether or not she tells the truth is another story."

"Whatever you say, you have to get in that house. Powell and I will take the back," Mills instructs. "If no one answers the front door, then we have a situation."

They're about four houses away. Preston and Myers go first. Mills and Powell watch as the men cross the yard and make their way to the door. They knock, and no one answers. They knock and wait. Again, nothing. As Mills and Powell approach from the side, the men continue to knock. Finally, the door opens, ajar at first. Mills can hear a woman's voice, a pleasant voice, but he can barely see her profile. She opens the door wider, lets the cops enter, and then the door closes firmly—as if she slammed it. There's a high fence blocking access to the side yard. Powell scales the fence first. Mills goes over right after her. The landing isn't perfect, but he's still on his feet. They stay low and scamper to the backyard. They crouch at the far corner of the house, where the side and the back meet. There's no sign of life. A light breeze pushes three empty swings as if the ghosts of children are haunting them. No happy shrill of toddlers plummeting down the slide, the whole play set abandoned. They round the corner and peer in through a back window. The room is dark, but a room toward the front of the house has light. A woman shouts. Mills can hear her roar, but he can't hear what she's saying.

"That our daycare owner?" Powell asks.

"I think so," Mills says. "But I don't think she's yelling at the children."

They inspect the back door. It leads from the patio into the kitchen.

Powell says it's an easy lock to disengage. Mills nods. Inside, the woman continues to shriek, her warnings coming in waves, rising and falling, as if there's danger, and then there's not. Powell works the door. This feels as if it's taking half a century, but it's actually less than two minutes before Powell cracks the lock and they're in. The first words Mills can hear are, "I don't care. I don't care what happens to me." As stealthy as scorpions, they quietly follow the woman's voice to a wall dividing the kitchen from the front room, Mills indicating with his hand for Powell to stay behind him. He takes a deep breath, listens to himself fully exhale. Then he gingerly puts a foot across the threshold and turns into the room, his gun drawn and aimed at Lee Leighton. Leighton is armed, as well. With a nod, she very simply acknowledges Mills, never pivoting from Al Torento, whom she has at gunpoint. The barrel of the woman's gun against his head, the congressman sits in a patio chair, slumped like a rag doll. But Leighton is surrounded. Like Mills, Preston and Myers have their Glocks pointing at her, too.

"She opened the door politely and led us in here," Myers explains. "Then she pulled the gun. So we pulled ours."

"No need to explain, Morty," Mills says as he carefully sidesteps the jagged pieces of a broken lamp.

A coffee table lies on its back, its legs up in surrender. A pair of potted plants are victims of a skirmish, as well. "Looks like there's been a struggle here," Mills says to the daycare owner. "I hope it wasn't the children." He now notices the handcuff latching one of Torento's wrists to the chair.

"It wasn't," the woman says.

"Is she alone in the house?" Mills asks the others.

"As far as we can tell," Preston says. "There appears to be no accomplices on premises."

The woman looks at Mills and says, "I'll tell you what I told your partners here. Put your guns down or I shoot the congressman."

Mills regards her gently, his eyes softening. "We don't want him dead," he tells her. "Whatever your grudge is with him, or the others for that matter, we don't want him dead."

"Why?" she asks. "Because he's such an esteemed statesman who's done so much for this country?"

Mills says, "No, that's not why. He's not and he hasn't."

"Now just a minute," Toronto protests. He's red-faced. His hair looks more strawberry than it does in pictures.

Leighton smacks his head, then waves the gun. "I could kill all of you. I should kill everyone in this house."

She's wearing a T-shirt that exposes her thick, muscular arms. Mills notices the tattoo on her neck. It's a butterfly. "You fire that gun, lady, or even point it at us one more time, and you're the one who will be dead. You understand?"

"Doesn't matter."

"Suicide by police?" Mills asks. "Not going to happen. I had you for braver than that."

She juts her chin. The muscles in her neck tighten. "You don't think it's brave to march these men to their deaths, huh? To lure them here, to make them comply with my demands? You should see how these powerful men become groveling little puppies once a gun is at their backs. It's almost hilarious. Davis Klink wet his pants. And I made him sit in it until it got dark enough to go to the cemetery."

"You lured two of the men to this house, and the others to elsewhere in the neighborhood," Mills observes. "Why?"

"Didn't want to establish a pattern," Leighton replies. "Plus, a Maserati on *my* street? No way. I told Barry to meet me at the PetroGo. That was our usual spot."

Without taking his gaze off the woman, Mills tells Preston to call in to the commander to request backup and a negotiator. Preston withdraws a few feet, his gun still fixed on Leighton. Mills can hear him murmuring into the phone, calm but firm, not changing the tenor of the room. And then Mills says, "I'd sure like to resolve this peacefully before we have a SWAT team out here. Could you answer some questions?"

"What questions?" Leighton asks.

"Is this all about money, Lee?" he asks plainly, casually, as if this is an interview, not an interrogation. "Some kind of blackmail?"

She brandishes her gun. "No!" she thunders. "Why don't you understand that? All the boys seemed to understand that." With her free hand she knocks the congressman in the head. "Right, Alan? Tell him, Alan."

Toronto shakes his head, says nothing. She knocks his head again. "The congressman's a baby boy. A baby boy who needs a diaper," she teases. And then, waving the gun again to punctuate her thoughts, she says, "This is not about revenge. This is about justice. And they all knew it. They all knew it when I forced them to their graves. They all knew it when they dug the holes. And now finally everyone will know it. I'm sorry I didn't do it sooner."

He looks at her dark hair and says, "So, I guess you're not a blond."

"I wear a wig when it suits me."

"Not that we'd get a DNA match anyway," Mills says, looking back at the squad. That's when he hears a door open and a quick rush of traffic from outside. Then footsteps.

"What the fuck is going on here?" It's the congressman's wife. She steps into the room.

"Who's she?" Leighton asks.

"I'm his wife. Who are you?"

"I'm his killer," Leighton says with a puff of her chest. She's a proud murderer. Valiant. She bends down and speaks in her hostage's ear. "Do you want to tell them, Al, or do you want me to do the honors?"

The room is getting warm. The shades are drawn. They're standing in a feebly lit airless box. The smell in here suggests the congressman freaked out and either shat his pants or came very close.

"Your esteemed congressman killed my best friend twenty-five years ago today," Leighton announces.

Toronto's wife shrieks. "*What?*"

Mills warns her to stay back behind Myers and Preston.

"And the esteemed doctor and the esteemed CEO and that slimy travel agent helped bury her body," Leighton continues, her eyes pooling. "They've kept me quiet all these years. They threatened me. They controlled me. They've kept track of my every move. But no more. They took

Kimberly's life. And they ruined mine. After twenty-five years, I'm done being tormented. They can't hurt me anymore if they're dead. And I don't care what happens to me. If I sit on death row, it'll be freedom."

"No!" the congressman's wife cries. "No, no, no. This . . . can't be."

"Ma'am, I need you to put the gun down," Mills warns Leighton.

"You'll have to shoot me first," she tells him.

He shakes his head. "No way. If what you're saying is true, then I need you alive. I need you alive if we want to put the congressman away for life."

Of course Mills has no idea if this woman has any deed to the truth or even a tether to reality, for that matter, but there's a discovery in Mills's gut, and it's tingling and rising, not unlike a Gus Parker epiphany, and in fact, Gus's visions are beginning to coalesce into a case with far greater implications than anyone would have guessed. His gun still aimed at Leighton, Mills takes a few steps closer to the congressman.

"Mr. Torento?" he asks with a mocking wide-eyed stare. "What can you tell us about this?"

"I have nothing to say."

"Is this perhaps the reason you never returned my calls?" Mills persists.

"No comment," the man says. "Get me out of here." He looks plastic but defeated. Perfect hair, smooth skin, perfect teeth. A good, strong chin that could probably still support a spring break smile. But he's not smiling. His head is down.

"You're in no position to give orders," Mills tells him.

"I have proof of their crimes," Leighton says. "Proof of what they did. I had a camera. The pictures aren't great, but I remember everything. They made me watch them bury her. It was by the ocean but far from Cancun. I'm sure of it. I've been studying the maps for years."

Jennifer Torento makes a choking noise and whispers, "Oh, my God." She then pushes past the detectives and into the room, standing there, a lone warrior in the line of fire. "So, *this* is why you insist on going to Mexico every year, Alan?" she asks him frantically. "To confront your guilt? Wash it out to sea? Or, what, to make sure no one's dug up that girl?"

"Or, more likely, to make sure erosion hasn't exposed parts of her body," Leighton says.

Jennifer, indifferent to Leighton's weapon, lunges at her husband, grabbing him by the collar. "*You're* responsible for the disappearance of Kimberly Harrington?" she asks. "It was you?" Then she slaps him, and the sound reverberates.

"Ma'am, I need you to step back from your husband," Mills warns her. "You need to wait outside."

"Yes, it was him and his spring break buddies," Leighton answers.

"If you had proof of their crimes," Mills asks her, "why didn't you go to the police?"

She lets out an acidic laugh. "If only it were that easy. They've been watching over me like a hawk. My every move. My every step. I get reminders almost every week of what will come to me if I ever go to the police. For twenty-five years!"

"Jesus Christ, Al!" Jennifer cries. "What did you do to this woman?"

Again, no comment from Your Pal Al.

"So, this isn't extortion?" Mills asks his suspect. "You didn't do this for the money?"

She looks at him astonished. "Money?"

"We know Davis Klink brought you a large sum of cash," Mills tells the suspect.

She laughs again. "Yeah. It's in a bag in another room," she says. "I just used the money to lure him here. Said I was finally going to go to the cops if he didn't bring me half a million dollars. I don't care about the money. I wanted to punish Davis and the others. He just happened to be the money guy."

"So how did you lure the others here?" Mills asks.

"Barry supplied me with good drugs whenever I wanted. All I had to do was call," she explains. "But he argued with me that night, and I told him if he didn't meet me with a full vial of Vicodin, I was ready to fess up everything and report them all to the police. And that dumb Joey had a stupid crush on one of the single moms who leaves her kid with me. So, I arranged for them to meet at the Taqueria over on Sixteenth for a 'blind date,' but when he got there I showed up instead. I told him she chickened out. Then I got in his Mercedes, and the next thing he knew he was trapped. I thought that was clever. Don't you?"

"What about the congressman?"

"Told him to double my allowance," she replies. "Told him to deliver it immediately or I'd not only go to the police; I'd go to the press, as well. Tonight! And look, to my surprise, we're all here! No need to call the police. No need to call the press 'cause I think this will all make headlines by morning."

Mills looks at the congressman and says, "There's one thing I don't understand, Al. Did you not pay attention to the murders of your old friends? Certainly you must have known you were on Ms. Leighton's list of targets."

Toronto says nothing.

Leighton scoffs and says, "He knew."

"Did you?" Mills asks the congressman.

Again, nothing from Your Pal Al.

"He knew," Leighton insists. "He came tonight to stop me, to put an end to it, once and for all."

"How so?" Mills asks.

"He brought a gun," she replies. "I disarmed him. I've been practicing. I put it in the other room. I suppose it's evidence."

Mills inches closer. "So, Lee, what will it take to get you to put your weapon down?"

She twists the gun against Toronto's skull. "Arrest the esteemed congressman for murder."

"I can't do that," he tells her. "I may want to, but I can't. It's not my jurisdiction. But I can call the FBI and have them stop by to hear your story. How about if I do that now?"

The woman looks around the room, considering her options, then tilts her head from one option to another. "Do it," the woman orders. "Call whomever you need to."

Mills turns to Preston. "Get on the phone with the field office. Let 'em know what's going on. Invite them to swing by if they're interested."

Preston nods and backs out of the room again.

"Put your gun down, Lee," Mills says.

"I prefer not to until we reach a resolution," she replies. "Your Pal Al is not going free after what he's done."

"If what you're saying is true, the congressman will be brought to justice and I will do whatever I can to help you. I promise."

"No!" the woman cries and raises the gun. She points it to the kitchen, then shoots out a back window. Glass explodes. "No, no, no!"

The tantrum is enough of a distraction to get Powell in the room, where she dives for Leighton's legs and tackles the woman to the floor. The gun rolls a few feet away.

"Cuff her, Myers," Mills says.

Powell sits Leighton against the wall. Myers clasps the handcuffs. Tears pour down the woman's face. She sobs loudly but says nothing.

"What about me?" the congressman asks. "How about letting me out of here?"

Mills kneels in front of him. "Sorry, Al. But you're not going anywhere."

The man snarls. "What do you mean? You don't believe the claims of a raving lunatic, do you?"

"Maybe I do."

"Get these fucking handcuffs off me," he growls.

Mills turns to Leighton and asks about the key.

"In the kitchen," she says. "In the silverware drawer. To the left of the sink."

Mills motions to Preston.

"You know how hard it was to cuff him while holding a gun to his head?" Leighton cries.

"Actually, I do," Mills says. "It sometimes comes with the terrain."

"You can't keep me here," Toronto insists. "You have no probable cause."

"The murder of Kimberly Harrington is not my case nor is it my jurisdiction. That will be for the FBI to decide, but I'm keeping you here because you're a witness," Mills tells him. "You're the primary witness to what happened here today. You'll need to give us a full statement. We want to hear everything Ms. Leighton did to you, said to you, and told you about her other alleged victims."

"But—but, wait, I have an event tonight," the man pleads. "Isn't that right, honey?"

Jennifer Torento glares at her husband and says nothing.

"I do," he insists. "I need to be at a fundraiser."

"Not going to happen," Mills advises him. "Now if you'll excuse me."

"Jen," the congressman screeches, "don't just stand there. Call my lawyer. Do something."

"Fuck you," she tells her husband.

Meanwhile, Mills switches places with Powell. He sits on the floor opposite Leighton and explains that he's arresting her for the deaths of Davis Klink, Barry Schultz, and Joe Gaffing Jr. He says other charges will be pending against her regarding Al Torento. He does a formal reading of her rights. She doesn't look at him. There's something about her brokenness that he can feel. "Whether or not you remain silent, Lee, I want to help you," he tells her. "And I promise you I can, but you have to tell me everything that happened in Mexico twenty-five years ago."

She shrugs. She's on the verge of a nod.

"I absolutely want to hear your story," he says like a shrink, like a brother, like a coconspirator. "I'm going to take you back to headquarters."

The woman lowers her trembling chin and sobs again.

Mills feels the presence of someone at his back. He turns. It's Jennifer Torento standing over him. "Ma'am, I really need you to wait outside. Okay?"

She kneels beside him and looks at Leighton. "I just want to tell Ms. Leighton that she's going to need a good lawyer. And I'm going to find her one."

The congressman protests with a bounce of the chair to which he remains bound. "You're going to do what?" he seethes at his wife.

"I'm getting her a lawyer, Al."

Leighton, suddenly tearless and placid, says, "I don't care what happens to me."

"But I do," says the wife of Congressman Al Torento.

39

On Mills's desk are printouts of what he considers the most critical excerpts of Lee Leighton's videotaped statement, edited—to the best of his ability—and transcribed in narrative rather than interview format. He and Special Agent Henderson Garcia, legal attaché, had been talking on Skype for days and poring over the information. Mills, to take the graveyard case to the county attorney, and Garcia, to present a possible case against Alan Torento to the Mexican authorities. The latter would prove far more difficult. But the ball's rolling, as homicide sergeant Jake Woods likes to say, and he likes to say a lot these days about Mills's work on the case. Mills shares the credit with his team, but it doesn't seem to matter to Woods; no more graves should be turning up in the Valley of the Sun. That's a huge political sigh of relief, even if the Phoenix Police Department could be the downfall of a sitting congressman. Yet no one seems to be jumping to Torento's defense, so perhaps Al wasn't such a great pal, after all.

Mills reads through the excerpts one final time before sharing them, along with other evidence, with the county attorney by way of Jake Woods.

VIDEOTAPED STATEMENT OF LEE LEIGHTON: TRANSCRIPT EXCERPTS

Edited by: Detective Alex Mills, Homicide
Case No.: C-FF-H-XXXXXXX

(A) Circumstances

Kimmy [Harrington] and I were roommates at Northern Arizona University. It was our junior year, and we were best friends. We heard about a spring break trip to Cancun, Mexico. Kimberly had to beg her parents to go. My parents were fine with it.

I remember it like it was yesterday. Why wouldn't I? It was the worst thing to ever happen in my life, and my life has never been the same since. I think there were seventy-five students on our segment alone. But there were tons of other companies doing tours down there. It was like an invasion. Everyone was drunk or high or both, and there was music day and night.

Kimmy and I first met the boys at a bar in town around midnight, maybe a little later, but it wasn't quite one o'clock, because I remember around one o'clock I said I wanted to go back to the hotel, and everybody started shouting me down and calling me a buzzkill, because we were already wasted. Anyway, I really wanted to go back to the hotel, so Kim finally said, "Let's go and bring the guys with us; we can party in the room." And I was, like, "Sure, fine." So we get back there, and Barry [Schultz] passes out on one of the beds. And Joey [Gaffing], whose uncle and dad are supposedly running the tour, is sitting on the floor, smoking a joint. And Davis [Klink] and me are kind of getting, you know, physical. I'm not proud of any of this. But I was nineteen. The next thing I know Davis is on top of me, and I was consenting at first, but then I heard Kim arguing with someone and I tried to push Davis off, but he wouldn't get off, and I said, "Something's wrong with Kim, get off me," but he wouldn't, so I tried to roll out from under him, but he pinned me and he ripped off my clothes, and that's when I kneed him in the balls and he rolled over and called me a cunt. Meanwhile, Kimmy is still yelling, and I find her out on the balcony with Al [Toronto], and he's calling her a cocktease and saying, "You better suck my dick; you brought me back here, and I could be with any chick right now at any of those parties." I remember this vividly because this was probably the worst example of frat-boy behavior I'd ever seen. So

I walked onto the balcony, and I said, "Shut up, Al, leave her alone." But keep in mind, there was a ton of music. There was music blasting from the other rooms, and there was all this music coming from a party on the beach, like one of those mariachi bands or something, and we could hardly hear each other. But I screamed so loud when I saw him slap Kimberly in the face. She just looked dazed, so I got in Al's face and said, "Get the fuck out of here," and he pushed me hard, and my head almost went through the glass door; then Kimberly turned to Al and said, "Why did you hit me, you fucking asshole?" And he said something like, "All I asked for was a fucking blowjob. You're making me miss out on all the fun out there; I could have any girl I want." And she said, and she's really screaming now, like drunk screaming, "Then go get any girl you want because I wouldn't blow you even if I was in the mood, because I don't waste my time on tiny dicks."

That's when he went into a rage, and he slammed her head into the balcony railing. And I was yelling, "Stay away from her, stay away from her, stay away from her." But he pushed her again. She was trying to steady herself, but instead she just leaned her whole upper body over the railing like a rag doll, as if she was going to throw up, and over she went. If she was screaming, no one could hear her because there was just too much music and rowdiness. It was like watching a murder in a silent movie.

(B) Disposition of Body

I figured she was dead, but I didn't know for sure. We were on the eleventh floor. I couldn't see how she'd survive a fall like that. So we rushed downstairs. All of us. Her body was in the bushes. There was nobody around. There were all these parties going on down at the beach, kids going wild like there was nothing wrong. [Not decipherable. Subject is sobbing.]

Al says we got to get her out of here. And Barry is all panicked and keeps saying, "What happened? What happened? What happened?" And Al tells him to shut up, and Davis says we have to move her someplace. And Al says, "Throw her in the ocean," and I start screaming, and Joey covered my mouth with his hand, and I couldn't break free. And he says he has a big carton in his room that's full of badges and T-shirts and some other trip items from the company, and he lets me go while he and Barry go get the box. I tried to get away, but Al grabbed me, and I will never forget what he said. He said, "If you do anything stupid, we'll dump you right along with her." I knew right then that he was serious. "You do exactly what you're told or you'll end up dead right alongside Kimmy," he said. I was terrified. I had my camera, one of those disposable ones. I was taking pictures of us at the bar and then in the room before everything got ugly. So I had grabbed it and tried to snap pictures when no one was looking, but I didn't have a flash, so most of them didn't come out, but some did, and I still have them.

Barry and Joey came back with the box, just like they were carrying supplies to set up an event for the next day. It was probably about two a.m. by then. Then Al and Davis slide the box into the bushes, lift up Kimmy, and put her inside. Then the two of them carry her on their shoulders to the parking lot. It looked like a coffin, really. But no one seemed to notice. Anyone who might have seen us on the way was probably as wasted as we were. [Sobbing.]

(C) Transportation of Body

Joey's dad had rented a minivan for the tour staff, so once we reached the parking lot the guys stuffed Kim inside the cargo area in the back, and then everybody got in the van. They made me ride in the back seat, closest to Kim, and I was losing my mind. I couldn't breathe. I begged them to let me go. I promised I wouldn't say a thing. But they weren't listening to me. That's when all the fighting started. Davis blaming Al for everything, and Joey saying none of them should have ever come back to the hotel because they weren't even on our tour. Barry wanted to back out and go to the police, and Al said something like he'd kill Barry before he'd end up in a Mexican prison. And Davis started crying like, "I have my whole life ahead of me. I can't throw it away on this. I'm going to business school." And Al said, "You won't throw away anything if we do this right." And I can't remember much else about who said what, but I remember them coming to blows. There were fists flying. College boys crying. Then we took off. I tried to observe everything. When I could snap pictures without being noticed, I did. Joey was the only one of the guys who had been to Mexico before, but he said he really didn't know anywhere else but Cancun. This was long before the days of GPS. So, Al just says, "Drive." And Joey drives. Al, who's sitting shotgun, basically navigates us as far outside Cancun as we can get until the road turned completely black, no lights, nothing, and we had no idea where we were going. Davis is screaming, "Where are we going? Where are we going?" I kept hoping Kimmy would jump out of the box and say, "What the hell is going on?" I wanted that desperately, but I knew better. My stomach was in knots. The first road sign we saw out on that deserted highway said, "Playa del Carmen." I made notes in my head. I think I'd heard it was another tourist area. Anyway, it was maybe an hour before we hit Playa del Carmen, and the boys said it was too dangerous because all of a sudden there were hotels and bars and we were back in civilization. They needed someplace deserted. And I started panicking, thinking we're going to be driving all over Mexico all night and we'll probably get pulled over and killed by some bandits. But at least, driving through Playa del Carmen, I could see for sure that we were right along the coastline. I remember making mental notes of all the signs we saw after that, just to get my bearings. A sign for Akumal came next. In all the years since, I've confirmed this ride from hell by studying road maps for that part of Mexico. That's why I know it was Akumal. I don't remember how close we were, because I can't remember the numbers on the sign—it could have been twenty kilometers or thirty—but it was the next major town we'd hit. I think maybe we'd been driving for about an hour when I said I needed to get out of the car and throw up. Barry said he had to do the same. Joey nearly swerved into a ditch. I could hear Kimberly shifting in the back. I bolted from the van, crossed the street—Barry wasn't too far to my side—and puked. Al stumbled out of the van and ordered us to come back. Barry complied. I refused. I ran along the roadway; it was rocky, and I remember there was a steep embankment. Then Al storms across the road, coming after me. And he's screaming at me. I'm not as fast as him, so he starts gaining, and just before he's about to grab me, Joey drives the van right between us and nearly runs Al off the embankment. I wish he had. I should've pushed him.

(D) Disposal of Body

Joey jumps out of the van and says, "We're not going any further." And Al says, "Why not?" Al wanted to go to Tulum. So Davis explained that Tulum might be farther away, but it's not a deserted area, far from it, with tourists coming to see the ruins. But Al said it would be cool to bury a body at the ruins; you know it would freak everybody out if it was ever found. Yes, he said "cool." And he was laughing. But Davis reminded him that the whole point was to leave the body someplace it would never be found.

Barry said it was too bad we didn't have a boat so they could have dumped her at sea. And Al said maybe they could steal a boat. There were plenty of boats up and down the coast. But Joey said her body would likely wash up someday. Then he said, "That's it, everyone in the van; we're leaving the body somewhere around here." He drove for maybe another mile until it was really dark again, and I remember we took a left somewhere, like we were heading closer to the water, 'cause you could smell the ocean air like you were practically on the beach. One thing I noticed when we turned onto the street that leads to the beach was a small sign that said, "Hurricane Evacuation Route," in Spanish. I remember it's the very first one of these signs after the sign for Akumal. I don't know if it's still there, but it was at the intersection of the main road and that small street. I'll never forget that. I always hoped I'd go back there someday and find her body. But these men wouldn't let me out of their sight. Anyway, we took the left off the main road, then drove maybe five minutes down this tiny street and came to a dead end. We all got out of the van and saw the sea was right below us.

The moon had come out from behind the clouds, and we saw several different walkways to the beach below. Joey pointed to one, and we followed. It was more like a tunnel between the cliffs than a walkway. And the beach below was actually not a beach. It was just a thin strip of mud and sand where the water hit the rocks, not a swimming beach anyway. Davis said that's even better, better chance Kim would get no visitors here. I tried to take some pictures when nobody was looking, but none of them came out because it was so dark, even with the moonlight. Barry says, "We obviously can't bury her in the sand or else she'll just be dragged out with the tide and wash up somewhere else." And Al says, "If the sea gulls don't get to her first." I wanted to kill him right then. Then one of the guys, I think it was Davis, says he found a spot in the tunnel between the beach and the road. The walls of the tunnel had these holes and craters on both sides. Davis climbed into one of the bigger holes and said, "She can go in here, and we can pack her in with sand and mud and close the whole thing up with rocks."

The other guys thought it sounded perfect, and I think they all even gave each other high fives, until Al pointed out they'd need a shovel to dig up the mud and the sand and the rocks. And he asked Joey, "You got a shovel in the van?" And Joey said, "No, why would I have a shovel?" And Al said, "Go find one." So, Joey takes off, and I remember sinking to my knees in the sand, kind of giving up at that point, you know, sort of surrendering because I knew there was nothing I could do. But, I also remember that it was at that precise moment when I resolved to get even. I couldn't imagine how or when, but I wanted these guys to pay. In the most violent way, I wanted them to pay.

Joey comes back about, I don't know, twenty-five minutes later with a shovel. He's got a big smile on his face, and he said he stole it from the back of a bodega, or something. Everyone kind of clapped, but no one else had a big smile on his face. And then I watched them bury her. But they picked a different hole, a bigger one than the hole Davis had found. But the idea was the same. They took the carton out of the van, kind of handing it off, two at it a time, until they got it down the tunnel, and then they all lifted it up to the ledge. It took at least an hour for them to get enough sand and mud and rocks up there. Some of the boulders were so big four of the guys together had to lift them. I'll never forget the sounds of them digging and packing her in the hole, like they were building her some kind of fortress.

Then we went back to Cancun. And Kimberly has been missing all these years. All these years. Only she wasn't.

(E) BLACKMAIL

They threatened to kill me if I said a word. It took a few days for the American authorities to come down and join the investigation, and the boys tried to stop me from talking to them. But they had no choice. No one had a choice. I couldn't leave Cancun until I talked to the FBI. But I was young and scared, and I really thought they would kill me if I told the truth, so I said nothing. Finally we all went back to the States, and I haven't been able to make a move since without them. They made it clear I'd end up dead if I ever breathed a word. But I had to tell my mom. It nearly destroyed her. She took the secret to her grave, terrified for me. But those guys, they just all went on with their lives. Davis became a business tycoon, Schultz became a doctor, and Alan Torento became a state legislator and later a member of Congress; like how the hell does he have the right to hold high office after what he did? I have their threatening letters and phone messages. It's been going on for years. They set me up with this crazy daycare business, and that's been my life. My whole damn life. They monitor me. These are powerful men. Every time I thought about calling the authorities, I thought about their power. They would crush me. They told me so. It's not even like they paid me off. They didn't have to. I got a thousand dollars a week for allowance, plus whatever shit change I get from the daycare. Big deal, right? And Kimmy never came home. [Undecipherable, crying.]

40

Woods is sitting at the edge of Mills's desk, peering at the computer. "That's all great stuff for the FBI, but you're not working for the FBI."

"I know that, Jake. But it shows motive for the graveyard murders, which she admits to! I sent you that file, as well."

"I know. I read the file," Woods says. "That's some crazy shit."

"No kidding. She fessed up to everything. That's huge!"

"Do you believe her?"

"Believe her? We got her gun. We found the shovel in her garage. It's covered in dirt and DNA. A fucking salad of DNA that *will* match our victims."

Sergeant Jake Woods folds his arms across his chest and bites his lip. "How do we know we can trust her version of everything that happened in Mexico?"

"Once we get all the emails and phone messages, hopefully the photos, into evidence, I think we'll be able to corroborate enough," Mills says.

"Too bad we'll never find that body."

"Don't be so sure."

Woods looks at him as if Mills just pulled a piñata out of his ass. "Oh, come on, Alex."

"Maybe not the body. But certainly some remains," Mills insists.

"I'll believe it when I see it."

"Send me down there," Mills says.

Woods laughs.

"I'm serious."

"I know you are. Ask your friends at the FBI," his boss says. "Or better yet, ask Mexico." Then he walks out of Mills's office.

Mills's friends at the FBI, namely Special Agent Henderson Garcia, call him a few weeks later to tip him off to the arrest of Al Torento. Garcia explains that the Mexican government has waived its right to prosecute the congressman, due, in part, to the abundance of evidence that is, like the key witness, impractically at arm's length. Mexico, however, has agreed to continue the search for Kimberly Harrington's remains. "We've been really careful around this," Garcia says. "But we're ready to go. Thought you'd want to know."

"He arranged to surrender?"

"Yes," Garcia says. "At his house stupidly. Agents out of our Phoenix office are handling this. He could have gone quietly to the office, but he wouldn't. Now they have to go out there and get him."

"Right. That is stupid. He can't possibly want a scene."

"It's his wife," Garcia says. "She wants a scene. She won't let him hide from this."

"You think she's leaking it to the press?"

"I know she is."

"Wow. What a difference a murder makes."

Garcia says his Phoenix colleagues will be at the Torento home at three o'clock. "Just in case you want to see the humiliation firsthand."

Mills opts to watch the humiliation later on the evening news, both local and national. And it's colossal. The video captures Torento in his complete walk of shame, from the doorway of his home all the way to the curb, where a car awaits to take him away. The zoom shows no mercy on the congressman's pouting face, his head bowed, his eyes heavy. And, oh, the money shot! The cuffs around Torento's wrists as the agents turn him around and lower him into the car. Your Pal Al tries to duck his head and cover his face as the agents drive him through the gaggle of reporters and cameras. But the duck and cover just makes it worse. Or better. Just depends if you're Toronto or the camera.

Mills flips from channel to channel, Kelly curled at his side, and watches essentially the same report with different screaming lead-ins.

Shocking news in Phoenix! Senator Al Toronto arrested for murder! Stunning! Startling! A missing person's case that's gripped the nation for twenty-five years.... Twenty-five years of intrigue ... of heartbreak ... of dead ends. Your Pal Al in handcuffs! The sensational Kimberly Harrington case comes to a close. Is your college student safe tonight? Is she???

Kelly squeezes his arm.

And then it happens. The one thing Alex Mills did not expect from tonight's clusterfuck of news reports. At one point in every story, on every channel, local and national, the videotape cuts to an FBI spokesperson holding a makeshift press conference opposite the home of Al Toronto. The spokesperson is visibly careful with his words, straining to convey the facts without releasing unauthorized details. None of that surprises Mills, but this does:

"If it weren't for the expertise of the Phoenix Police Department in their handling of a local murder case, we would not be standing here today sharing this very important news about critical developments in the case of Kimberly Harrington's disappearance. Had the Phoenix Police Department, homicide detective Alex Mills, in particular, not painstakingly investigated a string of murders in this city and located and apprehended the alleged perpetrator of those crimes, Mr. Toronto would not be in custody today for the crimes he committed relevant to the Kimberly Harrington case. I cannot and will not discuss specific evidence at this time, but I will say the suspect arrested by Alex Mills's squad provided extremely valuable information, which prompted the government to seek charges against the congressman."

Mills all but jumps out of his skin. Not with joy. Not with dread. Maybe a little dread. Mostly surprise.

"Oh, my God," Kelly cries. "You're a hero! What do you think Woods will say now?"

"He won't call me a hero. Because I'm not a hero, babe."

She jumps onto him. "You are if I say you are. I'm so damn proud of you."

She kisses him deeply. They writhe and grind for a moment, the moment almost certainly leading to something more, until Trevor emerges from his bedroom and says, "Jesus, you two, it's almost seven thirty. Can't this wait 'til after dinner?"

Can't this wait? The irony is stunning. Also shocking and startling.

41

This newfound notoriety, Mills realizes, doesn't have an expiration date. Especially now, almost two months later, when Mexican authorities make a discovery along a lonely stretch of beach highway between Cancun and Tulum. The news comes first from Special Agent Henderson Garcia, legal attaché. "I flew to Cancun with another agent, and we worked with the Mexicans," he says. "They could not have been more diligent. And it wasn't easy."

The Mexican authorities, according to Garcia, had availed themselves of the information provided by Lee Leighton in her statements to Alex Mills and the bureau. They gave Leighton's memory a two-mile radius and had determined three specific places to search. Mexican investigators had no trouble finding photographs of the coastline from twenty-five years ago, since the country's Ministry of Environment and Natural Resources had been monitoring erosion even further back than that. They searched the first site and found cliffs mostly untouched by the years of wind and salt and tides. They also found the divots, the craters, the gaps in the rock. And they combed and scoured just as they would any other crime scene. They turned up nothing but ocean debris, rocks, and grains of sand. The next day they blocked traffic and set up a search at the second site. It started raining, though, and it was too wet and slick for the team to lower itself over the cliffs or walk the tunnels between them. Instead, they went to the third site, which was just a wide-open beach and hotels where no hotels existed twenty-five years ago. They were there all day, through alternating hours of sun and passing storms. But nothing. Except frustration.

"We were really just there for moral support," Garcia tells Mills, "and that's what we did. We just told them to keep going. Don't give up. I had a much better feeling about the second site because it more closely matched the description that Leighton gave us both."

"Moral support? That's it?"

"Well, no," he replies. "We also had an agreement with the Mexicans that we'd bring her home if they were successful."

"And did you?"

"We thought we had about a sixty percent chance of finding her," Garcia says. "The Mexicans weren't so sure, but we decided that if she couldn't be found in one of those three sites, we'd be done. We'd pack our things and go back to La Ciudad."

Day three was not a charm. Day three was a complete washout. But day four brought a dry, hot day with clear skies and intense heat. Garcia and his associate met up with the Mexicans not far from Akumal. They found the "Hurricane Evacuation Route" sign at that fateful intersection of the highway and the smaller road leading to the sea. The Mexicans cordoned off the site. Here erosion had had an appetite. The photos showed it clearly. From above, looking down at the water, the team could see that the cliff to the left of the walkway had completely vanished during the past twenty-five years.

"My heart kind of sank right there," Garcia says.

But the Mexican team followed the path down toward the water and began searching the remaining cliff, working their way back up from the sand, to the rock, to the ledges, to the road. They dug into various divots and craters. Nine men and three women carefully scraped at the rock, crouched into miniature caves, and removed small boulders by hand. They were there for hours. Garcia and his team made several trips for water to relieve the workers.

"They were extremely dedicated," he tells Mills. "Like it was personal for them, you know. It was redemption for them to find this girl who'd gone lost in their country."

"That's what they told you?"

"Absolutely."

Returning from the fourth trip to fetch water, Garcia found the head of the operation, a woman named Sonia Ramos, waiting expectantly for him on the roadside above the cliffs. They had found something. She led Garcia down the pathway to a gully within the wall of rock. She pointed, then called to one of the workers. A woman emerged from a fissure in the cliff, barely large enough for her body to escape. In her gloved hands she held fragments of bone. And they knew. They all knew.

They would not find a skeleton intact, of course. Nor would they find a skull intact. So much was lost to storms and heat and the encroachment of a rising sea. But they found fragments in that makeshift tomb, most likely jaw, rib, hip. Enough to test conclusively.

"So I just found out about an hour ago we have a match," Garcia says. "We brought her home. Congratulations, man!"

"Congratulations?"

"Your arrest of Lee Leighton was the key to this case."

"So you've said. But you can spare me the attention this time around," Mills tells him.

"Too late," Garcia says. "Already prepared a statement for the media. Washington has already approved it. Can't change it now. Not even the punctuation."

"Jesus . . ."

"This is huge!" the man says. "We found Kimberly Harrington."

42

The next morning Alex Mills sleeps in late. He told his boss he wouldn't be at work until whenever o'clock. He'd been at headquarters until midnight, making the rounds of satellite interviews. By the end of the ordeal, he felt as though he had put his head through a cement wall a few dozen times. Actually banging his head against cement would have been more pleasant.

He doesn't hear Kelly get up. Doesn't hear her get ready for work. He has some fleeting memory of a kiss on his forehead. He brews a pot of coffee, gets in the shower, and avoids the TV and the newspaper. Yes, he knows what he and his squad have accomplished. He's proud of it. He understands the magnitude. But instead of the stream of accolades, he'd really like a lone hike up Camelback at sunrise (he hasn't climbed it in years) and the white noise of altitude.

When he gets to work, before he even gets to his desk, he's told he has a guest in the lobby. He detours for the front of the building and peers out from behind the reception cage, and standing there is Gus Parker. He does a big stride for the door and swings it wide open. "Hello, stranger. Long time no see. Not like you just to pop by unannounced."

"What have you done?" Gus asks.

"What do you mean?"

"Can we talk someplace privately?"

Mills leads him upstairs to his office, then shuts the door. They sit. "I saw you on TV last night," Gus says. "You mentioned my name. More than once."

"Is that a problem, my friend?"

"I just got home from LA this morning, and I have TV crews all over my front yard. Like, what the hell, dude?"

Mills laughs. "I'm sorry."

"Why? Why?" Gus begs. "Don't you think I got enough press from the Richard Knight ordeal?"

He's right. He did. "Oh, shit."

"Yeah. Oh, shit, Alex."

"I'm so sorry. But all your visions of Mexico led up to this."

Gus shakes his head, massaging the back of his neck. "Not really."

"Yeah, really. If we had connected the dots sooner, this would have been a slam dunk. But your visions, man, they were spot-on. You deserve some credit. That's the only reason I mentioned you."

"I deserve peace and quiet," Gus says.

"Okay. I'll have some patrols go over and keep the peace. That's the least I can do."

Gus rises. Smiles. He extends his arm for a handshake. Mills gets up, too, grabs Gus's hand, but instead of shaking, he pulls Gus toward him as he comes around the desk and forces the man into an embrace, the two of them slapping each other's backs. Gus says, "You mentioned taking Kelly to Hawaii."

"Yeah. Hopefully soon. We got to get out of this heat."

"Billie rents a house in Maui. She wants you to stay there."

"Seriously?"

"She watched you on the news last night, too. And we got to talking."

"Come on . . ."

"Yeah. She's going to fly you and Kelly to Maui. You're going to stay in her house. And Trevor's going to stay with us in LA."

"Are you kidding me?"

"No. I'm not."

"How long are you in town for?"

"A couple of weeks," Gus says. "Billie started her tour. So I get to have a normal life for a while."

Mills wonders if Gus understands the real meaning of what he's just said. And all of the implications.

Then Gus says, "Yeah. I know what I just said."

And Mills feels a small riptide in his chest. "Fuck you and your mind reading, surfer boy."

"It wasn't mind reading. It's just what I intuited from your silence," Gus replies. "Billie and I are fine. I got no predictions at the moment. No visions, really. Just a vision that we're fine."

They're walking outside to Gus's car. It's oven hot right now. One hundred eight degrees. The men reward each other with more slaps on the back.

"So, what's happening with Lee Leighton?" Gus asks.

"Man, it's too fucking hot out here," Mills tells his shaggy-haired brother. "I'll fill you in over dinner tonight. Kelly and I will pick you up."

"Do you believe her?"

"Believe her?"

"When she says she was too scared to go to the police all these years?"

Mills shrugs. "I guess . . ."

"Believe her."

As Mills heads back to his office, he debates just how much Lee Leighton should be punished. She killed three men. She killed three men who had tormented her for twenty-five years. She killed three men who were responsible for covering up Kimberly Harrington's death. But she killed three men. They stole her life. But she is neither judge nor jury. Jennifer Torento, from what Mills has heard, makes regular trips to visit Leighton, who is awaiting trial in a state prison. As promised, Mrs. Torento is paying the woman's legal expenses with the help of Carla Schultz, the doctor's widow, who, when hearing of Mrs. Torento's gesture, offered to match the donation with the money she's inheriting from the plastic surgeon and the money she's expecting from the pending sale of his prized Maserati. Davis Klink's wife is not participating in the legal fund.

Leighton, apparently, stands to gain quite a bit from her association with the Kimberly Harrington case. There's a plea deal in the works for a highly reduced (and no penalty of death) sentence in exchange for her testimony in the federal government's case against former US congressman Alan Torento. The widows are paying for a very good lawyer who's getting traction with the county attorney for both the reduced sentence and/or revised charges now that discovery of evidence shows a determined effort by Torento, Klink, Schultz, and Gaffing to prevent Leighton from telling the truth about the Kimberly Harrington case.

It's hard for Mills to stand at the intersection of the Torento and Leighton cases and not be furious. And distressed. He thinks he understands now why most women are fed up with most men. He wishes he had been around to smack those college boys upside the head, to knock their teeth out, break their faces, something. That's just the fury speaking. He's angry at a world that raises these boys. The antidote would be a good book. He thinks he'll start rereading all of the classics from his vast collection, though the boys (and the men) of great literature didn't always subscribe to the strictest moral codes, either. Still, some of them were heroes. He wishes his love for literature had rubbed off on his son. But they both like football, so there's that. It's remotely creepy that Trevor will be attending U of A, the alma mater of three murderers, in the fall. But he will. He's a man now who's not yet graduated from boyhood. It seems as if it was just yesterday that Mills was tickling a four-year-old to shrieks of laughter and shrieks of agony. Just yesterday they were writhing on the floor, the four-year-old begging him to stop. Just yesterday so many things. So many fucking precious things.

He calls his wife and asks if she's up for dinner out tonight. "I might even have a surprise," he tells her.

Then, as soon as he's off the phone, he goes to Google and, with a grateful nod to Gus Parker and Billie Welch, searches for Maui images. He finds a classic sunset over a shimmering sea, palms that bend so low they graze the water, a generic picture of beauty that could be paradise anywhere. He attaches it to an email and sends it to Kelly without a message of any kind in the body.

ACKNOWLEDGMENTS

I thank my family for their outstanding support of my work. My parents, Diane and Harvey, stand by me and always have. They both serve as de facto publicists, which you can't put a price on, and I'm glad they don't. My sister, Nancy, calls me every morning with her infinite wisdom, guidance, and, sometimes, just for a kvetch session. I treasure my daily dose of all of the above. My nieces, Marielle and Chloe, are always a source of great joy. My in-laws, Billy, Greg, Beth, Nate, and Ivette complete the family circle perfectly with their avid support. Mia and Ethan like to jump in my bed and cuddle. All writers need a Mia and Ethan. One of my oldest and dearest friends David O'Leary is my compadre and the brother I never had. I love him; his wife, Kathy; and all of their amazing kids.

I owe a big thanks to Sergeant Jon Howard and Sergeant Vince Lewis of the Phoenix Police Department. They've been invaluable guides to law enforcement, city and statewide. Their information has guided me well. But I, alone, am responsible for any mistakes or detours from official procedures. Also, a thank-you to Nancy Savage at the Society of Former Special Agents of the FBI. Again, I take responsibility for any errors.

Jean Stone is a great friend, and there's no one better with whom to commiserate. Thanks for all of the love and encouragement. Cara London has been a fan since our college days at Brandeis. The fandom is mutual. We have lots of stories that will never be published. Thanks for the love and laughter.

To my amazing editor, Dan Mayer, huge gratitude. I never get hung up on edits because I trust the man implicitly. I'm in great hands with my copyeditor, Jeffrey Curry. A genius. If he could copyedit my life like he copyedits my novels, I'd be a better man and I'd probably never lose my keys. Thanks to Jake Bonar, my publicist; Jill Maxick; Hanna Etu; Nicole Summer-Lecht; and all of the other professionals at Seventh Street Books, Prometheus Books, and Penguin Random House. My agent, Ann Collette, is a gem, and a hardworking gem at that. And to Hank Phillippi Ryan, your generosity is beyond. I'm so lucky we've connected. Your enthusiasm for other writers is a beautiful thing. Lori Rader-Day, the coaching has been good for my head and my spirit. You, too, are a generous soul.

Paul Milliken. Please stop making me eschew carbs. Can't I just eat Beth's brownies and drink Sangria every day? You are Sedona in the golden hour.

Last, but absolutely not least, thank you, the readers, for your precious time, your interest in my work, and your often very lovely reviews. You make this whole journey gratifying.

ABOUT THE AUTHOR

Steven Cooper is the author of *Desert Remains*, the first Gus Parker and Alex Mills novel, and three previous novels. A video producer and a former television reporter, he has received multiple Emmy Awards and nominations, a national Edward R. Murrow Award, and many honors from the Associated Press. He taught writing at Rollins College (Winter Park, Florida) from 2007 to 2012. He has also taught in the School of Communication and Media at Kennesaw State University. He currently lives in Atlanta.